They'll be home for Christmas....

He was born on Christmas Eve, and so was she.
Did that mean they were made for each other?
A hometown boy returns for the holidays,
in search of the girl he'd left behind, in
Ann Major's A COWBOY CHRISTMAS.

**"Full of sensual spark and fiery delight,
the works of Ann Major will brighten the darkest day."**
—*Romantic Times*

She came out of the blizzard, like his Christmas angel.
But could he get her to stick around once the tinsel came
down? The celebration may never end in
A COWBOY FOR CHRISTMAS by Stella Bagwell.

**"Stella Bagwell charms readers with inviting
characters and expressive emotions."**
—*Romantic Times*

ANN MAJOR

loves writing romance novels as much as she loves reading them. She is the proud mother of three grown children. She lists hiking in the Colorado mountains with her husband, playing tennis, sailing, enjoying her cats and playing the piano among her favorite activities. Readers can contact her through www.eHarlequin.com or her own author site, www.annmajor.com.

STELLA BAGWELL

sold her first book to Silhouette in November 1985. More than forty novels later, she still loves her job and says she isn't completely content unless she's writing. Recently, she and her husband of thirty years moved from the hills of Oklahoma to Seadrift, Texas, a sleepy little fishing town located on the coastal bend. Stella says the water, the tropical climate and the seabirds make it a lovely place to let her imagination soar and to put the stories in her head down on paper.

She and her husband have one son, Jason, who lives—and teaches high school math—in nearby Port Lavaca.

Christmas Cowboys

ANN MAJOR

STELLA BAGWELL

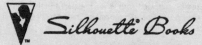

Silhouette Books

Published by Silhouette Books
America's Publisher of Contemporary Romance

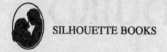

SILHOUETTE BOOKS

ISBN 0-373-21735-8

by Request

CHRISTMAS COWBOYS

Copyright © 2002 by Harlequin Books S.A.

The publisher acknowledges the copyright holders of the individual works as follows:

A COWBOY CHRISTMAS
Copyright © 1995 by Ann Major

A COWBOY FOR CHRISTMAS
Copyright © 1994 by Stella Bagwell

This edition published by arrangement with Harlequin Books S.A.

Visit Silhouette at www.eHarlequin.com

Printed in U.S.A.

CONTENTS

Dear Reader,

If ever there was a season of love, it is Christmas. How wonderful it is to share and give and think of others, especially those less fortunate. I love simple pleasures like decorating my tree along with my three cats while listening to carols. I like to bake iced cookies, make tamales, light a fire in our fireplace and string red pepper lights in the front yard. And, at least, at this time of year, I don't have to feel guilty about going shopping and spending money on beautiful things. My husband and I go to a lot of parties, so December becomes a time of reunion with our local community—which is nice.

But the most fun of all is having our children and their families home for the holidays. We always do some traveling to see more family, too. This last Christmas we had a surprise wedding, and we got a new son-in-law along with his little boy, Caleb, as new family members.

Here in South Texas, we almost never have snow. But we don't miss it. The Christmas spirit here is alive and well.

MERRY CHRISTMAS TO ALL,

Ann Major

A COWBOY CHRISTMAS
Ann Major

Prologue

The Dairy Princess, which served better gossip than hamburgers, never lacked for a crowd. That particular Christmas in Kinney, Texas, the hottest flavor on the DP menu was once again the latest development in the star-crossed romance of the local rich girl and the town's favorite bad boy cowboy.

"Did you hear that Leander Knight won Heddy Kinney in a game of five-card stud?"

An expectant hush fell over the DP.

"No!"

"And her supposed to marry that millionaire—"

"Well, she up and ran off to Mexico with Pepper—on her wedding night!" "Pepper" was the townsfolk's nickname for Leander.

As one-horse towns go in south Texas, Kinney was pretty dull. It had a rusty water tower that could be seen from the highway. It had a grocery store, a hardware store, a gas station, the Dairy Princess and two very disreputable bars.

Other than the fabled comings and goings at the big Kinney Ranch, there never was much to talk about. So, when Jim Bob Janovich phoned his mother on Christmas Eve from the French Quarter to say that Pepper had shown up drunk in the bar of the hotel where Heddy and her famous groom were about to take up honeymooning and had taunted the bridegroom into a card game while the bride was upstairs sprucing herself up for the big night, everybody got mighty interested. Especially after Jim Bob said Pepper had won her.

"Pepper always was a wild one."

"He was wild about Heddy, if that's what you mean," Flora Janovich said.

"You'd better worry about Old Man Kinney putting a bullet right between Pepper's pretty black eyes."

"No chance of that," someone else said. "I hear Heddy and Pepper hightailed it to Mexico."

The telephone lines buzzed. When the Kinneys returned New Year's Eve in a snit without Heddy, neither Barret, Heddy's father, who was usually a jovial fellow, but who'd been behaving mighty erratically of late, nor Tia, her imperious grandmother, would talk to a soul or show their faces in town.

So, without so much as a morsel of fresh gossip to chew on that week, all a curious body could do was rehash the old story that they all knew by heart about how Leander Knight and Heddy Kinney had got started in the first place.

They'd been born the same hour, under that same too-bright star, on that same Christmas Eve in Kinney, but nobody would have ever thought of matching them up then. For the golden-haired girl's birth had been looked forward to by her proud family, who were members of the local ranching aristocracy. Her birth was feted and written about even though her father, Barret Kinney, would have preferred a son.

The little boy, born less than a minute after she, was found half-dead in a garbage Dumpster by a wino who'd crawled inside to get warm that Christmas Day. Black-haired, black-eyed, swarthy-skinned, the infant was swaddled in a plastic garbage sack and rushed to the same hospital and laid beside her crib in the brightly lit, warm nursery. He began to kick the instant he was fed, his vulgar energy upstaging the pale little princess beside him and amazing and disgusting her family when they came to bestow their gifts of admiration upon her. But an old nurse, who loved both babies, would rock them together after all Heddy's fancy visitors had gone, and she told everybody who would listen that when Heddy was taken to her mother to nurse, the boy fretted till she was brought back and placed beside him in his crib.

Heddy was dressed in imported lace and taken home to a huge mansion decked in holly and ivy. The house sat on a low hill on her father's legendary ranch. There she was adored and petted, especially by her grandmother. Her family wanted only the best for her. Beneath their tall Christmas tree in the center of the ballroom, her gifts that had not been opened were piled high for her. Two hundred guests attended her christening the next month.

He was bounced from one shabby foster home to the next.

When her mother died the next year, and the little girl grew into a tomboy who preferred to run wild and free with her father and the vaqueros, Tia, her strong-willed grandmother, began to worry. For Tia, whose husband had recently died in a New Orleans hospital of a mysterious illness, had grand plans for her baby princess.

From their two separate worlds, these children came. They were ten years old when they met at school and were instantly attracted. He had suffered shame and loneliness and grown tough. Having lost her own mother, Heddy was drawn to Pepper, who had lost both parents.

He had just been adopted by the Widow Janovich, and it was his first day at school. Since she was a Kinney, she was the most admired child in their school. The bullies had knocked him and Jim Bob to the ground and were chanting at him, "Bastard! We don't like you! We won't play with you! Not ever!"

Heddy pushed through them. Two boys lay on the ground hemmed in by the hostile throng—the bigger of the pair, Jim Bob Janovich was red-faced and blubbering. But the center of attention was the slim boy lying in the dirt who hadn't given up the fight. When Tom Yates tackled him from behind, he fought back, rolling on the pavement, clawing and kicking like a wildcat until five more jumped him.

"Stop it!" she screamed.

The bullies scowled at her, but she scowled harder. Until finally, with blood trickling from their mouths, they slunk several feet away, leaving the stranger lying on the ground alone.

When she knelt closer he glared up at her, his insolent black eyes burning with a fierce animal excitement that sickened her. He was skinny, yet he was the most magnificently fearsome boy she had ever seen. For a long moment she studied his torn clothes, his dark sullen face that was somehow so incredibly attractive despite its bruises and cuts and that terrifying wildness that was so much a part of him.

She spun on her silent classmates. "You leave him alone. I'll play with him."

As if by magic his tormentors vanished. Not that the new boy showed any gratitude as she led him to a water fountain where she cleaned him up and told him he wouldn't look nearly as awful if he'd smile and say a thank-you.

"Who made you queen of the world?"

"I did," Heddy replied with a pert smile. "And my grandmother, Tia."

"So—does everybody always do what you say?"

"Mostly."

"Not me. I don't do what anybody says."

Her chin went up a notch. "We'll see."

He picked up a rock and threw it defiantly so that it arced high over the seesaws into the piercing blue sky.

She picked up one and threw it, and it sailed just as far. "I can catch fireflies, dozens of them, with my bare hands and not hurt them. I've got a pet snake and a pony I can ride better than any of the vaqueros. I can—"

"Who cares? What are you trying to prove with all your braggin', girl?"

"Same thing you are—that I'm just like everybody else."

"But you're not," he said. "You're different—like me. I'm all alone. I don't need anybody. And you're queen of the town."

"But I feel all alone, too."

She had looked into his dark eyes and been startled to find her own soul mirrored there.

When Heddy found out they shared the same birthday, she said, "That means our destiny's the same, too."

"That's silly."

They had become instant best friends, a relationship her

snobbish family considered undesirable. Especially when he grew more handsome as time passed and more acceptable to the other kids in their class. Especially when, except for the occasional lapses of youthful wildness, his career through school was amazingly honorable. When he wasn't studying or playing football, he worked to help Mrs. Janovich. He had a way with words and was always winning writing contests.

Every Christmas Eve, Leander always found Heddy and said, ''Happy birthday. Merry Christmas.'' Then they exchanged presents.

Not that their relationship was perfectly harmonious. She was outgoing while he was a loner. She was rich and headstrong and spoiled. He was sometimes defensive about his low position in the town compared to hers. Occasionally he got angry at her or her family for their imagined or real high-handed treatment of him.

But they were always so miserable when they quarreled that they made up quickly.

Eight years later, when Heddy's family sent her away to college and she made her debut in New Orleans, the Kinneys thought they had separated her forever from the cowboy who didn't have a cent to call his own and probably never would. Though they never said so, they thought he lacked everything that mattered most to them in a prospective son-in-law—breeding, moneyed connections and land. The fact that Heddy and he were soul mates and star siblings did not matter in the Kinneys' wealthy world of privilege. Nor did they wish to gamble on his innate talent and intelligence. They weren't impressed when he sold his very first short stories to good magazines. They believed writers were a starving, unpredictable breed and that their Heddy would be happier and safer with her own kind.

They thought she would realize that rich girls didn't marry poor boys like Leander Knight.

But in that they misjudged her....

Intermittent bursts of lightning lit the shimmering wet black windowpanes. Standing by the window, with her gleaming hair and violet blue eyes, Heddy was a vision of golden loveliness in her gossamer nightgown.

It was her wedding night, and her bridegroom had abandoned her. Most girls would have been devastated; Heddy Kinney was drinking champagne and enjoying the thunderstorm.

The New Orleans newspapers had called it the wedding of the century. They had described the groom's thirty-room mansion, his twenty-two polo ponies, with immense enthusiasm. Her ranch had been photographed with equal attention. She and Bronier DuChamp had stood arm in arm, staring at each other adoringly in countless pictures...at countless parties. As if being beautiful and rich and having lots of great stuff really meant they were the perfect couple.

Ha!

What would everybody think if they found out the lonely bride was getting herself thoroughly tipsy?

Some wedding night!

But so far it was better than she'd expected.

The champagne caught the light from the lamps as Heddy swiveled the crystal stem of her glass between her fingers. Her creamy skin glowed.

She wondered if Bro was ever coming.

Worse, she wondered if she even cared.

Heddy's travel alarm clock ticked steadily as she tipped her champagne flute to her lips. She'd been listening to the little black clock for over an hour—ever since Bro had misinterpreted her dread for shyness and offered to go down to the bar and have a drink with his best man while she got ready.

She went to the champagne bucket, pulled the bottle from the ice and poured herself another glassful. She wondered suddenly if he loved her, or if he was as scared as she was, if her marriage was doomed, as all her relationships had been since she'd left Kinney…and…Leander.

Outside in the Quarter, the rain drummed fiercely.

Last night had been beautiful and balmy.

Last night she had walked in the silvery moonlight with another man. She frowned slightly. She couldn't let herself think of that.

Instead she concentrated on the storm and the ticking clock. When she went to the window to watch the rain again, the night chill seeping through the windows made her shiver.

She heard the elevator bell, then a man's stumbling steps in the hall, his mumbled curses when he dropped something on the carpet—maybe his key.

When he fell against the door and then turned his key in the lock, she tensed.

Pretend you love him. Maybe someday you will.

She'd played the pretend game all this past year. Ever since that awful night when Jim Bob had called and told her that Leander had left her for a new girl.

No matter that Leander had shown up last night at the rehearsal dinner, swearing there had never been another girl, that he had only asked Jim Bob to call to make it easier for her to forget him and live the high life her family wanted her to.

He'd been passionately sweet, coaxing her out for a moonlit walk where she'd melted into his arms. One kiss, and he'd begged her to run away with him, swearing he'd been so lonely without her he'd nearly died. One kiss, and she might have gone if Bronier and Tia hadn't found her, and she'd recovered her senses.

The door swung open as Heddy took another gulp of champagne. It tasted warm and flat, and she felt a vague nausea as she smoothed her hair.

Instead of racing toward the door, she set her glass down.

Which was a mistake.

Because it was Leander, not Bro, who staggered inside. Leander, looking rougher and more unkempt, wilder and angrier and yet somehow more unsure of himself than she'd ever seen him. Leander, whose hot, insolent black eyes sent a paralyzing shaft of fear darting through her.

Other than her hand going to her throat, she remained motionless. Which gave him the precious seconds he needed to bolt the door and jam the key deep inside his tight jeans.

Dressed in the same black T-shirt and scuffed boots as last night, his expression was icily dangerous. There were smudges of exhaustion under his eyes, and black stubble shadowing his jaw.

His shoulders were wide; his biceps bulged. His wavy, coal black hair was uncombed and falling across his dark brow.

Her skin was bathed and scented; her long hair had been brushed a hundred times; her nails polished pearl pink. She was as meticulously groomed as he was uncouth.

"Howdy, Sugar," he drawled in a measured voice that told her he'd had too much to drink. He took off his hat, bowed in a mockingly respectful gesture and pitched it toward the nearest gilt chair. It sailed across the antique sofa and landed on a plump pillow of her magnificent bed.

"Oops." He grinned at her and stumbled forward.

"And happy birthday, and Merry Christmas and all that rot—"

Their old greeting. And yet it wasn't.

He held out two wrapped boxes.

"What are you doing here?" she whispered, aware suddenly that at the mere sight of him, angry and liquored-up though he was, her body had caught dangerously on fire.

When his devil black eyes went over her and lit with a fire of their own, she realized that her negligee and peignoir were so transparent she might as well be nude.

"This is my wedding night," she whispered, grabbing a blanket to cover herself.

"*Was* your wedding night, Sugar." His slurred, sexy voice was ice. "Don't remind me."

"You have no right."

He tossed his presents toward a low table and fanned four crumpled playing cards in her face proudly. "I won you, Sugar. Not fair and square. First time I ever cheated." He flipped the cards into the air. "Check out the winning hand!"

Not knowing what he was talking about, she stared as four cards, a pair of two's and a pair of three's, fell onto the carpet. "What did you do to Bro? Why isn't he here?"

"Your precious bridegroom can't hold his liquor. He's not much of a card player, either. He drank himself into a stupor after he lost you to such a lousy hand. I left him in the bar sprawled on the floor, holding a pair of jacks."

When Leander grinned cockily, she swayed toward him. "You bastard..."

"Now, go easy, Sugar." His gentle purr was savage now. "You know how I prefer *orphan* or *adopted* or some politically correct piece of garbage like *disadvantaged by birth.*"

When she lunged at him, he staggered backward against the wall. He grinned as he caught her wrists and hauled her into his arms. Then he glimpsed her wedding rings, and his smile died.

The circlets of platinum suddenly felt as cold as ice burning her finger. His narrow, hooded eyes pierced her soul. He held her firmly, yet he was careful not to hurt her.

Close up, his face was lean and hard, his carved features possessing a dangerous beauty that left her breathless. Close up he reeked of cheap liquor and sweat. But she didn't care.

"I wanted to put you out of my mind forever, Sugar. I hated always being told I wasn't good enough."

"I—I never—"

"Not you, baby. But everybody else in town thought you were grand and I was dirt. Especially Tia." His expression darkened. "I tried to forget you. I tried again last night after you left me for Bro. Then I watched you together."

His roughly callused hands were entangled in her golden hair, jerking her head back. "You looked so unhappy in his arms. I kept thinking how you lit up when you first saw me last night. How maybe your know-it-all family didn't know what was best for you after all. I went to a bar and damn near drank myself to death, but, drunk or sober, all I saw was your face. I couldn't live with the thought of you being unhappy."

Her pulses were beating heavily as he lowered his mouth to hers. "So, Sugar, is it really over between us?"

"Yes."

Then why was her voice so raspy and soft? Why couldn't she breathe? Why was her body tense with expectation because his mouth was so near?

"Or do you still have the hots for me?"

"Are you crazy? You smell like a brewery!"

"Sorry about that, Sugar. No toothbrush. Guess I'll have to borrow yours—" He dragged her toward the bathroom.

She should have slapped him or tried to run. But her body burned, and her heart ached.

He was spraying water everywhere when she turned the faucet off and took her toothbrush from him.

He turned back to her. She was tense and still. When he saw the hunger in her eyes, his voice softened. "I love you, Sugar."

Those four velvet words resonated in her soul.

She didn't move as his mouth met hers. His hands slid over her, molding her slender curves to his hard flesh.

"I've always loved you," he said as the warmth of his body engulfed hers. "I always will."

Then her heart began to beat violently.

She didn't know whether he was taking her to heaven or to hell—but she didn't care. She wanted his mouth on her lips again, his mouth all over her body.

Slowly he kissed her, a long, soft, undemanding kiss. But it seemed to her that the world shook and that he was the only solid thing she could cling to. And she knew that if his single drunken kiss could ignite such blazing need, her grand marriage to Bronier was a travesty.

When Leander picked her up to carry her to the bed, her arms wound eagerly around his neck. Her family, especially Tia, would do everything in their power to destroy them. But she didn't care. Tomorrow she would go down on her knees and beg Bro's forgiveness when she told him she couldn't be his wife because no matter how she had tried to pretend otherwise, she had always belonged to Leander.

Slowly she took off her engagement ring and her wedding band and laid them on the nightstand.

"Merry Christmas," she said as she'd said so many times during their childhood when they'd secretly exchanged forbidden presents. "Happy birthday." Her throat tightened. "I'm sorry I don't have presents for you."

There was an enigmatic darkness to his eyes. "Oh, but you do." He slid her peignoir from her shoulders and cupped her breasts. "You're about to give me the best presents I ever had."

"How do you know? You haven't unwrapped them yet."

"Ah, Heddy," she heard him say right before he pulled her under him. "You were always so sweet to me when we were kids. You could be a royal pain, too. But nobody was ever as sweet."

She fumbled urgently with his shirt, pushing it over his head, needing to feel his bare skin under her hands. He did not resist when she eagerly splayed her fingers through the crisp, black hair that matted his chest and then ran her hands downward, exploring the virile muscled contours of his body.

He felt so good. So perfect. With every passing moment, she grew hotter for him. She wished he would hurry, that his fingers and mouth would touch her more intimately. That he would take her fast and hard. And then make love to her again very slowly.

He smiled at her, laughing softly, pulling away a little, now that he knew she was as eager as he.

He began ripping at the snaps of his jeans, sliding them down, hopping on one foot, then the other to get out of them as he backed away from the bed.

"Hey, where are you going?"

"To take a shower. To brush my teeth."

"No—"

"Sugar, I slept in a storm sewer last night with three homeless guys that didn't smell too good."

She lay in bed, feeling lonely and restless while he showered.

He returned almost instantly, his black hair wet and shining as he lay down beside her. His minty-tasting mouth sought her lips, his tongue sliding inside.

"The first time I saw you, it was as if I already knew you," he said a long time later. "As if I'd lived somewhere in some other time or planet with you. As if you had always been a part of me and always would be."

She ran a fingertip down the length of his nose, liking the way he shuddered even from her light touch. "I felt the same way. But my family—"

He slid his hand under the straps of her nightgown. "What can they do, if we love each other?"

He pushed her nightgown lower and kissed each nipple. Her gown was only halfway off when she began arching her body against his and moaning his name. Sensing her need, he didn't bother to undress her. Ripping the sheets back, he lifted her gown above her thighs, searching out the hot damp sweetness between her legs. When she felt his hand there, she inhaled sharply. Then he was lowering his body to hers, and she was urging him inside her, her arms gripping him fiercely. When he thrust forward, ripples of pleasure convulsed through every part of her.

His heart pounded like thunder.

It had been too long for them both.

He moved once, and they exploded.

"Sorry, Sugar," he murmured, burying his face against her cheek.

She wrapped her arms around him, clinging to him, drawing him closer as he began to make love to her again.

She kissed his damp brow, ran her hand through his wet hair. He was everything. She loved him, and she was sure that her family, even Tia, would love him too once they realized what he meant to her.

Two weeks later, after her marriage had been annulled and she'd legally married Leander in Mexico, they went home to Kinney.

Shortly after that the trouble started.

Within a year, Leander was one of the richest and most famous horror novelists in the world.

But his marriage was over.

And he had an unsavory, if undeserved reputation.

It was a widely known fact that Barret Kinney thought Leander Knight had married his daughter for their ranch and that Barret hated him and berated him constantly. Thus, when Barret was found shot in the head after a quarrel with Leander, Leander was suspected of murder. Then Tia suffered a heart attack shortly afterward, and Leander was blamed for that, too.

Not that there had been a shred of evidence against Leander.

Not that he was ever formally charged.

Not that Tia, who hated him, or Heddy, who loved him, ever said a word in public against him.

The gossips tried him, found him guilty, and damned him.

But it was Heddy's coldness that drove him out of town.

Alone in New York, Leander wrote his first novel, *Dead Ringer*—to exonerate himself.

Leander hated the sordid publicity surrounding his

book, but it made him one of the hottest names in the publishing world. The journalistic slant was that he was a creepy killer who murdered his famous, wealthy father-in-law and wrote a novel about it to get rich.

He hadn't written the book to bring more scandal on the Kinney family. Nor to drive Heddy and his baby daughter even further away. Nor to make everybody in Kinney resent him even more. But that was what happened.

His fame soon grew to international proportions. Every time a new Leander Knight title hit the stands, the media rehashed the sordid story, magnifying the horror of Barret's mysterious death and implicating Leander as a gold digger and a murderer, as an opportunist who'd reaped fame and fortune after marrying into and then destroying one of the most famous families in Texas. Leander's early novels were reissued, especially the first. Nobody noticed that in his first novel, the hero had been framed.

The more successful Leander became, the more scary the media made him out to be. In the beginning Leander granted interviews in a naive attempt to clear his name. But his words were always twisted against him. The photographs of him that appeared in magazines were darkened to make him look more macabre.

In the end he grew so fed up with all the lies that he moved to a remote island in southern Alaska. And because it was impossible to hound anyone if he chose to flee to an uninhabitable winter wilderness where unpaved roads and ports were cut off by glaciers and snowstorms and mountains, where the few existing airstrips were fogged in by low clouds for weeks at a time, he escaped them.

For eight years Leander lived simply in Alaska and produced two megabestsellers a year, each outselling the one before. Each adding to his notoriety and his unsavory rep-

utation as a killer-writer. Each widening the chasm between himself and his wife and daughter. He was at the
top of bestseller lists all over the world. He reached the
fantasy level of success that all writers dream about.

But he despised his fame. Because it had cost him his
family and his reputation.

As for the writing—it was simply something he had to
do. He would have done it for nothing. But it was a lonely
occupation, and he was a lonely man. He was afraid to
drink because liquor loosened his inner control and made
his loneliness dangerously unbearable. Halfway through a
bottle something inside him would break and he would
feel a desperate, long-buried yearning for Texas and the
golden-haired woman he had loved and lost. For Christina,
their daughter, who had grown up without him.

He would have exchanged all his millions for an honorable life with the two of them.

One

The winter weather on the Alaskan island had been clear for a couple of hours around noon yesterday, so Leander knew the weekly mail plane from Juneau had probably been able to get to the village. He had a large house in Juneau, a computer, a secretary and a research assistant. Nevertheless, he preferred the isolation of his tiny cabin on the island and still spent as much time as possible there.

He came down by snowmobile, attentive to the familiar landmarks in the morning's dim winter light as he carefully approached the outskirts of the remote village which was a mere half hour upriver from his cabin even in bad conditions. Ivak, his Alaskan husky, loped happily behind him on the ice.

Usually Leander worked in his cabin till late afternoon. But his novel in progress had him stumped. He was nearly finished, and way before his deadline, but the ending lacked sizzle. There was no do-or-die climactic moment of choice for the hero, so that the reader could see what his character was made of and what his monster was made of. Leander had grown bored with his supernatural homicidal maniac, and he was afraid his readers would be just as bored if he didn't think up a new twist in the plot. So, he'd decided to break early and let his subconscious mind mull on the problem.

The icy wind slashed at him as the snowmobile flew over the snow. He welcomed the bracing cold; he welcomed the danger of it, the challenge, even as he looked forward to sharing a sandwich and a beer with Muz, and teasing Muz's pretty wife, Mara, and their little girl.

Unlike his own one-room cabin, the village, a poor looking town made up of small houses set in haphazard rows along unpaved streets, enjoyed the unusual luxuries of running water and indoor plumbing. The streets had lights, and every home had electricity and a telephone.

Despite such modern conveniences, despite having a wife who had yellow hair and a pretty smile, Muz tended to eat too much and to brood too much during the short dark days of winter. Mara was a simpler, happier soul. Leander enjoyed her company, although she never read anything other than the labels on cans or the recipes in her cookbooks. Neither she nor her husband knew or cared who Leander really was or what he'd supposedly done. They just accepted him as one of them—someone who, like them, lived on an icy fringe of the world because he was running from demons he didn't much want to talk about. Nor did fame like his have a place in a simple village like theirs.

Lori, their little girl, was the same age as Christina, whom he tried never to think about although Dean Shaw, his agent in New York, sent her mother a large support check every month and a Christmas present every year.

In Muz's cabin Leander could throw off his solitude for an hour or two and get a glimpse of ordinary life.

In the beginning, Alaska had seemed a place of exile. But now as he sped through the snow-covered trees, the silent white land was like his writing—a refuge. He had lived alone so long, sometimes he felt he was only half-civilized. He had grown used to the quiet, to the peace, to the awesome power of nature.

With a dashing swirl of ice and snow, he skidded up to the largest cabin on either side by fish houses in which dried fish and sealskin bags of seal oil were stored along with nets, floats and other gear. Two other snowmobiles and their spare parts were nuzzled close to the front door.

Inside Muz's cabin a tiny Christmas tree stood beside racks of radio equipment that buzzed with static. Muz set the headset to his radio down onto his counter when Leander stomped inside and went to the fire where he tore off his snow-encrusted, mountain-squirrel parka and gloves.

Ivak padded over beside his master, and Leander ruffled the big dog's icy gray fur. When Leander turned away, Ivak whined and made a pitiful face. Then he rolled on his back, and put all four of his feet in the air, so Leander could check his paws for ice balls or injuries.

"Faker," Leander whispered as he knelt and lifted each frozen paw while Ivak panted and thumped his tail happily against the wooden floor.

"You should tie him out back with the other dogs," Muz growled. "You spoil that mutt."

When Leander began scratching that certain spot behind Ivak's right ear where the big dog's soul was lodged, the heavy tail thumped even more ecstatically.

"Yeah. I guess I do. But he's more than just a dog. And, hell, it's almost Christmas."

"Which reminds me. You got a big package from New York yesterday. And the usual from Juneau."

With a silent nod Leander indicated he'd heard. Withdrawing his hand from Ivak and studying the well-stocked gun rack to the left of the stove, he edged nearer to the fire.

His fingers felt numb. The cold had sapped even his abundant strength. It would take him a minute to recover. It always amazed him that Ivak could run the three miles across the ice and snow as if they were nothing. But then Sitka, his mother, had been a famous sled racer in her day. Such dogs could run sixty miles a day. They could trot at twelve miles an hour and lope at eighteen. Leander knew because he'd put that fact in a book once.

Mara placed two bulging brown packages and a mug of hot coffee on the table nearest Leander and a bowl of warm water on the floor for Ivak. Leander seized the mug, cupping it so that the heat of it seeped into his cold skin. The first package was from his secretary. The larger one was from his literary agent.

He unsheathed a hunting knife from his belt and slit open the package from New York first. Staples went flying and so did little popcorn bits of packing foam from the envelope. Ivak got up, pawing and sniffing every single popcorn with curious fascination. The page proofs of Leander's next novel fell out. So did three smaller envelopes.

He picked up the letters.

One was addressed in a childish hand to Mr. Santa Claus, c/o My Daddy, Mr. Leander Knight.

The second, which was also from Christina, was addressed solely to him.

For an instant his blood seemed to cease its flow.

Christina had never written him before.

Then his black gaze narrowed as he instantly recognized the neat, elegant loops of pretentious blue ink that sloped backward across the third velum envelope. *Heddy.*

Her handwriting seemed fake and pretentious. Heddy had learned to write like that after Tia had sent her to private school in Switzerland.

A muscle pulled in Leander's stomach as he remembered her messy childish scribble. She'd had some sort of fine-motor coordination problem and had failed handwriting in third grade, but he'd enjoyed getting notes from her back then even though they'd barely been legible.

Well, she damn sure wrote like a great lady now. Tia had won that battle, too.

He shoved his chair back so hard it nearly toppled, then strode over to the counter, leaned over it, grabbed Muz's bottle of brandy and poured a double shot into his coffee.

"Sure—help yourself, why don't you," Muz muttered grumpily without looking up.

"Thanks." Leander raised his mug in mock salute and shoved the bottle across the counter toward Muz, who caught it. "Run a tab, why don't you?"

Then returning to the table, Leander pushed Heddy's letter aside and took another long pull from his mug.

With his knife, he ripped open Christina's envelope. Inside were a Christmas card, a gilt-edged invitation to the Kinneys' annual Christmas party, a single, tissue-thin sheet of sloppily folded paper and a photograph of Christina and her mother.

His dark gaze glinted as he studied the snapshot. Heddy and Christina were wearing red-and-green pullover sweaters over crisply pressed jeans. They were standing in what looked like a wide river of golden grasses edged on both sides by ancient sand dunes on which grew dense oak and mesquite. They were blond, slim, and so alike somehow. And so lovely with the sunlight and wind blowing in their hair. *And so beautifully dear to him, they put his soul in torment.*

Despite her jeans and youthfully trim figure, Heddy looked rich and sophisticated.

Why had he ever married her?

He ran his fingers through his black hair with a muttered curse. How many times had he told himself that he should have known from the first that Heddy Kinney had always been too rich for his blood. Still, even after he thrust their picture onto the table facedown, he couldn't shake off a powerful sense of despair and loss.

Eight years. How could it still hurt after eight years? It was a long time before he picked up his child's letter and began to read.

Big block letters ran crookedly up and down across the page, and since she'd used a pen and wasn't good at it, there were lots of scratch outs. Some of the *B*s and *P*s and *S*s were upside down and backward.

Dear Daddy, Hope you'll give Santa my letter since you live so close to the North Pole. Or, if you can't give it to him yourself, at least you oughta know his right address.

I sure hope you come to this party. I'm inviting you because my mommy said I could ask whoever I wanted and the only person I want in the whole world is you, Daddy.

I haven't written you before cause I wasn't good enough at writing. But I had to stay after school today cause I stole Attilla's chips at lunch, and my teacher helped me spell the hard words.

Guess what? I'm not an only child anymore. Which is good, because I got lonely with nobody to play with and with you never here. Mommy dopted two kids. They're fourth cousins. Or third. Twins. But they don't look alike. Their mother and daddy were in a wreck. So I guess I'm going to have a brother and a sister now. Their names is Cleopatra and Attilla. Cleo cries a lot. Mommy says cause she misses her mother. Attilla is mean. He says he might run away. And I hope he does.

Please, please come to this party so that I can show them that I do too have a daddy cause Attilla won't believe it less you do.

Luv, Christina Knight

P.S. I feel sorry for you cause you live in such a cold place and you can't play outside.

He read the "Luv, Christina Knight" again and again. It felt so natural, so good, her writing it with that childlike trust as if she considered his love an unconditional thing. Which he realized suddenly that it was. She seemed to feel close to him even though she didn't know him.

She wanted to see him. To show him off. She was proud of him.

It seemed incredible.

Equally incredible was his vague realization that he had similar feelings. He *wanted* to see her. He was proud of her.

Remembering his own fatherless and motherless childhood, he could relate to her need *to prove* she had a daddy.

Leander reread the letter a dozen times, stunned and baffled that he was so touched. He thought he was alone, invulnerable. And then this child had reached out and touched him. This child who seemed to take it for granted he would know how to act around kids, that being a father was an easy thing, that he'd fit right in because he was her daddy.

The party was a week before Christmas. He wondered how it would be if he just showed up.

Tia had already had one heart attack because of him.

But Heddy?

He flipped the photograph over and studied her blue eyes and corn silk hair. He pretty mouth still looked so kissable. Unbidden came the memory of how wild she had always been in bed.

Then he caught himself. She was Texas royalty. She thought he had used her as a step up the ladder to fame and fortune. He thought she had betrayed him by not believing in him. They had done one hell of a number on each other. For eight years he had told himself that he liked being alone, knowing that no one could get to him ever again the way she had.

No way could he go back. He didn't know the first thing about kids. And his relationship with Heddy was long over. All he'd ever known of normal family life was what little he'd had with Flora Janovich and Jim Bob.

He and Heddy had made their choices.

But now his kid was struggling to make hers.

Again he remembered how he'd longed for a father.

What the hell was he thinking about? He couldn't do Christina any good. Not when everybody thought he was even worse than any one of his fictional monsters. He had made the decision to stay out of her life a long long time ago—for her sake.

He finished his brandy-laced coffee before slitting open Heddy's letter.

Dear Leander,
I should have written you a long time ago and asked

for a divorce, but until I found Marcus, it never seemed like the right time. And Christina liked the thought of me still being married to you. Even if you weren't here—

She misses having a father—

The rest of the letter blurred. But he got the gist.

There was a new man in her life. Marcus. He loved children. Her family, which meant Tia, loved Marcus. Heddy wasn't really all that serious about Marcus yet, but there was the possibility. It was time for all of them to move on with their lives.

Leander wadded the letter and pitched it into the fire. Even though she hadn't actually said it, Leander knew that Marcus was some bloodless paragon who had been born rich, who had lived a sane dull life and, therefore, had a name that was unblemished by scandal and a soul unscarred by the ravages of poverty and illegitimacy and betrayal at the hands of his mother and then the woman he loved.

Leander borrowed a pen and several sheets of paper from Mara, but his large brown hand froze, and the tip of his pen dug into the paper so hard after he wrote "Dear Christina" that the sheet tore. He wadded it up and grabbed another.

Transfixed, he stared at the third blank page.

No words came. What could he say to this precious little girl he didn't know but he felt so much for?

To the wife who wanted her freedom but whom he loved still?

Loved? Did he love her?

And he had thought himself invulnerable and safe here. He looked down at the picture. His wife and his daughter were holding each other, laughing. They looked so happy—without him.

The lights on Muz's Christmas tree twinkled, mocking the lonely darkness his childhood had carved inside him. Leander had been born into the world alone and despised by his own mother. As a kid he'd wanted the same things all kids wanted—a family who loved him, friends and acceptance; and Christmas trees and Christmas presents. Not that he'd shown it. By the age of five he'd been so defiant and hostile that his foster home mothers had always given up on him and sent him back to the agency. When he was ten Flora Janovich had found him starving and hiding out along the creek that ran through her ranch. She'd run him down on horseback, lassoed him and thrown him kicking across her saddle, brought him back to her ranch house kitchen and fed him. Then she'd applied to the agency to become his foster mother. Early on she had proven she was even tougher than he was, refusing to take any of his nonsense. When he ran away, she always tracked him down. More than once they'd repeated that first ride with him bent double across her saddle. Finally he had realized that she really wanted him.

Flora and Jim Bob had given him so much, and, for a while, so had Heddy. But always Leander had known that he was different from other children—that he was more alone, that his own mother had abandoned him. No—that his own mother had thrown him away and left him to die. Then he'd lost Heddy.

He'd missed so much, so many years. So many Christmases. Everything. He had sworn to himself that never again would he reach out for the impossible.

A savage pulse throbbed behind his eyes as he imagined Heddy in another man's arms. As he imagined his child coming to think of another man as her father.

Damn brandy, he thought queasily, shocked at the depth of his emotion. All liquor ever did was open him up to the pain. So did writing, but in a different way.

Still, how could he hold on to a wife and child who were so far away? And there was no way he could go back. No way.

Not when he was despised as a murderer.

Not after the way Heddy had treated him.

She had thrown him away—as if he meant nothing—just as his mother had.

He forced his paralyzed fingers to move, to write a sentence that promised Heddy her freedom.

He kept it short.

Three words only, but they sucked him dryer than a nine-hundred-page novel.

"Divorce? Fine, Sugar." After that he could barely manage the rambunctious swirl of his gaudy signature.

He wrote Christina and said he couldn't come, but that she should give Attilla this letter so he would believe her.

He addressed both letters and gave them to Mara. When he returned to his table, he saw that Christina's letter to Santa Claus had fallen to the floor and lay between the radio equipment and the Christmas tree.

Indifferently Leander picked the envelope up and ripped it open.

The page began to shake as he read her first, childishly scrawled sentence.

He read no further.

But her plea to Santa changed everything.

Leander got up and stalked over to Muz and banged on the counter so Muz would look up. "If I go somewhere, will you take care of Ivak?"

At the mention of his name, Ivak shifted his golden eyes toward the two men and thumped his tail. Absorbed in his radio, Muz lifted his earphones only halfway off his head. "Juneau again? No problem."

"Farther than Juneau." *One helluva a lot farther.*

Leander paused, not wanting to say more. "You've gotta keep the ice out of his paws, and you can't let him stay out when it's too cold."

Muz's eyes rolled back, but his shaggy head lifted in an almost imperceptible nod. "It's damn silly the way you're so soft on that dog—"

"Yeah."

Good thing Muz didn't know what a fool he could be when it came to a woman.

Two

True, it was the week before Christmas, a hectic time for any successful shop owner. But that wasn't why the fitting rooms of Heddy's boutique were in an uproar.

True, Mary Ann, Heddy's sexy, redheaded assistant, who was writing a romance novel in her spare time, had had three very demanding customers trying on cocktail gowns for the past two hours. But other than the tapping of Mary Ann's spike heels as she rushed to and fro from the fitting rooms with chiffon gowns and rhinestone belts, other than the women's delighted whispers when they were thrilled, or their fretful sighs when they weren't, the four women scarcely made a sound.

No, the exuberant ruckus was due entirely to the children. Heddy and her seamstress, dear, plump Elvira Lopez, mother of eight, grandmother to twenty, had been closeted with Heddy's three darlings, doing fittings on the elf outfits that Tia had ordered from a catalogue. All three were to be dressed as Santa's elves in red suits with matching hats and shoes at the Kinney party.

The children had been wild even before they'd torn open the sacks that contained their suits and been metamorphosed into bright elves with tiny jingling bells.

In their new suits, everything—the other customers, the trinkets on the sale tables, Elvira—absolutely everything—became immensely more exciting. Tiring of making hand prints and nose prints and tongue prints on their reflections in the mirrors, they took off their hats and sank to the floor, peering under the cubicles, giggling as they watched the three ladies strip to their panty hose. After Heddy scolded them, they attacked one another.

"Make him stop, Mommy!" Christina said imperiously from the floor where she had been coloring when Attilla waggled a long red sleeve with jingling bells in front of her crayon. Not touching her. Not causing her to make a mistake. Just almost.

Attilla whose hair was as red as a carrot and as curly as corkscrews, had been full of himself all day. He had been whirling like a dervish in front of the mirror, dizzily slapping the other three children with his sleeves until Heddy had reprimanded him quite sharply. He was now prancing about like a boxer, his pants drooping and tangling around his ankles.

"Ouch!" Cleo screamed when she darted out of Attilla's way and stomped down onto a pin. "Aunt Heddy, get it out!" Big tears welled up in the child's huge, dark eyes.

"All right. All right," Heddy said, easing the pin out and holding it so that the weeping little girl with the ink black hair that fell like a curtain down her back could study it.

"If you would wear your shoes this wouldn't happen, Cleo."

Cleopatra was rubbing the tears off her cheeks. "I can't find them!"

"I think I saw you take them off under the Christmas tree."

Cleopatra was always taking her shoes off. Heddy was always looking for them.

"Kids, if all of you could just hold still, we'll be through in a jiffy," Elvira murmured.

How many times in the last hour had she said that? Heddy wondered.

Not that it mattered. The children paid not the slightest attention.

Attilla zoomed up to Cleo and swiped at her with his sleeve again. Not touching her hurt foot. Just teasing.

Maddened, Cleo shoved him into Christina whose purple crayon wriggled across Santa's plump pink face, ruining all her careful work. In a rage Christina yanked three orange corkscrews of hair. Attilla pinched both girls, and all three toppled like bowling pins.

"Attilla!" Heddy cried.

"Mrs. Knight, I think I can sew the outfits without fitting them."

"Bless you dear, talented Elvira."

Cleo was rubbing her foot and crying again, and the doorbell buzzed, which meant more customers. Christina, who had a flare for badly timed drama, chose that moment to look up from her coloring book and say softly, "Guess what! My daddy is coming to our Christmas party!"

Despite the confusion, the phrase *my daddy is coming* registered.

Heddy spun. "He's what?"

"Attilla didn't believe I really had a daddy so I wrote him and invited him. My teacher helped me."

"Christina—you had no right."

"You said I could ask whoever I wanted to."

"Whomever."

"Whomever," Christina repeated ungraciously.

"But I didn't mean *him*."

"If you don't let him come, I'll hate you forever and ever." Christina picked up her coloring book and stomped out of the room.

"Christina!"

They exchanged heated glances. Then Christina just ran faster.

They were outside now, mother and daughter, their matching golden heads huddled on the bench on the wide sidewalk in front of Heddy's shop. A single, very bright star, glowed in the purpling twilight sky.

Elvira was inside, helping the other elves get dressed. The sounds of their hilarity were muted by distance and glass windows, by the ringing of a bell by a fat woman across the street soliciting donations.

Christina was a sensational seven-year-old. She had very blue eyes, bluer even than Heddy's; translucent skin and a delicate bone structure that lent to her every movement a fluid, ballerina grace. She was an original—fey and dramatic or imperiously bossy—depending on her mood.

"I can't believe you wrote your daddy, honey."

"I wrote 'cause you wrote him about Marcus."

Heddy blushed, wondering how much Christina, who was a precocious reader, had understood. "Yes, I did write him."

Christina's eyes blazed rebelliously, yet she was very pale. "Are you going to marry Marcus?"

"I—I— We haven't talked about it," she said gently. "Right now Marcus and I are just friends."

"Good."

"Marcus loves children. He's very nice—"

Christina stiffened and thrust her chin higher, and Heddy was reminded of how she had rebelled when her family had tried to force her to be friends with children other than Leander.

Teasingly Heddy touched the defiant chin. "Honey, I just don't want you to be disappointed when your daddy doesn't come."

"He'll come," Christina stated with absolute faith.

Once, Heddy, too, had believed in Leander, even though her family had warned her against him. He had broken her heart.

"Honey, I—I don't think he can. He lives a very long way from here. He hasn't been back since— He and I, we made a deal—"

"He will. 'Cause I want him to so much. 'Cause I wrote Santa, too, and told him I wanted my daddy to come home for Christmas. Santa can make anything happen."

"Not this, honey."

"Then how come that guy from New York called and said—"

Heddy was about to argue, but a horn tooted, impatiently, and Christina looked past her and jumped up when she saw her great-grandmother's blue Lincoln. "Tia..."

As the automatic window on the passenger side lowered, Christina ran eagerly to the car, squealing when she saw the Christmas presents piled high on the back seat.

"Is one for me, Tia? Is—"

Tia's silver head nodded and she smiled. Her wrinkled face was alight at the sight of Christina.

"Which one, Tia? Which one? *Please*... Tell me."

Tia was as devoted a great-grandmother as she had been a grandmother. She supervised every detail of Christina's life.

Heddy felt a pang of guilt. The reason Tia was so overly concerned was because she believed she had failed with Heddy.

Deciding she'd have to talk to Christina later, Heddy got up reluctantly, spoke to Tia and then went inside to get the other children. She had forgotten Tia had promised to drive them to have ice cream at the Dairy Princess and then to the ranch after she finished shopping so Heddy could work late.

"I hope he does come," Mary Ann said dreamily from behind the cash register after Tia had driven away with the children.

Mary Ann had sold more merchandise today than she ever had before. Even though she had a talent for putting rich women into flattering outfits they would never have had the nerve to choose themselves, her mind was never really on the shop. When she wasn't flirting, she was daydreaming about her novel.

"You hope *who* comes?" Heddy asked, wishing Mary Ann would concentrate on closing out the day's receipts.

Mary Ann punched buttons haphazardly on the cash register, and long coils of tape began spilling from the machine and falling to the floor in messy tangles.

"You could be fanfolding the—" Heddy began.

"Your husband. I hope he—"

"He's not really my—"

"But he's a writer! And not just any writer!" Unconsciously Mary Ann stepped on the tape. "He's famous."

Heddy bit her lip. "Are you watching that tape?"

"Oh, sorry." Mary Ann moved aside. "I couldn't put

Midnight Eyes down. I mean he's really talented at creating a brooding mood of horror.''

''Yes…'' Heddy's faint voice trailed into nothingness.

''You know I'm almost finished with my own book.
Maybe he can tell me what I have to do to get it published.
I've heard you have to have an agent. You have to know
people in New York. I bet he has connections—''

The cash register had quit clicking, and the thick white
coils hung motionless. Not that Mary Ann noticed.

''He's not coming,'' Heddy said stonily as she punched
a button to clear the machine.

''But Christina said she—''

Heddy ripped the tape out of the machine so savagely
that it tore. Then she marched toward her desk and turned
her slim back to Mary Ann. ''He wouldn't dare.''

But he did…dare.

Leander parked Jim Bob's truck a mile from the house,
off the narrow ranch road and behind a tall hedge of salt
cedar. Then he loped up the blacktopped drive. Keeping
to the shadows of the stunted trees, he sneaked around to
the back of the tall three-story mansion. There he waited
for several guests to descend before he crept up the stairs
to the darkened verandah and stared through the tall windows into the brilliantly lit ballroom.

Even though it was late December, and a norther was
in the forecast, the air was damp and unpleasantly warm.
A sharpening southeasterly breeze was gusting across the
flat savannahs from the Gulf, snapping the party tents in
the garden and rustling the palm fronds briskly.

It was so different from Alaska. And yet so familiar.
So poignantly home, even after all the years.

He never dressed up in Alaska. His rented tuxedo bound
him too snugly across his wide shoulders; his pleated shirt

made his neck itch. He wanted nothing more than to rip at the starched collar and send studs flying.

A huge Christmas tree with sparkling white lights and silver bows stood in the center of the ballroom. Four huge chandeliers lit the room. Long tables that stretched against the far wall were laden with fancy pink linen and silver candelabra. Crystal bowls and plates were piled high with catered delicacies.

The three-piece band was loud, but Leander felt as cut off from the dancers as if he were encased in a glass bottle with no holes punched in the lid. Other than the beating of his heart, there was absolute silence. And no air.

The glittering people in the ballroom seemed to move noiselessly, without echoes. In their glittery world that was so far removed from his, they laughed easily, noiselessly. They belonged; they were happy while he was an outcast.

Then Heddy came into the room. Heddy with her radiant, glorious face, with her pale shimmering hair forming a halo around her face. She wore a red silk sheath that fit her like a glove. But no jewels. She was so stunning, her image burned into his retina with such absolute clarity that when he shut his eyes at her unbearable beauty, he saw her still.

His Heddy, his very own Heddy, lovely, warm and so much more alive than anyone else in that room. And yet beneath her beauty he sensed a sadness in her, a loneliness that mirrored his own.

The years they had been apart were as nothing to him. More than anything he wanted to go to her. He had to know whether her face would light up with joy or go dark with sorrow. Would she ache for his kisses or despise him? And he hated himself for the fierce burning need to know.

Leander took an involuntary step toward the door, intending to join her. Suddenly a tall blond man came out of nowhere and gathered her into his arms, sweeping her onto the dance floor and vanishing with her behind the Christmas tree.

It was then that Leander remembered that there was no way he could approach her without crossing a barrier of immense pain. She believed he was a murderer, and he almost loathed her for thinking him so low. He had built walls to protect himself, and he did not want to let them down.

The couple whirled around from the other side of the tree. That look of sadness had left her face. Flushed and laughing now, Heddy tilted her head up to her partner's whose lean golden features were warm and caressingly tender.

Leander drew a harsh breath and forced himself to study his adversary. The man appeared rich and dashing, his custom-made tux the height of style and tailoring. He danced flawlessly, with the confident air of a man who'd inherited his money. He had the affable appearance of someone who found life an easy voyage. He could offer the woman he chose what he himself possessed in abundance—happiness and security, acceptance by society. There were probably few women who could resist his charms when he chose to exert them. And Heddy, who placed her head against Marcus's elegant shoulder, did not look like she wanted to resist them.

The other guests stopped dancing and made a huge circle for the glamorous couple who spun faster and faster around the large tree under the sparkling chandeliers. When the onlookers began to clap enthusiastically to the beat of the music, Leander's heart began to hammer at the same desperate tempo.

Because of this man, Heddy wanted to divorce him.

He left the dark verandah and went to the front of the house and joined the party.

When Leander strode tigerlike into the ballroom, a dozen pair of eyes turned and watched him.

Dramatically tall and broad-shouldered with his piercing dark gaze, he was used to stares, especially from women, the most beautiful of women—at his publishers' parties—everywhere. But this was different.

There were horrified gasps from the women and hostile scowls from the men.

"Murderer," someone hissed.

The cruel word tore through Leander.

"That bastard's one scary guy."

Leander forced a tight smile when he saw Tom Yates.

"Of all the nerve. Do you think Heddy knows he's here?"

More heads turned his way.

Leander felt like he was a kid in school again—friendless and helpless, about to be set up by Tom. As sheriff, Tom had made Leander's life a living hell before he'd left town. Leander knew he'd better make his move—fast.

"Oh my," the beautiful redhead in a low-cut green gown who was clinging to Tom cooed. "Will you get a load of that? Rich and famous and dangerously drop-dead gorgeous to boot."

"The key word for that lowlife is—*dangerous*. I'd like to give him the boot. Watch yourself, M.A., or you may be the one to drop dead next," Yates warned.

"Oh, pooh, Tom! The way you hate him, if you'd had a shred of evidence, you'd have put him away for life!"

"He hid behind Tia—"

"I thought a man was innocent till proven—"

"In the eyes of the so-called law maybe."

"Well, I told Heddy I simply had to speak to him if he came!"

Leander hesitated at the sound of Heddy's name. Which gave the redhead with the amazing cleavage time to pounce on him.

"Mr. Knight! I've read all your books! I absolutely adored *Midnight Eyes!* I can't believe you really came! Welcome home."

When she seized his hand, Leander tensed. She was sexier than hell. Not that he felt particularly interested. He was too aware of the buzzing whispers around them, and far too aware of Heddy.

"I'm sorry," he said, trying to shrug loose. "Do I know you?"

"You could…" She thrust her amazing chest even closer. "I'm Mary Ann!" she gushed.

Leander shook his head, puzzled. "Sorry?"

"I work for Heddy—in her shop. But, you see, I'm not just a salesgirl. I'm a writer, too. Romances. Or at least I want to be. I'm just starting. I thought maybe you could tell me how I could sell—"

An unpublished writer, and a romance writer at that— a desperate breed. He'd met her type hundreds of times in the past—at signings, in bookstores, at parties. She was one of those predictable creatures who could become instantly infatuated with any writer whom she believed possessed the secret of publication. As if publication were some sort of magic attainment.

Imperceptibly he relaxed. Both her gushing admiration and her questions were routine. Hell, it wasn't that he didn't empathize. He could be as neurotic and insecure about his writing as anybody. He felt vaguely guilty that his only real interest in her was her connection to Heddy.

She began describing every detail of her manuscript.

He nodded mechanically, hoping he'd plastered a suitably sympathetic expression on his face as he strained for more glimpses of Heddy.

The glamorous couple whirled from behind the Christmas tree.

Did Heddy have to stroke that rich wimp's throat in front of the whole world? Did she really have to wind a strand of his yellow hair around her fingertip? Had she forgotten that she was still married—to him?

The voluptuous redhead asked who his agent was, where he got his spooky ideas—the usual. Leander answered her. She said if someone would only read her book, would only tell her what was wrong with it—

Hardly aware that he spoke, his entire attention focused on Marcus's hand wandering through Heddy's golden hair, on Heddy nuzzling her head against Marcus's shoulder, Leander promised to read the book.

When the couple vanished again, and Mary Ann squeezed Leander's hand in thanks and pressed her incredible bosoms closer, he wondered what exactly he'd promised her.

The beautiful couple swirled out from behind the Christmas tree once again. The crowd parted. Suddenly as Mary Ann was kissing his cheek—Heddy seemed, at last, to feel the burning pull of Leander's gaze.

Slowly, as if in a dream, she turned.

Her eyes locked with his.

It was as if they were the only two people in the room. The music faded to a murmur.

His heart began to beat erratically, and not because the writer had draped her sexy body all over him.

It was because of Heddy that he couldn't breathe.

Apparently Heddy couldn't get her breath, either.

Numbly he watched her hand go to her mouth in horror.

Numbly he watched her try to push herself free of Marcus. If Leander didn't stop her and fast, she was going to run before he had a chance to talk to her.

Mary Ann was happily babbling as Leander said an impatient goodbye. Then he rushed toward Heddy, reaching her just as she was about to run.

The music stopped in the middle of a measure, punctuating the dramatic moment.

Tom Yates and his hostile gossips buzzed as angrily as a swarm of killer bees.

On the other side of the ballroom, a pale Tia placed a shaky hand over her heart.

Thunderstruck, Heddy stood as if paralyzed while Leander slowly took her slim hand and forced her into his arms, dragging her against his hard body.

Close up, Heddy looked even better to Leander than she had from the verandah. Her warm flesh was creamy soft and seemed to flow over her bones. Her trembling lips were full; she smelled like fresh flowers after a rain. Her long sleek legs, which were aligned against his, seemed to go on forever.

He felt the heat of her as he drew her closer. The excitement of her. And he got hot in spite of himself.

As he drank in that first long look before her eyes frosted over, he knew that she was every bit as lonely as he, and that no matter how she might pretend otherwise, she had missed him as terribly as he'd missed her.

Then Heddy's eyes went bluer than polar ice chips.

Several of Tia's friends including a man dressed as Santa Claus were leading Tia to Santa's throne where she collapsed.

Marcus was the first to recover. "What is the meaning of this?" he demanded. "I say—"

"Do you mind if I dance with my wife," Leander

drawled in a softly resonant, well-modulated tone that was somehow dangerous.

"Your what?" Marcus stared at Heddy, who had gone white and was clinging to Leander as if she might faint.

"But we...we're getting a divorce," Heddy said furiously.

"We're still married, damn it," Leander repeated.

Marcus bowed his head politely and backed out of their way as Leander dragged her nearer and signaled curtly to the musicians to begin.

"What if I don't want to dance with you," Heddy whispered, yanking at his hands.

"Don't make a scene. Wherever you go, I'll follow." He swept her with the music into a quick turn.

"Why?" she asked. "Why are you doing this?"

"You wrote. So did Christina."

"I wrote for a divorce."

"She invited me to come tonight."

"But...she's just a child."

"Exactly. Our child. It's Christmas—a special time for us. Maybe I felt homesick."

"How could you, when you know what people think of you—"

"Yes," he said, unable to conceal his dark pain as he glared down at her. "And I know who made them think it."

"Leander—"

They were dancing now. The long windows that were decorated with ivy and mistletoe and red ribbons were swirling past them. So were three bright elves who were madly jumping up and down in excitement in Santa's chair. One elf had long golden braids and blue eyes.

And then suddenly Leander saw Tia slumping weakly

into the big red chair, looking paler and more fragile than Leander had ever seen her.

The old lady watched them with dark, hooded eyes, like a tragic queen at the center of a kaleidoscope. Her arched brows lifted faintly. She was struggling to hold her chin high, to smile calmly, to maintain some semblance of regal control, but she was trembling.

The elves were dancing. Other couples began to dance.

Leander couldn't see Tia any longer, but he could not forget her any more than he could forget the hostile crowd massing around them. Tia controlled the town. Even though she had pretended to back him all those years ago, she had deliberately made everyone hate him.

Maybe she was older and frailer, but nothing had changed. All the old forces that had driven him away and destroyed his reputation and marriage still existed. He looked down at Heddy's pale face and saw that she was still afraid of him. And it was her fear—not the town's hatred or Tom Yates and his goons constantly harassing him—that had driven him away.

"You shouldn't have come," Heddy said, but breathlessly now. "They hate you. They might even hurt you."

"So what," he said in a deep dark voice. "At least then you'd be rid of me."

"I don't want that."

Her glance lifted to his, and in her eyes he saw some strange emotion. When he gently folded her closer, she didn't stop him.

They danced as they had always danced, as if they were made to dance only with each other, and their dancing brought that old familiar intimacy, that natural easiness that had always been between them even though they were in public.

"I didn't want to feel anything for you," she said several minutes later, her eyes still shining strangely, her fear of him gone now.

"I know." But he felt caught in the same spell. He didn't care what the whole world thought of him, if only she—

She had turned her back on him. No way was he going to make a fool of himself over her again.

But the passionate music carried him on magic wings, suspending reality.

"I don't ever want to stop dancing," she said, her feet floating through the steps.

He whirled her out onto the moonlit terrace where they danced in the warm night air and deserted shadows. One star was brighter than all the others. Lightning crackled to the north. The music was muted now, but the magic closeness between Heddy and himself held.

At last he stopped and was not surprised when her arms tightened around him. An odd shiver darted through him when he saw that she was crying.

"I've had dreams like this sometimes, of you coming back, of everything being like it was when we were so happy," she said through her tears. "It's so good to see you, Leander."

"It's good to see you too," he said gently before he thought. "You're still the most beautiful—" He broke off.

"I thought we'd be like strangers."

"I hoped we would be."

She touched his raven hair with the tips of her fingers— as she had touched Marcus's. But Leander forced himself not to think of that.

"You're beautiful, too," she said. "But...but we hurt each other."

"Yes. Don't think about it," he commanded roughly.

For some reason he was no longer in the mood to dwell on bitter memories.

"All right," she murmured, melting into him on a sigh, her closed lashes feathery crescents against her pale cheeks, her scent heavy and fragrant.

Neither of them knew how or when their lips came together and fused in that warm frantic darkness. Above them high clouds were whirling. Lightning flashed against the northern horizon.

Neither of them heard or cared when the music stopped. She was kissing him with an ardor he couldn't resist. His heart was beating like a drum. When his mouth fastened on hers with a greedy passion as if he wanted to devour her, she opened her lips to his endlessly.

He knew he should stop, but he had neither the will nor the self-control to resist her.

It was she who finally pulled away, quivering, smiling up at him in that beguiling way that compelled every emotion in his soul. His body tensed when she moved closer and her moist lips found the base of his throat and began to nibble. His heart slammed in fast, heavy strokes.

"It's been awful…without you," she muttered, shuddering against his collar, her hands clutching him now as if she would never let him go, her warm breath on his skin firing shafts of desire through him. "Awful. God, how I missed you, Leander."

"I don't want a divorce—not yet, anyway," he said a long time later, admitting too much because he was drugged from the taste of her honeyed lips and his own hot need.

"It's not that easy." But her mouth was seeking his frantically. In the next breath the wet wildness of her tongue inside his lips again brought ecstasy. He closed his eyes and surrendered to the bittersweet pleasure of her.

When coyotes yelped in the faraway gloom, nostalgia washed through him. He was a kid again, and she had sneaked out to meet him in the oak mott near the house. She loved him. There had been no pain then. Only the wild glorious beauty of her. Only the naive, youthful certainty he'd felt every time she'd sworn she was his destiny.

He held her tightly, his loins aching now for far more than chaste kisses, his soul aching for an end to his loneliness.

She wrapped her arms around him, as caught as he was in their dangerous embrace until Tia's thin voice shattered their dream.

"Heddy!"

Guiltily Heddy pushed Leander away, her face blanching in the moonlight.

"What do you think you're doing?"

Heddy's low whisper was shaky. "Oh, God…"

Leander grew cold. As always, one word from Tia could destroy everything Heddy might feel for him.

"Oh, God, Tia. I—I don't know," Heddy said.

Tia was leaning heavily on Tom Yates's arm as she walked toward Leander, her eyes icy, her imperious nose high.

She still thought she was a queen and he was dirt.

Leander swore viciously under his breath.

Reality was back with a vengeance.

Again Leander noticed that Tia couldn't walk without support. It seemed an effort for her just to keep that haughty lift to her chin so she could stare down her nose at him. Her bones were more prominent; her pale skin was a web of wrinkles. The thin hand she pressed to her heart was shaking.

But before Leander could ask the older woman if she

was all right, a mischievous elf with bouncing blond braids skipped up. She was trailed by two other elves.

"See, Attilla," the lead elf taunted the freckled-faced hellion behind her. "I told you so!" And in a softer voice of pure awe and intense love—to Leander alone—Christina said, "Merry Christmas, Daddy!" Softer still and warmer, "I saw you kissing Mommy! Does that mean you're going to stay? Oh, I hope so. 'Cause that's what I want."

Leander sank to his knees. He felt weak and tired suddenly. Yet his heart thundered at the sight of the golden little girl who approached him with such imperious confidence. He was thrilled when Christina crawled into his arms, usurping her mother's spot. Without a shred of shyness, she snuggled close and pressed her childish mouth against his ear so that only he could hear her secret wish, "I want you to stay with me and Mommy more than anything in the whole world."

Her warm breath tickled his earlobe. Her slim fingers tightened possessively around his neck as if she assumed he was hers to command.

His throat was too choked for him to answer.

"Christina, it's past your bedtime," Tia said frigidly. "Heddy, dear, I'm afraid Marcus is looking quite lost without you. I really think you should—"

"Of course. I'll go at once, Tia."

Heddy had barely managed a robotic half turn before Leander's husky voice stopped her.

"No," he said quietly. "Stay." He rose easily even though he was still holding Christina and extended a hand to his wife.

"Please, don't go, Mommy," Christina begged. "Not if Daddy doesn't want you to."

Three

The freshening wind had changed direction. High silver clouds, backlighted by the moon, were rolling to the north where occasional bursts of lightning exploded.

Not that Leander, whose eyes were glued on his wife's white face, was thinking about the weather.

"Heddy— Don't go." His voice was no more than a whisper, but its gentle warmth stopped her cold.

"Are you forgetting how this smooth-talking, scary bastard married you for your money and then killed your daddy, girl?" Tom snarled. "How he got rich and famous writing that book that made the Kinney name the biggest joke in Texas?"

Heddy paled.

Rage blazed through Leander that she could believe that. "Damn it, Yates!"

"No, Daddy!" Christina whispered frantically when

she felt Leander tense. "He's the *sheriff*. He's got a *big* gun."

Leander said tightly, "That's a damned lie, Yates, and someday when you've completely ruined things between Heddy and me and Christina, I'll probably be able to prove it."

"Yeah. Right. Maybe Heddy and your kid'll buy that, but it'll take more than a few hot words to make me see you as a saint."

"This is a family matter, Tom," Tia warned in her soft commanding voice. "We'll settle it ourselves like we always do."

"By condemning me to a lonely hell in Alaska without Heddy or Christina for the rest of my life. I know your tactics, Tia. You won't say a word against me. You won't have to. But you'll have Heddy feeling guilty and believing the worst of me again. From the first day you ever saw me you set about trying to make her see me as her inferior."

"Which you are," Tia said faintly.

Heddy was staring from Leander to Tia in confusion.

Damn those blind eyes of hers for not seeing the truth. Those gorgeous luminous windows into her softhearted soul. Leander hated the way he could see both Heddy's longing for him as well as her fear of him. He hated the way the two things twisted inside him like a knife and her pain became his.

"I don't know who to believe," Heddy said at last.

Leander mood darkened. "So what's new?"

As always Tia took charge. "If you're confused, Heddy, dear, imagine how Christina must feel," Tia said gently. "Take her inside. Leander, you'd better leave. Christina—"

"When you were a kid, you never let anybody tell you what to think," Leander said wearily to Heddy.

"I only acted like that at school to impress you," Heddy sighed. "Leander, maybe Tia is right, at least for tonight. It's late. We can talk tomorrow."

Tomorrow. But would she listen? Tia was so clever—so smooth. She always convinced people that she was acting in the best interests of everybody, especially Christina. In the past, he'd been too confrontational. Tia had used his hot-headed outbursts against him. Maybe it was smarter to appear to back off tonight. If he did, he might have a better chance with Heddy.

Leander nodded and then sank to his knees, saying bleakly to Christina, "You'd better do as Tia says—for now. Go on inside with your mother."

"But, Daddy, I don't want to!" Christina declared passionately.

"Neither do I, but I'll be back to see you both tomorrow, honey."

"Promise?"

He looked up at Heddy as he spoke to Christina. "Honey, the only reason I came to Texas was 'cause you asked me to. I'm not going to just leave—"

"I want you to meet Mayflower, my dog. She's part coyote."

"And I want to meet her. I like dogs."

"She used to be my only friend—before Attilla and Cleo came. She kills rattlesnakes. Even great big ones—"

"Tomorrow, honey—"

"She bites their necks and shakes 'em—"

Leander grew quiet, and he took his time straightening Christina's elf hat, tweaking it so he rang the little bells and made her smile. He traced the soft length of a golden braid with his thumb. Then very gently he pushed her away and rose.

But Christina stared up at him, her eyebrows drawing together to form one ferocious brow, her bottom lip sticking out like a bulldog's.

"Go with your mother, sweetheart," he ordered, his voice soft.

She sucked in a huge defiant breath.

"Christina—" Heddy begged.

Grudgingly Christina began backing slowly until she came within inches of her mother whose hand she then crossly refused. But when Heddy tried to coax her toward the house, the child didn't budge.

Only when Heddy turned back toward Leander did Christina bound after her.

Heddy put a soft anxious hand on his forearm. "Leander—"

He couldn't have been more stunned when she said, "You'll be careful? There are people around here who don't like you much."

Those gorgeous blue eyes of hers again, working their magic on him as she stared up at him. Christina was looking at him, too, with identical blue eyes.

Heddy was worried. For his sake. As she'd been that first day at school. As she'd been throughout their childhoods.

For eight long years who had ever given a damn whether he lived or died. No human being.

Only Ivak, his husky.

And his publisher and agent, whom he rarely saw. They cared, but for financial reasons.

Nothing on earth but Heddy's soul-deep gaze and his daughter's pinched face could have shown him what a lonely, pathetic existence his life in Alaska without them had been.

Before he thought, his large brown hand gently cupped her chin. She was such a little thing. Ever since she'd rebelled and married him, she'd had a self-destructive tendency to try to make up to Tia by letting her bully her. Heddy was trying to raise three children without a man to help her. He knew she had a tendency to work too hard when she wasn't happy.

Tenderly he brushed a golden tendril out of her eyes. "I'll be careful, Sugar," he promised. "Now you go on. I'll call you tomorrow."

She smiled, a sad smile that stung him the same way her eyes had.

"You too, Christina," he whispered.

When Marcus met them at the door, Leander whirled on Tia. Forgetting the old woman's frailty, he said bitterly, "You've been running the show a long, long time, Tia. Did you ever stop and ask yourself if you know what the hell you're doing?"

Marcus was folding Heddy into his arms in the doorway.

Tia's color had heightened. "I know exactly what I'm doing. You'd better go, Pepper. You shouldn't have come. And don't you come back. I won't have you snooping around on this ranch, pestering Heddy, confusing her. You've made her miserable. She's better off with Marcus."

"Last I heard, Tia, I was still her husband."

"Stay away from her."

Stonily furious—hell, worse than that—green with jealousy at the thought of Heddy obediently returning to Marcus, Leander turned his back on Tia and stomped down the steps that led from the terrace to the drive. But he didn't head for Jim Bob's truck as she'd ordered him to. As soon as he was out of her sight, he doubled back and took the trail through the high brown grasses into the brush that led to the ravine where he'd found Barret's decaying body all those years ago.

For eight long years Leander had wanted to forget the nightmare that had destroyed his life.

No longer.

Tonight he wanted to remember—everything.

When he reached the steep-sided cliff that plunged to a dry creek bed, the past came back with a vengeance.

The first sign of trouble had been the gunshots. The instant he'd heard them, Leander had spurred his palomino, galloping away from the cows he'd been working, reining in only after he'd gotten close enough to catch the boys' high-pitched, quavery voices.

"You...you reckon somethin's dead down there?" Mickey McKamey had asked.

"Stinks mighty bad. Why don't you find a stick or something and crawl down there and poke it."

"No—might be more snakes. Maybe a whole swarming nest of them this time. You do it!"

"Chicken!"

"I ain't no chicken, Amos!"

"What's going on here, boys?" Leander had shouted as he'd ridden up. "You boys been shooting?"

Both boys, who had been leaning down and peering avidly into the ravine, jumped and tried to tuck their guns under their belts. Not that it was any use their trying to hide them. Leander, a dead shot himself, had eyes like a hawk.

"You boys been poachin' on the ranch again?" Leander demanded sternly. "How many times do I have to—"

"We didn't hit nuthin', Mr. Knight. Not anything you'd mind about leastways."

"That wasn't exactly what I asked, now, was it, Amos?"

"Show 'im that rattle you got in your back pocket, Amos," Mickey ordered.

After Amos dug out the rattle, Leander leaned across his saddle scabbard and took it.

"It's got nineteen joints! That sucker was as big around as your arm!"

"Where'd you shoot him?"

"Over there by your windmill. He was lying on a big rock."

Leander turned the rattle over in his palm, studying it like a virtuoso examining a fine instrument. "Very impressive." He looked Amos in the eye. "How far?"

Amos beamed. "Thirty feet. One round."

Leander nodded approvingly and returned the rattle. "So—you two been shooting up the windmill blades again?"

Both boys flushed.

"How many times do I have to tell you boys not to come on Kinney Ranch with those guns?"

"There's something mighty dead down there, Mr. Knight," Mickey said to distract him again. "Something mighty big. Maybe a cow— Stinks something awful. I was about to crawl down and check it out when you come up."

And as Leander's palomino shifted closer to the edge of the rocky ledge, the wind changed and Leander caught a whiff of a powerful stench that almost gagged him. The brush must have been too thick for the buzzards to get to whatever was down there and pick it clean.

Dismounting and scrambling down through the dirt and

rocks and prickly pear cactus, heedless of the rough branches tearing at his shirt and chaps, Leander had already known it wasn't going to be a cow.

He'd known—even before he saw his Beretta half-buried in the gravel and sandy loam.

Even before he saw the skeletal hand that had been gnawed half off by coyotes thrusting up from the rocks. Even before he recognized Barret's navy checked shirt— the one he'd been wearing the afternoon they'd quarreled in the library.

"Boys, y'all get on back to the big house and call the sheriff," he'd said in a harsh low tone. "Hurry up now. You bring Mr. Yates back here—right away. Along with the coroner and an ambulance."

"Gosh almighty, Mr. Knight! What's down there?"

"You and Mickey just get, Amos, and do like I said."

Leander hadn't touched the Beretta; he'd just knelt and stared at it. Picking up a handful of sand and sifting it through his fingers, he'd known for sure the gun was his. Just like he knew even before Heddy came flying and stumbling down into the ravine like a wild woman with Tia right behind her that everybody would think for sure, now, that he'd gone and killed Barret in a rage. Because it was a well-known fact that Barret had hated Leander with an insane passion ever since he'd married Heddy. Just like it was a well-known fact that Barret had berated him constantly and that Leander had a dangerous temper and was better than anybody with a pistol....

All these years after the fact, staring into the dark nothingness, it was easy for Leander to see where he'd gone wrong.

God. He stared up at the big black sky. The clouds parted. The constellation Orion was straight over his head. If only he'd gotten up and walked out on the old man that awful afternoon in the library. If only they hadn't quarreled.

Leander had been paying the ranch bills, when Barret had stormed in and started accusing him of getting a bang out of signing all those big checks.

"That's not your money, boy. And this isn't your ranch. And it never will be. Not if I have anything to do with it."

Leander's tight-lipped silence had made Barret angrier.

"You think you're high-and-mighty now—sitting there under my granddaddy's portrait? At his desk? I've seen the way you lord it over all the vaqueros. Well, you're nothing but a low-born bastard. Nothing but a two-bit, trashy gold-digging hustler who married up. You aren't half good enough to be married to a Kinney. You're stupid and lazy—the way you sit around staring out the window and writing all the time. You don't know the first thing about ranching or anything else that counts. Everybody laughs at me 'cause of you, boy."

"Why the hell did you come back early from San Antonio?" Leander had demanded, too furious to look up.

"You quit college. The only way you could think to make it was to marry my damn fool daughter."

"I quit school to help Mrs. Janovich," Leander rasped. "I've been going to night school ever since. I'll get a degree—no thanks to you. And from the looks of these bills, I know a helluva lot more about ranching than you do. And for what it's worth, I love your daughter."

"Her and who else? Damn it, Knight, you and I both know the way women chase you. You cheat on Heddy every chance you get. It's in your sorry blood."

"You shut your mouth, old man."

"Why? You just married her because of the ranch. Why

don't we finish this once and for all? I'll give you what you really want. And you can go.''

Leander should have walked out. Instead he had shoved the account books aside so recklessly they'd crashed to the floor along with the lamp. ''All right, let's finish it.''

Barret grabbed the open checkbook and then threw it down and went to the wall safe. ''No, I'll pay you in cash—however much you want—if you'll just clear out and never come back.''

''Damn it, Barret. There's not enough money in that safe to buy me.''

''Then I'll go to the bank and get more.''

''Get this, old man—I married her, and I intend to stay married to her!''

''No, you get this!'' Barret had swung his fist into Leander's jaw so fast that Leander had crashed to the floor. Then Barret had jumped him.

Even then Leander hadn't fought back. He'd only defended himself, crossing his arms in front of his face to ward off the worst blows, crashing into the desk when the older man threw him against it again. Then he fell into the broken glass from the lamp on the floor, into the bookcases. Though Leander was younger, Barret had attacked him like a demon, his maniacal fists pounding into him. Finally Barret had picked up the broken lamp and swung it straight at Leander's face.

In that last second before he ducked, Leander had been sure Barret had gone completely crazy and was going to kill him. Then the lamp smashed into the back of his head, and he had blacked out. But when Barret had raised the lamp again Heddy had come in and screamed.

Everything might have been okay if the servants had kept their mouths shut. But, no, they had told how Barret had staggered out of the library covered in Leander's blood, about how Leander had suffered a concussion and gotten the worst of it, about how the desk had been turned over and the lamp broken.

About how Leander had called the old man crazy, and Barret had screamed that theirs was a fight to the death right before he hit him with the lamp. And every time the story was retold, it got worse.

When Barret didn't come home that night, people got curious. When Leander's gun turned up missing, they started talking.

Worst of all, to Leander, had been that Heddy was so shaken by the fight. She'd been guiltily withdrawn as she'd tended Leander's injuries. Then Tia had come into their bedroom and told them that Leander's gun and Barret were both gone and asked Leander if he had any idea where they were.

He'd retorted caustically, "How would I know, Tia? He hit me so hard I've been in bed all afternoon."

"Oh, so…that's your story," Tia had said, staring pointedly past him to Heddy.

The servants had reported everything. When Barret didn't return, tension built both on the ranch and in town.

Leander stared into the dark ravine and forced himself to remember the awful sense of doom that had engulfed him after Amos and Mickey had hightailed it back to the house while he'd waited with the body.

He'd stared at his gun and sifted sand endlessly through his fingers until he'd heard Heddy's terrified scream above him. She'd stumbled and fallen down the cliff, practically landing in his arms.

With a single frightened gasp she'd pushed him away and crawled through the dirt to her father's body.

Staring into his open lifeless eyes, she had begun to sob. "Oh, Daddy, you look so dead."

Tia had simply asked, "What's your Beretta doing here, Leander?"

Heddy had stared at the gun and then at him, her eyes dazed, unfocused. "Tia's right. If I hadn't married you, this never would have happened." Her low tone was more guilt stricken than ever.

"I didn't kill him, Heddy."

"I—I wish I could believe you. I'd give anything, if only I could, but Tia—"

"Damn Tia, what does she—"

"Heddy," Tia said, "I want you to believe him. Leander is your husband, and if we don't stand behind him and convince our friends and family to do the same, who else will?"

"I—I... But you—"

"Do you want Leander to go to prison?"

Heddy buried her head in her hands.

"He will, if we aren't strong," Tia said. "People will say he married you for the ranch and killed your father for the same reason. Do you think your father would have wanted more scandal?"

Heddy's face was white when she looked from Tia to him and then back to Tia.

"Damn it," Leander said. "I didn't shoot him. Neither of you have to cover up a damn thing."

When he reached for Heddy, she backed toward Tia.

"This is going to be difficult for all of us, Leander," Tia said, her voice very soft, almost exultant as she petted Heddy's bowed head. "But we are both behind you completely."

"The hell you are."

Then the sheriff had come and made a pretense of investigating the shooting. Friends and relatives had gathered in the big house and helped Tia plan an extravagant funeral that even included the governor.

The guests, some of whom stayed for more than a week, were supportive of Tia and Heddy, and of Leander, at least on the surface, but their incessant small talk and guarded silences when he was around wore on Leander's badly frayed nerves.

Heddy was thin and pale—guilt stricken because of her belief that her marriage to Leander was the cause of her father's death.

He overheard a guest say sympathetically to Tia, ''It's so wonderful what you're doing for him and Heddy. I don't know if I could stand by someone who—''

''It's not easy—you see—tying myself to him forever. If only Heddy had stayed married to Bro.''

Then the guests were gone. Barret was buried beside his father, and the big house was empty and lonely and more tension filled than ever. Heddy was unable to let go of her feelings of guilt and love him again.

Unless forced, Heddy would have nothing to do with Leander. If he walked into a room, she ran from it. She spoke to him only when he asked her a direct question. She would listen to his explanations and say nothing.

Yates came every day. He made it clear he detested Leander, just as he made it clear he would handle everything the way Tia wanted. Thus, Yates's investigation was at best halfhearted. Still, to pacify the gossips who were yammering for Leander's hide, Yates put a deputy on Leander's tail every time Leander left the ranch.

At first Leander hoped that Yates might accidentally stumble onto some shred of evidence that might exonerate him. But Yates allowed his deputies to contaminate the crime scene. Then they lost the bullet that had killed Barret as well as the coroner's report. When Tia replaced the servants who had gossiped, and Yates didn't even try to find them, everybody knew the Kinneys had bought the "justice" they wanted.

"Pepper did it, or Tia wouldn't be working so hard to protect him," they all agreed.

When somebody shot at Leander one night, Yates had stuck his finger through the bullet hole in Leander's truck and laughed. "Damn shame whoever did this wasn't as talented with a pistol as you, Knight!"

Even after Heddy moved out of their bedroom, Leander had hung on a while longer, hoping for a miracle. Finally they quarreled for the last time, and he had walked.

He had returned to Kinney once and begged her to come with him and start over somewhere else. But she wouldn't leave Tia. Months later when Heddy had come to New York seeking a reconciliation, Leander had known it was too late for them because by then *Dead Ringer* was about to hit the stands. But he had incautiously slept with her and they had conceived Christina.

Not that Heddy told him about the baby. Nor had Jim Bob gotten around to calling until the day Heddy was admitted to the hospital in premature labor. Leander had rushed back to Kinney for what turned out to be the last time. For two days he had paced the waiting room until Christina was born.

When he had begged Tia to tell Heddy he was there and that he wanted to see her, Tia had promised she would. A few minutes later she had come out of Heddy's hospital room and told him that Heddy, who had nearly died during the difficult birth, didn't want to see him and that it would be better for everybody if he didn't see the baby, either.

"All Heddy wants from you is a divorce," Tia had said quietly. "And I don't blame her."

At the time, Leander had been staring out a window at the pale flat prairie through the blinds and the stunted patches of trees, at the land and sky that seemed to stretch forever, thinking how this was the only place in the world that would ever feel like home, thinking how Heddy was the only woman he would ever love.

"Okay," he'd finally said in a weary voice. "I think you know that I didn't kill Barret, but you win. I lose. If she doesn't believe in me, our marriage is over. Tell her she can draw up the divorce papers."

Tia's eyes flashed with triumph. "How much will it cost me?"

"What?"

"How much will it cost me to be rid of you?"

"I don't want a dime."

"Of course you do. That's all your kind every wants."

"My kind?" His bitter voice had been edged with sarcasm. "Wrong. All I want is to get the hell out of here. Away from *your* kind. But...you'd damn sure better be good to Heddy and my daughter."

The funny thing was that Heddy had never asked him for a divorce.

Until Marcus.

High white clouds raced overhead. He glimpsed Orion again. Coyotes yelped at the moon and sent thin, quavering howls floating over the flat lonely land. A gust of cool damp air fanned Leander. The norther was due to hit any minute now.

With a polished shoe he kicked a rock into the dark ravine and heard the rapid scuttling of feet. Some varmint was prowling down there, probably an armadillo.

Leander thought of Heddy in her tight red sheath back in the ballroom dancing with Marcus. He kicked another rock over the edge and listened to it crash against brittle branches.

Damn it. He couldn't endure thoughts of that rich wimp pawing his wife.

Never had Leander felt sicker or tighter or more isolated. Not even in Alaska.

What he needed was a drink. And some company.

When he turned, he saw the brilliantly lit third story of the mansion hovering over the tops of the trees.

For him booze was always a dangerous mistake. It would be more so in some cheap beer joint in Kinney, Texas, with the locals after him.

But what the hell. He loped back toward the house in a dead run.

He needed a fight. A helluva lot more than he needed a drink.

And he found one, too. Right off—soon as he stepped into Rita's. Mac Benson, a former schoolyard bully, jumped him, shoving him drunkenly against the rough oak wall. Men were laughing and swearing, smoking and drinking. Not that he could see much in the gloom other than a tiny glittering Christmas tree over by the bar.

Not that Leander paid much attention to the bar's seedy ambience with Benson's brawny hand knotting the pleats of his dress shirt; with Benson's other fist aimed at his jaw.

Yeah, Leander would have had his fight. Only Mr. Q, the big bartender, decided to play vigilante. Mr. Q snapped the plug of the jukebox out of the wall, vaulted over the bar like a giant ape, and stuck his broken nose right in Mac's ugly potato white face even before Mac got through bellowing, "We don't want no truck here with no rich writer-murderer. You better git, Pepper—"

The crowd cheered Mac on drunkenly. "Get 'im, cowboy!"

"I'm the bouncer here, Mac. And I say you ride your horse off into the sunset. Knight stays." The silence in the bar was thick and hostile; everybody, even Mr. Q held his breath. "Or—you kin stay if you jest set yourself down again real friendlylike and shove that big nozzle of yours back in your own mug where it belongs, Mac."

The fickle crowd guffawed.

Somebody plugged in the jukebox. Music filled the room again, and everybody relaxed.

Mac flushed as Mr. Q methodically loosened Mac's black-nailed fingers—one by one—from the ruined white pleats of Leander's shirt.

Leander swallowed, once he was free, and shrugged his wide shoulders so the wrinkles could fall out of the starched white cotton.

Mac wiped his forehead with the back of his hand. "You just got lucky, Pepper. But—"

"Anytime, Benson," Leander drawled nonchalantly. "And just so you know—I'm bunking in that old cabin out back of Jim Bob's."

"Maybe you think you're something 'cause you're rich and famous. But folks around here know who you really are, where you come from."

"Right."

As Mac sank grudgingly into a chair and lit a cigarette, Leander strode past him to the bar where he turned his broad, arrogant back on Mac and his sullen crowd in an attempt to ignore their glares and whispered jeers. Then he ordered a double Scotch on the rocks.

Mr. Q poured the whiskey very slowly. "A thank you would be nice, Pepper."

Leander bolted his whiskey—very fast. "I don't like

people fighting my battles, Q,'' he muttered under his breath as he slid his empty shot glass toward the big man again.

"Then you shouldn't have come in here, Knight. I don't like fights."

Leander tapped the rim of his shot glass.

Q looked him in the eye as he poured. "Stay mellow, my friend."

Leander raised his hands innocently. "Hey—I'm not looking for trouble."

"Then why the hell did a famous writer like you come back to this one-horse hellhole when you know you ain't exactly the favorite hometown boy?"

The door opened as if in answer, and Q said, "Will you get a load of what the storm just blew in? It's your wife."

Leander turned and froze.

She might as well have been naked standing there with her red silk dress plastered wetly against her body.

Leander felt like he'd been hit by a cyclone. He sucked in a deep breath and then tossed down the second drink before he dared to look at Heddy again.

She was standing under the yellow neon glow of the beer sign, shivering and dripping water everywhere. Her damp hair spilled in wild tangles, long strands of it sticking to her bare shoulders. Her wet dress so transparent he could see her nipples. So could every other man in the bar.

When her soul-deep eyes zeroed in on Leander like radar, the blood rushed to his face.

She looked sexier than hell. And scared.

Almost as scared as he suddenly felt as he grabbed for the bottle of Scotch. With a shaking hand he made her a mocking salute. "You want to hear the joke of the century, Q? I came back because of her."

"Then you were damn sure lying when you said you weren't looking for trouble. 'Cause that's all that rich debutante's ever been to you."

"So, what else is new? Merry Christmas, Q." Leander took a lengthy pull from the bottle. "I was born on Christmas Eve. Did anybody ever tell you that? Same night she was. She used to say that meant she was my destiny. What kind of crazy sucker would fall for a corny line like that?"

Reflections from the Christmas lights gleamed in Q's steel gray eyes.

"You tell me—sucker."

Four

Churning fear. Heddy stared through the downpour at the bar. As one of Kinney's most respectable citizens, Heddy had driven past Rita's all her life without ever once considering going inside. The dive had an evil reputation and was frequented by border trash—smugglers, hard-drinking rednecks, and the lowest cowboys. The dearest tenet of their macho philosophy was that any woman dumb enough to come into Rita's was fair game.

Oh, God. Was she ever asking for it!

Tia would be furious if she ever found out that her granddaughter had gone inside such a place.

Heddy eyed Jim Bob's empty truck and then the squat frame building with the crooked line of Christmas lights dangling from its roofline and the tacky fake snowdrifts sprayed on its windowpanes. The jukebox was belting out hard rock so loudly she could feel the muted vibrations even in her Suburban with the windows rolled up and the rain streaming in torrents across her windshield.

She lowered her head and sagged against her steering wheel. All her life she had lived to please her family. An only, long-awaited child, their expectations, especially Tia's, had been so high for her. And she had failed them.

The sky went opalescent white and then inky black again. Flash; dark. Flash; dark, blinding her, causing her heart to race and her breath to quicken as she reconsidered her options.

Maybe she shouldn't have been so fast to abandon Marcus on the ballroom dance floor and follow Leander into Kinney. But when she had seen him coming from the path that led to the ravine, looking so dark and tormented, it had seemed imperative to follow him.

She'd been so miserable dancing with Marcus. There had been no magic in his cool, light touch. No soul-deep fire in his gentle brown eyes. She liked him. But only as a friend. Which wasn't nearly enough after Leander.

Suddenly Heddy had been unable to continue the charade—even for Tia, who'd been watching them. Heddy had made some excuse to Marcus and run outside.

Maybe she could have fallen in love with Marcus if Leander hadn't come back and held her in his arms and kissed her. If she hadn't seen how wonderful he was with Christina.

But it was too late now.

Leander had come home, and nothing would ever be the same for her again. She was no longer a child, no longer so easily led in her thinking by older people.

Leander had always said he was innocent.

She remembered how he'd always avoided fighting with her father. How he'd begged her to believe him. How he'd always faithfully sent generous support payments for

Christina and demanded nothing in return. People had called him a gold digger. But the truth was he'd been prouder than any Kinney when it came to money. He'd worked hard for the ranch when they'd been married. After their separation, he'd never taken a dime. And now he was a wealthy man in his own right.

Why had Leander come back when it would have been so much simpler for him to divorce her? Why had he kissed her with such tenderness and passion, as if he cared for her with every atom of his being?

Then, later that night, just when she'd been crazy from thinking about him, he had burst out of the stunted trees with the look of a man chased by demons from hell.

She had known that path. Where it led. Where he'd been.

Suddenly she had wanted to discover the truth. About her father and about Leander's true feelings. About her own.

Just as she'd climbed into her Suburban to follow him, the norther had blown in with gusting winds and big drops splashing and starring her windshield. Once she'd caught up to him, she'd kept his bobbing taillights in sight until he'd veered from the highway into Rita's. She'd hit her brakes and U-turned it, her tires skidding off the shoulder and howling. She'd parked between his empty, mud-spattered truck and two big black motorcycles.

As she sagged wearily against her steering wheel, the canvas awning over the front door shredded in the wind.

Don't go in, a silent voice warned. *They'll tear you apart.*

Afraid she'd lose her nerve, she slung open her heavy car door into the wind. Her sodden skirts were plastered to her legs even before she reached the entrance.

Music and smoke and men's laughter and drunken wolf whistles blasted her the minute she stepped inside.

"Sit here, baby," yelled a florid-faced biker in black leather.

"No, over here, sexy."

The smoky bar was so dark, she couldn't see. But she had the impression of several men in black leather crowded around small tables, drinking and smoking, swearing and shouting to be heard over the blasting music. There were half a dozen kickers in sweat-stained Stetsons at another table.

Then a Texas-sized barrel of a man with a fat potato face and a straw Stetson shoved a chair back and staggered toward her, his hot, narrowed eyes too interested. She caught a whiff of beer on his breath as he reached her.

She *had* to find Leander. *Fast.*

"Well, well. Just look what the cat dragged in," a familiar voice said suggestively against her ear.

"Hi, Mac," she breathed, relaxing a little since she knew him.

"Hi, back," he said, leaning closer, his eyes on her breasts instead of her face. "Thought you was having a big old party out at the ranch."

"It's still going on."

"But you came looking for a crowd that's more fun?"

"Not exactly, Mac."

Her eyes had grown accustomed to the smoke-filled gloom. She scanned the nearby tables first. Then the rest of the bar.

She was near panic when suddenly she recognized Leander's crisp crop of black hair and his tall, linebacker's physique across the room near the Christmas tree. He had stripped out of his tuxedo jacket and was hunched over the bar. His pleated white shirt was unbuttoned at the collar and rolled up to his elbows, revealing tanned, muscular forearms.

"I—I was looking for my husband."

Desperate to attract Leander's attention, she raised her hand to wave at him.

Mac grabbed it, crushing the bones of her wrist, stepping between her and the bar, blocking her view of her husband before Leander could notice her.

"Let me go, Mac. Please—"

Reluctantly the big man obeyed. But the minute she pulled free, he leaned toward her again, and with a lewd gesture, used his thick middle finger to unstick a tendril of wet hair from her cheek. "Now ain't that too bad. The rain done messed up your hairdo. I was just saying what a damn shame it is for a pretty little thing like yourself to be mixed up with a nut case like Pepper, who shot your daddy and then got rich bragging about it in a novel."

She pushed his big hand away. "Nobody ever proved that."

"'Cause y'all covered for him. Maybe it's about time we got some real justice around here."

Leander had looked up and was watching her now. She waved at him, and he saluted her by tipping his liquor bottle ever so slightly.

"Y'all leave him alone, Mac," she pleaded before turning and heading toward the bar.

Wolf whistles and hot stares followed her the entire way.

Leander watched her, too, but in a nicer way that caused every nerve in her body to prickle pleasantly.

"You look a little breathless, Sugar. And you damn sure know how to stir up a ruckus," he said edgily, pulling a stool out for her. "Why don't you sit down and put on my coat?"

He leaned toward her and picked up his jacket.

His white shirt was unbuttoned halfway down his bronzed chest. She remembered how hot he always got when he wore a coat or tie, how anxious he always was to strip out of them. He smiled, a slow lazy smile that transformed his carved features.

Her throat tightened. He seemed so primitively male, so powerful and dangerous—so sinfully handsome.

"I wanted to talk to you," she whispered.

Leander was studying her intently, too, as he draped his coat over her shoulders. When he was done, he took another long pull from his bottle. Then he hooked his other wrist casually and yet possessively over the backrest of her stool. "You should have caught me before I started drinking. I'm too far gone to think. Much less talk."

"Maybe you should slow it down," she said.

"Maybe." With a mocking grin he took another pull.

She watched his lips on the rim of the bottle. When she caught a glimpse of his tongue, unwanted heat climbed her neck.

Nearby someone muttered, "You wouldn't think she'd have anything to do with a loony who killed her father."

Leander's jaw tightened. With an effort he kept his tone casual. "What the hell do you think you're doing—coming here?"

"What will you have, little lady?" Mr. Q interrupted.

"Nothing." Leander's whisper was suddenly tense. "She's leaving."

"Whatever he's drinking," Heddy countered, pulling the black jacket closer around herself. "I'm staying."

Mr. Q pitched three ice cubes in a glass. Then he grabbed Leander's bottle. "Double Scotch on the rocks for the little lady."

"Thanks, Q. I'm *very* thirsty." Her sip began nonchalantly enough. But when the Scotch scalded her throat, she suddenly lurched forward, sputtering and gagging. Leander patted her on the back. She would have taken another sip if Leander's long fingers hadn't curved around her glass.

"Easy does it, Sugar. Maybe you should slow it down."

At the rasping brush of his fingers, she spilled her drink all over the counter.

A hostile murmur went through the crowd as Mr. Q mopped it up with a towel.

"You're attracting attention again," Leander said, a warning in his low tone.

She pulled her glass free of his grip and lifted it to her lips again. "So? Maybe I was trying to."

"I don't like it. You're making them madder. Mac and those jerks are staring at you. You shouldn't have come in here."

"Neither should you. But we're here, aren't we? Together. The question is—what are we going to do about it?"

"I think you should get the hell out of here before this place blows like a keg of dynamite," he said.

"Maybe I feel more like a party." His coat slid off her shoulders as she picked up one of the quarters he'd left on the bar for a tip and handed it to Mr. Q. "Play something we can dance to. Something slow. Something country. Better yet—" She leaned forward and whispered a specific title into Mr. Q's ear before she turned back to Leander. "I want to finish what we started."

"What was that?"

"We were dancing. Remember?"

The music started—slow, twangy—country, but with a heavy beat. She looked everywhere except at him. His bronzed masculinity was evoking a pagan response. Her senses were fighting a losing battle against the desire to be crushed against the muscular strength of his chest.

She slanted her eyes to him. "Well, what do you know?" she said silkily. "They're playing our old song."

Behind the bar, the lights of the Christmas tree winked at her. For a long moment the years slid away and they were young and in love.

He was staring into her eyes, forgetting himself. Then his black gaze left her face and roamed over the shapely length of her body as if he, too, found her irresistible. "That's one helluva dress," he muttered. "You'd better put my damned jacket back on."

"I'm glad you like it," she said without pretense... without reserve.

"That's not what I said. I said put—"

When she tentatively put her hand on the white cotton covering his broad shoulder, one of his nerves jumped. His incredible body heat seeped through his damp sleeve into her fingertips. "Dance with me," she whispered, leaning so close that her breath beat upon his face. "For old time's sake."

One minute stretched into two.

"No way, Sugar," he finally said, jerking away from her touch. "Not here. Not to that song."

She lifted her head and their eyes held again. "Then somewhere private."

"Look, Sugar. You were right. I was wrong. I shouldn't have come back. Nothing's changed except my hide isn't as thick as it used to be. I don't like people thinking I'm this weirdo writer who killed Barret when I didn't. I especially don't like you thinking it. I'll give you your divorce whenever you want it. It'll be my Christmas present."

She swayed even closer. "You didn't used to be such a coward, Leander Knight."

"I was too damn dumb to know to be scared."

When she touched him again, he shot off his stool like her hand burned him, the same as his heat burned her.

"I don't want a divorce for Christmas, any more than you do," she whispered fiercely.

He grabbed her wrist. "Look—don't come on to me. I don't like to be teased."

Her seductive glance flitted to the sensual line of his lips. She ached to feel his mouth on hers, to know that she inflamed him as he did her. "Leander," she said simply. "I'm not teasing."

He let her go and threw down a twenty-dollar bill.

When he slammed his stool back under the bar and strode toward the door, she raced after him.

He plunged out into the thick sheets of rain.

So did she.

When he hopped in his truck and locked the door, she beat on his window in frustration as the thick, cold rain blasted her.

He took his time lowering the glass. "You're getting drenched. Give it up, Sugar." As he backed out slowly, careful not to hurt her, she banged on the side of his truck with her open palms.

He waved goodbye as he revved the engine, his tires spinning gravel and pellets against her bare legs as he kept backing.

The rain was thicker than ever, colder. She'd left his jacket inside and was soon so thoroughly soaked, she was shivering. As he pulled out onto the highway, she got in her Suburban, scooped her keys off the floorboard and sped after him.

Not that he made it easy for her. By the time she swerved onto the highway, his truck had vanished.

She floored the Suburban, her transmission screaming. And a few seconds later she saw the red glare of his brake lights as he swerved too fast to the left off the main road.

His tires hit fresh gravel. She held her breath when his truck slewed violently. Geysers of water shot from his back wheels as his vehicle skidded off the road.

Oh, no... She eased off her accelerator and took the turn slowly, carefully pulling up on the shoulder behind him.

She flashed her headlights on and off.

Ignoring her, he restarted Jim Bob's truck. His engine roared, but his right wheels spun uselessly in the mud.

She laughed.

She had him now.

After two jaunty toots of her horn he didn't get out, so she jumped out into the icy deluge.

When she banged on his window, she saw he was on his car phone. He stared down at her. For a second she thought he was going to stay where he was. Then he cut his engine and threw open his door.

Very slowly he got out, too.

"You should be glad I'm here to rescue you," she said almost lightly.

His mouth was set in a straight line, his eyes dark and empty before her words relit that swift light of anger in his face. "I told you to go home, Sugar."

"You used to drive better than that," she mocked.

He caught her arm and slammed her against his truck. "You didn't used to chase me so hard."

"You never ran," she said.

His savage gaze glittered. "I wasn't on to you, back then."

"I don't think you really feel like running tonight," she said.

There was the barest tightening to his jaw. He might have argued that point, too, but she kissed him.

Lips against lips. Although the contact was brief, it set her pulse racing.

"You're wrong, baby," he muttered, jerking away. But even as his words defied her, his gaze was dwelling on her mouth as if he couldn't forget the taste of her.

Her arms went around his lean waist, her fingers splaying as she drew him toward her. "I don't think so, Leander."

The rain was cold as it blasted them, trickling through their hair, down their spines in icy rivulets, plastering their clothes to their bodies.

But his reluctant lips were hot when he forcefully caught the back of her neck with his hand and, tilting her face, lowered his mouth to hers. His tongue was hot, too, when it invaded her lips and filled her mouth. His arms tightened around her like steel bands as he shoved her against his truck.

She gasped at the sudden heated contact with the rock wall of his chest. For a long moment his mouth smothered hers, and she couldn't breathe. She saw a thousand pin pricks of brilliance behind her closed eyes before blackness swirled around her.

"Ah, Heddy—" he groaned. "I swore I'd never let this happen again."

She caught her breath and sighed as she looked at the rough carving of his dark features. "Me, too."

The icy rain beat down. She was standing ankle-deep in a frigid puddle. Every time she moved, water sloshed inside her sodden designer shoes. But she didn't care.

His warm hand was suddenly on her breast, kneading

her warm flesh through the wet transparent silk. Her nipple was swelling and hardening against his palm. She'd never felt so hot, so purely a creature of animal instinct, her body open and quivering with wonderful, glorious, burning needs.

"I'm not running now—though God knows I should," he whispered, still kissing her, his arms locked around her in a stranglehold of desire as he picked her up and carried her to her Suburban. "What do you say we get the hell out of here?"

Inside her car he placed her across the back seat and devoured her mouth hungrily for a long moment. His deepening kisses touched off the passionate core of her body and set her on fire. When he began lifting wet silk out of the way and touching her intimately, her icy skin turned to flame. Not once did she try to stop his roaming hands as he molded her curves to the hard contours of his male length.

Another car swept past, showering the Suburban with a wave of water and gravel and brilliant headlights.

His voice was husky as he lifted his mouth from the warmth of her throat. "What the hell are we doing, Sugar? Making love in the back seat of your car like teenagers when anybody might drive up?"

On a harsh shudder he let her go. Draping a long arm over the front seat, he jingled the keys in her ignition.

"Climb on over, Sugar," he ordered softly.

Pulling herself up on her elbows, she stared at him dazedly.

"You'd better drive. You've had a helluva lot less than I've had to drink." He spoke in an offhand manner. "I'm staying in that old cabin behind the Janovich place."

"What?"

Another car rushed by peppering them with gravel and brushing them with a brilliant arc of white light again.

In the darkness that followed, she wished he would touch her or hold her, that he would show some small sign of tenderness or affection. But he was frowning. His dark face was harsh; his smooth tone too cynical. "I'm asking you to spend the night with me. No strings attached."

She felt an empty ache in the pit of her stomach.

"I want to sleep with you, Sugar. Don't look so shocked. That's why you came on to me in the bar, wasn't it?"

When she turned her back to him, he yanked her around and kissed her again. His kiss was lush, intimate, from the moment his mouth covered hers.

He tasted of Scotch whiskey and sublime temptation.

"I may not be good enough to be your husband. You might even believe me capable of murder. But you still want me in your bed, don't you? And I'm so desperate for any scrap of affection—I'll take what I can get."

Murder? She had forgotten all that. For a numbed moment she cringed as she guiltily remembered her father.

Leander's black eyes blazed darkly. His wet hair was plastered against his inky brows. His chiseled features were etched with the harsh determination to have his way no matter what.

Was he guilty? Or innocent?

In that moment he seemed so hard. When she scooted away from him, recoiling from the ruthlessness she saw in him, his lips thinned.

"You put me in hell, too, Sugar," he whispered, seething. "For years I was the poor boy bastard your family said wasn't good enough for their rich, blue-blooded princess. Then you and the gossips of this little burg convicted me on a rumor for a murder I didn't commit. I've tried to hate you. I buried myself alive. But you haunted me. No matter how hard I tried to forget you, I couldn't. As for Marcus—'' Leander's curt voice broke abruptly as his arms tightened around her. ''Tonight, you're mine.''

Five

Leander felt like he was coiled tighter than a spring as he stood beside Heddy's stiff figure and fumbled for his key.

"Damn it, I said I was sorry," he whispered.

"Right. Technically I suppose you did."

"What more do you want?"

"Oh—nothing. Or…or maybe just for you to mean it."

More silence. From her.

From him, too.

"You just don't get it. Like I'm really sorry that it gets to me that you desire me even though you still think I'm a killer."

As he shoved the door open, he pitched his key ring past her, scarcely noting in his frustration that it fell between his suitcase and his laptop computer. She stepped inside hesitantly, freezing when she saw the bed. He stopped, too, suddenly seeing his drab room through her aristocratic eyes.

The cabin had ancient cowhide lamp shades with scorch marks. A wagon wheel with deer antlers and little lamps swung over the dining room table at a cockeyed angle. A threadbare Indian blanket had been thrown across his bed.

"Sorry...about the cabin, Sugar. You're used to a whole lot better—"

"No—I was remembering how it was when we came here as kids. You were so messy then. But I loved coming here, being alone with you." Her voice had softened. Some of the strain had left her white face.

"You were sweet to me back then. At least most of the time."

"Life seemed so simple then," she agreed.

Flushing, he pivoted abruptly. His heels made hollow sounds on the scuffed oak floor as he walked over to the pine dresser. There he pulled open a drawer so that she could see it contained plenty of blankets that they could use to wrap up in after they'd stripped out of their wet clothes.

She didn't smile or even look at him as she took a blue one. "Everything's happened so fast. I don't know what to think, Leander."

For a long moment there were only the sounds of his magnified heartbeats and their breaths.

"You could give me the benefit of the doubt, for a change."

She squeezed her eyes shut and nodded. "I am trying to."

"Hey," he murmured. "I'm sorry I yelled at you." When she turned away, his arms went around her in a vise. His hand pressed her golden head against his chest, holding her possessively against him. "But this is hard for me, too," he said gently, lowering his lips to her throat, nibbling until her heartbeat skittered madly. A wild peace enveloped them for an endless time.

She turned to face him, placing her cold hands against his warm cheeks. "Why are you always so hot?"

"High metabolism. I eat a lot. Remember how you used to steal food off my plate."

Her lips parted. "You never minded."

"I used to wish so hard that I'd been born rich or even born legitimate—just so your family would approve of me. Why would I care if you stole my food? I always wanted to give you the world, Heddy." With heated fingertips he tilted her chin up and stared at her. "I didn't kill your father. I would never hurt anyone you loved."

She was silent. And beautiful. So beautiful with her luminous, sapphire eyes, with her long, inky lashes and her slanting brows. Her delectable mouth was gently curved, her nose straight and finely boned. Her breasts rose and fell as she breathed in and out. She was both innocent and voluptuously sensual. He could hardly think, so powerfully was he attracted to her.

But she didn't believe him.

Which was the reason he'd left her and stayed away and sworn never to come back.

He had two choices—to drive her home or to take her to bed.

Her lush mouth parted again, and she moistened her lips with her tongue. The shattering kisses in her Suburban came back to torment him.

Hell. For eight years he'd dreamed of that mouth, of her body. Of her.

There was no choice. He was too far gone to let her go—no matter what she thought of him. No way could he face the bitter loneliness of Jim Bob's cabin without her.

If he didn't take her, he'd torture himself for the rest of his life with the fantasy of what he'd passed up.

Leander knew he was going to kiss her, and there wasn't a damn thing he could do about it.

And the instant his mouth brushed her upper lip and her fingers curled tighter into his chest, he knew that this kiss was like none of the others because they both knew where it would end.

His mouth was tender and yet eager. He didn't rush— it was a kiss of considerable restraint and yet of deep hunger.

When she opened her mouth to accept his tongue, he knew a soul-jolting thrill.

"You'd better take off that wet dress," he said, after the first taste of her tongue and teeth started his heart beating too fast. He sucked in a gulp of air. "Before you catch your death—"

"I don't care, Leander."

"I do," he muttered hoarsely.

Breaking free, she tiptoed with elfin grace to the bathroom.

While she undressed in his tiny bathroom, Leander phoned a cousin of Jim Bob's who had a tow truck and asked him to pick up his truck on the side of the road. Then he stacked logs and lit a fire in the fireplace, so that the room was aglow with a rosy warmth when she came out bundled in the soft blue blanket. He was still so worked up from their kiss that when she accidentally gave him an eyeful of long shapely leg as she settled down by the fire, he craved nothing more than a session of hot, dangerous, all-or-nothing sex. Yet, he was afraid of sex with her. He was afraid it would suck him in too deep.

She didn't help much when she looked up at him dreamily, her eyes pulling him into her in that soul-deep way, like blue magnets. "Why don't you get out of those wet clothes and come sit by the fire?"

"Hey, that's supposed to be my line."

"I'm already undressed." Her damp shoulders were bare. Her wet hair slicked back. She looked young and vulnerable and sexily wanton. "Take your clothes off."

"Good idea," he rasped. "But—"

She felt his hesitation. "Leander, I'm still your wife."

"Technically maybe. But we've been separated more years than we lived together."

Her lovely eyes shimmered with loneliness. And with desire. "I never slept with anybody else. Does that count?"

Yeah. It counted. Too much.

"We still have a very complicated relationship. There's Christina. And Tia."

"Leander, is there…is there somebody else?"

"Hell, there's the whole damned town." He paused. "For the record—I haven't slept with anybody for a long time, either," he breathed.

Her sudden smile was radiant. "Good."

Why the hell had he admitted that? "Not that it's any of your business."

She smiled again when he reddened. "Go take a hot shower. And hurry back. I'm already feeling lonesome."

He took his time. Not that it mattered. As soon as he returned and hunkered down by the fire, she was all over him, snuggling close, smelling fresh and clean and feminine.

"Women are always after you. Are you telling me the truth about your not sleeping—"

He flushed darkly. "I wouldn't make too much of it if I were you. There aren't enough women in Alaska to go around. Especially on the island."

"If you had wanted another woman, you'd have had one." She touched his tanned face, traced the line of his jaw, the hollow of his throat, not saying anything more. She didn't have to. Her eyes spoke volumes. So did the magic fingertips that fired his warm skin.

He could see that she wanted him. Every bit as much as he wanted her. And suddenly nothing else mattered.

She kissed him, her firm lips warm and light in the beginning, but things heated up fast. Within seconds they were stretched length to length, and he was breathing as hard as a marathon runner. He was soon so hot he was peeling off their blankets. Hers first, unwrapping her gorgeous body as if she were a priceless Christmas present, tracing the curves of her exquisite breasts with his palms until she made small gasping sounds of pleasure.

"Heddy—"

"Relax," she whispered, placing his hands back on her creamy flesh, running her own fingers over his hair-roughened arms and torso.

Her skin felt as smooth as satin. Her wet golden hair streamed out over the blue blanket and oak floor in silken waves as she lay back, guiding him toward her, letting his hands move between her thighs, touching first all the allowable spots before those crying out to be touched.

She pulled his blanket off, too, kissing his dark body, his wide shoulders, his taut stomach and sinewy muscles. Her hands followed the path of her lips, stroking lower, down the length of his abdomen, as if she were polishing a living bronze statue. And then finding his manhood, her fingers circled it, sliding back and forth until he groaned aloud.

A few minutes later he jerked away from her. For a second or two she whimpered while he fumbled with a box in the darkness.

"Leander?"

He held up the box of condoms so she could see what he was doing. When he had one on, he rolled back over and feathered her damp brow with kisses. With a silent moan of helpless surrender, she arched her body up to meet his.

He murmured an inarticulate sound of passion. Then with a single thrust he was inside her, binding them body and soul, whispering her name as he tenderly kissed her lips and throat. He began rocking back and forth, driving ever deeper, giving himself shatteringly to the ardent task of satisfying her. Her fingertips tunneled into his black hair. She was whispering his name, clinging, sighing, pleading.

As always, her body was a perfect fit. As always, she excited him as no other woman could, drawing him out of the lonely depths of his solitude. His breath grew heavier as his fever for her rose. And soon, sooner than either of them wanted, swift, hot waves of carnal excitement were sweeping them both to dizzying heights that were greater than they'd ever known.

His head came up in that last moment, and he looked into her unwavering jewel-dark eyes. Tilting her head back, he fused their mouths, his lips grinding against hers, his tongue mating with hers.

He was out of control.

So was she.

And when she found shattering ecstasy, she sent him spiraling over the edge, too.

For a long time after their shared bliss, he lay on top of her, crushing her damp body beneath his. For a timeless moment all their tensions were suspended, and he savored the comfort of her warmth and nearness.

Only she could repel the darkness inside him. The loneliness and pain of the past, all that stood between them, dissolved in that moment of blistering glory.

She was all that had ever mattered to him.

When they were children she had diminished the agony of his lonely childhood, just by being there. Before her he had felt that he was less than nothing because his own mother had thrown him away. Then Heddy had befriended him and made other children befriend him. Because she had believed in him, he had started believing in himself. All that he had ever accomplished was due to her. That was why her betrayal had hurt worse than anything in his whole life.

Outside the wind and rain raged. Inside the fire died down and they lay together in secret, loving peace. He fell asleep still holding her, clinging to the fragile dream that he hadn't come this far to lose her again.

And then the telephone rang.

Dimly he felt Heddy's warm body untangling from his as she reached an arm lazily across his chest to lift the receiver.

Leander's stomach tightened at the instant guilt in Heddy's muted voice when she said, "Tia!"

His eyes opened. As he studied the ceiling, his temples began to pound—from the Scotch, from the long airplane flights, from the sex—or maybe just from listening to the strain in Heddy's voice.

Shapes lit by the dying embers of the fire came slowly into focus. He made out the hideous antler chandelier, the gleam of Heddy's tangled hair. Most of all he felt the heaviness of Tia's spirit coming between them again.

"It just happened, Tia. He ran Jim Bob's truck off the road," Heddy was saying in that hollow tone he hated. "I couldn't very well just leave him there when it was pouring."

Leander's opaque eyes glittered in the dark. "Why don't you tell her you were chasing me when I ran off the road, Sugar?"

With a shudder Heddy clamped her hand over the receiver. "Hush." She removed her fingers, one by one. "I—I don't know, Tia. I—I just felt like a drive."

"Sugar, why don't you tell her how you were feeling when you came on to me in the bar in that wet, skin-tight, see-through red dress—"

"Mac called?" Heddy said sharply, whitening. "Yes, I did go there." Her remorseful voice was nearly inaudible. "I know. It was kind of a crazy thing to do."

"Not any crazier than coming here, Sugar. Not any crazier than…this." Leander's hand moved under the sheets and ran up her silky, naked thigh.

She jumped away from his heated fingers with a startled cry. "No, Tia. It was nothing. I—I just…saw a mouse. I'm okay. I—I swear."

Heddy hung up and sank stiffly against her pillow. When he started to roll on top of her, she backed away. "I have to go."

"Heddy—" He ached to hold her again, to know the warm bliss of her body in the darkness again. But instead of reaching for her, he got defensive, too, which made him retreat into that place deep inside himself that was like a frozen ice cave where he could shut out everyone who rejected him, even her. He found angry words and forced them out.

"Right," he began. "Tia called. And she doesn't like it that you're with me. So, what's new? You're torn between the two of us again. And you'll choose her because you always do. But before you go, could you forget Tia and tell me what you feel about what happened here tonight?"

Heddy's pale expression was unreadable. "Tia wants to know why. She wants to know how—how I could be here with you. I guess maybe I do, too."

"You tell me, Heddy. You followed me to that bar. You asked me to dance. You kissed me in the rain. Did you want sex? Or did you want something more?"

Heddy sprang off the bed. Then realizing she was naked, she yanked the sheet off him and wrapped it around herself.

His muscular body lay sprawled across the bed without a stitch on. "What gets you hot, Heddy? My bad reputation...or me?"

"Shut up," she whispered, dragging her gaze from him with an immodest reluctance that fired his blood. "Just shut up. This isn't helping." Her voice was quavering with anger.

"Are you mad because you like sleeping with me? Or because Tia has you back to thinking I murdered Barret?"

She compressed her lips and turned away again. He watched her, wanting to push her even harder and demand answers.

She whisked her dress off the chair by the fire. When she disappeared into his bathroom, he got up.

Seething, he yanked clothes off hangers in his closet, pulling on his jeans and a Western shirt. Then he rummaged on his closet floor for his belt and boots.

When she came out of the bathroom, he was grabbing his black Stetson hat from a peg on the wall by the door.

She stared at him, her anguished face darkening with embarrassment as she realized his intention. "Where do you think you're going?"

"I'm driving you home, Sugar."

"Not in my car. We can't be seen—"

"Together?" he mocked, finishing her thought. "By

Tia or somebody else? You ashamed of me, like before?"
He felt a muscle ticking savagely in his neck.

She blushed, equally furious. "Yes! Yes! I'm embarrassed they'll know—" Her eyes darted to the tangled white sheets and Indian blanket on his bed.

"Sugar, it's a little late to worry on that score. Tia already knows about us, and the whole town'll know tomorrow you chased me out of the bar. I don't want you out this late alone. You could have an accident. Somebody might chase you and run you off the road. I don't want just anybody…rescuing you."

She stood stock-still, her eyes wide as he leaned down and scooped up his keys.

"Leander, I hate this as much as you do."

He let a moment of silence pass. "Somehow I doubt that."

"But if—if you didn't kill my father, who did? Is it so terrible that—that I just want to know what really happened to him?"

All the warmth he'd felt for her congealed. He hated her thinking him that low. And because his own emotions were so ravaged, because he had retreated into that dark cold part of himself, his voice came out harsh and razor sharp with sarcasm.

"Don't we all, Sugar. But what I wanted more than that was for you to believe in me. You don't. You won't ever. Which means our marriage is over. What galls me the most is that I still give a damn. But for the record—I don't intend to for long."

He strode toward the door and shoved it open for her. When she stayed where she was, he stepped quietly outside into the wet, wild night without her.

Some instinct warned him of the danger.

He heard shouts. Then flashlights blinded him.

There was a deafening shotgun blast. Another gunshot. "Don't come out!" he yelled, reeling backward as a steel bullet creased his temple, snapping his black hat off. Blood spurted from his hair and streamed into his eyes.

"Got the creepy bastard," someone screamed.

Blinded by blood and the darkness after the flashlights, Leander crawled back inside, shouting hoarsely to Heddy to get down. When she didn't obey instantly, he grabbed her ankle and pulled her beneath him, blanketing her with his own body.

There was a final shotgun blast as he kicked the door shut. As they lay in the darkness, his larger body almost completely smothering hers, he heard racing footsteps outside, shouts, and a truck engine and a motorcycle roared to life.

Still shielding Heddy, he dragged her to the window and cautiously watched a late-model sedan and a big motorcycle race away in the wet darkness.

When his assailants were gone, Leander slumped against the wall, all his emotions draining out of him as his blood dripped from his brow onto the carpet. He felt dizzy, sick. He saw Heddy's face, heard her frantic whispers before he lost consciousness.

When he gradually came to a few seconds later, his head hurting like it was going to split in two, Heddy was kneeling beside him, bathing his face with a cold towel.

"I think it's just a nick," she said soothingly.

He heard her through a mist of pain and nausea.

When her wet rag stung him again, he grabbed her wrist and opened his eyes. "Just a nick?" he howled fiercely.

"A scratch," she confirmed, her tone gentle. "Did… did you see who shot you?"

He touched his hand to his face and found only a trace of sticky blood.

"No. It could have been anybody."

He lay back, relaxing, his anger for the moment gone, not caring if the whole town wanted him dead if she cared this much, liking her gentle fingers smoothing his black hair away from his brow so that she could apply the gauze dressing.

When he winced, she murmured anxiously, "Are you okay? I—I don't like hurting you."

"Yeah. Right." The constriction in his throat made his deep voice sound weak.

Her pale face grew very remorseful. Her lips bent to kiss the bandage. "No, I don't. I really don't like hurting you," she repeated dully.

"Then it was almost worth getting shot up," he said. "To know you care, even if you don't believe—"

When her fingertips stroked his rough cheeks, his heart began to pound.

Her dark lashes fluttered. "I care," she whispered. "Too much."

"It always was fun—making up after one of our fights."

"Yes, it was."

"Heddy," he said hoarsely. "Do you ever think— Do you ever hope that—"

He stopped himself and wearily closed his eyes. For years he'd schooled himself not to dream the impossible.

For a long moment it was enough that they could share the darkness together, that they could find comfort if not peace once more in each other's company.

When the phone rang again, he knew even before Heddy picked it up that it would be Tia.

Six

Wind lashed the palm fronds in front of the big house, but the fury of the storm was nothing compared to the turmoil Tia felt as she stood in the arched doorway and watched the rain batter the thick palms in the middle of her circular drive.

As always her annual Christmas party had been a huge success, the last of her glittering guests having been whisked away by limousine to the airport hours ago. But Tia was not thinking with either pleasure or pride of the ball she had carefully orchestrated.

Her aristocratic features were set in an icy mask. Every time Tia remembered Heddy abandoning Marcus on the dance floor and running after Leander, her heart rushed with an odd pain that took her breath away. She felt weak and old—and very ill equipped to deal with her impossible grandson-in-law.

But she had to fight him one last time.

Tia had sensed he'd be trouble when Heddy had rushed home from school and told her about the poor boy she'd saved from a fight. The minute Tia had seen him, she'd known at once he was a cocky, self-serving upstart who had befriended Heddy solely because he was impressed with her money and position. Later he had married her for the same reason and had used the scandal and tragedy following Barret's death to promote himself into a world-famous writer.

Tia remembered the first afternoon Heddy had brought him home. He'd been a skinny ten-year-old with holes in his jeans. Tia had hidden on the second-floor landing and observed him. His black eyes had gleamed as he'd stared at the black-and-white marble floors in the foyer, the three-story spiral staircase and the enormous chandelier that hung in the foyer.

Tia remembered Heddy's almost feverish excitement as she had dashed about, letting him turn the chandelier on and off, letting him handle all the house's treasures. He had been clumsy and self-conscious, not wanting to touch anything, but Heddy had made him.

How Tia had relished his terror when he and Heddy had dropped a priceless Dresden porcelain figurine. He had wanted to confess at once, swearing he'd work for her grandmother forever to pay for it, but Heddy had insisted on hiding the broken bits under a table—an action that had proved to Tia the boy was a corrupting influence.

Tia had swept down the stairs then, pretending to know nothing of the Dresden figure, inviting the scarlet-faced children to tea and cookies on the terrace, only noting the absence of the figurine after she had lulled him into a false sense of security.

When they were once more in the foyer and she was showing him out, she had innocently commented that the

Dresden piece wasn't there. He'd flushed as Tia had pretended to search the china closets. Tia had been haughtily magnanimous when he'd confessed and shown her where the broken fragments were. She had soothed the embarrassed boy. At the same time she had let him know how irreplaceable the figurine was. She had made him see that he shouldn't play with things he couldn't afford. Secretly she had hoped to make him feel so outclassed and uncomfortable that he would realize he didn't belong and would never return.

And he never had come into their house again until that disastrous day when he'd returned as Heddy's husband. Tia remembered how happy the young couple had been, how full of young love and hope. When Tia had greeted them coldly, Pepper had sworn that he knew he wasn't good enough for Heddy in her eyes, but if she'd just give him a chance, she'd soon see that no man could ever love her granddaughter as he did.

Not that either she or Barret had believed him. From the first, Tia had been determined to find some way to break them up. And since she had known Heddy so well, she had known just how to manipulate events to diminish Pepper in her eyes. How Tia had loved having the kind of parties and inviting snobs she'd been sure would ask the kinds of questions that most embarrassed and infuriated him. She had used pretended kindness to destroy him.

And now the bastard was back.

When Tia saw the arc of white headlights at the gate, her heart jerked painfully again and began palpitating with sharp fits and starts when she got a glimpse of the tall man in the Stetson beside Heddy.

Tall and lean, still the rangy cowboy, Leander jumped out of the Suburban and helped Heddy down. Tia hated the way he bent his dark bandaged head so attentively to

Heddy's, the way she smiled so sweetly up at him as they joined hands and ran together through the rain toward the house.

The disgusting display of affection between them could mean only one thing—that Heddy had given into the wild, headstrong part of her nature that had been such a problem when she'd been a girl. She had slept with him again.

Thinking themselves alone, the lovers melted together under the awning, their mouths clinging for an endless time before reluctantly breaking apart. Tia's hand went to her chest. Her eyes grew as hard as stones as Heddy touched the white bandage at his temple and smoothed the damp lock of black hair that was falling carelessly across his forehead.

They were more in love than ever.

The storm door whined as Tia pushed it ajar and stepped out of the darkness, her intent to drive him away.

The wind was like a physical blow, banging the door back into the stucco wall and unbalancing her so that she teetered as rain blasted her.

Odd—how the cold air made her heart tighten and turned the joints of her knees to jelly, how her old eyes had trouble focusing on Heddy and Leander, who were now peering up at her.

"Tia?" Leander demanded.

The bruised center of her chest tightened again, this time radiating sharp, paralyzing wavelets of pain. When she tried to catch a breath, she couldn't.

"Tia, I didn't see you there," Heddy began in a frightened rush. "Is anything the matter?"

Tia clutched her chest, gasping for air. Heddy's lovely face began to swim in a sea of raindrops and darkness as she fought to speak.

An iron band wound around Tia's chest, crushing her diaphragm so tightly she couldn't breathe.

Her heart was beating violently now; her gown was wet with perspiration. And she felt heavy. Too heavy to stand.

"Dizzy," she said in a weak, baffled voice as her knees buckled and she grabbed for the railing.

As the polished wood slipped from her grasp and she staggered, Leander plunged toward her through the darkness.

Their eyes locked.

His expression was kind, almost gentle; hers aflame with implacable hatred. Even so it was she who recoiled.

"No—" She pushed herself away from him, stumbling backward.

In terror of him.

Her mouth went dry as he caught her, cradling her gently as he lowered her to the ground.

"Tia, Tia—" Heddy was sobbing now, truly terrified.

The wind and rain were whipping the house. But the burning pain in Tia's chest obliterated everything.

"Call 911," Leander barked at Heddy.

Only dimly, as if he were shouting from a long way away did Tia hear him.

"Am I dying?" Tia managed in a shaken voice.

Leander turned back to her, his eyes very kind, his gentle tone reassuring. "It's going to be all right. There's nothing to be afraid of."

But he was wrong.

Tia buried her head in his shoulder and wept. They were tears of despair and agony. But there was something else—fear. The most terrible fear she had ever known.

Fear of what she had done.

Never before had she been afraid to die. And it was all Leander's fault.

Pictures from the past flashed before her. She was remembering the sanitarium, the patients roaming the wide halls, their vacant stares, the wild horror of her husband's illness and his rampages. She saw scraps of paper blackening in the library trash basket, and then the thick noxious smoke filling the library. Next she saw Barret's decaying body in the ravine and the Beretta lying in the sand by his skeletal claw.

For years she had never once allowed herself to think of these things. But now she was too weak to suppress the terrifying memories.

A crushing wave of pain spiked from her chest down her left arm.

Heddy knelt and kneaded her age-spotted hand. "The ambulance is coming—"

"Too late," Tia gasped. And then she looked straight at Leander and spewed all the jealous venom in her heart. "This is your fault. First you took Heddy. Then you murdered Barret. Now, you have killed me. Why couldn't you just stay away?"

Tears sprang to Heddy's eyes.

Leander's gaze hardened, but he didn't speak.

Tia was suddenly too exhausted to say more. She saw the blackened ashes at the bottom of the library trash can. She remembered opening the windows to get rid of the smell of smoke.

And then she felt herself slipping into darkness.

"If I die, promise me, Heddy darling, that you won't take him back."

Only dimly was she aware of Heddy's face crumpling as she made a sharp little cry.

"Promise me."

Heddy was very pale as she leaned down and whispered brokenly. Tia smiled faintly at her granddaughter's words.

She had won. Now—at last, she, Tia, could rest. She wanted peace. Oblivion.

But when she closed her eyes that was not what she found.

One minute she was drifting into darkness with the memories of her long life passing before her.

In the next she was being sucked into a vacuum of fire and sent hurtling into a blazing hell.

Waves of flame writhed like snakes around her.

Terrified, she screamed.

The snakes slithered closer, wrapping themselves around her ankles, pulling her deeper into the inferno.

She heard Leander's kind voice through the spiraling orange tongues that coiled ever tighter.

But she couldn't see him. She couldn't find him.

And she had to.

She opened her eyes, but he wasn't there, either.

She was lost in a sea of fiery darkness.

"Leander—"

"Don't try to talk," he said soothingly.

But she had to talk. She had to tell him.

Before it was too late.

But just as she was about to explain, the sky seemed to crash down upon her, and she was trapped in a fiery pyre with the burning writhing snakes.

Seven

There was a roar from the angry crowd when Leander emerged from the hospital into the grayness of the day.

"Knight!"

Leander didn't hear them at first as he raced down the steps. The rain had stopped. The gray clouds were higher, and the sun had broken through.

The Santa Claus and his sleigh that was set up in front of the hospital looked oddly out of place on the lush green lawn. The day was almost balmy—at least to someone used to the bitter winter of southern Alaska.

Not that Leander even noticed the weather. Or the Christmas decorations.

His skin was sallow, and there were dark smudges of sleeplessness under his eyes.

"Knight! Murderer!"

Leander's mouth went dry when he heard his name; it

grew absolutely parched when he saw the stampeding army hurrying angrily up the steps toward him.

Townspeople with raised fists were waving handmade signs. Yates and his deputies in their uniforms trying to hold back the crowd.

Photographers screamed abuse and curses, so Leander would scowl their way.

Two smiling reporters rushed through the melee with raised mikes. One of them was a tall, slim woman with curly black hair. She had a nice smile and nice eyes. A rhinestone snowflake was pinned to her lapel. In other circumstances he might have liked her as a friend.

"Bastard! You belong in a cell!"

Leander ducked the mikes and cameras.

"Murderer!"

Venomous insults erupted like lava as he bolted for the rear parking lot where Jim Bob's cousin had sworn he'd left the truck.

"Get the bastard!"

More shouts. Thundering heels on pavement. Storm troopers right behind him. In hot pursuit.

They were catching him.

"You deserve the same thing Tia got!"

They closed in around him when he reached Jim Bob's truck.

"Murderer!"

One of the photographers cursed him vilely.

Leander's lips curled back from his teeth. He grabbed one of the signs and, raising it, turned on the photographer. His black eyes lit dangerously. He made an inarticulate animal sound of rage and drew back the sign as if he might strike.

The photographer laughed gleefully. Flashes blazed. Cameras clicked.

"Got the bastard!"

More creepy photographs for the tabloids.

"Why did you come back to Kinney?" the nice reporter asked.

"Because that's what my kid wanted for Christmas. Because I thought I was still in love with my wife."

"Did you kill—"

"Go to hell. All of you."

Leander threw down his sign and got in his truck, slamming the door as the pretty young woman scribbled and the photographers got shots of the sign he'd thrown down.

He fumbled on the floorboard for the keys. His heart was pounding at a terrific rate and with such terrific force that his whole body shook. He couldn't believe he'd answered the woman's question.

His tormentors got on either side of his truck and began rocking it back and forth. Suddenly he felt exactly like one of his heroes in a novel, hemmed in by enemies.

Trapped. Claustrophobic.

At the sound of breaking glass he jumped. He felt a small sharp pain in his left cheek. Touching the place with a fingertip, he drew back a splinter of glass and blood.

The bastards had smashed out a back window. A flying shard had cut his face.

Somehow he managed to start the truck and back out of the parking lot without running over one of the jerks.

Once he'd escaped them, Leander drove slowly. The road was straight; the south Texas landscape bleak and endless. The sky was huge.

He mopped his brow. He could feel his pulse pounding under the bandage over his temple. His blood pressure was probably off the charts.

For eight years Heddy had put him in hell. After the way she'd treated him last night, he was finally through.

Tia had hovered in intensive care on the brink of death all night, her condition too unstable for surgery. Leander had stayed in the hospital to be with Heddy. Not that she had wanted him there.

Heddy had neither looked at him, nor spoken to him. Every time he'd tried to comfort her, she'd pushed him away with a wild desperate look and curled up in a vinyl chair, hugging herself quietly or silently weeping.

Her tears would have been bad enough, but what killed him was the way she'd kept staring at him with her soulful blue eyes and repeating, "I should never have chased after you. I should have stayed with Marcus last night. If I had, Tia would be all right."

She wanted Marcus! That pale, bloodless, aristocratic wimp!

Finally she said that one time too many. Or maybe he'd just had one cup of coffee too many.

Whatever. He'd flung his coffee cup in the trash and erupted.

"Fine," he'd yelled. "Go back to Marcus. I'm sick of the way you let Tia run your life. Not matter what I do, I can never come up to your high standards or hers. You want Marcus? You want a divorce? Okay—you've got it."

When she'd chased after him, he'd shrugged her off and sworn to her that this time he was really through.

Half an hour later when he got to his cabin and his phone was ringing, he was so worried about her, fool that he was, he raced inside and grabbed it.

A brutal masculine voice that sounded a whole lot like Benson's blasted him. "Bastard! Get out of town. Next time we won't miss."

Leander turned on his television and Yates was there, expounding pompously from the hospital steps. Leander punched the remote and was stunned to find Mary Ann giving an idiotic critique of his novel *Dead Ringer*.

Then Heddy walked into the shop, and the reporters pounced on her.

"Tell our viewers about your famous husband."

Heddy's eyes were swimming with tears as she looked directly into the camera. "Would you please just leave us alone?"

On another channel he saw his own haggard image swinging a sign that read Murderer, Go Back to Alaska. He listened to the pretty reporter ask him why he'd come back to Kinney. He heard himself say, "Because I thought I still loved my wife."

Leander caught his breath. He couldn't stand it.

His agent called next.

Partly to express concern.

Mostly to inform him that his publisher was putting a rush on a huge reprint order to get more books out to meet the demand.

"They're selling like hotcakes!"

Leander went ballistic. "You just don't get it, Shaw. Nobody does! I'm not some psycho killer. I didn't come here to get shot at or to terrorize an old lady into a heart attack just to sell a few lousy books. I came here to try to save my marriage and get to know my daughter."

"Sure. Sure. I'm on your side. But, hey, nobody up here is complaining if we sell a few million more copies of your novels just because a few idiots believe—"

Leander swore viciously and slammed the phone down.

He was losing it. And there wasn't a damn thing he could do about it.

When the telephone rang again, he picked it up, intending to force out some sort of apology to Dean.

"Shaw, look, I'm—"

A deep voice cut in, "Leave Heddy alone! Go back to Alaska, killer!"

This time Leander didn't bother to hang up.

Heddy wasn't going to call. She didn't believe in him. She never would. She didn't give a damn what he might be going through.

Hell. He had said he was going to divorce her.

It was about time he got smart and stuck to what any fool could see was the only rational solution to their crazy marriage.

Maybe he still loved her. Maybe she still felt something for him.

So what? He couldn't live on *maybe*.

She was worse than the jerks who had mobbed him at the hospital. Her only concern was Tia, and Tia ruled her the same way she ruled the town. If Tia died, Heddy would blame him for her death, too.

Leander sank onto his bed and stared up at the crooked chandelier. The caller had it right. The only smart thing to do was to get the hell back to Alaska.

Who would miss him?

He thought of Christina. Of Heddy.

He was only making their lives worse by hanging around. He was mortally sick of the whole mess.

Not that he could go before Tia's crisis was resolved.

Still, he got up and began listlessly stacking his things in a pile, so they would be easy to pack when the time came.

As he grabbed an armful of hangers from his closet, he heard tires crunching into his shell drive. Tensing, he backed warily away from his window. But the footsteps running lightly up his steps and across his porch were a woman's, and the knock at the door was gentle enough to be Heddy's.

He felt a sudden tearing pain. His whole being ached for her to walk through that door and tell him that she loved him and believed in him.

Cautiously he went to the door and opened it. But his smile died when he saw the beautiful woman standing there.

In the slanting afternoon sun, Mary Ann's lush hair looked like flyaway plumes of fire. Her beige sweater was too tight across her beautiful breasts. She was as brightly painted and as ravishingly aglow as a stage actress. There was a sexy interplay between her mouth and eyes that probably caught most men.

He froze, unable to think of a thing to say to her.

With a bat of her long lashes, she cued him boldly. "I'm sure you don't mind if I come in."

"Anytime." He held the door for her.

"Hey," she said softly, touching his nicked cheek and bandaged temple. "This town isn't so good for your health."

"I'm not the town's most popular citizen."

"With me you are."

She squeezed past him then, letting her lush body brush his.

"Sorry," she whispered.

But she wasn't, and her warm smile made him uneasy.

"You're here because..."

"Oh, er, yes. I—I brought my book."

He relaxed just a little when he saw the fat brown package she was carrying.

"You do remember you promised to read it?"

He didn't, but he nodded anyway.

"I just think it's terrible what everybody's saying about you. I don't believe you'd hurt a fly. Much less blow out your father-in-law's brains and leave him for the buzzards to eat.''

Leander's mouth tightened. ''You said you came because of your book?''

''I know it's probably a terrible time for you, but I want you to tell me every little thing that's wrong with it,'' she purred. ''I can take criticism.''

''Sure. I'll get to it when I can.''

''I—I thought maybe we could read it...together?'' Her voice was throaty.

''Like you said—it's a bad time.''

''Oh.'' Her painted lips pouted prettily.

He didn't reverse his position.

''I tried to call, but your line was busy.''

''Write down your phone number and address. I'll get back to you when I'm done,'' he said in a businesslike tone.

She wrote quickly. ''I'll be waiting...breathlessly for your call.''

''It may be a while,'' he warned dryly.

Her teasing eyes were too intimate as he escorted her outside. Just as he was putting her into her car, Heddy drove up.

She looked pale and exhausted as she cut her engine. But Leander's throat went hot at the sight of her.

Heddy had come to him. Why?

He would have rushed to her if he hadn't played the fool for her so many times before. With an effort, he forced himself to pretend indifference and concentrate on his first guest. He kept talking to Mary Ann even though his real attention was riveted to the solitary woman in the Suburban.

His flirty grin produced a dazzling smile from Mary

Ann. Heddy whitened and pulled down her visor and fluffed her fingers through her hair.

When Mary Ann made him an illicit proposition, Leander leaned deeper into her car, kissed her cheek and whispered his regrets that he was a married man. As he did it, he relished the way Heddy slammed the visor back in place, the way her face tightened.

Was she jealous? Did she feel something for him after all?

He beamed brightly and waved at Mary Ann as she drove away. Only when she was out of sight did he lower his hand and walk slowly over to Heddy's Suburban.

"You getting out? Or are you just going to sit there fiddling with your hair all afternoon?"

"You didn't look like you would welcome an interruption," she retorted icily.

"Didn't I? Sorry."

"Mary Ann told me she was going to the bank."

"I assure you, her visit was strictly professional," he said mildly.

"I'll bet."

"Would you care if it wasn't? I mean, since you're so determined to blame me for everything that goes wrong—"

She didn't answer as he helped her down from the Suburban. Instead she looked at the bare branches of the large oak tree to the right of his front door. One of the branches had broken in the storm and had collapsed against his roof. Dead brown leaves, soaked by the rain, littered his porch and shell drive.

"Either you or Jim Bob needs to do some serious pruning—"

"It'll have to be Jim Bob. He's hell with a chain saw."

Leander was leading her inside his cabin. "Besides, as

you can see—" Once inside, Leander turned his broad back to her and made a careless gesture toward the messy pile of jackets and jeans and luggage by his computer and manuscripts. "I'm leaving just as soon as we know what's going to happen to Tia."

He heard Heddy sink to the bed. "Oh. I—I..." Her distressed voice sounded almost faint.

Still, he kept his back to her and continued to pretend indifference. He was divorcing her. He was through with her *forever* he reminded himself. It didn't matter that she had come to see him.

"Leander, I came here because—I know I made you feel terrible. I want to thank you for being so sweet to Tia last night and to me when we were both so awful to you. Whenever I'm around her, it's like I—"

"You can only be loyal to her by hating me," he said, finishing her sentence and turning to face her at last.

"That's what Mary Ann said to me this morning. I guess, in a way, you're right. But, I don't know what I would have done without you. You were wonderful in the ambulance. I totally panicked— And when you blew up and left the hospital a while ago, I panicked again. I—I don't think I can go through this without you."

Leander stared at her in amazement. "Even if it means more scandal and publicity, and making Tia unhappy?"

"I can see that the publicity is worse for you than it is for me."

That admission, as well as her gratitude, further stunned him.

"And Tia?"

Guiltily she looked away.

He gritted his teeth. *He was through, damn it.*

"Most of all, you need to stay for Christina's sake," Heddy continued on a different tack. "I just left her. I'm afraid she's seen the television coverage, and she's very upset and confused. Until Tia's better, I'm going to have to be at the hospital a lot, and Christina needs somebody to stay with her. I think it should be you.''

He nodded wearily. She wanted him to stay more for Christina than for her.

''There's something else. Tia has been asking for you. When we try to distract her, she gets very agitated and starts repeating your name over and over. Sort of like a chant.''

Leander stared at her angrily. With her dying breath, that domineering old witch still wanted his hide. ''Wait till the press hears this,'' he muttered, furious. ''It's not enough that she nailed me to the cross for Barret's death. She's not about to die until she makes damn sure she's convinced everybody—including you—that I brought on this heart attack. Or maybe she's going to say I poisoned her.''

''Leander, she really is so pitiful.''

''Yeah, sure.'' His low voice was harsh.

''I—I don't blame you for feeling—''

Confusion, grief, pain—he saw them all in her luminous eyes. If he was going to divorce her, it would be easier if he hated her.

His fury left him.

Slowly he crossed the room and sat down on the bed beside her, enfolding her in his arms. She laid her golden head upon his shoulder.

''Forgive me. I shouldn't have said that. You know I hope Tia gets better.''

''I'm so afraid she won't,'' Heddy whispered in a small voice. ''I feel like I'm losing everything.''

''I can relate to that.''

With an effort he put Tia out of his mind and concentrated on Heddy. She was shivering as she huddled against him. He drew her deeper into his arms, warming her, soothing her. Then he buried his face in the wealth of her hair and murmured reassurances that everything would be all right, even as his own doubts tore at him.

She moaned softly and clung to him.

"Lie down with me," he prodded gently a little while later.

"No. I—" She shivered and tried to pull away.

"Heddy," he whispered softly. "I just want to hold you for a little while. I swear I won't touch you in any other way."

She sucked in a hesitant breath. "I don't know—"

"One last time."

She looked into his eyes.

As always, even though she looked pale and exhausted, he found her beautiful. As always, in her gaze he saw her soul.

God, he'd had her last night. Since then she'd put him through hell. He was going to divorce her. But even as he longed to despise her, he was starving for her.

"I won't touch you," he said, swallowing hard.

She bit her lip. "That's okay," she whispered, her voice as low and choked as his.

Very slowly her arms went around his neck, and she allowed him to ease her down on the bed beside him.

As she stretched her cool, pliant body against his warm length, he was sure he'd never known such exquisite torture. He closed his eyes to shut out the vision of her lush beauty; he clenched his fists so he would not run them over her body. He was determined not to let his desire for her break the tenderness of this short time they had together.

She snuggled closer against him, sighing, as if she felt

warm and safe in his arms. Gently he brushed his lips against her hair, then her brow.

He had wanted a life with her so desperately. It broke his heart that he might never hold her like this again, that he would probably never make love to her again. But he couldn't go on like this.

It would tear him apart to leave her, but as he pressed her closer, he knew he was at the end of his rope. He was through fighting a losing battle.

Baby-sitting had to be the most stressful job in the world, Leander thought, eyeing his wristwatch as he had dozens of times before, glad that it was about time for Heddy to return.

"Can I wear your hat, Uncle Leander?" Attilla asked very politely—which would have warned Leander that the brat had something up his sleeve. "I want to see the bullet hole in it again."

Attilla was hanging his last Christmas ornament on the almost leafless, stunted mesquite tree that Leander and the children had chopped down. They had hauled it up three flights of stairs to their playroom, leaving a trail of mesquite twigs and thorns that had kept two housekeepers busy with brooms and sweepers for an hour.

Christina pranced saucily over to the window in her daddy's Stetson. "No! You had your turn, Attilla!" She shivered involuntarily in spite of the thick blue sweater she was wearing.

Cleo who was standing by the tree, threw down the little cowboy hat that she'd been making for a miniature Santa and dashed up to Christina on swift bare feet. "I haven't had my turn yet!"

"That's because my daddy's hat is way too big for you,

Cleo." At just that moment, the Stetson tumbled over Christina's brow and hid her eyes.

"See there. It doesn't fit you, either," Cleo said importantly.

Christina pushed the black brim back up. "Does, too!"

"Children, I may just have to wear my hat myself—if you all can't share."

The quick treble of worried voices rose in volume as each child pleaded his case to Leander. All afternoon they had besieged him with questions. And with demands that he settle countless circular arguments. Attilla and Christina had almost come to blows about which baby mesquite tree would make the perfect "Cowboy Christmas" tree. Then Cleo had to be comforted and bandaged with three Band-Aid strips after she got a mesquite thorn wedged under her thumbnail.

Never had Leander felt more powerful. Nor more important.

Nor more stressed out. Maybe because he was used to so much solitude. Maybe because he wasn't used to so much energy.

This fatherhood bit could be nerve shredding. Each child had a totally different personality. Attilla was a hyperactive dynamo who turned into a bully if he didn't get constant attention. Christina was bossy, selfish and passionately stubborn. Cleo tended to whine about the smallest injury, imagined or real, and she couldn't keep up with her shoes to save her soul.

All three were daredevils. All three were argumentative. All three were full of ideas. But their way of viewing the most ordinary things in life with a marvelous, wide-eyed wonder sparked his creativity.

Leander had thought he was messy, but these kids were as hard on a neat house as three miniature cyclones. Nev-

ertheless, the pluses of fatherhood outweighed the mi-
nuses. At least that's what he thought until Attilla yanked
the Stetson off Christina's head, jammed it on top of his
own red corkscrews, raced out onto the landing, jumped
onto the banister and slid recklessly all the way down to
the foyer, screaming, "Yahoo, ride 'em cowboy!" at the
top of his lungs. His oversize athletic shoes hit the black
and white marble floor running.

Leander was about to race after him. But Christina's
question stopped him cold.

"Did you really kill my grandpa?"

Leander heard the front door bang which meant Attilla
had escaped. Christina watched him, her blue eyes charged
with passionate curiosity.

"Who told you that, sweetheart?" he demanded mildly.
"Your mother?"

"No. Kids. People in town. Mr. Yates on TV. I saw
you, too, and you looked mean."

Leander sank to his knees and ruffled her hair. "It isn't
true, and someday everybody will know it isn't."

"A kid at school told a lie about me once."

Leander nodded sympathetically.

"And everybody believed him instead of me." A pause.
"Does my mommy believe you?"

"No. And I'm afraid that when she does learn the truth,
it'll probably be too late for us."

Christina chewed her lip. Big-eyed, Cleo was listening
to them and studying her bandaged thumb.

"I believe you, Daddy," Christina said at last.

Christina climbed onto his knee and put her arms
around his neck.

"I believe you, too, Uncle Leander," Cleo said in a
hushed voice. When she came up to him cautiously, he
pulled her into his arms too.

"And, girls, that means a whole lot to me," he said, his voice oddly muffled. "More than you'll ever know."

Christina who could not stay serious long wriggled to the carpet. "You're the best baby-sitter we ever had. Are you going to whip Attilla when we find him?"

Cleo said, "It was my turn to wear your hat. And he made me hurt my thumb."

Leander had the distinct feeling he was being manipulated by minds that were far more clever than his. But there was no way he could disappoint his only two allies.

"Let's go get him!" he whispered.

The girls were out on the landing in a flash. And before Leander could groan "Not the banister" they had straddled it and were flying down the three flights even faster than Attilla had.

What the hell? If three brats could do it—

Leander climbed on the polished railing and sailed after them.

He came flying into the marble-floored foyer just as Heddy, her arms full of packages, burst through the front door.

"Leander! What do you think you're doing?"

"Er…baby-sitting."

The little girls giggled madly from the corner where they were turning a crystal ball upside down and then setting it upright, so they could watch tiny flecks of fake snow shower down on the brightly painted Santa Claus inside.

"Mommy—" Christina was shaking the ball vigorously. "Daddy's going to catch Attilla for us and spank him."

"I thought I told you that we don't allow corporal punishment in this house," Heddy said primly.

Leander sprang from the banister. "I wasn't going to spank him. I just wanted to find him."

"And the banister?"

He grinned sheepishly, charmingly. "I couldn't let the girls escape, too."

Heddy relented and gave him a soft smile. "You're as incorrigible as Attilla." A pause. "So, how did it go to-day?"

"A piece of cake," he lied.

She smiled. "Hey, you're getting pretty good at this."

"Kids take some getting used to when you've lived alone like I have for so long. But I think baby-sitting might grow on me."

For an instant her glowing face looked delicate and vulnerable, and he allowed himself to dream that they could be a real family. That she could really be his wife again. That he could take care of her and the children.

Leander swallowed, fighting the constriction in his throat.

A frown chased away her own smile.

"How's Tia?" he asked, growing serious, too.

"Better."

"Then?"

"We have to talk," she said, her voice faltering.

"Okay."

The afternoon sun was streaming across the verandah as Heddy led Leander outside. But the horizon was dotted with dark clouds.

"So why do you look so worried if Tia's better?"

"She's conscious," Heddy said evasively.

He pressed her hand. "I'm glad."

Heddy tugged her hand free of his. "Conscious. But...restless. Not quite herself. She won't talk to anybody but you. She keeps talking about hell and damnation and the devil…and—"

"And?"

"And then you. All in the same breath."

"That figures," he said bitterly.

"She says she won't say a word unless Tom Yates and the press are there, too. She wants them to hear what she says to you. Because she might only have the strength to say it once."

Leander sucked in his breath. It had to be a real bombshell then. Dear God. What was left for her to do that could possibly make things worse between himself and Heddy? After all, they were getting a divorce.

"Do you have any idea what she's going to say?" he asked dully.

Heddy shook her head, but he could tell by her pale face that she was just as worried as he was.

The old witch probably had a vial of arsenic or something tucked away in a bedroom drawer somewhere with his fingerprints all over it. She'd probably say he held her down and forced her to drink it.

With an effort he suppressed his novelist's imagination. "Let's go then," he whispered. "We might as well get it over with."

Eight

The crowded hospital room, which smelled faintly of antiseptic, had gay pink wallpaper and was cheerily lit.

Heddy's heart was full of dread as she stepped inside.

"Tia, look who's here," Heddy said in a soft tone as she led a grim Leander past Tom Yates, Marcus, and a pretty journalist with curly dark hair to the thin figure in the bed.

Tia's skin was the color and texture of parchment, and her thin strands of gray hair were glued to her skull. Her droopy eyelids and the blue rings under her eyes made her look wan and exhausted, even though she was wide awake.

In contrast, Leander, who was huge and dark and muscular, exuded robust health and strapping energy as he loomed over the elderly woman.

What could Tia be thinking of to demand to see him

when she was so ill? When their mutual dislike was so evident.

Tia's rheumy, sunken eyes regarded him warily. Leander's jaw muscles trembled despite his efforts to set his teeth.

When he pulled up a chair to sit down beside her, Tia recoiled weakly, an exertion which brought on desperate choking sounds.

"Tia! Nurse!" Heddy cried, pushing Leander aside and attempting to soothe her grandmother. "There's nothing to be afraid of, Tia. I'm right here. Leander's not going to hurt you."

Lights danced frantically across her four monitors. An alarm went off. White-coated nurses came running in to adjust tubes and dials.

"I'm sorry, folks," the R.N. said, regarding them all, especially Leander, with immense suspicion. "We have too many visitors." Her tone sharpened. "You, Mr. Knight, definitely have to go."

Leander's dark face hardened. But when he started to rise, Tia's gnarled hand seized the nurse's skirt and sent tongue depressors flying out of her coat pocket.

"Make him stay. I *have* to talk to him in front of all these people. And I don't care if it kills me."

"There! There!" Heddy whispered pleadingly. "There's no need to be so melodramatic, Tia."

Tia clawed at her, too.

Heddy took her palsied hand. "We can do this tomorrow just as well as today."

"No...no..." Tia's faint grip tightened. She began mumbling, rapidly, hoarsely. Most of what she said was gibberish. What came through was her fear and her fierce determination to speak to Leander.

"I hate you, Pepper Knight. I do hate you," Tia whispered, her voice so low it was almost inaudible. "But I'm going to hell if I don't tell these people the truth about you."

A muscle in Leander's jaw ticked violently under his dark skin as he leaned closer to his old adversary.

"She's delirious," the bossy nurse said tartly. "Mr. Knight, you need to go."

"No—" Tia rasped. "I do hate him."

"With good reason," Yates encouraged.

"Let her talk," Leander said forcefully. "Can't you see she isn't strong enough to argue with all of you?"

Tia looked into Heddy's eyes pleadingly. "I've done your husband a...a terrible wrong."

"How, Tia?" Heddy prompted gently.

"He... Pepper didn't kill your father."

The room went deathly quiet as everyone waited in breathless suspense for Tia to continue. Yates stepped closer to the bed.

She took her time; sometimes her words were slurred and halting. Sometimes her tired voice was so low she had to repeat whole sentences. But her listeners hung on her every tortured word.

"I—I knew Pepper was innocent, but I kept silent. Not because I wanted to protect him and the Kinney name. But because I wanted them, especially you, Heddy, to *think* he was guilty and that I was covering up for him because he was your husband. Because I wanted to protect the Kinney name."

Leander's color had heightened.

So had Heddy's. "Tia, no. You couldn't have deliberately—"

"I—I did. I loved you, girl. A fool could see Pepper wasn't half good enough for you. I wanted the best for you. Not some…some poor nobody with no family like him.''

''What are you saying?''

''Barret shot himself!''

The floor seemed to rock beneath Heddy's feet, and Heddy had to lean heavily against the bed to steady herself. ''I don't believe it!''

''I knew he killed himself.'' Tia's pitiful voice cracked. ''And I knew why. I knew everything. But I kept it to myself.''

''Oh, Tia—''

''You see, I found Barret's suicide note after that awful fight in the library. You had taken Leander upstairs. I discovered Leander's gun was missing, too. Barret said in his note he'd taken it and was going to kill himself in that ravine so he wouldn't make a mess near the house, and so Heddy and I wouldn't have to find him like that.''

Leander was innocent!

And all these years she hadn't allowed herself to believe him! All these years she'd felt sorry for Tia and had tried to be the perfect granddaughter to make up for bringing Leander into their lives.

Heddy's heart screamed in silent joy and agony. She had hurt Leander terribly. She had driven him away. Why? Why had she so blindly believed Tia? Why had she listened to all the mean things the small-minded gossips had been so eager to say against him?

He hadn't cared about what any of them had thought. Only her. And she had let him down in the most terrible way a wife could let her husband down. She had banished him to that lonely hell in Alaska. She had kept Christina from him. Her crime against him was a thousand times worse than Tia's.

When Heddy put a soft, apologetic hand on Leander's

wide shoulder, he stiffened as if her touch were now repugnant to him.

"I want to hear it all," he said, his swarthy face grimly fierce, his dark eyes cool and emotionless as he regarded her. "Let her finish."

Heddy's hand fell limply to her side.

Tia went on with her confessional. "I knew what Barret intended to do, and I didn't try to stop him. I didn't send anybody after him. If anybody murdered my son, it was me. In his note he begged Pepper to forgive him."

"Why, Tia? Why would Daddy, who had everything—"

Tia's guilty voice was muffled. "Barret had gone to see a doctor in San Antonio and found out what we both suspected, that he had a rapidly growing tumor in his brain. He knew just how terrible it would be because his own father had died the same way."

The blood drained from Heddy's face. "I—I should have known. He'd been acting so strangely. He lost his temper at the least little thing."

"How could you have known? We never told you the truth about your grandfather. We took Gerald to a hospital in New Orleans. Gerald was so violent at the end—completely out of his mind. He hated me, Barret, everybody. Barret said he could feel the sickness in his brain getting worse. In his note he said that every day he felt a little crazier, a little more prone to irrational rages. He knew from what had happened to his father what would happen to him. He said in his note that if you hadn't come into the library when you did, he would have kept hitting Leander with that lamp till he killed him. His last words were, 'Forgive me for this act of selfish cowardice, but remember that if I were a horse, you'd put me out of my misery.'"

"Oh, Tia, why didn't you show us the note?"

"Because I saw my chance to get rid of that cocky upstart you'd so foolishly married, once and for all. I burned it in the library fireplace. I thought I was doing the smart thing. I thought it would be best for everybody—especially you."

Leander got up. Towering over everybody in the room, his frozen face was a dark unreadable mask. Heddy felt a shaft of real fear as he avoided touching her or looking at her.

"Well, now you know, don't you, Sugar?" His mouth was a thin cruel line; his wide-shouldered body rigid.

"Leander, I'm—"

"Don't start! Not now when it's too late."

Her blood ran cold at the grimness in his tone. "Leander, please. You have to forgive me. This changes—"

But he was already gone.

Heddy was about to run after him, but Marcus grabbed her arm gently. His brotherly voice was kind and mild. "Let him go. He needs time alone."

"I—I thought it would be for the best." Tia's thin voice trailed off miserably as Marcus led Heddy back to the bed.

"But it wasn't, Tia," Heddy whispered.

"When you were in labor with Christina, you sobbed so brokenheartedly for Pepper. You wanted him back so much, I thought I would go mad. But when Pepper came to the hospital and begged to see you, I told him you didn't want to see him."

When Heddy gave a cry of loss and desolation, Marcus circled her with his arms. And because his embrace held friendship and nothing more, she welcomed it.

"Forgive me?" Tia whined in a strangled whisper, fretfully clutching for Heddy's hand. *"Please."*

Suddenly Heddy's eyes were swimming as she thought

of the terrible burden her grandmother had carried all these years.

"Oh, Tia. My guilt is so much worse than yours."

The pretty journalist rushed out with her story.

Nobody saw Leander when he returned to the door a minute or two later. Nobody saw him stop dead still in the doorway, his black eyes fierce, not a muscle flickering in his face when he saw Heddy wrapped in Marcus's arms.

Nobody saw him leave without saying a word.

A cool sea mist was rolling in from the bay when Heddy drove past the reporters and television crews, who were besieging the guards she had posted at her ranch gates. The fog was swirling thicker when she reached Leander's cabin and parked her Suburban.

For two days she had waited in an agony of suspense for Leander to call her at the hospital or to come by the ranch. Since her confession Tia had improved rapidly. It was Heddy who felt sick and tired and more afraid than she had ever felt in her life.

She was being vilified in the press as the rich wife who hadn't stood by her husband. But it wasn't the unflattering publicity that was killing her, it was Leander's cold withdrawal.

Marcus had advised her to wait, to give Leander more time.

But she simply had to try to see him. If necessary she would gladly go down on her knees and beg his forgiveness. She had to tell him how desperately sorry she was.

If only he would listen. If only he would believe her.

For more than eight long years she had refused to believe him. And now he said he wanted a divorce.

Heddy quietly went up to his door and laid her hand

upon the rough wood. She was about to knock, but when she touched it, it swung open a little.

She heard a woman's voice and then Leander's husky laughter.

She couldn't see them, but she knew they had to be sitting on the small red couch by his fireplace. Mary Ann's voice was low and vibrant. She was speaking with such intensity that Heddy caught every syllable.

"You've been so wonderful, Pepper."

"My pleasure, M.A."

They were using pet names for each other.

"You're so experienced. So talented. How can I ever repay you?"

"Easily," he murmured. "So easily."

The intimacy and warmth in his husky voice wounded Heddy greatly. She imagined any of a dozen ways a woman as beautiful and flirtatious as Mary Ann could please a man of Leander's virile appetites.

In the silence that followed, Heddy envisioned them embracing, kissing. And much more.

A log crackled in the fireplace.

A plume of gray smoke erupted from the chimney and swirled upward in the fog.

Heddy shrank away from the door, feeling lost and hopeless.

Then without uttering a sound to let them know she had ever been there, she fled hurriedly down the steps into the mist.

The central heater in the big house was broken, and Heddy and her two little girls and Mayflower, Christina's golden dog, were huddled in blankets on the carpet around a Chinese checkerboard in the playroom.

"Mommy, do you think the poor children will like all their presents?" Christina demanded with shining eyes.

Heddy looked up from their checkerboard to the messy pile of gifts that were under, or rather stacked around, the leafless "Cowboy Christmas" tree.

"They'll love them, darling."

"They'd better, even if my bows aren't good, 'cause my thumb hurts," Cleo complained, sneaking her marble an extra space since they weren't looking. "It hurts something awful from wrapping so many. And I'm cold." She opened her mouth so Heddy could see how dramatically she could make her teeth chatter.

"This year there's more than a hundred gifts," Heddy said, pulling a second blanket snugly over Cleo.

"A hundred and seven," Cleo stated proudly.

Heddy and the girls knew this because Attilla had counted the gifts five times. He was a slow, meticulous counter. He'd spent more time racing about, hollering numbers out, than wrapping. Which had brought complaints from the more dutiful girls.

"When is the fat church lady coming by for them?"

"Girls, if dear Mrs. Gumphrey heard you call her fat, she would be so hurt."

One minute Heddy was laughing and telling the girls they needed to carry all the gifts down to the foyer. In the next she heard a man's heavy boots on the stairs and Christina's joyous scream nearly piercing her eardrum.

"Daddy!"

"Uncle Pepper!"

The checkerboard went flying, and so did the marbles. Mayflower galloped after her miniature mistresses and jumped up on Leander, too, big friendly paws leaving gray smudges on his white shirtfront.

Heddy got up from the floor slowly, miserably, and then

just stood there, curling her bare toes into the carpet as she watched Leander bend his tall body down to pet the dog and embrace his daughter and Cleo—and deliberately ignore his wife.

Heddy was barefoot, in old jeans and an old yellow sweater, with masses of gleaming tangles flowing over her shoulders like molten gold. If only she'd known he was coming today, she would have combed her hair or put on makeup. Then he couldn't have resisted looking at her. As it was, she was as pale as a rabbit. The cold was penetrating the soles of her feet and her thin jeans and causing her to shiver.

When he raised his black head from the children, his eyes locked with Heddy's for a long moment. She willed one kind word, one tiny sign that he still cared as their gazes held.

But his dark face was shuttered and colder even than the chill of the unheated house.

"Oh, hello," was all he said—casually in that tight, controlled tone she hated.

Her blue eyes narrowed. Suddenly she was remembering that Jim Yates had told her that Leander had driven Mary Ann into Corpus Christi for a late dinner the night before, that they hadn't come back till dawn.

Everywhere she had gone that morning to do her last-minute Christmas shopping, everyone had sneaked sidelong, curious glances at her, and every busybody had seen fit to repeat that story or add to it.

"I saw Jim Bob's truck parked under the water tower last night till all hours. Looked to me like there was a man and a woman inside."

"Couldn't see much of 'em though."

That was something Heddy hated about Kinney. If ever a person took a false step or a husband did something a wife wouldn't like, there was no keeping discreetly silent about it.

"You're shivering," Leander said awkwardly to Heddy.

"The heater's broken. A repairman's coming." Heddy's voice was as strained as his as she picked up a blanket and draped it around her shoulders.

"Daddy, can I wear your hat?" Christina asked Leander.

He smiled and handed it to her.

Peeping out from under the wide black brim of his Stetson, Christina asked him, "Why haven't you been by like you promised?"

The two adults stared at each other in mute dismay.

Only when Leander realized he was looking at Heddy, did he pull his eyes away and answer his daughter.

"Well, sweetheart, I'm here now," Leander said lightly, offering no other explanation.

"Are...are you in love with Mary Ann? Have you been visiting her instead? Are you going to divorce my mommy?" Christina asked. "Everybody in town and on TV says that Mommy was mean not to believe you—"

Heddy's fingers tightened on the soft woolen blanket. *Oh, how fast the gossips forgot their own fault. Oh, how much more fun to make her the new villain.*

People had always talked about her and all the Kinneys. But it was different now with the truth out about Leander's innocence. He had the town's sympathy, indeed the whole country's, while she, the wife who had not stood by him—

"Everybody in town should keep their damn mouths shut," Leander began impatiently, taking Heddy's side, before he caught himself.

"Christina," Heddy protested. "You shouldn't listen to idle gossip."

"How the hell can she help it in this town?" Leander demanded. "When everywhere you go—"

"You know what else they say, Mommy? They say you're going to divorce Daddy and marry Marcus 'cause Tia wants you to," Christina persisted.

"Maybe the gossips have it figured for once," Leander said grimly.

"No," Christina said. Her voice was a murmur, but her blue eyes were fierce as she looked from him to her mother. "'Cause if you divorce him, I'll run away!" Drama and passion were carrying her away. "I'll run all the way to Alaska! Even if I freeze...and die. Even if...even if I miss Christmas and don't get a single present."

"Can I come, too?" Cleo begged in a small lost voice. When she paused to catch her breath, her teeth began to chatter. "But can I bring...just one little-bitty Christmas present?"

Nine

Leander gave little heed to where he was going as he strode down the circular drive past the palms to his truck. He was intent on only one thing—getting away from Heddy. She had been laughing and playing happily with the girls before he'd come in. Then her smiles had died.

All it had taken to convince him once and for all to head back to Alaska was the way her lovely face had been pale with misery every time she'd looked at him. Her obvious agony at his presence had been almost worse to endure than the contempt she'd felt for him when she'd believed he was a killer.

"Daddy!"

He spun around. Yellow braids flapping, her cheeks red, Christina was racing out of the house as fast as her short, sturdy legs would carry her. Her blue eyes were hidden by the black brim of his cowboy hat, but she had such a glorious smile on her face, it nearly broke his heart.

"Watch where you're going, sweetheart!"

When she skidded up to him, he swept her high in his arms. She wrapped her arms around his neck and locked her legs around his waist as if to never let him go.

"You forgot your hat, Daddy."

He took it from her and placed it on his head.

"Thanks, sweetheart."

"And I wanted to ask you to come for Christmas dinner."

"Well, I don't know that I can promise that. The way things stand between me and your mother, I may be going back to Alaska before—"

"Mommy's coming out to ask you, too."

Leander looked toward the big house and saw the slim, hesitant figure in a tight yellow sweater and jeans at the front door. He caught the gleam of her lovely golden hair. She'd put on lipstick, and she had her purse.

He smiled warily at Christina. "You little manipulator."

Heddy started to rush toward them, walking fast, and then she began running.

"I need to talk to your daddy alone," Heddy said breathlessly, her face prettily flushed. She did not look at him, though.

"Sure," he said offhandedly, hugging Christina tighter, not looking Heddy's way, either.

"We need to have a rational conversation. I mean, after all, we are Christina's parents," Heddy said. "Can we go somewhere?"

"Sure." He set Christina down and opened the door of his truck.

Heddy knelt and kissed the little girl goodbye and sent her back to the house to check on Cleo. Both he and Heddy watched fondly as she ran the entire way. Only when she turned and gave them a final wave before disappearing into the house, did they turn back to each other. Even then they avoided eye contact.

Lounging negligently in the lee of his open door, Leander purred lazily, ''After you, Sugar.''

She got in silently, and then he circled the vehicle and got in, too. For a while they drove in silence.

But the silence got to him. Big-time.

Leander pulled his black Stetson lower to shade his eyes from the glare coming off the road. To hide from Heddy, too. His stomach tightened; his throat knotted next. He grew increasingly uneasy and suspicious of Heddy as they drove toward Kinney in his truck.

She'd said they had to talk.

Yeah. Right.

Then why had she brushed against him climbing into the truck if talk was all she had on her mind?

We need to have a rational conversation.

Right. That's why she'd darkened her eyes with that blue war paint and put on blush. That's why she'd tied her hair back with a yellow ribbon and splashed herself with that flowery perfume. That's why she was wearing those skin-tight jeans that showed off her tiny waist and the curve of her hips.

I mean, after all, we are Christina's parents.

Right. Motherhood and apple pie.

That's why she'd dressed sexily, leaving several buttons of her yellow sweater undone. That's why she'd gone bra-less so that she could tempt him with tantalizing glimpses of her pale throat and creamy cleavage, so that every time she moved or leaned toward him, he'd be aware of her breasts.

He hadn't even touched her. Hell, he'd barely looked

at her, and she had him as hard and as hot as a brick in a kiln.

Where the hell could they talk? Without her coming on to him and getting the upper hand?

I made a rational decision to go back to Alaska and divorce her.

He caught the dizzying smell of her and cursed himself for still wanting her.

Damn. Just this once he was going to do the smart thing where she was concerned.

And then he saw it—the giant vanilla ice cream cone suspended high against the cobalt blue sky, a white jet trail streaming off to one side of it.

Bingo!

Better than bingo!

Salvation!

When he braked and put on his right turn signal, she made a soft little honeyed sound of dismay.

He felt her blue eyes burning into him as she said a single desperate word. "Here?" And then when he said nothing, she pleaded, "Leander, why here?"

"You said you wanted to talk," he replied as dispassionately as he could as he swerved under the huge fake cone into Kinney's only fast-food establishment. "Besides—I'm hungry."

That was a bald-faced lie.

"What have you got against the Dairy Princess anyway?" he murmured dryly, inordinately glad his choice had so displeased her. "This used to be our favorite place when we were kids."

Another bald-faced lie. They had always preferred being alone.

"It is *the* most public place in town," she said. "Everybody comes here to talk about everybody else. Why don't we just skywrite our conversation over the town square, so everybody can read it. Or better, paint a banner and hang it from the water tower?''

''Good idea.''

She scowled. He grinned.

He forced a flippant lightness into his tone. ''Now you're getting the spirit of this gossip thing, Sugar. If we can't lick 'em, we'll just have to join 'em.''

''What?''

Leander tossed a cynical smile toward Yates and the fat deputy in the next car, who were drinking coffee from heavy mugs. Both officers were now staring at them in bug-eyed curiosity. ''Guess y'all could hear better if I rolled my window down a bit,'' he hollered, as he lowered his glass.

''*Leander!* Don't!'' she begged as he smiled and waved at the law officers who lifted their mugs and waved back.

''I wasn't serious,'' she hissed.

''Everybody's been talking about us ever since we were born, Heddy. Maybe it's about time we gave 'em box seats to the show.''

''Not right now. Not this afternoon. Not when—'' her voice faltered ''—when our marriage is at stake.''

''Sugar, whoa! Let's get something straight up front— our marriage is over.''

''But,'' Heddy began, ''doesn't what Tia said change everything?''

He was grateful for the waitress's voice blasting statically from the rusty speaker under his window.

''You want anything, Sugar?'' Leander asked in a disinterested tone, interrupting her, as if his primary interest was food.

''No!''

Her brows swept together as Leander hollered down at

the speaker, placing an order for two burgers, three sacks of fries, a black cow, a chocolate sundae and a small root beer.

"You can't possibly eat all that!"

His eyes slid lazily over her and then away, but not before he felt an almost overpowering urge to slide his fingers inside her sweater and touch her luscious skin. He grinned in spite of himself. "You steal."

"Not today. How can you even think of food? I'm too upset to eat a single bite."

"You always say that." He stared straight ahead and then yawned, as if he were bored. "You were saying, Sugar?"

"Leander, I know the truth now. And that changes everything. For me…at least."

The soft pain in her voice cut him to the quick.

Fool, for once play it smart.

"Maybe for you, but not for me," he said harshly. "I never laid so much as a hand on your father. I always knew that. You should have, too."

"But I didn't," she said, her voice low and choked.

"Well, maybe you should have figured it out. I never, not once in my whole life, ever hurt anybody weaker or older or poorer than me. You know how I always hated bullies."

"Leander, I do know the truth now. I'm so sorry that I ever doubted you." Again that fragile sound of pain in her soft voice tore at him, because it made her seem so vulnerable and in need of his protection.

Desire for her raced along his veins and lit fires in every nerve.

Smart. Be smart. Use your brains.

"So am I," he said roughly. "But we can't undo the past."

"I love you."

God. The clincher to claw out his heart.

Smart. Be smart. Use your brains.

He stared at Yates and the deputy who were straining to hear every word.

"Yeah—till the next time you decide to turn on me." Leander's voice was as dry as dust. "You're like a light switch—on, off. On, off. Most of the time it's been off, Heddy."

"Not anymore," she pleaded.

"No?" He closed his eyes, so he wouldn't be so aware of her. Not that he could shut out the smell of her or the magnetic pull she exerted by just being there. But when he spoke, it was not of the present, but of past emotions he'd felt.

"You know, Heddy, I grew up loving you. Only you. Even though everybody, especially your folks, were always making me feel I wasn't good enough for you. Sometimes you were kind of snooty, too, especially when you were around Tia."

"I never meant—"

"Hey, let me finish." He waited till he was sure she was quiet. "It wasn't easy, growing up with nothing, with nobody, not even knowing my real name. But then I *had* to go and fall in love with the town goddess."

She reddened.

"Not only did everybody figure I had an ulterior motive, Sugar, but I had to learn so much—what fork to eat with, what to say in 'polite' company when some rich jerk asked me what my daddy did. I used to pore over etiquette books in the library, trying to learn all sorts of stupid rules that didn't make a lick of sense to me—just so I wouldn't embarrass you in front of Tia's fancy friends. Then you went off to those European private schools. After that you had to be a debutante. I stayed home, going to school, working my guts out just to pay bills, writing in my spare time. But most of all I went crazy with jealousy every time the gossips told me about some rich guy escorting you to one of those debutante balls. I needed you so much back then! You had everything—you didn't need me. And yet I couldn't let you go. It was the battle of my life. Every time we'd fight, I always wondered if it wouldn't really be better if we broke up. I got real real tired of it, Heddy.''

"Leander—"

He held up his hand. "Hush, Sugar. Let me finish."

She sighed as he continued.

"Then after I pulled that damn fool stunt in New Orleans and we got married, I tried my damnedest to make it work. But the whole town turned against me—even you. Everybody said I married you for the ranch. Then your daddy died, and suddenly I was a murderer, too. I brought scandal to the sacred Kinney name, and you couldn't stand that. You treated me like I was less than the lowest vaquero. You—nobody else—drove me away. I can't forget that."

"I know that, Leander. And I'll never be able to forgive my—"

"Then I came back when Christina was born. The gossips told me how you nearly died having her—naturally they blamed me for that, too, of course. So did Tia. I wanted to see you so bad. I could have forgiven you everything, because I was so glad you were alive and that we had a healthy daughter, but you refused even to see me. After that, it was like something broke in me—"

"I didn't even know you came…till Tia told me in the hospital today. Oh, Leander. I'm so sorry."

"Well, it doesn't matter now. What I guess I'm trying to say is that I can't ever be sure how you'll treat me.

When I came back this time, it was the same thing all over again. You were glad to see me and hot at first, chasing me down the road. And then all Tia had to do was call on the phone. You turned on me before she even had her heart attack. And then you promised her—''

''Because—''

''Look, we've spent most of our marriage apart, maybe it'd be a whole lot easier on everybody if we went on that way. I just can't take any more.''

He stared past her, tight-lipped and unbiddable, not wanting to dwell on how translucently pale she looked. On how her fists were knotted weakly in her lap. On how her thick silence and despair made him feel like he was suffocating.

''What about Christina?'' Heddy asked in a low desperate tone.

He hated the thought of kids suffering, especially his kid. ''She'll adjust,'' he said harshly. ''Same as half the kids in America do. Same as I did.''

''She needs a father.''

''Maybe you should have considered that before. Besides—she has one. It's you who won't have a husband. Leastways, not till you marry Marcus.''

''But I'm not going to marry him.''

''That's not what I hear. He's over at the house and with you at the hospital all the time.''

''He's a friend.''

''Yeah. Right.'' He paused. ''Look, Heddy—''

A buxom waitress in a short skirt brought out the order. Leander forced himself to turn away from Heddy and to flirt and laugh with the other woman while they raised and lowered the window to get the tray attached. He put a burger, a sack of fries and the root beer on the dash where

Heddy could reach them and kept the rest on the tray for himself.

When he wasn't looking he heard the paper bag on the dash crinkle as she took a fry.

"See, I told you you'd steal."

"Is…is it Mary Ann?" Heddy's voice was very small, very tight.

He was munching into mustard, onions, pickles, burned meat and a soggy bun. Food he had no appetite for. "What?"

"Is she the reason you won't give me another chance?"

He chewed thoughtfully for a while before saying, "Good Lord, no. The last thing I need is another woman working me over."

"Everybody says—"

"I thought you told Christina not to pay attention to gossip."

"You went out with her last night."

"I was helping her with her novel."

"All night? Under the water tower?"

"She's not a very skillful writer. She needed a lot of editorial advice."

"I'll bet she has other talents—"

He swore softly as he set his burger down. "No! It's not Mary Ann!"

"Then why are you dead set on going back to Alaska?"

Hell. He turned. From the deep shadow of his wide-brimmed hat, he stared straight into her beautiful blue eyes.

Which was a mistake. Because just looking at her like that always formed that soul-to-soul connection that had hooked him in the first place. Because the sunlight was shining in her hair and her yellow knit top was stretching tightly across her breasts leaving next to nothing to his imagination. And because the longer he let himself be with her, the more he felt like staying and the less he felt like going.

Smart. Be smart. Use your brains.

"'Cause I think maybe we've caused each other enough grief, Sugar."

He took a long swig of his icy black cow, praying that the cold drink would cool him down.

When she thought he wasn't watching, she snitched two more fries.

"I agree," she said softly, nibbling a juicy golden fry.

He was stunned. "You *agree?*" Odd, how his deep voice was suddenly so unsteady. He found he couldn't take his eyes off that fry disappearing inch by inch inside her pink lips.

"Yes," she breathed, sucking in the last of that fry. "I think it's time we gave each other joy." She licked the salty tip of her second fry.

"Whoa!" He drew in a harsh breath and slammed his black cow down on the dash, sloshing foam all over the top of the mug. "It's been so long, I wouldn't know where to begin," he said, mopping the mess with a wad of paper napkins.

"But I do." She scooted nearer, reaching for him.

"Heddy—" he said hoarsely.

But she buried her face in the hollow of his neck. Every muscle in his body bunched when her tongue flicked across the base of his throat.

Leander strangled a curse. "What the hell do you think you're doing now, Sugar?"

She lifted her beautiful gaze to his, but she didn't speak. She didn't have to.

Through thick, downcast lashes her jewel blue eyes blazed softly with love—for him. Her slim fingers curled tighter into his chest. A warm, staccato breath of air escaped her lips and feathered across his, causing every male sensory receptor in his body to come alive, as little frissons of desire raced along his heated nerve ends.

Damn those eyes of hers, for making him know how starved he was for her. Damn her lithe sensual female beauty. With a supreme effort he willed himself to resist her.

"What am I doing?" she whispered silkily. "Just the same thing you did that night in New Orleans when you won me in that card game. You fought for me that night, Leander. You were poor and drunk and scared, but you came to that posh hotel and gambled against incredible odds. You knew I was making a mistake, and that we would both be miserable. Then you married me. You were good to my family, and we were terrible to you. Well, you're not poor anymore. Nobody's ever going to say you came back to me for the ranch." A beat passed. "I've made my mistakes…lots of them. I've hurt you. So has my family. But I'm sorry. If you leave me now, when we might finally have a chance to be happy, you'll be making the worst mistake of all."

Her words touched him; he felt a wave of emotion stronger than any he'd ever known. For days he hadn't been able to get her touch, her smell, the heat and shape of her body out of his mind.

But it wasn't enough. Not if he couldn't trust her. Not if she would just go back to her old ways.

His voice was rough, he pushed her hands away. "That's a crock of horse—"

He would have opened his door and gotten out, but she moved faster than quicksilver. Her mouth fastened over his, devouring his swearword in one last desperate attempt to change his mind.

Quiet tears filled her eyes and beaded her lashes.

"*Please,* Leander. *Oh, please—*"

Her plea seemed wrenched from her tender soul in those final seconds before her soft mouth seized his again. "Please, give me another chance."

He inhaled the dizzying scent of her perfume. Golden clouds of sweet-smelling hair foamed silkily against his cheek and throat. The instant she fused her gentle mouth to his and he tasted her, pleasure and desire saturated his body.

He wanted to believe her. He wanted to so desperately. *Smart. Be smart.*

But she was kissing him in a frenzy of hope and despair, and his brain short-circuited.

He had no illusions as to their future happiness. But her lips were molten hot as her soft body melted into his.

When her hands moved over the corded muscles of his shoulders, kneading and then tightening as a passionate little moan of ecstasy escaped her lips, she set him aflame.

A shudder went through him. Her moist velvet tongue dipped into his mouth and he was lost.

His hands began to move down her body, gently exploring, as he molded her flush against himself. Soon he forgot everything except the familiar pleasure of touching her and kissing her, and she withheld nothing, surrendering herself with a wild, reckless abandon. Every single day since he'd had her that night, he'd craved her.

He had no sensation of time or place or of their avidly fascinated audience as he pulled her onto his lap and washed her throat and nape with his tongue. He had no sensation of anything except the exquisite rapture she aroused. He began to shake. More than anything he wanted to make fierce, wild love to her.

Then dimly, very dimly at first, Yates's voice penetrated Leander's bedazzled consciousness.

"What are they doing now? Did you see that? *Hot damn!*" A veritable yelp of pain, followed by howls and curses, erupted from Yates's car.

"Bill! This coffee's boiling!" Yates was bellowing now, squirming to unzip his slacks. "Get me a towel! Get me a damn waitress! Quick! Myrtle! Over here, girl! Your damn tray fell in my lap!"

"Da—amn," Leander muttered in broken syllables. "Damn." Reluctantly Leander kissed the golden curls on her forehead as he gently began easing her off himself. "Heddy, Sugar…"

"Mmmmm." Her beautiful blue eyes were feverish and confused.

He traced his callused hand through her tangled hair. "Sugar, er…I…we've got to stop…for now."

"Why?" she asked, her tone soft and slurred with desire as she attempted to kiss his bottom lip searingly again.

"No…Sugar, look over there. Yates and that lard-of-fat deputy of his and damned near everybody else in Kinney are watching us."

"So?" She looped her arms loosely around his neck and kissed his mouth again. "You were the one who wanted to give them box seats."

He strummed her hair back behind her ears and cupped her chin lovingly. "I changed my mind, Sugar. This definitely has to be a private showing."

Ten

They were in his cabin, and the fire he had lit made a flickering orange glow against the stone walls and wooden floors. Not that either of them needed a fire, Heddy thought unsteadily. The sexual tension sizzling between them, ever since they'd kissed at the Dairy Princess, was as hot and dangerously electric as a live wire.

And now at last—she had him alone.

It was a good thing she'd told her housekeeper she might be out all night, she thought, as she went to his stereo and put on a compact disc. In an instant a wild, haunting love song washed over them.

She felt the magnetic pull of Leander's burning black eyes as she turned toward him. The warm flush that ran through her body was terrifying in its intensity.

Still wearing his hat and jeans and boots, he lay sprawled across his bed, staring at her as if she were already naked.

''Strip,'' he ordered in an uneven whisper.

Her heart was beating too fast and too loudly, as she shyly began to pace the small room. Her ribs felt squeezed, and she kept taking deep breaths.

This was her chance. Her one final chance to win him. She could run.

Or she could play it for all it was worth.

A quietness fell over her that had nothing to do with the wild melody.

When she began to undulate, slowly at first, to the beat of the music, Leander tensed, stretching his frame like a panther before he forced himself to relax again.

His eyes never left her face as she reached above her head and languidly untied the yellow ribbon in her hair, so that the loose silken waves fell down around her shoulders in a cascade of golden flame. ''Throw me your hat, cowboy,'' she whispered.

He cocked the brim back from his forehead with his thumb and then, with a practiced flick of his wrist, he caught hold of the edge and sailed it to her like a Frisbee.

She caught it and put it on—slowly, slanting it at a rakish angle.

Then she lowered her hands over her body, sliding them down her hips, slowly running them back up her waist over her silky smooth breasts to the buttons of her yellow sweater as she swayed provocatively to the beat of the music.

A muscle ticked savagely along his jawline as he stared fixedly at her from beneath his heavy black lashes.

''Take it off—cowgirl,'' he drawled in a husky timbre. ''Take it all off.''

She felt dizzy, strange. But she said teasingly in a trembly voice, ''Can I leave your hat on?''

He nodded with an enthrallingly intimate smile.

She moved closer to the fire, and with deft, quick fingers, undid each tiny yellow button, moving and twisting, causing firelight and shadow to flicker across her body. Slowly, very slowly, she released the last pearly button from its buttonhole.

As she peeled the edges of yellow wool apart to reveal a strip of honeyed skin, he gasped expectantly. But just as the gap widened to give him more than a tantalizing glimpse of her breasts, she turned the slim curve of her back to him and slipped her sweater down so that it fell halfway off her shoulders.

"Turn back around," he commanded quietly.

For a long moment she hesitated—teasing him instead with the slender curve of her naked spine instead.

Then suddenly she whirled and faced him again. She cocked his Stetson at a more coquettish angle. With her lashes downcast and her head held back, her fiery hair tumbled down her back. She planted both hands on her hips in a seductive pose and thrust her breasts forward. In that swift fluid gesture the sweater that had been clinging to the jutting tips of her soft pink nipples succumbed to gravity and fell from her body to the floor.

"Come over here, Sugar." This time his voice was deep and very gentle. And very hot. As hot as the fire warming the bare skin of her back.

She stepped daintily over the pool of yellow wool. "But I haven't taken off my jeans."

His black eyes glittered.

She slipped her fingertips down her abdomen and then beneath her frayed denim waistband, unsnapping the single metal button. Then slowly she inched the zipper down, so that her partially opened jeans exposed a resplendent V of rosy flesh above her sex.

Her graceful young body, thus revealed, twirled closer to him, and then retreated.

"Heddy—"

She began pushing her jeans down, rotating her hips from the waist, undulating with the wanton expertise of a natural; instinctively knowing just how to sway that which would most excite him.

"Come here, damn you!"

Startled, she disobeyed on a nervous giggle, undressing more slowly.

When her jeans lay beside her sweater, she wore nothing but his black hat and a pair of minuscule black lace bikini panties. The flickering firelight played across her tawny skin and glimmered in her hair.

"Where the hell did you learn to do that?" he groaned.

"Nowhere. You are the only man I've ever had, Leander." Slowly she closed her eyes and danced to the hypnotic tempo of the passionate music, deliberately arousing him. "There has never been anyone but you."

Her voice was a honeyed caress; her innocent face glowed like an angel. But it was the wanton invitation in her brilliant blue eyes as she opened them that sent him over that fatal edge.

In a single leap he was off the bed and she was crushed in his powerful arms. Shoving her against the stone wall, he tore his hat off her head and pitched it to the wooden floor.

She had confessed that there had never been anyone but him. For all his passion, she felt a fleeting sadness that he did not make the same oath to her.

But the hard, hot feel of his hands moving over her naked flesh rocked her senses. The musky scent of him enveloped her. He caught her wrists and raised them above her head and caught her in a passionate embrace. Slowly his hand traced down the length of her arms. Then his fingers grasped the thick golden coils of hair at the nape of her neck and forced her head back. With ruthless mastery he pressed bruising kisses on her lips, her throat, her breasts.

Breathing hard, he savagely wrenched his jeans and shirt off, stripping out of his clothes with a great deal more haste than she had. Then he forced her back against the cool stone wall, parting her thighs with his leg, his hands sliding under her hips, cupping her, positioning her, lifting her around his waist. With her spine against cool stone, her legs locked around his back and her arms around his neck, he drove into her.

''Ah, Heddy. My beautiful Heddy—''

If he was wild for her, he made her wilder. Crying out softly, she gloried in all the sensual pleasures of their love-making—in the way his breathing had roughened, marveling at the heated textures of his bronze sculpted muscles moving against her softer flesh. She ran her hands over his ribbed chest that was thickly carpeted with black hair, savoring his masculine beauty. As always his skin grew increasingly hot, and soon her own temperature rose.

A warm blush of color spread across her pale skin, tinting her cheeks, her throat, her breasts, but she would not let him linger at any point. The rapidly increasing beat of her pulse raced in tempo with his. He drove into her again and again. When she began to shudder and moan, returning his kisses wantonly, he lost all control. Feverishly in that last moment before the cataclysm, he fused his mouth to hers in a final long hot kiss.

''Heddy. Ah, Heddy,'' he groaned as he began to shudder.

Afterward, she felt drained and faint from the pleasure, too dizzy even to stand. So he picked her up in his arms and carried her to the bed. They lay down together, and she curled against his body, nestling there until she fell asleep in the warmth of his arms. Later they woke and showered, lathering each other with soap, making love again against the tiles while they were still wet and slick.

Once more they showered and made love again until all the hot water was gone.

The next time, he took her on the floor by the fire with his lips and tongue. As she did him. His body heat was at his usual high, and she found this sort of sex exquisitely delicious.

He drew the infinitely tender, profoundly intimate, process out until her whole body seemed a mass of nerve endings all quivering for release. Until she felt hotter and closer to him and more cherished by him than ever before. Still, he made her hover on that titillating edge of erotic delight for hours. Then he satisfied her with a single deft flick of his warm tongue which sent spirals of pleasure radiating throughout her limbs. And when he finished, she was left with the pleasant salty aftertaste of him lingering in her mouth. Afterward she felt so utterly sated and tenderhearted as she lay beside him that she wept from the sheer beauty of it.

Beside them in the hearth, the fire had dwindled to glowing coals. Above them the misshapen antler chandelier loomed.

He pulled her golden head into the curve of his shoulder and draped his arm over her. She lay in the darkness and reveled in her newfound happiness, believing that at last she had made him know that she truly loved him, believing that he had to love her in return.

But he dispelled that illusion with a casual sentence or two, thanking her for the good time.

She blushed miserably, longing for words that would

betray the depth of his love and give spiritual meaning to the act.

When he said no more, she whispered gently, "I love you. For me…it wasn't just sex. It never could be. Not with you."

"Wasn't it?" he murmured darkly, getting up then.

"Leander—"

"Don't start!" His voice cracked like a spark, across the firelit darkness. "Tonight was good." He yanked on his jeans but didn't snap them. "Too good." Next he shrugged into his shirt. "Let's leave it at that."

"But, I can't."

"Sure you can, Sugar."

"Leander, *please*—"

A muscle jumped convulsively at the corner of his mouth. His shirt unbuttoned, the edges of it hanging apart to reveal a strip of dark brown muscles, he got back in bed beside her. "Shhh."

"But—"

"Shhh. I can't bear it." He smiled so tightly that white lines radiated about the edges of his lips. When she tried to tell him again how she felt, he kissed her into silence.

She began to touch him, caressing his naked skin beneath his open shirt with shaking fingertips. He shuddered but remained tense, his passion toward her under control now.

Frustrated that he would neither make love nor talk, she finally gave up and lay still. It was enough that he was beside her. Surely he would listen when she tried to explain in the morning. She lay her head on his pillow and let herself drowsily succumb to the drugging bliss of his blazing warmth. She couldn't expect miracles overnight.

Her last sleepy thoughts were about how good he was with the children, even Attilla. About how thrilled Christina would be when she told her that her father was staying.

Heddy fell asleep, certain of their reconciliation. In the morning she would make him eggs and coffee like a real wife. She would tell him how much she loved him. He would listen and smile. Perhaps he still wouldn't quite believe. But she couldn't expect him to trust her immediately. It would take time, but she had time. She had the rest of their lives.

Heddy was determined to make up to Leander for all the hurt she had unintentionally caused him. She would nurture him, adore him, spoil him—in bed as well as out of it. And someday he would have to forgive her and come to love her again as he had in the past. As she loved him.

She was sure that at last, everything was going to be wonderful between them.

She slept so soundly she did not hear him get up in the night.

The next morning she woke up gradually, perceiving in her first hazy moment of consciousness only that she was bathed in the golden warmth of sunlight. Then languidly she stirred and reached toward his pillow, her heart filled with the warmth and love she wanted to bestow upon him.

Instead of silky black hair, her fingers brushed a hard, felt hat brim.

Startled, she jumped up and stared at the black Stetson lying in the indentation where only hours before Leander's head had been.

Where was he?

In a panic she saw that his suitcases and laptop were gone. Frantically she wrapped a sheet around herself and ran to the porch. Jim Bob's truck was gone, too.

Oaks and mesquite stood like silent sentinels. Not a

breath of air stirred through their leafless branches. High above her a solitary buzzard made lazy circles.

The stillness and the quiet settled oppressively upon her spirit.

She was all alone. Leander had left her.

Feeling desolate, she wandered aimlessly back inside. Shakily she went to the bed and lifted the black Stetson from the pillow.

A single white slip of paper fluttered to the floor and landed beside her discarded yellow sweater and jeans.

For a long moment she was afraid to pick it up. When she did, she sobbed when she saw that his note was for Christina, and not her.

Heddy stared at the black swirls of ink, her mind a disbelieving blank.

The words ran together in an unintelligible blur as she began to read. Only with great effort did she manage to focus.

He told Christina he'd left his hat behind for her, so that she could wear it whenever she missed him. But that she had to let Attilla and Cleo take turns wearing it. He said he'd left Christmas presents for her and the other children under their "Cowboy Christmas" tree. He invited her to come to Alaska for the summer. He promised her a long letter explaining why he had to divorce her mother.

Divorce?

When Heddy saw that he had not written a single word to her, not even goodbye, despair opened before her like a chasm.

Eleven

Forsaken.

For the first time in her life Heddy felt completely alone.

Completely abandoned.

Even though she was surrounded by people.

She had been a foolish, vain creature who had overestimated her desirability. She had also overestimated Leander's ability to forgive her for not standing by him when he'd needed her. For more than eight years she had let Tia persuade her to doubt Leander and thereby had condemned him to exile. She was sorry now, sorrier than she'd ever been for anything.

Somehow she worked, putting in long days at her busy shop, selling and wrapping Christmas presents. Somehow she found time to visit Tia and care for the children. She cooked and told bedtime stories. She showed endless items to exasperating last-minute shoppers, but she existed in a numb, zombielike state.

Mommy, you're not listening!

Heddy, dear, would you bring me my walker?

For the third time, do you, or do you not, have this red blouse with the cute little ruffles down the front in a size twelve?

Someone was always demanding something of her.

But she was only half there.

Leander didn't call.

He didn't write.

Not even to Christina who jumped as she herself did every time the phone rang, who raced down the long blacktopped drive every afternoon wearing his cowboy hat to check their rural mailbox for a letter.

The tension inside Heddy mounted until finally one morning as she folded a sexy nightie in tissue for an embarrassed husband in a black Stetson who was shopping for a wife he obviously adored, she burst into tears. Tossing the nightie and gift box on the counter in front of Mary Ann, Heddy raced out of the shop.

She couldn't put the beauty of her last night with Leander out of her mind—when she had tried to show him how completely she loved him. When she had thought he had showed her the same thing. After such shared intimacies, some part of Heddy marveled that Leander could coldly walk out on her.

And yet some part of her understood.

Once he had tried to describe his feelings for the woman who had given birth to him and then left him in a garbage Dumpster to die. He had wanted to know what kind of coldhearted monster could give birth and then throw her own baby away.

"I used to dream about her when I lived in those awful

foster homes. She was always beautiful—like an angel. She would come back for me and I would be so happy to see her at first. Then I would ask her, 'Why did you leave me? Why didn't you love me?' I always woke up before she answered. And you know something—I was always glad I did.

"She was *my* mother," he had said, "and I loved her and wanted her, no matter what she'd done. But at the same time I was glad she never came back for me, because I wouldn't have trusted her, and I was afraid that I might be like her."

As a boy Leander had possessed a vein of ice in him that enabled him to withdraw into himself and reject people. She had seen him do it with the bullies at school and with Tia's snooty friends. It was a survival technique he'd learned in those first bitterly lonely years of his childhood before Mrs. Janovich had adopted him. Now Heddy wondered if he wasn't doing the same thing to her.

Was he afraid of her love? Was he afraid of getting in too deep and losing her again? Or was he capable of turning his emotions off the same way his own mother had when she'd left him to die?

Maybe Leander could survive alone. Maybe he could survive without their love. But Heddy knew she couldn't. Not again.

Maybe he thought he could use her for a wild, wonderful night of soul-shattering sex, and then pack his bags, and go back to Alaska. Maybe he was even trying to get even.

Heddy didn't blame him. But understanding his possible reasons didn't lessen the hurt.

After Christina read her Leander's note, she'd cried, "This is all your fault, Mommy!"

"No—"

"Yes!" she'd screamed, tears streaming down her cheeks. "Everyone in Kinney says so!"

Christina ran to her room and locked herself inside, refusing to answer Heddy when she pleaded with her through the door. The next morning a pale, red-eyed Christina emerged. Sweeping down the stairs, she avoided her mother, choosing to hold court instead on the huge flowered couch in the parlor where she shared her father's note with Cleo and Attilla. Attilla who had trouble concentrating except on his very favorite stories, made her read it three times.

Then the children solemnly marched into the library. There they tore through the drawers of the ormolu escritoire to get stamps and stationery and pencils so they could write Leander—even Attilla, who could barely sit still, much less hold a pencil and concentrate on one thing long enough to write a letter. Nevertheless, in between grinding three pencils down to their nubs and jamming the electric pencil sharpener and then spilling pencil shavings all over the carpet, he laboriously managed two lines, a postscript, at the bottom of Christina's letter—"Come back soon, Uncle Pepper. We miss you lots."

A day or so later Tia came home from the hospital, but she was so weak and breathless, a hospital bed had to be set up downstairs. Ironically, as soon as Heddy finished arranging her pillows, the old lady demanded to see Leander.

For a long moment Heddy just stared at her, not believing what she was hearing.

"Well then, where is your impossible husband?" Tia demanded restlessly.

An immense weariness of spirit engulfed Heddy. "He's…gone, Tia. Back to Alaska."

"When did this happen?"

"A few days ago."

"Why didn't anyone tell me?"

"I—I just couldn't, Tia."

"You'll have to speak louder. I seem to be having trouble hearing."

"I—I said, I just couldn't."

"Well then, what are you going to do about it?"

"Nothing."

"That doesn't sound like you."

"I—I thought you hated him, Tia."

"Well, I suppose...I do," Tia declared but without much of her former conviction. "But..." Her voice quavered. "The ranch could use a man to run things...at least while I'm down. Not that I won't be up and around by spring."

"Of course you will be."

"Then there's Attilla. Give him another year or two, and you'll never be able to manage him without a man."

"Leander is gone, Tia. For good."

"I thought you loved him."

"What's love got to do with it?"

Heddy hired round-the-clock nurses and therapists to care for Tia. Even so, when Heddy was home, it was Heddy's attention that the difficult old lady constantly demanded. And much to her surprise Tia badgered her incessantly to go after Leander.

Heddy couldn't eat. Or sleep. She couldn't bear the thought of Christmas without Leander. Nor could she think of her approaching birthday without bursting into tears. She couldn't turn the radio on in her car because the Christmas music made her feel even sadder. Finally she left her shop in Mary Ann's hands because everything there reminded her of Christmas.

Even the children lost their joy in the holiday. They were angrier at Santa Claus than they were at her.

"Why are you mad at Santa Claus?" Heddy asked when they rebelled in the grocery store, refusing to let her buy chocolate chip cookie ingredients because they weren't going to bake any cookies on Christmas Eve for Santa.

"Not a single cookie!" Attilla swore vehemently, throwing the package of chocolate chips back on the shelf.

For a long moment his freckled hand lingered on the package, as if he was sorely tempted to put it back in the shopping cart when nobody was watching. He adored stuffing himself on cookies almost as much as he adored making mischief.

Christina crossed her arms across her chest. "If Santa really was very magic, he would have made my daddy stay in Texas. Santa has been very bad this year, and he doesn't deserve a cookie."

"He's too fat, anyway," Cleo said, not to be left out.

"Let's leave him switches," Attilla suggested, "'cause that's what you're always saying he'll leave me if I'm bad."

Anytime they were all home and the phone rang, Heddy and the children would race to get it, hoping it would be Leander.

Then one bright sunny morning, while she and Tia were making out the final grocery list for their Christmas dinner, a lawyer called and said he had been hired to represent Leander in the divorce.

"But…but I don't want to divorce my husband," Heddy had whispered into the phone as the three children and Tia hung on her every word. "The situation is—" Heddy's voice cracked.

"Unremediable, I am afraid. You see, Mrs. Knight, my client wants to divorce you as soon as possible."

Sunlight streamed into the yellow-papered kitchen as a thin-faced Heddy, her three unusually quiet children and Tia sat tensely around the table. That morning there were no sounds other than the burble of the coffeemaker, an occasional spoon clinking against china, or the slurps of a child's mouth wet-vacuuming the very last drop of orange juice from his glass.

Attilla turned off his suction hose and banged his empty glass down with a vengeance. "It's nearly Christmas. We have to go get *him*."

All eyes locked on Attilla's freckled nose to which a toast crumb clung. Everybody knew who *he* was.

"Oh, dear," said Tia, seeing all the pale, unhappy faces. "Oh, dear."

Heddy set her coffee cup down very carefully. "How, Attilla? *He* is in Alaska."

"We..." Attilla grew silent and sucked in his bottom lip thoughtfully. After a long moment of intense concentration during which he amazed everybody by licking his nose clean with the tip of his curled tongue, he burst out with an idea. "We could take a rocket or a missile or maybe a jet to Alaska! We could whoosh up there, get him and bring him back!" Attilla turned his hand into a jet and made impressive blasting-off sounds with his talented tongue. "Or...maybe we could call him on the telephone. Maybe he's just sulking the way Christina does when she wants us to beg her to do something. Maybe if we talked to him real nice and said *please*—"

Christina, who was shoveling eggs into her mouth with obscene amounts of grape jelly, nearly choked. "I don't either sulk!"

"Do, too," Cleo affirmed matter-of-factly, twirling a bacon strip. "Can I ride on the tail of the rocket, Aunt Heddy?"

"I say we go up there and bring Uncle Pepper back," Attilla said, making rocket sounds again.

There was a moment of charged silence, unbroken by the clinks of spoons or the vacuuming slurps of orange juice.

Heddy felt an attack of conscience as the children stared at her with round, expectant eyes, as if Attilla's off-the-wall suggestion really was the solution.

Despite the warm sunlight streaming across the table, she shivered. "But he doesn't want me." Lamely she added, "Besides, kids, we don't have a missile."

"Then you can get one!" Tia pulled herself up until she was sitting as stiffly erect in her wheelchair as a displeased queen. "I expected more from my granddaughter!"

"More?" Heddy repeated in stricken amazement. "I threw myself at him…and he left me."

"Because he's as stubborn as we are. It's hard to back down, Heddy. Believe me," she added quietly, "I know. You get an idea in your head…but never mind. People fly in planes to Alaska every day of the week! It's almost your birthday, Heddy. Dear! It's almost Christmas. I remember another Christmas when you and Pepper set this town on its ear."

"You mean when he won me playing poker on my wedding night and we eloped to Mexico?" Heddy flushed hot pink.

"Maybe it's time you acted like a Kinney and made a real play for him. Do something wild. Take the bull by the horns. Go after him, dear. Unless you want to lose him."

"Yahoo!" Attilla whooped. Then he folded his paper napkin into a rocket with lopsided wings and pitched it high into the air.

Ivak lay on the wooden floor beside his master's heavy boots, the tip of his tail flicking tensely as he pretended to sleep. In reality he was watching Leander through his narrowly slitted topaz eyes.

Muz's half-empty bottle of whiskey stood at the ready—beside Leander's empty shot glass.

"Would you like some biscuits and tea?" Mara asked gently. "It's getting dark. You might need a little something to warm you before you set out for your cabin."

As if tea or biscuits could warm him. As if anything in the whole damn world could warm him except—

Leander saw golden hair fanning over his pillow. A tawny body with curved hips undulating before a flickering fire. He saw Heddy wearing nothing except his black cowboy hat. He saw her lips parting in a seductive smile.

Leander shook his head and reached blindly across the table for another cigarette. When he found the package empty, he wadded it up and pitched it toward the trash can. Mara picked it up when he missed.

As he leaned forward he peered glumly through the ice-encrusted window. The dim light was fading into darkness fast. Too fast. The night would be long and fiercely cold. And dark. He needed to go home before the last of the light went. Instead he got up and bummed another pack of cigarettes from Muz.

Leander had quit smoking when he was eighteen.

He had a headache from too many cigarettes and too little sleep.

Leander avoided liquor because it opened him up to the

*bleak feelings of loneliness and abandonment he'd had to
fight ever since his childhood.*

Yet when he stomped into Muz's cabin early this morning, as he had every morning since he'd returned to
Alaska, and reached over the counter for Muz's bottle, he
had told himself just one small shot—just to get him over
the headache from another sleepless night and too many
cigarettes. Muz had reminded him he'd used the same line
yesterday.

But one drink had made the headache worse. So had
two. He had four more drinks and dozens of cigarettes to
get him through the morning.

Somewhere after the sixth shot, he'd stopped counting;
his headache was no better, but he'd stopped caring.

"Mara, tell Muz to call Juneau. I want two cases of
whiskey and cigarettes sent up here on the next mail
plane."

"You're killing yourself," Mara said from the kitchen.

"So, the hell, what."

Leander heard her footsteps padding toward him. Not
that he looked up as Mara pulled out a chair and sat down
beside him. "Do you want to tell me what happened in
Texas?"

He drew a deep shuddering breath. "Not really. I'm
getting a divorce. That's all. And, no, I don't want to talk
about it."

"Maybe you should think about it then."

He fell silent.

"The decision to divorce her doesn't seem to be making
you very happy. The fact is, it's killing you."

His morose black eyes impaled her with shards of ice.

"I'm divorcing her. And that's final. She turned on me
one time too many—just like my mother—"

"Just like—"

"Hell, just leave me alone," he snapped.

Everything was oppressive to him—the gray skies, the snow, the long black nights, and even Mara's pretty hurt face, which reminded him of Heddy. Most of all he felt oppressed by the utter aloneness he now experienced without Heddy. Not that he shouldn't be used to it by now.

Why the hell had he gone back to Texas, anyway?

What had he been trying to prove? If he hadn't gone, he would never have known for sure what he had lost. Seeing Heddy again had opened him to the pain, even worse than the booze did.

He got up and yanked his parka off the peg.

"I know I've been hard to take. Don't worry. I won't be back," he said. "Not till that mail plane gets in with my whiskey and cigarettes Saturday. I've gotta handle this alone."

Alone. The feeling smothered him and froze him like the great lonely cold.

All his life he'd been alone.

Even though he was rich and famous, for the rest of his life he'd be alone.

He kissed Mara goodbye and stepped outside into bleak, wintry, bone-freezing whiteness with Ivak trotting faithfully along behind him.

He threw his long leg across the seat of his snowmobile, smiling grimly when the image of flying the little machine off a cliff or smashing it into a rock flickered in his imagination.

No more pain.

No more fame. No more hassles.

No more aloneness.

He started the engine.

The minute he was out of the village, some self-destructive impulse in him screamed for more speed.

Leaning forward, his whole body charged with the vibrations, he pushed the snowmobile for all it was worth until he was flying way too fast through the bone-numbing cold. He skidded wildly down an embankment onto the ice and snow of the frozen river that wound through the forest the short distance to his cabin. For a brief moment Leander lost himself in the exhilaration of pure speed as he blasted through a huge snow drift that normally he would have avoided.

Snow and ice exploded, showering him. The wind cut through his parka.

He was cold. Too cold.

Ice was forming all over him, on his parka, his gloves, even on his eye lashes.

Faster.

He hit the slick ice and skidded wildly. He raced up a drift, and for several seconds he and the snowmobile were airborne—an out-of-control rocket flying into the blackening sky.

Then the snowmobile hit the ice heavily, lurching, nearly rolling. And then he got control.

Not that he slowed the speeding machine.

He held on to the handlebars, so cold now he was numb and shaking, and pushed the thing faster than ever.

Hell, maybe he did have a death wish.

Right now he just wanted to end the pain.

"Did you hear that Heddy Kinney chartered a Lear jet to go to Alaska and fetch Pepper?"

"No!"

"You can see it from the highway—just settin' parked out there, plain as day on the ranch runway."

"She's taking all three kids. Attilla's even got himself

a rope. He says he's gonna lasso and hog-tie his Uncle Pepper and bring him home where he belongs.''

"It's about time Heddy came to her senses.''

"About time Pepper came to his.''

"But it was terrible the way Heddy didn't stand behind him when Barret died. The way the press made him seem so spooky and mean.''

"I knew all the time Pepper was innocent.''

"So did I. So did everybody.''

"What's Tia got to say about it?''

"The jet was her idea. She said it was her Christmas present and birthday present to both of them.''

"Times change.''

"For the better sometimes.''

"Hey, did you hear that the city's floating a bond to paint the water tower?''

"About time.''

"Like a lot of things.''

The early-morning sky was a purple dome above a broken land that seemed from the mail plane to be endless ice and snow. A mountain loomed to one side of the tiny shuddering plane, its jagged face scarred with naked rock and broken trees that marked the monstrous path of a recent avalanche.

There was a strong crosswind. The plane flew at an angle fighting the wind with the bright blade of its propeller.

"You're lucky as hell, little lady, that we can even get in today,'' the bearded pilot with the parrot's beak nose yelled over the roar of his engine. "All our airplanes have been grounded for the better part of a week—till today. Too dangerous to fly.''

"Too dangerous?'' Heddy was gripping the edges of

her chair as the plane jounced in the nearly constant tur-
bulence. "But…it's safe…today?"

"It's great. A few bumps maybe."

The plane hit a pocket of nothingness and plunged.

"Yahoo!" Attilla cried, rocking back and forth in his
seat, urging the plane down faster, loving it.

"That boy of yours is a natural-born pilot!"

"Are we going to crash, Aunt Heddy?" Cleo asked
quietly, hiding her eyes.

"No, scaredy," Christina snapped imperiously as the
plane leveled out. "We're going to get my daddy!"

"We've had nothing but weeks of pea-soup fog, black
ice, and blizzards," the pilot explained.

The vibrating walls of the plane were eggshell thin.
Heddy and the children were cold in spite of their heavy
ski clothes. Nevertheless, Attilla's nose was glued to the
icy window even though it was too fogged to see much.

"You can't tell it now, but it's pretty here in the summer," the pilot yelled. "Lots of creeks and forests and
alpine meadows. The forest is alive with bears…"

"Bears!" Cleo gasped, opening her eyes, her pupils
dilating until they were huge. "Are bears nice?"

"I wouldn't want to tango with 'em, hon. Here we go!"
the pilot yelled spotting a clearing between the trees.
"Hang on to your britches, babies. It always gets a little
bumpy getting into the village."

A little bumpy… If ever there was an understatement.

For the next five minutes the pilot was totally absorbed
in landing the plane. Every time he banked, Heddy's nails
clawed the armrests as the small aircraft bucked like a
bronco through wind shears and air pockets. Her ragged
nails were still digging in long after they'd slid smoothly
to a stop on the icy runway.

When they were on the ground and the pilot had shut

the engine down, Attilla was in her face, his green eyes alive with feverish excitement. "Can we do it again?"

Cleo was whining, "Aunt Heddy, Attilla hid my shoes. And I have to find 'em. 'Cause I want to walk back to Texas."

Muz's phones and radios had been dead all morning, so it was impossible to reach Leander by radio. Muz had kindly offered to lend Heddy his snowmobile despite Mara's protests.

"Hell, he's been here practically every day till today," Muz explained impatiently to Heddy. "He didn't say nothing about any wife coming for Christmas. In fact he said just—"

"Muz—" Mara warned gently. "Heddy, I could tell Pepper missed you. He came into the village every day like he couldn't stand being alone out in his cabin."

Muz gave his wife a long look, and she answered it with an equally eloquent silence, defeating him in a curious battle of wills. Surrendering, Muz sat back down grumpily in front of his racks of radio equipment and put on a headset. He shook his shaggy head in frustration. "Dead as a dodo!" He pounded a fist on the counter. "What good is this stuff when it's out just when you really need it?"

"That's okay," Heddy said. "It's not your fault. I know you tried. I'm just so grateful you said you'd loan me your snowmobile."

"I really think you should go with her, Muz," Mara coaxed. "It's clear, but it's awfully cold. You know how fast the weather can change—"

"I have ridden snowmobiles lots of times when I've gone skiing in Colorado."

"But Muz knows the way," Mara persisted.

"You said it wasn't far. From the map it looks very easy to get there," Heddy said, rolling Muz's map back up.

"Believe me, in the snow, when you're out there alone, it's harder," Mara said.

"It's just a straight shot up the river," Muz repeated for the third time. "She'd have to be an idiot to miss it. And like I said, the kids can spend the day with Lori at her school. Mrs. Asuluk, their teacher, is having them clean the room and then they're having that Christmas party."

"You are all so sweet," Heddy said gratefully.

"Pepper's been our best friend for nearly eight years," Mara said. "We know how thrilled he'll be to see you."

I hope, Heddy prayed.

The weather had been clear when Heddy had zoomed out of the village on Muz's snowmobile.

But gray clouds had formed, and it was snowing now. These light flurries were accompanied by sharp frozen winds, and the falling snow made it difficult to see through the fringe of trees that lined the bank of the river. The cold numbed her muscles, especially those in her hands, and made it more difficult to control the snowmobile.

Not only that, but the river was more narrow and circuitous than Muz had led her to believe. Afraid she'd miss Leander's cabin, she kept a constant eye over her right shoulder. Which made it impossible to pay close enough attention to where she was going.

Thick snowdrifts and logs on the frozen river were a constant hazard and had to be dodged.

Crouching forward, she raced on through the freezing cold.

It seemed to be taking longer to get to Leander's cabin

than Muz's map had led her to believe. She was constantly thinking that his cabin would be around the next turn. And then the next.

But it never was.

The sky was darkening, and it was growing harder and harder to see. Her adrenaline began to pump as she considered frightening possibilities. What if she had ridden past his cabin and was speeding into empty wilderness? What if she got lost in the dark?

Then she rounded the next curve and saw a light in the trees. And smoke curling.

In the next instant the light and smoke weren't there.

Had they just been illusions?

She slowed the snowmobile and struggled to focus, but the snow was falling too thickly for her to see much.

She was straining over her shoulder so hard that she didn't see the mountainous snowdrift and logjam in front of her. Not until her snowmobile slammed into them.

Snow and rocks and ice and wood erupted. The snowmobile spun crazily, and her hands were too numb to hold on to the handlebars. When she fell, the snowmobile skidded off on its own toward the embankment.

Her head struck the ice as her unmanned snowmobile crashed into a tree.

She lay in the snow, too dazed by the force of her fall to get up.

The snow fell thicker. Vaguely she felt the sharp, icy wind and the cold seeping up from the frozen river, piercing her thick ski clothes, chilling her to the bone.

At first she was afraid. Then she began to feel very sleepy. She closed her eyes, intending to lie there just for a minute, until she felt stronger.

She had read somewhere that one should dig a hole in the snow to keep warm. But her head ached. When she tried to sit up, her muscles were too numb to obey the command of her brain.

She had been so determined to reach the cabin, she hadn't realized she was so cold.

A great weariness settled upon her as the snow swirled thickly around her. The sky was almost black now. The frigid temperature of the ice numbed her brain as it did her body, lessening her terror, weakening her instincts for survival, making her feel incredibly lethargic.

Vaguely she realized that it was her birthday. And Leander's too. And that Christmas was the next day.

Her last thoughts before she fell asleep were of Leander.

She heard a sound and opened her eyes.

Was someone shouting her name?

She cried out softly, but her faint voice was lost in the wind.

For a moment she thought she saw him standing above her in the snow. He was holding out two presents. "Happy birthday. Merry Christmas, Sugar. I love you. I love you."

She had come so far to hear him say those words.

"Leander," she whispered faintly, reaching for him. "I love you, too. Leander—"

But when she opened her eyes, he wasn't there.

Twelve

He could live without her. He could live without anybody.

At least that was what he'd believed until now.

The pain without Heddy was unbearable, and Leander hadn't even endured it a week. He felt like he was losing his mind. Was she all right? Was Christina? No matter how hard he tried he couldn't stop worrying about them. He couldn't stop caring.

He had been at his desk all morning, accomplishing nothing. Usually he wrote his first drafts on a long yellow pad with a soft black pencil, skipping every other line. Usually his pencil flew like lightning—he was either writing or furiously erasing and rewriting.

Today more than a dozen crumpled yellow balls lay at his feet. He hadn't written a coherent sentence.

All he'd managed were doodles and nude sketches of Heddy. He was driving himself crazy.

But at least he was sober.

Suddenly there was a roar. And then a crash.

A tree falling? No... He didn't think so. Someone was out there.

Ivak got up and bounded to the door, barking ferociously.

"Hush!"

Ivak could not resist one final howl before settling on his haunches excitedly, his alert amber eyes glued to Leander, his intelligent gray face looking as worried as any human's.

Curious, Leander glanced at his watch as he rose and went to the window. Not that he could see anything through the frosted panes.

Ivak put a tentative paw on the doorknob, whining as Leander pulled on his parka. When he opened the door, Ivak bounded outside, disappearing into the trees.

Leander stepped out onto his porch and watched the snow swirl and listened to the eerie shivering of the trees. It was barely noon, but the snowfall had thickened. It was almost completely dark when Ivak raced back barking.

At the same moment static buzzed loudly over the radio from inside the cabin.

"Muz to Pepper. Damn it, would you come in? Over."

Ivak barked more frantically in acute disappointment as Leander went back inside. Picking up his headset, he snapped down the transmitting button. "This is Pepper. I read you. Over."

Almost instantly Muz's deep voice crackled back to him. "Did you wife make it? Over."

Leander's hands began to shake as he felt the vague beginnings of fear.

Ivak nudged the door open and trotted tensely over to the fire and whined.

"*My wife?* Not sure I read. Over."

"Heddy? Is she there yet? Over."

Leander broke into a cold sweat. "Muz what the hell are you talking about? Over."

"Your wife came in on the plane from Juneau this morning—along with those cases of cigarettes and whiskey you ordered. When I couldn't contact you by radio, I loaned her my snowmobile and gave her directions to your cabin. She kept saying it was your birthday and that it was urgent she see you. She should have been there by now. Over."

"Tell me everything! Over."

Leander was pulling on his gloves and snow gear while Muz spit out the rest of the details in between intermittent bursts of static. Then Mara got on the radio, too, assuring him not to worry about the children, that she would take care of the kids for as long as necessary.

She'd brought the kids, too?

Suddenly Leander remembered the sound he'd heard outside in his woods a few minutes before—and prayed that it was her.

Nothing mattered. Nothing in the whole world.

Except finding her.

Except telling her he loved her.

The afternoon seemed much colder than the actual temperature readings of the thermometer on his porch. An unprotected amateur couldn't survive in a blizzard like this. He considered the vastness and the danger of the island's wilderness and the smallness of a single human being. Of a woman.

The chances of a woman unfamiliar with survival training lasting long were extremely slim.

He had to find her—fast. Muz had been out of his mind to let her come.

He had been out of his mind to leave her in Texas.

Especially after that last night they had shared, when she had done everything in her power to make him feel loved.

He trudged through the trees in the direction of the sound he'd heard. But it was slow going in his snowshoes.

He had been a blind stubborn fool, bent on proving what he'd always been determined to prove as a child—that he could survive without anybody.

But he couldn't. *Dear God.* Had he learned that too late?

He never prayed.

But suddenly he felt compelled to sink to his knees in the snow. "God, *please,* let me find her."

Unaware that he was crying as he got up, he plunged through the forest toward the river, calling her name.

"Heddy!"

There was no answer—just the empty sound of his own voice echoing through the trees, and the heavy silence of the great aloneness.

Ivak raced around him in ever-widening circles, his nose in the snow. For ten long minutes, they wandered aimlessly.

The gray day was so quiet and cold, so without life or color anywhere—exactly as his life would be if he lost Heddy, if he could never kiss her again, if he could never make love to her again. If he lost her now, after all they'd been through, he would feel worse, worse even than he had in those early lost years of his childhood.

Suddenly the husky stopped and sniffed the air alertly. A ridge of fur stood up along the middle of his back as he turned to his master, howling with immense excitement. Then he dashed down to the river and began barking furiously.

Hope burst in Leander's heart.

Dear God, let it be Heddy.

Leander took off, running clumsily in his snowshoes.

First he saw the overturned snowmobile, its handlebars snagged in a leafless tree branch. Then he saw the prone figure lying perfectly still on the frozen river.

"Heddy!"

He raced toward her and then knelt, pulling her limp body into his arms.

He brushed the snow off her face. He thought her unutterably lovely. She seemed to have only fallen asleep, her thick lashes lying quietly against her pale cheeks.

Terror gripped him as he kissed her blue lips. He pulled her lifeless body into his arms, cradling her head against his chest as he lifted her gently.

"Live!" he whispered hoarsely. *Live! Because I love you more than anything on earth and I'll die if you don't!*

Her lips moved, but she made no sound.

Leander.

Was he really there this time?

Was she dead or alive?

As if in a dream she heard a dog barking.

"Go away," she whispered drowsily when a warm tongue bathed her stiff face.

"No—"

Then Leander was there.

Vaguely she was aware of the great passion in his voice when he spoke, although his voice seemed to come from far, far away. Vaguely she was aware of being lifted and carried. Of her name being said over and over as he laid her on a bed and built a roaring fire. Vaguely she was aware of sips of warm brandy being forced through her frozen lips.

"I love you," Leander said gently. "I love you."

"Why did you leave me then? Why didn't you love me?"

"Dear God." His tone was low and agonized. "Those are the same questions I used to ask my mother every time I dreamed she'd come back for me when I was a kid." Gently he placed his hands against her forehead and cheeks. "My darling, I do love you. More than anything. So much it scared me. I was angry and hurt. I hated thinking you only changed your mind because Tia gave you permission to. Maybe I just wanted to prove I didn't need anybody. I don't know. But I found out I was wrong. I can't live without you. I wouldn't have hurt you for the world. I swear I'll never leave you again."

"But can you ever forgive me?" she breathed, too weak and sleepy still to open her eyes. "I was their only child. Their last hope. Only children have a lot to live up to sometimes. Barret and Tia loved me so much. They expected so much. Too much sometimes. I felt guilty every time I disappointed them. But no more. You will always be first now, I swear."

"You believed your family, and since I didn't have a family, I ran away and played tough guy. We were both wrong. I would forgive you anything," he whispered fiercely. "Anything, Sugar."

"I never stopped loving you, Leander. Even when I doubted you. Not once during all those years even when I thought—"

"I loved you, too. And never more than when you were far away and I was all alone pretending I didn't need anybody. Nothing will ever matter to me again but you. I was too hard. You showed me you loved me that last night, and I abandoned you. If you had died in the snow, I would have died, too."

"Happy birthday," she murmured, her teeth chattering

as he bundled her trembling body under the covers. "I lost your present somewhere on the ice…"

"You have given me everything that I ever dreamed of, everything that I ever wanted. Love. A daughter. A family."

"Will you stay with me this time? Will you promise never to leave me? Will you—?"

"Forever. Until we die. And after. We are star mates, remember? You are my destiny."

"You used to say all that was silly."

"I'll never say it again."

She smiled weakly as he left her just for a moment to radio Muz and Mara and tell them that he had found Heddy, but that they couldn't get back to the village until the next day. Mara reassured him again that they were having a wonderful time with the children.

When Leander came back to Heddy, she was trembling and blue with chills. He stripped off their clothes and pulled her against his body under the thick covers of his bed.

And still shivering, but warming slowly, she fell asleep against his heated length.

Hours later she awoke, the warmth of his body drawing her like a magnetic force. She felt gloriously hot. Gloriously alive. Gloriously his. And incredibly in need of his love.

"Leander—"

Her husky tone had him instantly awake.

She let her hands trail across the broad expanse of his chest, twining her fingers into the silky carpet of black hair. "Leander, I want you to make love to me."

In an instant he was fully roused.

"Are you sure, Sugar? You nearly died out there in the snow."

"I'm fine." Her eyes sparkled in the dark. A lovely tawny-pink flush tinted her cheeks. "In fact I never felt so deliciously hot and wild to—"

He bent his head over hers and crushed his lips to hers. His hands caressed her.

One kiss and she was moaning softly and breathing hard.

Two and she was frantic.

"Now," she urged. "I can't wait."

Her breath stopped as he lowered his black head and placed his open mouth over her breast. His hot, moist breath burningly caressed her as his tongue teased her nipple.

She wanted him with a fierceness that shocked her.

"Now." Her voice sounded strangled. "Oh, Leander, please, now!"

He pushed her underneath him and with a violent thrust joined his body to hers.

When she gasped in pleasure, his head came up and he met her brilliant gaze. His lips fashioned her name in wonder.

"Leander. Oh, Leander," she said softly, eagerly.

Quiet tears of happiness clung to her lashes. "Don't ever run away from me again. I was so afraid I'd never see you again."

"So was I." He hesitated for a long time, savoring that first moment of sexual possession, not wanting to rush. "I can be a stubborn idiot, but I love you, Heddy."

"I know," she said, her low voice trailing away on a note of tempestuous excitement as he began to move.

Wrapping her legs around him, she drew him deeper and deeper inside her as his body surged into hers. Finally she could stand no more. All the pleasure that had been denied to her for so long burst gloriously inside her, and she cried out against his lips. He felt her joy and began to shake as the same shattering wave washed him.

They lay together, sated, in that golden afterglow of their love, knowing that finally they had come home. She had been waiting for this moment all her life.

He was as incomplete without her as she was without him. He was hers—forever.

Just as she was his.

Together they were whole.

"You are my destiny," she whispered in wonder, kissing his mouth lightly.

"Ah, Sugar," he murmured, tiredly, contentedly, burying his face in the sweet-smelling hollow of her neck. "As you are mine."

"Merry Christmas," she said. "And Happy Birthday."

They fell asleep in his warm cabin in that snowy wonderland, wrapped in each others arms and in each others love, their hearts filled with ecstasy.

Epilogue

One year later
Christmas Day

Mayflower and Ivak were prancing back and forth, barking excitedly on the verandah. Their golden eyes held both love and canine torment as they studied the human family they loved from their place of temporary exile.

Heddy's tender gaze met her husband's, and her heart leapt at the depth of emotion she read in his eyes. She would never get used to the wonder of just looking at him. He was stunning in a navy suit even though his black hair was as unruly as ever as it fell across his dark brow. Even though the Santa Claus tie Attilla had given him and insisted on tying for him was not as crisply knotted as usual.

"Should we let them in?" she whispered, indicating the two desperate dogs who whined even more pitifully when

Leander glanced their way. Ivak held up his paw as if to plead mournfully to his master.

"Faker," Leander said to the dog. And then to his wife he murmured, "No way, Sugar. I'd say we have enough chaos already."

"But—"

"I have everything I need, everything I want, right here." He pulled her into his arms and kissed her, and for the length of that lingering kiss it was as if they were the only two people in the world.

Neither of them had the slightest awareness that everybody else stopped what they were doing to watch as they kissed and clung.

"I like it when they do that," Christina said with a quiet smile.

"They do it all the time," Attilla remarked impatiently as he tossed a present into her lap.

"I like it, too," Cleo said softly, unbuckling a shoe strap and then stealthily sliding the red slipper off her heel and tucking it under the plump sofa cushions.

Tia just watched them, trying to suppress a smile as Leander gripped Heddy more tightly.

"Heddy...ah, Heddy," Leander whispered against his wife's warm throat and heavy golden hair.

"Leander...my darling Leander...I never thought I could be this happy."

"It took us a while, Sugar."

His mouth sought hers again. Only when his lips at last released hers did she come back to the golden glow of the parlor, to the sound of their two dogs barking and scratching frantically on the door again, to their children and Tia.

Heddy felt very loved as Leander hugged her closer. Attilla was dashing about again, stumbling over the litter of boxes, wrapping paper, pieces of ribbon and parts to new toys as he searched for presents with tags that had his name on them. Their new baby, James Robert, a darkly handsome miniature version of his father, squealed from his bassinet every time the big star on top of the tree blinked. Cleo and Christina sat on either side of Tia as she helped them undo the gold foil bow on Cleo's giant red package.

Yes, it had taken them a while to make a life together.

But the wait had been worth it.

The past year had been full of delights. She thought of the nights they had shared in the bed upstairs, their bodies entangled even when they slept. How wonderful it was to know that if she awoke in the dark, she would find him there. He had been with her for the birth of their son. He would be with her always.

"Happy Birthday," he murmured huskily, his voice low and intimate, for her alone.

"We said that last night," she whispered. "This is Merry Christmas."

"Yeah. Right." A crooked smile lifted the corner of his sensual mouth. "Merry Christmas it is then."

He leaned down and kissed her nose. "I love you, Heddy." Suddenly his arms came around her possessively. "I love you more than I ever thought possible."

With her hands, she framed his dark face, searching his black eyes and finding, as always, her own soul mirrored there. "I love you, too."

And, of course, after such a tender, heartfelt, soul-to-soul confession, they couldn't resist another kiss.

And once again the glory of their mouths coming together made it seem that they were the only two people in the world.

The only two people in the universe, for that matter.

Until Attilla stumbled against the bassinet and James Robert began to cry....

*   *   *   *   *

Dear Reader,

What a special treat this is for me to be able to wish each and every one of you a "Merry Christmas!" When I first learned that *A Cowboy for Christmas* was going to be reissued, I was thrilled. Of all the holiday stories I've written for Silhouette, this one happens to be a favorite.

Lucinda Lambert has always been alone. She has no idea what it's like to have the support of a family, much less what it means to share in the Yuletide cheer. But when a cowboy named Chance plucks her from a blizzard and takes her home to his ranch, she quickly learns that Christmas means far more than the giving or getting of material gifts. As for Chance, he's a man haunted by the past. The coming holiday means little to him—until Lucinda fills his heart and opens his eyes to the shining star of Christmas hope and the joy of everlasting love.

I hope you enjoy reading Lucinda and Chance's story and that you all can celebrate this holiday season with the ones you love!

God Bless, and Merry Christmas,

Stella Bagwell

A COWBOY FOR CHRISTMAS
Stella Bagwell

To my editor, Mary-Theresa Hussey,
for her patience, guidance and friendship

Prologue

Lucinda Lambert stared cautiously at the brightly wrapped package on her coffee table. It was long and slender in shape, the paper printed with Santa Clauses and reindeer. She'd found it on the back steps of her apartment when she'd arrived home from work. That was enough to alarm her. No one had access to the inner courtyard of her apartment building, except the other tenants. Could she be that lucky? Was it possible the gift had merely come from a neighbor?

Seeing no other way of finding out, Lucinda reached for the small card that was slipped beneath the red ribbon. Her fingers shook as she opened the envelope, then everything inside her went cold and still as she read, "Merry Christmas, my darling Lucinda. All my love, Richard."

Fear clutched her heart, drained the blood from her face and left her hands clammy. It had been almost a week since her telephone had rung in the middle of the night, or an unmarked police car had followed her home from work. The small reprieve had led her to hope this horrible nightmare was going to end, that Richard was finally going to come to his senses and realize she was never going to love him, much less marry him.

Lucinda could see now that she'd been crazy to hope. Christmas was little more than a week away, but obviously Richard wasn't going to use the holidays to spread cheer and goodwill. No, she thought sickly as she glanced once again at the wrapped package, he was going to use Christmas to spread his own special brand of evilness.

As if on cue, the telephone rang. Lucinda stared at it a moment, then with a small groan hurried across the room to pick up the receiver.

Perhaps it was Molly. She'd left her friend working late tonight at The Fashion Plate. There was a chance she might be having problems with the mohair cape she'd been sewing.

"Hello," Lucinda answered warily.

"Hello, sweetheart. Did you get my Christmas package?"

The mocking masculine voice sent shivers of pure terror along her spine. Without saying a word, she slammed down the receiver and backed several feet away from the telephone.

Before she could reach the kitchen, it began to ring again. Lucinda did her best to ignore the demanding sound and tried not to think of the caller, who might be far across town, or perhaps just across the street from her.

The doors and windows are locked, Lucinda. He can't get to you, she fiercely told herself. But deep down, she couldn't make herself believe that she was truly safe. If, or *when* Richard finally decided to get to her, he could easily do it. Being on the Chicago police force had taught him all the ins and outs. It had also left Lucinda without any protection at all. No one believed she needed to be protected from one of their finest homicide detectives.

Finally the incessant ringing stopped. But by then, Lucinda was shaking all over. She was also furious. She was sick of being afraid. She was tired of constantly looking over her shoulder and dreading the ring of the telephone.

Chicago was the only place she'd ever lived. But it wasn't a home to her anymore. It was a cage of fear and would be as long as Richard continued to harass her.

Squaring her slender shoulders and lifting her chin, she walked to the bedroom and pulled several suitcases out of the closet.

It was time she found a real home.

Chapter One

Lucinda leaned over the steering wheel and squinted through the small circle she'd just swiped upon the windshield. The misty rain that had been falling for the past fifty miles had turned into snow. Not just a few fat flakes drifting along in the wind; this stuff was coming down by the bucketfuls, turning the night into a white blur and making it impossible for her to see more than a few feet in front of the car.

For the past fifteen minutes she'd been straining her ears to catch a weather report on the radio. So far the only thing she'd managed to pick up from an Amarillo station was a cowboy humorist telling a story about a bull and a greenhorn rancher. And now, thanks to the fading radio station, she'd even missed the end of that, drat it!

The windshield fogged over once again and Lucinda flipped the defroster on high. It was the middle of December. She'd expected Texas to be cool, but a blizzard? Not in her wildest dreams. This was a southern state! At least it was far south of Chicago!

Lucinda supposed she should have stayed at Amarillo and gotten a room for the night. But ever since she'd crossed the line from Oklahoma into Texas, she'd felt the urge to press on. California was still more than a thousand miles away. The longer she could stay on the highway, the sooner she could get there.

But Lucinda hadn't planned on driving straight into this foul weather. Now she was going to be lucky if she made it to a town large enough to have a motel or a place of lodging. If she made it to a town at all!

"You've lost your mind, Lucy. Moving to California isn't going to make your life all sun and roses," her friend Molly had told her the minute she'd heard Lucinda was leaving. "Richard can always follow you out there."

"He won't follow me all the way out to California," Lucinda had protested. "Surely he's not that obsessed."

Molly glumly shook her head. "I'm beginning to think the man is crazy. He might do anything."

"That's why I'm leaving and you're not to tell anybody where I'm going."

"If you'd let the police—" Molly began only to have Lucinda interrupt her with a mocking snort.

"Do you hear yourself, Molly? Richard *is* the police."

Maybe her friend Molly had been right, Lucinda thought as she fiercely gripped the steering wheel. Richard could possibly follow her. But she had to take that chance. She had to find a new life for herself. Whether it was in San Diego or Los Angeles, she didn't know yet. She only knew that she was finally putting Richard and the hellish months of his abusive threats behind her.

"—snow and sleet with high winds and dangerously low temperatures. This winter storm—"

Apparently the weather was playing havoc with the antenna on her car. The man's voice faded into nothing.

Lucinda desperately twisted the tuning knob, but it didn't help.

Oh well, she thought wearily, from the dim view she had before her, she didn't need a meteorologist to tell her it was bad out there. The wind had picked up considerably, slashing snow straight into her little car. The tall, yellow grass on either side of the highway was bent flat under the merciless gale, making Lucinda wonder how soon it might be before her car was blown off the road or into the path of a passing vehicle.

Perhaps she'd be better off if she stopped the car and waited for the storm to abate. But where? From the sketchy glimpses she could catch outside the windshield, there was no place to stop. This was a rural area she was traveling through, much of it open farm and ranching country. The four-lane highway had ended several miles back, leaving her on a narrow highway with hardly any shoulder.

"Damn!"

She shrieked the word as suddenly a loud pop exploded at the front of the car. The steering wheel jerked violently against her hands. Instinctively Lucinda reacted by stomping hard on the brake pedal, jamming it nearly to the floor. In response, the wheels locked and sent the car skidding sideways on the ice-slick road.

Frantically Lucinda jerked on the steering wheel to right the car back on a straight course. But it was too little too late. She was going to crash and there was nothing she could do about it.

"What the hell?" Chance Delacroix muttered as he topped a rise in the road and saw a small red car buried nose first in the ditch.

Quickly he eased the pickup off to the side of the highway and dug a flashlight out from under the seat. More than likely the car was empty, left by the owner until the weather cleared. But Chance couldn't, in all good conscience, pass it by without checking first. If someone was still in the car, it would only be a matter of minutes before hypothermia set in.

The moment he stepped out of the shelter of his warm pickup, bits of ice and snow smacked him straight in the face. Cursing, Chance tugged the brim of his cowboy hat lower onto his forehead and hurried across the wide ditch to the wrecked car.

It had Illinois plates and the back seat was piled high with bags and suitcases, but more important, a head of dark hair was pressed against the driver's window.

He rapped his knuckles against the window. "Hey in there! Can you hear me?"

There was no response. Or at least Chance couldn't hear any over the sound of the driving wind.

Gently, in case the driver was unconscious and not belted in, Chance opened the door.

Lucinda immediately felt something wet against her face and for a moment she thought she'd been dreaming and had woken up crying. But then a hand touched her forehead. A big, callused hand that smelled like man and snow.

Slowly she opened her eyes and found herself looking into a darkly shadowed face.

"Who—what happened?" she asked fuzzily.

"Looks like you met up with a patch of ice. Are you hurt?"

The voice was deeply masculine, very Texan and oddly soothing. She took a deep breath and tried to pull her senses together.

"I don't know." Frowning, she touched her fingers to

her forehead as her eyes swept frantically around the dark interior of the car. "There was a loud pop and then—did I—" her gaze swung back to the stranger's shadowed face "—did I hit something?"

"I don't see anything else around here, lady, but you and a ditch."

Lucinda groaned as her wits gathered and reality began to settle in. "Is the car ruined?" She fumbled with the seat belt while inwardly cursing the fact that the interior lights had obviously gone awry.

Chance hadn't spared an extra moment to pull on his coat. Now he was getting wetter and colder by the second. Didn't this woman realize they were out in a blizzard? he wondered irritably.

"You can worry about the car later, ma'am," he said, raising his voice above the wind. "Are you all right?"

The belt finally snapped free. She pushed it out of the way. "I'm fine—I think. Except for my right foot. It feels like I must have twisted it, or banged it against something."

"My truck is just a few yards away. I'll take you to a doctor."

"Oh, do you think that's necessary?" She knew she was in a predicament, but that didn't necessarily mean she wanted to put herself into the hands of a total stranger. And she certainly didn't want to go to a hospital emergency room where they'd charge her several hundred dollars for five minutes of service. Money that she didn't have to spare.

She had a Midwestern accent, but Chance would have known she was a Northerner even without hearing her voice. She had that attitude about her that Texans like himself described as standoffish.

"Look, lady, you can't wait here for a tow truck! I.

could be hours before one is available. You'd freeze to death before then.'' He put one hand on her shoulder and another on her arm. ''The D Bar D is only about four miles from here. We'll call a wrecker from there.''

Lucinda grabbed her purse and coat from the passenger seat.

''The D Bar D?'' she asked, darting him a frantic glance as he began to virtually lift her up and out of the seat, pulling her coat over her.

''My home.''

Suddenly she was outside the car, cradled in his arms. Ice and snow pelted her face and the streaks of pain shooting through her ankle felt as angry as the freezing wind howling around them.

Even though Lucinda couldn't see her rescuer's face under the brim of his black Stetson, she could feel his chest and shoulders were wide and his arms strong as he began to carry her easily across the wide, soggy ditch to his vehicle.

Once he'd placed her on the bench seat and hurried around to the driver's side, Lucinda had collected herself somewhat. Pushing her dark hair behind her ears, she bent forward and tried to examine her foot.

''Do you think it's broken?'' he asked gruffly.

The dome light came on and she jerked her head in his direction. ''I hope not,'' she said through chattering teeth. ''I don't think...'' Her voice trailed off as she looked at him beneath the glow of the dome light.

That drawling, sexy voice had a face that was equally disarming. Crow black hair hung in wet curls around his angular features. Bits of ice and snow glistened on his tanned skin and spiked the thick sooty lashes that were now drooping over his gray eyes. Which, at the moment, were looking back at her, waiting for her answer.

Yet Lucinda couldn't get a word past her lips. All she could do was stare at him. Her eyes felt glued to his roughly hewn mouth, the long hawkish nose, the cocky jut of his jawline. Unable to suppress a shiver, she hugged her arms to her.

"I don't know. I've never had a broken bone. Have you?"

He took off his hat, quickly dusted the snow from the brim, then socked it back onto his head. "A couple. They hurt like hell."

He put the pickup into gear and carefully pulled back onto the highway. White sheets of snow slashed horizontally through the air, making visibility practically nil. Lucinda didn't know which was more threatening, the violent weather or this dark stranger who was taking her to God only knows where.

"Is this weather—isn't it unusual for Texas?"

Shaking his head with disbelief, he switched the wiper blades to a faster rhythm. "In case you hadn't noticed, Texas is big. What goes on down in the south is nothing like here in the Panhandle."

So he was telling her that blizzards were a normal happening around here. He must be thinking she was an idiot for driving in one.

"It was misting rain when I left Amarillo, I never thought I'd run into snow like this," she felt compelled to explain.

Chance didn't say anything, but he wanted to. It was damn stupid for a woman to be traveling alone at night. And in this weather! She had to be one of those flighty females who never thought before they acted.

"You must be in a hell of a hurry to get where you're going," he muttered. "Does your husband know you're out in this?"

The heater was running full blast but Lucinda felt cold in spite of the warm air rushing over her feet. "I'm not married."

Chance darted a quick glance at her. She wasn't married, so who or what was she trying to get to? A job? A lover?

"Well, I can tell you the highway on down to Roswell is a solid sheet of ice. In fact, parts of it are closed. But you would have never made it that far. You have to have a four-wheel-drive vehicle to travel on this stuff. Were you headed in that direction?"

Lucinda bit her lip. This man had just rescued her from a wrecked car in a freezing blizzard. She shouldn't mind his asking questions. But she was loath to tell him where she was going. She didn't want to leave any sort of trail behind her that Richard could follow.

Her eyes traveled over his dark face as she tried to decide whether he was a man to be trusted. "Yes. I'm working my way south to Interstate 10."

That didn't tell Chance much, but he didn't question her further. She looked frazzled, but then he supposed any woman who'd just slammed her car into the ditch would be a little distracted.

She was pretty though, Chance concluded, and young, too. He doubted she was a day past twenty-five. Straight brown hair spilled over her shoulders and down her back. Her eyes were also dark, but whether they were brown or green he couldn't tell.

At the moment he could feel those eyes studying him warily. "Well, miss, you haven't told me your name."

Lucinda looked away from him. She didn't want to tell him her name. That was too personal. And he didn't really need to know it, did he?

''You do have one, don't you?'' he prompted when her silence continued.

Her eyes straight ahead, she nodded. ''It's Lucinda Lambert. Lucy to my friends.''

''Well, Lucy,'' he said as he carefully guided the pickup onto a graveled lane, ''I'm Charles Delacroix. Most everyone calls me Chance.''

From the corner of her eye, Lucinda noticed his snow-dampened shirt was white and obviously for dress wear. Gold-and-onyx cuff links glinted at his wrist while the toes of a pair of fancy black cowboy boots extended beneath the legs of his dark trousers.

He'd taken a chance on ruining his expensive clothing to rescue her from the wrecked car. That surprised her. All the men she knew would have stood back and waited for an emergency unit to arrive.

She let out a sigh. Maybe this man could be trusted. She prayed to God that he could be. ''I've obviously interrupted your evening. Were you going to a party?''

''I was at a party. Until I went out for more lamb fries.''

''Lamb fries?''

From the look on her face it was obvious to Chance that she didn't know what he was talking about.

''Yeah. They're, uh—a certain part of the bull that's considered a delicacy. Sarah Jane just had to have them. It's her engagement party, you see. She doesn't realize there's a blizzard going on out here.''

He motioned to a grocery sack sitting between them. ''Once the guests finish these off, that's it. I say let 'em fill up on steak.''

Some woman named Sarah Jane wanted lamb fries, something that had nothing to do with a lamb, so this handsome hunk with his molasses voice had braved a blizzard to go get them and had rescued another damsel in distress along the way. Were all Texas cowboys like this one? Or was Charles "Chance" Delacroix something special?

Chapter Two

The home Chance Delacroix called the D Bar D turned out to be a sprawling Spanish-style ranch house. Along the driveway leading up to it, a maze of vehicles were parked at every available angle. It looked as if some guests had just left and others were in the process of leaving.

Lucinda stared in awe as Chance brought the pickup to a stop behind a dark green Jaguar. She'd known, just by looking at his clothes and the luxurious pickup they were riding in, that he wasn't a poor man. But she hadn't expected him to live this well!

"Do you think you can walk? Or do I need to carry you into the house?"

She darted him an anxious glance. "Do I have to? Go in there, I mean?"

He frowned as she inclined her head toward the brightly lit house.

"Where the hell would you want to go? Other than the house, there's only barns and stables and they aren't much warmer than being outside."

Lucinda had driven well over a thousand miles in the past two days. She was bone weary and now her car was wrecked and her foot was throbbing. She wished he could see that she wasn't in any shape to walk into the middle of an engagement party.

Clutching her coat protectively against her, she said, "I—I'd really rather—could I just sit in the kitchen while you call a wrecker?"

Biting down on a curse, Chance started to point out that she was being ridiculous, but something on her face stopped him. There was a haunted, vulnerable look in her eyes that tugged at him in spite of the fact that he normally couldn't abide a helpless woman.

Without a word, he jerked the gearshift into reverse, pulled away from the Jaguar and started around a driveway that led to the back of the house.

Oh brother, now he thought she was being ungrateful, Lucinda thought with a silent groan, and that was the last impression she wanted to give him.

"I'm sorry. I know I'm being a bother. It's just that I'm not up to meeting a roomful of strangers."

Her apology made Chance feel like a heel, though he wasn't quite sure why.

"Hell, don't apologize," he said more gruffly than he intended. "It isn't your fault that a party is going on."

He killed the engine and Lucinda scooted to the edge of the seat.

"It isn't your fault that I ran into the ditch, either," she told him. "I don't know what I would have done if you hadn't stopped to help me."

By now the inside of her car would be ice-cold. Even if the motor had started, she wouldn't have been able to drive it out of the ditch. And trying to walk in the blizzard with an injured foot would have been asking for deep trouble.

The sobering thought sent a shiver of fear through her. She looked at him and tried her best to smile, though she could feel her lips trembling. "I'd be glad to pay you for all your trouble. But that sounds pretty pathetic, doesn't it, when we both know you probably saved my life?"

Chance frowned at her. She was making him out to be some sort of hero. And that made him very uncomfortable. The last thing Chance could ever be was a hero. Especially to a woman.

Turning away from her, he reached for the door handle. "Keep your money. You can repay me by staying off the roads in weather like this."

Before she could say more, he climbed out of the truck and came around to her side. Lucinda quickly opened the door and lowered her feet toward the snowy ground below.

"Wait," he said as she started to slide out of the truck. "You'd better let me carry you."

Lucinda didn't want him to carry her. She wasn't exactly sure why. She only knew that he was big and strong and male. The idea of being that close again to him left her feeling awkward and hot faced.

"I—I can probably walk," she quickly blurted, and slid the rest of the way to the ground before he had a chance to reach for her.

"Ooh!" The one word came out in a shocked gasp as her injured foot took her weight.

Cursing under his breath, Chance didn't wait for her permission; he swung her up into his arms and started toward the house.

"It always feels good to prove a point, doesn't it?" he asked mockingly.

Trying her best to ignore him, Lucinda gritted her teeth as the pain in her foot shot through her leg, then gradually began to subside.

"I know you're anxious to get back to your fiancée," she told him. "As soon as you get me inside to a telephone, I'll be all right and you can return to your party."

As Chance stepped upon the porch and walked along its length to his private entrance, with Lucinda still in his arms, it dawned on him that she believed he was celebrating his own engagement. Which didn't really matter, he supposed. He didn't know this woman and she'd be leaving as soon as a wrecker pulled her car from the ditch. Still, he didn't like her thinking he was engaged. He wasn't a marrying man and he made sure everyone knew that.

"Sorry, but you're wrong on two counts. I don't have a fiancée and a telephone isn't all you need."

He walked through a side door leading from the porch, fumbled for a light switch, then carried Lucinda inside. From her lofty perch in his arms, she could see they were in a bedroom. From the masculine look of the pine furniture and sparse decorations, she could only guess the room was his.

Knowing that only made her feel more awkward as he gently placed her down on the bed.

"Now," he said, taking a step back from her. "Stay right there and I'll go get the doctor."

Lucinda's heart gave an odd little thump inside her chest. He was looking at her as if he were almost pleased to see her lying on his bed. But that couldn't be. He didn't know her and it was hardly likely that he welcomed the intrusion she'd made on his evening.

"Did you say doctor?"

Before he could answer, she planted both hands on the

mattress and vaulted to a sitting position. "Oh, please—I don't want you to go back out in this weather. It's too dangerous! Besides, I'll be fine. Really. I don't need a doctor."

She was practically pleading with him and Chance got the impression that she wasn't at all used to having anyone help or look after her. But that could hardly be right. She was a beautiful woman. She'd probably always had men at her beck and call.

Shaking his head at her, Chance put his hand on her shoulder and pressed her gently back down on the bed. "You let me decide what you need."

As Lucinda looked up at him, she was struck by how much larger he was than she'd first imagined. He had to be at least two or three inches over six feet and carrying two hundred pounds of pure muscle. Just looking at him sent a surge of adrenaline pouring through her, making her heart gallop beneath her breast. Not with fear. No. This man didn't scare her. He excited her in a way that made her feel warm and womanly and totally foolish.

"Do you always have a habit of ordering women around?" she couldn't help asking.

One corner of his mouth lifted as though he found her question amusing. "Only stubborn Northerners. The women around here know when to let a man take care of them."

Certain that all the oxygen must have left the room, Lucinda drew in a deep breath. "And you know how to do that? Take care of a woman?"

His eyebrows peaked as he slowly took in her long, disheveled hair, pale face and, finally, the shape of her legs encased in bright red leggings.

"I guess I should know. I've been doing it for years."

Lucinda didn't know exactly what he meant by that and

she certainly wasn't going to ask him. Just having him
look at her in such a possessive, male way was enough to
stain her cheeks with bright red heat.

Chance could see that he'd embarrassed her and that
surprised him. Modesty seemed to have gone out of style
with most of the women he knew. Seeing the uncomfortable color on Lucinda Lambert's face made him wonder
just what kind of life she'd led up until now.

"Don't worry, Lucy," he said, suddenly struck with a
need to reassure her. "The D Bar D isn't a bad place to
be stranded."

Before Lucinda could say anything to that, he went on
out the door that led into the main part of the house.
Which was probably a good thing. Getting personal with
a man like Chance Delacroix would be inviting trouble.
And she already had enough of that to deal with.

Sighing heavily, she looked around the large room. Sur-
prisingly, most of the furniture was old. Since it was all
in excellent condition, Lucinda knew it was very valued
and had probably been handed down through family gen-
erations.

A denim shirt was tossed across the arm of a wooden
rocker, and several toiletry items were scattered on the
dresser top. Photos looked at her from different perches
around the room, but Lucinda was too far away to see
them clearly, though she suspected they were probably all
family. Chance Delacroix seemed that sort of man. Even
if he wasn't married or engaged.

Closing her eyes, she rubbed her hands over her face.
Dear God, how had she ended up here in this strange
house, in the bed of a man she didn't know? Her car was
probably out of commission and from the way it felt, her
foot, too. What was she going to do?

She'd barely had time to consider the question when

Chance walked back through the door. A tall, gray-haired man followed closely behind him.

"Lucinda, this is Doc Campbell. He likes partying better than he does doctoring, but I talked him into looking at your foot."

"Hello, Doctor," she greeted, grateful for the kind smile on his face.

"Don't listen to this one," he told Lucinda, while jabbing his elbow back at Chance's rib cage. "If he's got his mouth open, he's lying. And I ought to know, 'cause I delivered him into this world."

Expecting him to look at her foot first, she was surprised when the doctor came and sat down on the side of the bed.

Taking her hand in his, he said, "Chance, if you'll be kind enough to go get my bag from my car, I'll check this pretty young woman over."

To Lucinda he said, "Don't worry your little head about a thing. You couldn't have picked a better place to mend than the D Bar D."

To mend? She had no intentions of staying here long enough to mend, and from the scowl on Chance's face, she knew he had no intentions of letting her.

"What's the matter with you?" Doc asked, glancing up at Chance, who was still standing a few steps away from them. "Are you waiting for the molasses to run? Get gone, boy."

Chance left the room and Lucinda was relieved to feel her heartbeat slow to a more normal pace. She didn't know what it was about the man, but he definitely unsettled her.

"Now tell me about this car accident," the doctor spoke up. "Chance mentioned that you were a little rattled when he found you."

Glad to put her mind on anything other than her dark rescuer, Lucinda nodded and proceeded to tell him what had happened up until the moment Chance had found her in the car.

She'd barely gotten the whole story out when the door leading from the porch opened and Chance entered the bedroom. Snow and sleet covered his clothes and the black bag he handed to the doctor.

The older man grabbed the medical bag and shook it in a way that reminded Lucinda of a dog ridding its coat of water. "You'd better get out of those clothes, Chance, or you'll be in bed here with Miss Lucinda."

"If that's the case, maybe I should leave them on," Chance said.

Lucinda's gaze whipped over to where Chance was hanging his snow-damp Stetson on a hat rack. There was a smile on his face. Or maybe it was closer to a mocking grin, she thought. Either way, it was the first one she'd seen on the man tonight.

If his words and the twist to his lips hadn't been so suggestive she would have let her eyes linger on the raw good looks of his face. But the idea of being in bed with him was such a provocative one, she had to lower her eyes back to the doctor and safer ground.

"Get out of here, Chance, and let me examine my patient," Doc told him. "And when you get done changing your clothes, bring us back some brandy. I expect this young woman could use a bit of warming."

Chance winked at Lucinda. "Doc, you're gonna give Lucy the wrong impression. She'll be thinking you're the boss around here instead of me."

Lucinda couldn't remember when a man had ever winked at her. Was he actually flirting? Or had he simply been trying to tell her that Dr. Campbell was a longtime friend and that's why he put up with the old man's orders? Whatever the reason, that wink had left Lucinda feeling strangely hot and bothered.

Dr. Campbell chuckled softly. "Maybe if your mama would marry me I'd help you do a little bit of bossin' around here. But as it is, I guess you're the only top dog on the D Bar D."

Crossing to a closet, Chance pulled out a pair of jeans and a red shirt. "I wouldn't worry, Doc. Mama will come around to marrying you one of these days," he said, then added as he started out the door, "I'll bring that brandy back in a few minutes."

Once Chance was totally out of sight, Lucinda exhaled an unconscious sigh and closed her eyes. That man had about as much presence as the winter blizzard wailing out there over the plains. And she was stupid for letting it affect her.

Dr. Campbell pulled out a stethoscope and a blood pressure cuff. While he wrapped it around her upper arm, he glanced at her swollen ankle. "I know you're more worried about your foot than anything. I'll get to that in a minute."

Lucinda tried to relax as he pumped up the cuff and listened to the fold of her arm. After a moment, he gave a satisfied grunt. "Just a little elevated, but I'll blame that on Chance. He seems to do that to all the women."

"He's—certainly not like any of the men I knew back in Chicago."

The doctor laughed. "No, I expect not." Flashing a pin light in her eyes, he continued to talk. "Chance isn't always easy to read. But he's a good man. I used to be a bit like him myself. But thirty-five years does a lot to a man. I'll bet you wouldn't believe I was a favorite beau among all the young ladies in this county."

"I'm sure I could believe it," Lucinda said politely, while thinking she'd never had a doctor like this one. Even though he was obviously in his sixties he was still a handsome man. His clothes were expensive and tasteful and she knew in spite of his casual demeanor he was a very educated man.

"Is—Mr. Delacroix always this way?" she asked as the doctor put away his light.

With his palm, he pressed down on her abdomen. "What do you mean?"

Lucinda licked her lips. She shouldn't be asking the doctor anything about Chance Delacroix. But since she was now in the man's house, she didn't think a question or two was that out of place. "Well, I mean, does he go out of his way to help people? He could have driven on by me tonight."

"Like I said, Chance is a good man. He doesn't know it, but he is. His father was a generous man, too. God rest his soul." The doctor suddenly looked up at her. "You're not pregnant, are you?"

The question left her with an overwhelming sense of relief that things between her and Richard hadn't gotten that far. "No. There's no possibility of that. Why, is something wrong?"

He gave her a reassuring smile. "Nothing is wrong. I just wanted to make sure there wasn't a little one in there that had been shook up."

The doctor turned his attention to her foot. Lucinda winced with pain as he took it between his hands and flexed it first one way and then the other.

"You trying to break it more, Doc?"

Through the pain, Lucinda heard Chance's voice coming into the room. She opened her eyes to see he was carrying a tray holding a cut glass decanter, three matching glasses and a plate of food.

Lucinda had thought him attractive before in his dress shirt and trousers, but now in jeans and a red cotton shirt with its long sleeves rolled back against his forearms, he looked like a handsome devil. One that knew it perhaps, but would never think of flaunting it.

"I've been a doctor for nearly forty years, Chance. I think I know a little bit about what I'm doin'."

Chance placed the tray on a table beside the bed then stood by Lucinda's shoulder as the doctor finished his examination. While he'd been out of the room changing clothes and waiting for his mother to fix a plate of food, he'd kept telling himself that the little northern snowbird he'd found in the ditch wasn't really that pretty. She was just an ordinary young woman who didn't have enough common sense to stay off the highway during a blizzard. But now that Chance was close to her once again, he had to admit to himself that there was nothing ordinary about her.

The red mohair coat she'd hurriedly thrown around her shoulders was now tossed, along with her purse, to one side of the bed. The loosely knit sweater she was wearing came down to her thighs and was black. Buttons lined the front of the garment and all were fastened, except for the top three where the collar fell away from her throat. Her skin was ivory pale, making the red velvet ribbon she wore as a choker around her neck even brighter.

If Chance allowed his eyes to dip lower, he knew he would see the faint shadow between the slight swell of her breasts. But he didn't allow himself that pleasure. It had been a long time since he'd been interested in a woman, physically or otherwise. He certainly wasn't going to let a total stranger change his habits.

"I called the wrecker service," he told her. "It will probably be tomorrow afternoon before they can get your car to you."

Her dark eyes jerked up to his and Chance was taken aback by the desperation he saw in them.

"Tomorrow afternoon!" she gasped. "But that's—I have to be gone before then!"

Chance exchanged glances with Doc, who'd also noticed the frantic sound in her voice.

"Why?" Chance asked. "Do you have a family emergency?"

Lucinda was in an emergency all right. But it had nothing to do with family and everything to do with getting as far away from Chicago as she could possibly get.

"I don't have any family," she said.

Chance had long considered himself tough hided and he intended to stay that way. As far as he was concerned, getting sentimental and soppy made a person vulnerable. But hearing Lucinda say she had no family tore right into him. A beautiful little thing like her surely had folks out there somewhere who loved and looked after her.

"You don't have anyone you need to notify and let know you're safe?"

Lucinda shook her head, wondering what Chance would think if he knew she'd just severed all ties with the only home and friends she'd ever had.

"No," she told him. "I have a friend who's expecting to hear from me tomorrow or the next day. But that's all."

Dr. Campbell eased her foot back onto the bed and stood up. "Well, you're going to need to take it easy on that foot for the next few days. It isn't broken, but the tendons around your ankle have had a pretty nasty wrenching."

Now that she knew her foot wasn't actually broken,

getting back on the road was her major concern. "How soon will I be able to drive?" she asked him.

"I wouldn't advise it for two or three days. Even then I certainly wouldn't drive for long hours. Keeping your foot in that same downward position will only cause it to swell and ache."

What little bit of hope Lucinda had been desperately trying to hold on to vanished with the doctor's warning. What was she going to do now? The nearest town with a motel was Hereford and that was probably a good twenty miles back toward Amarillo. Even if she had her car and was able to drive, the roads were probably already becoming impassable.

Dr. Campbell moved to the nightstand and poured a small amount of brandy into one of the glasses. "Drink this," he ordered, handing it to Lucinda. "And try to relax. In a few minutes Chance can find you some good oldfashioned aspirin for your pain."

Lucinda thanked him, then took a careful sip of the brandy.

Satisfied that his patient was going to follow his orders, the doctor left the room. However, the moment he was out of sight, Lucinda sat up and swung her legs over the side of the bed.

"Where do you think you're going?"

The authoritative tone in his voice took her by surprise. As Dr. Campbell had said, Chance might be the top dog here on the D Bar D, but he definitely wasn't her boss. After the torment Richard had put her through, she wasn't going to take any man's orders.

"I'm getting up. I've got to figure out how to get to a motel." She took one last sip of the brandy, then placed the glass on the nightstand. "Surely some of your guests will be going home soon. Perhaps I could catch a ride with them to the nearest town?''

His mouth compressed to a disapproving line. ''Most of the ones who live in town have already gone home. The rest are ranchers who live even farther out. Besides, with weather like this, I'm sure all the motel rooms around here are already filled.''

And you should have thought about all of this earlier, his expression said. Well, maybe she should have known better than to keep driving after dark and straight into a snowstorm, Lucinda thought, but her predicament wasn't entirely her fault. She wasn't familiar with Texas or its violent weather.

''Then what do you suggest?'' she asked.

Before he could answer, her face brightened with another thought. ''Could *you* get my car out of the ditch? I'd pay you double what a wrecker service would charge.''

That desperate sound was back in her voice again, and Chance could only wonder who or what was making her so frantic to leave his home.

Pulling a bottle of aspirin from a drawer on the nightstand, he shook three of them into her palm. ''Here, take these and forget about your car. It wouldn't do you a bit of good tonight, anyway.''

Clutching the aspirins tightly in her fist, Lucinda stared at him. ''But I can't stay here!''

She'd barely spoken above a whisper and, if anything, her face had gone even whiter. Chance was beginning to wonder if she was one of those women prone to hysterics. If she was, then she'd come to the wrong place.

''Why not? The D Bar D isn't the Ritz, but it's comfortable. And we have plenty of room.''

Lucinda couldn't remember one person back in Chicago being so generous to her. Nor could she think of anyone who would trust a total stranger to stay overnight in their home.

Chance could see that his invitation had overwhelmed her. Along with gratitude, there was a lost, wary look on her face that made Chance want to take her in his arms, smooth his hand over her long hair and assure her that she would be all right. It was an awkward feeling for him and one that he didn't welcome, but it was there just the same.

"But you don't know me," Lucinda pointed out. "I could be a dangerous person."

Chance figured Lucinda Lambert *was* dangerous. But not in the way she meant. The only thing around here she might be a threat to was his common sense. But he could hardly tell her that. No more than he could send her out in a blizzard to find her own way to Roswell, or wherever the hell she'd been headed for tonight.

One corner of his mouth cocked upward into a wry grin. "I'm a big guy. You don't scare me too much."

He was trying to ease her mind, and for the first time since he'd pulled her out of the car, she felt a little better. Surely Richard couldn't track her down tonight, and tomorrow afternoon she'd have her car back. By then the sun might even be out and the snow would begin to melt.

Lucinda had to look at things positively. More than anything she didn't want to fall apart in front of Chance Delacroix and have him thinking she was a totally helpless female.

Moistening her lips, she lifted her eyes back up to him and was immediately struck by how familiar he already seemed to her. No matter where she went in the future, or how much time passed, she had a feeling she would never forget this man's gray eyes or slow, sensual voice.

She cleared her throat, then said quietly, "Thank you for—helping me like this. I—"

Her words trailed away in awkward silence and Chance suddenly realized he didn't want her to be grateful, he wanted her to be happy.

"Don't think anything of it. Christmas is just a few days away," he said, "and I'm in a generous mood. If you want to thank me, take those aspirins and eat the food Mother fixed for you."

"I will," she promised, then smiled at him. A wide, generous smile that lighted her green eyes and dimpled her cheeks.

Chance didn't smile back. He was too struck by her beauty and the knowledge that he really didn't want to leave the room. He wanted to stay here, keep looking at her, talking to her. He wanted to know exactly where she'd come from and where she was going. Most of all, he wanted to know why she was alone and why he cared that she was.

"Good night, Lucinda."

"Good night."

Chapter Three

So what now, she asked herself after he'd closed the door behind him. Are you supposed to stay here in this room? In *his* bed? Even if it was nearly Christmas, she didn't think he intended to be that generous.

It finally dawned on her that she was still holding the aspirins Chance had given her. She swallowed them down with a sip of brandy, then reached for the plate of food on the nightstand. There were several finger sandwiches filled with an assortment of meat, crackers slathered with dip, several types of cheeses and a slice of chocolate cake.

She'd started one of the sandwiches when the door opened and a tall, auburn-haired woman stuck her head inside the room. "Do you feel like company?" she asked.

"Of course," Lucinda told her while thinking the woman could only be Chance's mother. Other than the color of their hair, the resemblance between the two was very strong.

"I'm Dee, Chance's mother. I'm sorry I haven't been in to see you earlier, but my daughter's engagement party was going on and most of the guests decided to say their goodbyes about the time you and Chance got here.''

It seemed incredible to Lucinda that this woman would even think it necessary to apologize to her. "Oh, please— don't think you need to treat me like a guest. I'm more of an intrusion than anything.''

"Don't be silly,'' Dee said with a smile. She took a seat on the bed beside Lucinda. "Anyone who's a friend of my son's could never be an intrusion.''

"But we're not friends,'' Lucinda felt obliged to point out. "I just met Chance when he stopped on the highway to help me.''

Laughing, Dee reached over and patted Lucinda's hand. "Doc says you need to rest your foot for a few days. By then you'll be a friend to the whole family.''

It was on the tip of Lucinda's tongue to tell Chance's mother she had no intention of staying on this ranch for a few days, but she kept the words to herself. Dee Delacroix was being warm and gracious, and right now Lucinda thought it best to simply accept her hospitality.

"I told your son I didn't want to be a bother.''

A smile still on her face, Dee shook her head. "And you won't be. What with getting ready for my daughter's wedding in May and Christmas and having you as a houseguest, well, this is going to be an exciting place for a change. I love it,'' she said happily.

Yes, but would Chance? was all Lucinda could think about.

"Now,'' she said, rising to her feet. "I'll go get you some things of Sarah Jane's so you can change and be more comfortable. There's a private bathroom right through that door.'' She pointed to Lucinda's right. "And while you're changing, I'll start getting the spare bedroom ready for you. Is there anything special you need in the meantime?''

At the moment, Lucinda felt so bewildered by all that had taken place this evening she could hardly think, period. ''No, thank you. I'm fine.''

Out in the kitchen, Chance poured himself a cup of coffee and carried it over to the breakfast counter. The entire room was a mess. Dirty plates, glasses, cups and partially emptied containers of food took up every available inch of counter space, besides filling the sink and covering the top of the cookstove.

Chance cleared a spot for his elbow, then straddled one of the bar stools. He was just lifting the cup to his lips when his mother came into the room carrying a tray loaded with party leftovers.

''There you are,'' she said brightly. ''I hadn't seen you in the past few minutes. I thought you might have already gone to bed.''

He couldn't go to bed. Or at least not his own bed. The Chicago snowbird was in it. He'd have to carry her to her own room first. ''Not yet. I thought I was hungry, but after seeing this mess I've changed my mind.''

Dee emptied the tray into a garbage pail. ''There's some chocolate cake left around here somewhere.''

''What about the lamb fries?''

Dee laughed. ''They ate them as fast as I could fry them. Not a crumb left.''

Chance frowned. ''Well, it was sweet of Sarah Jane to remember and save some for me. I guess it slipped her mind that *I* was the one who braved a blizzard to go get them for her.''

Still chuckling, Dee began to fill the double sink with warm water. ''A lot of things slip Sarah Jane's mind here lately. But that happens to a person when they're in love and about to get married. Or have you forgotten?''

Chance grimaced. It wasn't like his mother to bring up Jolene. She knew it brought back painful memories to him. ''I've made a point to forget, Mother.''

Dee looked over at her son. ''You know, I used to think you were right. That you should try to forget everything that happened with you and Jolene. But after your father died I learned that trying to block out memories just doesn't work.''

He didn't say anything. Dee squirted liquid soap into the water, then tossed in a sponge. After a moment she said, ''You know, it was a good thing Sarah Jane begged you to go to the grocery store. Otherwise, that young lady would have more than likely froze to death.''

''I wouldn't go so far as to say that. Someone else would have probably stopped to help, eventually,'' he told his mother. But to be honest, each time Chance thought of Lucinda being stranded in such dangerous weather, it sent a shiver down his spine. He did thank God that he had stopped to look in her car.

''Someone else didn't. You did.'' She picked up a scouring pad and scratched at the skillet. ''She sure is a pretty little thing.''

''There's pretty women around here, too, Mother,'' Chance pointed out.

''That's true. But Lucinda is one of those with true beauty. She doesn't need to paint it on.'' She glanced at her son. ''Did she tell you much about herself?''

Feeling edgy and restless, thinking about carrying Lucinda from his bed and into another, Chance left the bar stool and carried his coffee over to a plate glass door that looked out onto the back porch. ''Not really. Just that she was headed south. And she seemed to be in an all-fired hurry to do that.''

''Hmm. Well, she's probably anxious to join her family for Christmas. It's so lonesome to be away from your loved ones at this time of the year.''

Chance stared at the thick, blowing snow, but in it he was seeing Lucinda's face when she'd confessed that she had no family. ''She doesn't have any family. She did say that much.''

''You don't mean it?''

Chance nodded grimly at his mother's shocked question. ''That's what she said, and I can't think of why she would lie about such a thing. But then people are strange these days. She might be on the run from the law or something and just doesn't want anyone to know where she is.''

Her dish washing momentarily forgotten, Dee frowned at her son. ''You'd never make me believe that. She's as innocent as a lamb. I can see it in her eyes.''

''You think everyone is good,'' Chance told her.

''They are. I made a point of taking you to Sunday school year after year just so you would know that.''

Chance didn't bother asking his mother if she thought rapists and murderers were good, too. She'd merely remind him that all human beings had to have some redeeming qualities hidden away in them.

''You're too trusting, Mother. It's a good thing we don't live in a high-crime area. You'd be in trouble before you turned around.''

Dee made a clucking noise with her tongue. ''Chance, you've gotten so cynical. Your daddy would hate that if he knew it.''

Stan Delacroix had died ten years ago. Chance had just turned twenty-one at the time. And though he hadn't been emotionally ready to take on the responsibilities of running the D Bar D, he'd made himself rise to the task. His mother and sister had looked up to him, depended on him to make sure their home and financial security would always be there for them.

It had been a big task for a young man who'd already had his hopes and dreams shattered with the loss of his young wife and child. If Chance was cynical, as his mother had said, then he felt he had a right to be.

"I'm not cynical, Mother, just realistic." Turning away from the glass door, he placed his cup with a pile of dirty dishes on the end of the cabinet counter. "By the way, where's Sarah Jane? Isn't she going to help you with this mess?"

"I sent Sarah Jane to bed after she helped me get the spare room set for Lucinda. She was tired."

Chance groaned. "You spoil that girl rotten. It wouldn't hurt her to do a little work around here."

"She worked like a dog getting things ready for this party tonight. Besides, she'll be gone in a few months and I won't get to spoil her anymore," Dee said wistfully.

"Well, don't stay up too long." Chance leaned over and kissed his mother's cheek. "I'm going on to bed. Feeding tomorrow is going to be hell. I just hope I don't find any dead calves."

Dee patted his shoulder. "You worry too much, son."

It was his job to worry, his responsibility to see that the ranch and his family remained intact. And sometimes the load made him feel very old.

"Chance?" Dee twisted her head around to her son as he started out of the room. "Do you think the highway will be passable tomorrow?"

"Maybe in a Jeep, but not for regular car travel. Why? Did you need something from town?"

"No. I was just wondering about your new friend's car. I'd like her to stay a few days. It would be nice to have a fresh face around here at Christmastime."

Fighting the urge to smile, Chance rubbed his hand over his chin and jaws. His mother would never change. She was hopelessly lost with a checkbook, she never remembered dates or appointments, and after thirty-some years on the ranch she still wouldn't climb onto a horse, but she loved people and if she could manipulate them to her way of thinking she'd go at it gung ho. In spite of all that, Chance wouldn't change a thing about Dee. He loved her just as she was.

"She's not my new friend, Mother. And as for her staying, I wouldn't put any stock in it. She's got all the markings of someone on the move. As soon as the highway clears, you can bet she'll be gone."

Dee pushed absently at the curls across her forehead. "Oh well, maybe we can change her mind about that. You will try, won't you?"

It had been a long time since he'd spent more than a few minutes with a woman who wasn't kin to him. He'd almost forgotten what that felt like. Until tonight when he'd brought Lucinda home with him.

Maybe it would be nice to have Lucinda Lambert's company for a few days, he thought. She'd definitely be a treat for his eyes. And as for him being tempted to flirt with her? Well, what would it hurt if he did? He was a man, after all, and it wasn't as if he were going to do anything foolish like fall in love with the woman.

"I'll see what I can do," he told his mother.

When Lucinda woke the next morning the bedroom was cast in a gray, eerie light. She felt groggy. Probably because for the first time in months she'd slept deeply all through the night. Maybe it had been those three aspirins that had knocked her out so completely, she thought. Or maybe she'd simply felt safe here in this house that Chance Delacroix called home. Whatever the reason, Lucinda felt more rested than she had in a long time.

Throwing back the covers, she sat up and swung her legs over the side of the bed. Her ankle still looked swollen and was painfully sore when she attempted to move it in any direction, but at least the constant throbbing ache had stopped.

Carefully she raised herself off the bed and hopped on her good foot until she reached a pair of long, arched windows.

The view outside the paned glass surprised her as much as the sight of this house had last night. From what she could see the D Bar D wasn't just a fancy ranch house pretending to be a ranch. There were barns and sheds everywhere she looked and an endless maze of holding pens and corrals. Numerous herds of black Angus cattle stood huddled together in the falling snow. Some of the luckier ones were being driven by cowboys on horseback to a long feeding shed with a roof over it.

Lucinda peered closely at the cowboys, trying to see if Chance might be one of them, but they were too far away for a clear look. Which was just as well, she told herself, turning away from the window. She'd gone to sleep last night with the man on her mind, now he was right back on it again this morning. She didn't like the idea of thinking about Chance Delacroix that much, but that was hardly enough reason to make her stop.

Hopping back to the bed, she tried to assure herself that it wasn't strange that she found him attractive. Any woman with eyes would. On top of that, she'd never known a cowboy before, or any man who worked with animals and the outdoors. That intrigued her about him. That and a whole lot more if she were honest enough to admit it.

Lucinda was sitting on the side of the bed, rummaging through her purse for a powder compact when a light rap sounded on the door. She pulled on the blue robe Dee had brought to her last night and tied the sash before calling, "Come in."

A tall, young woman wearing a long corduroy skirt and matching rust-colored sweater entered the room. She was carrying a tray with an insulated coffeepot and a thin china cup. A warm smile spread across her face as she spotted Lucinda on the side of the bed.

"Good morning," she said cheerfully. "I'm Sarah Jane, Chance's sister. Sorry I didn't make it in to meet you last night. How are you feeling this morning? Did you sleep well?"

Obviously Sarah Jane was just as warm and gracious as her mother. "I'm feeling much better. Your brother told me it was your engagement party last night. I hope my being here didn't create a problem," Lucinda told her.

Sarah Jane laughed and Lucinda realized the woman was younger than herself, perhaps not much older than nineteen. Yet she seemed uncommonly poised for her age. She had copper red hair almost as long as Lucinda's. The natural curls were tied back at her nape with a black velvet ribbon, and just looking at this young woman made Lucinda feel very unkempt.

"Not in the least," Sarah Jane assured her. "We hardly ever have the treat of having visitors here on the D Bar D. I do wish the snow had held off for a while, though. Everyone got worried about the roads and left the party early."

She set the tray down on the nightstand. "Would you like me to help you walk to the bathroom?"

"Oh, yes!" Lucinda said with relief. "I was just sitting here wondering if I could make it across this big room."

As though she'd known her for years, Sarah Jane put her arm around the back of Lucinda's waist and gently helped her to stand on one foot. "Chance told us how he found your car. Lord, I'm glad I begged him to go after those lamb fries. Otherwise, you might have frozen out there!"

"I'm very grateful to him. To all of you for your kindness," Lucinda told her.

Sarah Jane waved away her thanks. "It's nothing. Really."

But it was something to Lucinda, who'd spent nearly all of her growing-up years in an orphanage. Without the kindness and generosity of strangers back then, she would have been lost and alone. The same way she would have been last night if Chance hadn't come to her rescue.

With Sarah Jane's help, Lucinda managed to walk to the bathroom. While she made use of the facilities, Sarah Jane stood outside the door and chatted.

"Doc says you should be walking fine by Christmas."

"Well, I guess that's something to look forward to," Lucinda said as cheerfully as she could. Though it was hard to look on the bright side when she knew her Christmas would be spent entirely alone.

There was a hairbrush on the vanity. Lucinda pulled it through her tangled hair. It needed shampooing terribly, but she supposed that could wait until she got to a motel room. Which might be as soon as this evening, if the weather cleared and the wrecker service delivered her car.

"Chance said you were from Chicago," Sarah Jane spoke up again. "Are you vacationing?"

"No." With her hair finally free of tangles and brushed away from her face, she moistened a washcloth with warm water and pressed it to her eyes. "I'm actually—moving."

"Oh, really? How exciting! I've lived in this same house ever since I was born. I can't wait to move."

Lucinda's mouth twisted wryly at Sarah Jane's comment. For so many years she'd longed to have a family and a real permanent home such as this. But that would be hard to explain to someone who'd never been without such things.

"You don't think you'll miss your mother and brother?"

"Oh, sure I will. But I'm only moving about five miles from here. If I want to visit, all I'll have to do is ride or drive over."

Lucinda couldn't imagine what it would feel like to have such a network of family and friends, to know that if she had any sort of crisis in her life, there would always be someone close to help her through it.

"I'm sure your family is pleased about that."

"Oh, yes. Especially Chance. He thinks I'm too young to be married anyway. And this way, he'll be able to keep an eye on me."

Lucinda frowned at her pale image in the mirror. "Doesn't that bother you?"

"Not really. Oh, he's overprotective most of the time. But he's only that way because he loves me."

Yeah, Lucinda thought wearily, she'd heard that all before. Each time she'd caught Richard watching her every move, he'd told her he was doing it because he loved her. Well, as far as Lucinda was concerned she could do without that sort of love.

Finished in the bathroom, Lucinda opened the door to find Sarah Jane waiting to help her back across the room.

At the bed, she picked out a skirt and sweater from the things Dee had brought her last night and carried them behind a dressing screen.

Sarah Jane made herself at home on the foot of the bed. "What did you do back in Chicago, Lucy?"

"I design clothes."

Sarah Jane let out a small gasp of surprise. "Oh my, you must be very talented to make a living doing that. I mean, that's not the sort of thing just anybody can go out and do."

Lucinda pulled a rose-colored sweater over her head. It fell past her hips and over a full skirt printed with tiny matching roses. "Don't get me wrong, Sarah Jane, I'm only small-scale. But I sold enough things out of a little shop in Chicago to make a living for myself."

"Well, that's certainly a start! A pretty grand one, I'd say." She clapped her hands together. "Wait till Mother hears about this! She'll love it!"

Lucinda stepped from behind the screen and Sarah Jane immediately laughed. "I guess I'm a little taller than you."

Laughing with her, Lucinda glanced down at her borrowed clothes. "Only about five inches, but long hemlines are in style now. Especially when they hide a swollen ankle."

"If you'd rather, I could get you a pair of jeans," Sarah Jane offered.

"Oh no," Lucinda assured her. "The skirt is very nice. I love the colors."

"You look very pretty in it." Sarah Jane left her seat on the bed and began to carefully pull Lucinda's hair out from the neck band of the sweater.

Lucinda was touched by the simple gesture and wondered if it might have been like this if she'd had a sister.

"Thanks," she murmured once Sarah Jane had freed her hair, then hobbled over to the dresser where she'd left her purse and what little makeup she carried in it.

While she dabbed on a bit of face powder and lipstick, Sarah Jane asked, "Are you married?"

Lucinda shook her head. The word *marriage* left her cold now. She knew she shouldn't feel that way. But she couldn't help herself. "No. I think it's not meant for me to be married."

Sarah Jane clucked her tongue, then laughed softly. "That's what Chance says, too. But I think he's wrong. I think you're probably wrong, too."

Lucinda smiled wanly. It was obvious that Sarah Jane was young and in love and marriage seemed like a bright, beautiful union of two hearts. But that wasn't the way it would have turned out for Lucinda.

A few minutes later, the two women left the bedroom and went down to the kitchen where Dee had a cup of coffee and a wooden cane waiting for Lucinda.

"I thought it would get you around until you're able to put a little more weight on your foot," she said of the cane.

Lucinda was once again amazed. These people didn't know her. They didn't know what sort of life she'd led, or what kind of person she might be. But they treated her warmly and generously just the same.

"Thanks, I'm sure it will be a big help," she said, taking a seat at the breakfast counter.

While she sipped the richly brewed coffee, Lucinda looked around the long room, which was actually part kitchen, part dining area. It was decorated with all sorts of Christmas items. There was everything from a tablecloth printed with prancing reindeer, to Santa Claus-shaped pot holders. Real spruce, pinecones and holly berries made up a huge centerpiece in the middle of the dining table, while poinsettia plants ranging from deep red to pale white sat on worktables, cabinet counters and atop the refrigerator.

"This is all so beautiful," Lucinda exclaimed. "I've never seen a kitchen decorated for Christmas before."

Dee smiled at Lucinda's awed expression. "After you drink your coffee, you should go in and look at the living room, while Sarah Jane and I get breakfast ready. Chance should be in from the feedlots soon and then we'll all eat."

The rest of the house turned out to be just as beautifully decorated as the kitchen. She was staring up at the huge Virginia pine in the living room when Chance's voice sounded behind her.

"We normally don't put up the tree until a few days before Christmas, but this year we made an exception because of Sarah Jane's party."

Lucinda turned to look at him and instantly felt her heart begin to hammer with foolish anticipation. She was glad to see him. There was no way she could deny it. Dee and Sarah Jane had been nice and helpful to her, but Chance was the one who'd gotten her out of the car and carried her through the snow, twice. He was her rescuer and she couldn't help but feel a little bit close to him.

"It's magnificent. Did you help decorate it?"

His gray eyes roamed over her rather than the tree. Lucinda didn't know if the path of his gaze was intentional or not. But either way, she felt touched by him.

"My job is to put on the lights. Mother and Sarah Jane do the rest."

He was wearing jeans and boots and a dark blue denim shirt. At the open throat she could see the banded neck of a thermal undershirt, to help keep him warm. This morn-

ing he was wearing a black hat similar to the one he'd
worn last night, only this one was stained around the band
with dirt and sweat. The brim was bent in places and
rolled up in a tighter curl on the sides. Lucinda thought
the hat fit him perfectly. It had much more character than
the one she'd seen on him last night. Maybe that was
because she somehow knew this particular hat was probably always on his head or in his hands.

"I see you've been out working. Is the weather getting
any better?"

He shrugged. "Well, it's not blizzard conditions anymore, but it is still snowing." He took a few steps toward
her. "How's your ankle? Do you think you should be
trying to hobble around on it this morning?"

"If it hurts, I'll quit," she assured him.

Chance was close enough to her now to see the infinite
shades of green in her eyes, the smooth porcelain quality
of her skin and the dusky pink color that stained her lips.
He had a thousand things to do, but right now looking at
her seemed to be the most important.

"You don't take orders very well, do you?"

Lucinda had never heard a true Texas accent until she'd
driven into the state yesterday and stopped in Amarillo to
eat and service her car. Yet none of the men she'd encountered there had sounded quite like Chance Delacroix.
His voice was deep, rich and slow. It shivered over her,
curled around her with a warmth all its own.

That warmth melted the cool distance she wanted to
keep between them, and before she knew it, a smile was
tilting the corners of her mouth. "Actually, I don't."

"Then how are you with invitations?"

Her eyebrows lifted. "You're inviting me somewhere?"

He held his arm out to her. "To breakfast. Have you ever eaten chorizo and eggs?"

She took his arm and instantly scolded herself for liking the feel of it beneath her hand. "No. I haven't."

"Do you like things hot?"

Just what sort of things? she wondered, and glanced up to see a grin on his face that could only be described as sexy. before she could stop it, a deep blush of red swept across her cheeks.

"Your food, Lucy. Do you like it hot?"

"Sometimes. But I've never tried it for breakfast. Usually I'm in too big of a rush to eat anything in the mornings."

"Sounds like you've been living too fast," Chance said.

Lucinda had never considered her life fast. Back in Chicago she'd spent her days at work and her nights at home, alone. She'd certainly not had a man like Chance Delacroix inviting her to breakfast with him. And even if there had been an invitation from a man, Richard's stalking would have made it impossible for her to accept it.

Yet here she was in Texas, hanging on to Chance's big arm and blushing like a schoolgirl. Had she lost her mind? Or had she just now become brave enough to live again?

Chapter Four

Scrambled with Mexican sausage and served with soft tortillas, the eggs were very hot, and equally delicious. Instead of the small breakfast counter, the four of them ate at the dining table.

Lucinda sat at Sarah Jane's right and directly across the table from Chance. She caught his eyes on her often and, each time she did, it jolted her right down to her toes.

"Chance, did you know that Lucinda designs clothes?" Sarah Jane spoke up between bites of food. "She sold her things out of a shop in Chicago. Isn't that the most exciting thing you've ever heard?"

Chance glanced from his sister to Lucinda. "Is that what you were doing when you left Chicago?" he asked.

Lucinda nodded, wondering why she found it so difficult to think of Chance Delacroix as any other man. What was it about him that made her insides hot and shaky? Why did she notice every little thing about him?

She didn't know why she was intrigued by the way his black hair waved away from his forehead, the way his

darkly tanned skin had been bitten by the cold wind and
was now flushed red from the indoor heat. He hadn't
shaved this morning and she could see his beard was black
and heavy. If she were to rub her cheek against his, she
knew it would scrape her skin. Yet she knew it would be
a pleasant sensation.

"I—yes, I was," she answered as she desperately tried
to shove aside the thoughts running through her head.

"Is that what you're planning to do when you get to—"
His brows lifted in question. "You never did say where
you were going, did you?"

Lucinda took a deep breath, then let it out slowly. She
knew he was purposefully trying to pull information out
of her. And she supposed she shouldn't blame him. If a
stranger was staying in her house, she'd probably feel she
was entitled to know a few things about the person. Still,
she wasn't used to confiding anything to anyone. Especially these past months when she'd had to watch everything she'd said and done in fear that Richard might pick
up the information through a mutual friend.

"No. I guess I didn't say," she told him.

Chance frowned and reached for his coffee cup. Across
the table, Sarah Jane said to him, "Lucinda is moving."

"Moving? Where?" Dee asked curiously.

It was obvious she could no longer avoid their questions, and perhaps it wouldn't make any difference anyway. If she made it to California without Richard tracking
her, then she could probably lose herself in one of the
state's major cities.

"California," she answered. "I've always wanted to
see the West Coast."

Chance eyed her over the rim of his coffee cup. "So
you're going to design clothes and try to sell them out
there? Isn't that an iffy thing to do? If you were making

a living in Chicago, looks like you'd want to stay where you already have customers who know you."

Damn him, why did he have to be so smart and nosy? Dropping her eyes back to her plate, she scooped up a forkful of eggs and lifted them to her lips. "I guess moving is a chancy thing to do. But I think my clothes will sell better out West. California's economy hasn't been all that good in the past few years and I think the women out there are looking for more affordable fashions."

Pleased with her quick thinking, Lucinda chewed the eggs, then reached for her coffee. While she carefully sipped the rich brew, she felt Chance's gaze lingering on her. Was he suspicious of her, or did he merely like what he was looking at? Whatever the reason, Lucinda knew that she was definitely going to have to watch herself around the man.

"You might be right about that, Lucy," Dee spoke up. "Course, around here, we women just go to the closest mall and buy our clothes off the rack. Unless there's a special occasion going on and then we have something made."

"Like my wedding. I'm getting married in May," Sarah Jane said, her face suddenly glowing as she turned toward Lucinda. "I've already chosen the fabric for my gown. I'd love you to take a look at it, Lucy. I'd value your opinion."

Lucinda shook her head. "I've never done bridal gowns before."

"But I'm sure you know all about fabric and lines, how it will all look when it comes together. You—" Sarah Jane stopped abruptly, then quickly asked Lucinda, "Did you bring any of your work with you?"

"Yes, several pieces are in my car. The woman who

worked as my seamstress is going to send the rest to me once I get settled.''

Sarah Jane turned a pleading look on her brother. ''Chance, will you please go get Lucinda's cases from her car? I'm dying to see her work!''

Chance grimaced. ''I've got cattle to feed, Sarah Jane. Several herds, in fact.''

Sarah Jane pulled a face at him. ''You have hired hands working, Chance. Surely they can make it without you for half an hour. Besides,'' she went on before Chance could argue, ''if Lucinda is going to stay here with us, she needs her own things.''

He turned a pointed look on Lucinda. ''Is that right?''

When he looked at her, she couldn't think, much less know what she needed. ''I—well, if the wrecker gets my car this afternoon there's no need for you to—''

''Lucy, don't you let him off the hook!'' Sarah Jane practically shouted. ''Mike's the only wrecker service around here for miles. It might be tomorrow, or the next day before he gets around to getting your car out of the ditch. Especially if he knows you're here on the ranch and not absolutely stranded.''

But she *was* stranded, Lucinda thought. She looked to Chance. ''Is she right? Could it be tomorrow before I can get my car?''

Chance nodded. ''Possibly. It's still snowing outside.''

''Forget about the snow, Lucy. Your foot is hurt. You can't go anywhere until it gets better.'' Dee spoke in a persuasive tone.

Never having had a family to ply her with opinions and advice, Lucinda had always made decisions on her own. It more than bewildered her to have the Delacroix taking control of her plans.

''I think I can drive if—''

"Hellfire, woman!" Chance suddenly barked. "Didn't you learn anything last night? There's at least three or four inches of packed snow and ice on the highways! How long do you think it would be before you'd wind up right back in the ditch?"

Lucinda might have made a foolish judgment in the weather last night, but that didn't mean she was stupid. She shot him an annoyed look. "Don't you people have snowplows out here?"

Frowning at her, he said, "I'm sure the road graders are out at work, but I imagine the snow is falling about as fast as they can push it off."

So that was that, Lucinda concluded. She was going to be here on the D Bar D whether she wanted to be or not. "Then it looks like I will need my suitcases."

Sarah Jane began to giggle. "You're not going to tell Lucy you have to work now, are you, Chance?"

Ignoring his sister, he said to Lucinda, "After breakfast I'll warm up the Jeep. Would you like to go with me?"

Go with him? She did, and she didn't.

The indecision must have shown on her face, because Chance went on before she could give him an answer. "You don't have to worry about wrecking again. We should be safe traveling in the Jeep."

Yes, but would it be safe traveling with him? she wondered. Aloud she said, "I'll be ready."

A half hour later, bundled in her long, red coat and a white woolen scarf, Lucinda stood beside Chance on the back porch and looked out at the Jeep. Between it and her were several yards of knee-deep snow. How was she going to hobble through all of that?

Reading her thoughts, Chance stooped over and lifted her into his arms. "Don't worry about my back," he said before she could put up a protest. "You hardly weigh more than a couple of sacks of good horse feed."

Instinctively Lucinda looped her arms around his neck and pressed her face dangerously close to his. "Good horse feed doesn't weigh the same as bad horse feed?" she couldn't help asking.

Chuckling, he stepped off the porch with her and into the deep snow. "No. Bad horse feed weighs more 'cause it has worms in it."

Beneath the brim of his Stetson, she could see the sky was lead gray and snow was falling thick and fast. She should have been worried at the sight. The more it snowed, the longer she would have to stay here on the ranch. Yet all she could think at the moment was that Chance didn't smell like soap or cologne. His scent was pure man and so intoxicating she hardly knew where she was until he'd placed her on the Jeep's bucket seat.

"Thank you," Lucinda murmured as he carefully pulled his arm from beneath her knees.

"You're welcome," he said lowly.

Her heart going in a mad gallop, Lucinda's eyes inched upward to find his face hovering just inches away from hers. The tempting sight crumbled her common sense. And though she knew it was crazy, more than anything she wanted to cup her palms against his jaws, feel his skin, his whiskers, draw his face to hers and kiss his lips.

"I think—" With one hand he reached above her head. The movement caused his face to dip even closer to hers. Lucinda drew in a sharp breath and gripped the edge of the seat. "You'd be safer belted in," he finished, drawing the belt across her lap.

"You're probably right." Her voice was barely above a whisper, but at some point during the past few minutes she'd forgotten to breathe.

As he snapped the seat belt against her tummy, she let out a long, burning breath, then waited until he'd stepped back from her before she drew in a fresh one.

You've gone crazy, Lucinda, she scolded herself after Chance had shut the door and gone around to climb into his own seat. She'd spent the better part of this whole year in misery because of a man. How could she look at Chance, a man she didn't really know, and feel such strong erotic urges?

"You've certainly got Sarah Jane stirred up," Chance told her as he carefully put the Jeep into motion. "If I hadn't agreed to go get your suitcases, she would have probably tried driving herself."

Even though Lucinda was wearing gloves, she jammed her hands down into the deep pockets of the coat. Maybe there, her fingers would forget all about touching Chance Delacroix.

"You make her sound headstrong."

Chance grunted. "She is at times. But I try my best to keep her reined in. Which hasn't always been easy to do. A brother isn't the same as a daddy. But I've tried to be both to Sarah Jane for the past ten years."

They were out of the ranch yard now and headed down the lane. Lucinda noticed it was lined on both sides by huge cottonwood trees. Like most of the other trees in this part of the country, the bare limbs had been permanently whipped to the north by the relentless winds. At the moment, the trees, as well as the railed fence that followed the arrow-straight road, were decorated with snow.

"Your father has been dead that long?" she asked.

He didn't look at her. Nor did his expression alter as he answered, "Yes. He died suddenly. An aneurysm in the brain. He was still a young man at the time."

Even though his face didn't show it, Lucinda could hear

the pain of loss in Chance's voice, and it told her that he'd obviously been close to his father.

"I'm sorry you lost him. But at least you have your mother. And she's still a young, vibrant woman."

A fond smile crossed Chance's face. "Mother is one of a kind." He glanced at Lucinda. "And she very much wants you to stay on the ranch for the holidays."

Lucinda pushed her hands deeper into the coat pockets. "What about you? Dr. Campbell said you were the top dog around here."

Chance laughed and Lucinda felt herself melting at the warm sound. "Being the top dog doesn't necessarily mean anything. Not when the dog has two women to keep happy."

Sighing, Lucinda looked out at the golden plains that were now covered in a sea of white. It was a very beautiful sight to Lucinda. But last night she'd learned just how harsh and unpredictable this country could be in spite of that beauty.

"I wouldn't blame you if you weren't keen about me staying in your home," she told him. "For all you know I could have a very sordid past."

Chance didn't believe her past was anything close to sordid. At least he didn't want to think it was. However, she did seem secretive about herself. But rather than putting Chance off, her evasiveness had only made him more intrigued with her.

"Are you warning me that I might wake up one morning and find that you've skipped out with all the silverware and every last Christmas gift under the tree?"

Lucinda couldn't help but laugh at his ridiculous question. "Maybe I should wait until you open your gifts first. I might not bother taking the things I don't like."

"Well, I don't imagine you'd like the box of farrier

tools Mother got me. Fashion designers probably don't shoe horses.''

Smiling, she glanced at him from the corner of her eye. ''How do you know that's what she got you?''

''Because I told her to.''

Lucinda shook her head with wry disbelief. ''That couldn't be any fun. Your gifts are supposed to be a surprise.''

Chance kept a tight grip on the steering wheel as the Jeep plowed through the deeply rutted snow. ''Oh, you can rest assured Mother will have plenty of other surprises under the tree.''

Yes, Lucinda figured Dee was the sort of person who loved Christmas and gave as much as she could to everyone around her.

''What are you going to get for Christmas, Lucinda?'' he asked a bit impishly. ''Have you already told Santa what you want?''

If there truly was a Santa Claus, Lucinda would have simply told him she wanted someone to love her, to share her life and make a family with. But the possibility of there being a real Santa out there somewhere was about as remote as her finding a man she could trust enough to give her heart to.

''Santa forgot about me a long time ago. So I guess I'll—'' Actually Lucinda wouldn't be getting anything for Christmas. But she didn't want to admit that to Chance. It was too painful to think about, much less share with a man who'd never known what it was like to be really and truly alone. ''I'll have to wait and see what my friend in Chicago sends me. Probably a box of chocolates. She thinks I'm too thin.''

She. Chance shouldn't have been so pleased to hear that Lucinda's friend was female. But he was. He couldn't help wanting to believe that she was completely unattached. He wanted to know that every time he looked at her, he wasn't looking at another man's woman.

"Last night I got the distinct impression you were running from Chicago," he said.

Inside the coat pockets, Lucinda's hands tightened into fists. Her gaze remained fixed on the windshield. "I didn't run from Chicago. I simply left."

"And you left because of a man. Didn't you?"

Was she that transparent? Lucinda wondered. Dear Lord, had he been able to read the wanton thoughts going on in her head a few minutes ago when he'd set her in the Jeep?

Slowly she moistened her lips, then glanced over at him. He was watching the road ahead, but she knew he was expecting her to answer. She also knew that if she didn't give him one, he'd continue to pester her about it.

"What makes you think I left Chicago because of a man?"

His mouth twisted. "Because I figure you had to work long and hard to build up the sort of clientele you need to make a living in your business. You wouldn't just up and leave all that for a change of scenery."

"I told you—"

"I know what you said at breakfast. But I wasn't born yesterday, Lucy. You might have fooled Mother and Sarah Jane with all that business about the economy, but you didn't fool me."

Turning her head, she frowned at him. "I didn't know cowboys played detective."

"Now you're being flip," he accused.

"And you're being nosy," she shot back.

He suddenly braked the Jeep to a halt and Lucinda looked out to see they'd reached her wrecked car. Good, she thought with relief, maybe he'd go after her cases now and let this whole conversation drop.

Her hopes were quickly dashed when Chance squared around in the seat to face her.

"Maybe I am nosy," he conceded. "But I just don't see how running across the country could cure you of a broken heart."

He thought she had a broken heart? Before she could stop herself, she let out a caustic laugh. "I'm not moving across country because of my heart. I—" She broke off, then heaved out a sigh as Chance patiently folded his arms across his chest.

"Yes?" he prompted.

Why was he doing this? she wondered. She was just someone he and his family had befriended. In a few days she'd be out of their lives. It shouldn't matter to him why she'd left Chicago. But it seemed to, and that shook her.

As far as she knew, no one had ever really cared what happened to Lucinda Lambert. Some, like Richard, had pretended to. Others, like those at the orphanage, had cared for her because it was their job. So why should she think this man was any different?

Tossing her hair away from her face, she let out a weary sigh. "I left Chicago because—well, a whole lot of bad memories were there and I wanted to get away from them. I want to start somewhere fresh."

"I can understand that," he replied, his voice much softer than it had been moments ago.

Could he really understand? she wondered as her eyes slowly searched his strong face. She couldn't imagine him ever feeling so desperate that he wanted to leave his home. He'd always had a family who loved him.

Swallowing down the sudden lump that had collected in her throat, Lucinda turned her gaze back outside the windshield. "Last year at this time I was engaged to be married."

His jaw tightened. "What happened?"

She shrugged as though none of it mattered, but Chance could tell from the distant look on her face that she was back in a painful time and place. He could only wonder what sort of man could have hurt this woman. Moreover, what kind of man could ever have given her up?

"Things didn't work out. He was—very possessive and I—well, I broke off our engagement and ended the relationship."

She'd pulled her hands out of her pockets and removed her gloves. Now they were on her lap, clasped together so tightly her knuckles were white. Chance wanted to reach over, unclench her hands and press them between the two of his. He wanted to reassure her, make her smile, make her glad that she was with him and not that man she'd once promised herself to.

"Do you regret that it's over?"

Chance's question pulled her gaze back around to him. If only he knew how desperately she wished the whole thing with Richard was finally and truly over.

"No," she said with a shake of her head. "It was the only choice I had. Now I want to put all of that behind me."

Maybe her heart wasn't broken and maybe she was moving simply to have a fresh start. But he wasn't blind. The shadows that haunted her eyes told him she was troubled about something and that bothered Chance. More than he cared to admit.

He opened the door, but before he climbed to the ground, he looked at her and said, "Then I hope you can leave all those memories back there, Lucy. I really do."

As Lucinda watched Chance wade through the snow to

her car, she realized she was shaking. It wasn't strange for a woman to want to kiss a man as attractive as Chance Delacroix. But now her wants were going a step further. She'd told him a part of her past and had wanted to tell him more. She'd wanted to lay her head on his chest, hang on to his broad shoulders and tell him the fear and helplessness she'd been living with these past months. What did it mean?

Don't think about what it means, she silently whispered. Don't think about him or the way he smells and looks and talks. Just because he was a big, physically tough man didn't mean he could protect her, or that he'd even want to.

No, she thought, the only person who could take care of her and keep her safe was herself. She had to remember that.

Chapter Five

"Lucinda, these are the most gorgeous things I've ever seen in my life! Look at this blue crepe suit, Mother. Wouldn't it be great for traveling?"

The three women were in Lucinda's bedroom, where Sarah Jane had scattered Lucinda's fashions all over the bed, dressing table and a stuffed armchair.

Dee picked up the Wedgwood blue jacket lying on the bed and held it out in front of her.

"It's very nice," she agreed. "What size is it, Lucy?"

"An eight, I think."

Dee shook her head. "Forget it, Sarah Jane. That's too small for you."

"Oh, but I love it. I wish you could make another for me," she told Lucinda, who was sitting in a nearby rocking chair with her injured ankle propped on a footstool. "Or do you ever duplicate your pieces?"

"Of course I do. But I didn't actually sew—"

Before Lucinda could finish, Sarah Jane whirled around to her mother. "Can I have the suit, Mother? Better yet," she said, her voice suddenly squeaking with excitement, "can Lucinda design a few more things for me to wear on my honeymoon?"

Dee cast her daughter a doubtful glance. "The cost, Sarah Jane. We're already spending so much for the wedding."

"I'll leave something off," Sarah Jane quickly suggested. "Like the band and the champagne. We can dance to recorded music and drink fruit punch."

Dee groaned helplessly. "I'm sure the men will all love fruit punch."

"We'll give the men beer. That's what all of them are used to drinking anyway."

Dee laughed. "You're right about that. But serving beer at a wedding? People will say we're uncouth."

Sarah Jane picked up a green silk dress and waltzed over to a cheval mirror. "Since when have we Delacroix worried about what other people say? And James certainly won't care, especially when he sees how beautiful I look in the clothes Lucinda designs for me."

Tossing the dress over her arm, Sarah Jane went to kneel beside Lucinda's chair. "You will design some things for me, won't you? I'd be forever in your debt!"

How could Lucinda say no? Chance had rescued her from a potentially dangerous situation and his mother and sister had already gone out of their way to make her feel at home. Besides all of that, Sarah Jane was so young and beautiful and excited about getting married that Lucinda didn't want to be the one to spoil anything for her.

"You'd have to find your own seamstress. I'm not that good at it," Lucinda told her.

"There's Margie. Over by Friona," Dee said thoughtfully. "She's very professional. And in the end, we'd probably save money having the clothes made, rather than buying out of those expensive boutiques in Amarillo or Fort Worth.''

Lucinda smiled at Sarah Jane, who was breathlessly waiting for her answer.

"I'd be glad to do it. On one condition," Lucinda added.

Sarah Jane clapped her hands together gleefully and Lucinda wondered sadly if she would ever feel that light-hearted and happy. Would there ever come a time in her life when she'd be planning her own wedding to a man who really loved her?

"What's the condition?" Dee asked.

Lucinda looked at the older woman. "That I do a dress for you, too, Dee. And that you'll accept my work as a Christmas gift."

"That's asking too much!" Dee began with a shake of her head, but Sarah Jane was already flinging her arms around Lucinda and smacking a kiss on her cheek.

"Oh, thank you, Lucy, you're wonderful!" Sarah Jane exclaimed.

Lucinda had been praised for her work before. Coming from paying customers, the compliments had meant much to her. But seeing the genuine joy on Sarah Jane's face, the gratefulness on Dee's, stung Lucinda's eyes with tears.

Clearing her throat, she warned jokingly, "Maybe you should see how the clothes turn out before you call me wonderful."

Sarah Jane went back to the bed, held up the Wedgwood jacket and sighed with pure appreciation. "Just wait till Chance hears what you're doing. He'll probably kiss you, too, for saving him so much money."

Lucinda couldn't stop the blush she felt creeping across her cheeks. The idea of kissing her would more than likely never enter Chance's head. But it had definitely gotten into hers and she couldn't seem to get it out.

"That would be the day," Dee said glumly. "As far as I know it's been years since Chance kissed a woman."

The happy glow on Sarah Jane's face suddenly vanished. "That's true, Mother. I guess he—well, with everything that happened with Jolene. He doesn't want anything to do with women."

With a deeply resigned sigh, Dee swiped her tousled red hair off her forehead. "Well, he's wrong and I've told him so. But hearing it from me hasn't done any good."

Lucinda's gaze swung curiously from mother to daughter. Who was this woman they were talking about? And why had she ruined Chance's interest in women? The questions whirled around in her head, demanding an answer.

"Was Jolene an old flame of Chance's?" she finally asked.

Dee shook her head. Sarah Jane said, "Jolene was Chance's wife."

Later that night, Lucinda sat quietly in her room near a window overlooking an east pasture. A sketch pad lay open on her lap, while several colored pencils were scattered atop a table beside her chair. For the past hour she'd been trying to concentrate and do a little work toward the clothes she'd promised Sarah Jane. But her mind refused to cooperate. All she could think about was Chance and that he'd once been married.

Where was Jolene now, she wondered. And why had the marriage ended? Lucinda had been about to ask those very questions this afternoon, but the phone had rung, interrupting the moment. Sarah Jane had rushed out of the room to answer it. Dee had quickly fled, too, saying she had to check on the beans she'd left cooking on the stove.

By the time things had quieted back down, Lucinda had decided not to bring up the subject again. Sarah Jane and Dee would probably think it odd that she would be that interested in Chance's past life.

And it was odd, she told herself as she looked up from the sketch pad for the umpteenth time. Chance was none of her business. Nor would he ever be. The sooner she got that through her head, the better off she'd be.

A light knock suddenly sounded on the door. Grateful for the interruption, Lucinda called, "Come in."

To her surprise it was Chance who strolled into the room. He'd changed from the denim shirt he'd been wearing this morning. Now a plaid flannel shirt of reds and greens flapped open against his thermal undershirt. The battered hat was gone. Without it, she could see that his black hair was shiny wet and combed neatly to one side. Lucinda could only think how solid he looked, how strikingly male, and how just looking at him made her stomach flutter.

"I wanted to see if you're ready for supper," he said.

Quickly Lucinda placed her sketchbook on the table with her pencils and reached for the cane Dee had given her. "I hadn't noticed the time. I hope you haven't been waiting on me."

Chance watched her hobble toward him. She seemed determined to get around on her own steam and he liked that independence about her. Especially when he knew how much pain it must be costing her to walk.

"It's only you and me," he said.

A look of utter surprise came over her face. "It is?"

Chance's mouth twisted wryly. The last thing he'd wanted was to be left alone with Lucy. Or so he'd thought.

Now that he was looking at her, he was glad the house had emptied, except for the two of them. "James has taken Sarah Jane over to his parents tonight."

"On these roads?"

"It's not that far and he has a four-wheel-drive vehicle," Chance explained. "As for Mother, she just left with Doc. It seems they have a mutual friend who needs his medical attention."

So it was just the two of them, Lucinda thought, trying not to let the idea of being alone with him shake her. After all, she wasn't afraid of him. On the contrary, she instinctively knew she could trust her very life with him. But what about her? She couldn't even look at him without going a little bit crazy!

"I see. Well, I'll be perfectly fine making myself a sandwich. You don't have to go out of your way for me."

He took her arm and guided her from the bedroom. "Supper is already on the table. Chili beans, corn bread and apple cobbler."

"Did you cook it?"

He chuckled and Lucinda decided the sound was as warm as the feel of his fingers on her arm.

"No. My cooking is limited to opening cans or frozen dinners."

Because of her ankle, she was forced to walk slowly toward the kitchen. Chance seemed content to go at her pace and lend her the support of his arm. Last night he'd told her he was used to taking care of women. Tonight she realized he'd probably been speaking the truth.

"I guess it wouldn't be the macho thing for a cowboy to cook," she replied.

"The reason this cowboy didn't learn was because he never had time."

They reached the kitchen, but Chance didn't release his

hold on her until she was securely settled in one of the chairs.

As she waited for him to take his own seat, Lucinda thought about the tiny apartment she'd had in Chicago. She'd rarely cooked there, and when she had, it had been simple things. There hadn't been much point in cooking a meal just for herself. Most of the time she'd simply settled for something from a nearby deli. But being here with Chance like this made her realize how lonely and isolated her life had become.

"What about you, Lucy? Can you cook?"

She shrugged one shoulder then the other as he filled her bowl with chili beans. "A little. The nuns in the orphanage would take us into the kitchen at times and teach us basic things."

He handed the bowl to her. "I remember you said you didn't have family. You grew up in an orphanage?"

She nodded. "I can only guess that my mother must have been Catholic. When she was killed in an auto accident, I was placed in a Catholic orphanage in Chicago."

"How old were you then?"

"Going on five, I think."

Surprised, he glanced at her. "So you can remember your mother?"

Nodding, Lucinda took a square of corn bread from a cloth-lined basket. "I can remember a few things about her. She was blond and pretty. She always smelled like flowers and at bedtime she sang lullabies to me."

Chance couldn't imagine how sad it must be for her to only have those few precious things to remember her mother by. He'd had years with his father and with them so many wonderful memories. He'd been young when he'd lost his father. Yet compared to Lucinda's life, he'd been very blessed.

"What about your father?" he asked after he'd taken a few bites from his bean bowl.

Lucinda's eyes dropped to the tabletop. "As far as I know, I never had one. My mother was never married."

Sensing her awkwardness, Chance said, "That's nothing to be ashamed of. You were just an innocent child."

The gentleness in his voice brought her eyes up to his. She smiled wanly, "I'm not ashamed. I'm just not used to talking about these things with anyone."

There was an insulated pot of coffee on the table. Chance filled two cups and pushed one over to her. "What about your friends back in Illinois? You didn't talk to them about growing up in an orphanage?"

Lucinda took a bite of the beans, then tried the corn bread. Maybe if she kept her mind on the food, she could forget about how good he looked sitting across from her with the dim light throwing shadowy angles over his face. Maybe if she kept talking, she wouldn't think about how quiet the house was and that the two of them were completely alone.

"Chance, except for Molly, most of my friends weren't family-oriented people like you. Whether I had a father, or grew up in an orphanage didn't really interest them."

"Some friends," Chance muttered.

"At least they didn't judge me because of it."

"And you think I do?"

As her eyes connected with his, Lucinda felt something inside slipping away, leaving a part of her exposed to him. "No. I think you've never known anyone like me before."

She was right about that, Chance thought. None of the women he knew would take off driving across the country by themselves. None of them were as beautiful. And certainly none of them stirred him the way she did.

"You mean someone who doesn't have a list of aunts, uncles and cousins a mile long?" he asked.

She nodded and he grinned at her. "Well, think of all the money you save each Christmas by not having to buy ties and fruitcakes for them."

He truly wasn't looking down on her because she didn't come from a long family lineage. Knowing that warmed Lucinda's heart and drew her to him in spite of all the warnings going off in her head.

They continued to eat and talk of the weather and the stress it put on the cattle. Afterward, Chance carried their coffee into the living room, where the lights were twinkling brightly on the Christmas tree.

Standing beside it, Lucinda breathed in the faint scent of pine and took pleasure in looking at all the ornaments hanging from the branches. Many of them were obviously old and a little ragged. A little brown teddy bear had a missing ear, and a toy soldier had lost the end of his rifle, but she knew that being perfect had little to do with finding a place on the Delacroix's Christmas tree.

One particular glass ball had been glued with rows of colored rice and macaroni. She glanced over at Chance, who'd taken a seat in a recliner. "I'll bet you made this when you were about eight years old."

He rose from the chair and came to look. "That's my work all right. I was a trusty Cub Scout then. We made those ornaments to give to our mothers. I guess it's pretty obvious that Dee is sentimental."

She was beginning to think that he was sentimental, too, but she didn't say so. On the outside he was a tough cowboy, and she didn't expect a man like him would appreciate her insinuating that he had a soft spot.

"If I'm ever lucky enough to have a child who gives

me an ornament for Christmas, I'll be just as sentimental about it as your mother," Lucinda told him.

As Chance watched a wistful sort of yearning come over her face, he felt ashamed of himself. Which didn't make sense. It wasn't his fault that Lucinda had grown up without her mother or any sort of family to share Christmas with. Still he couldn't help thinking of all the times he'd felt bitter about losing Jolene and their newborn daughter. Many times he'd felt as if he were the only person who'd ever suffered that much loss and loneliness. Lucinda was making him see just how wrong he'd been.

"Mother told me about the clothes you're planning to do for her and Sarah Jane. It's a very generous thing for you to do."

He was standing so close to her that her shoulder was brushing his chest, and even though she wasn't looking directly up at him, Lucinda knew his eyes were gliding over her lips and throat and downward to where her sweater clung to her breasts.

The feel of that hot gaze traveling over her left Lucinda's knees spongy and made her voice unusually husky when she spoke. "It's not that big of a deal. I'm not an Anne Klein or Liz Claiborne."

One corner of his mouth curled in a half grin. "No. You're Lucy. Maybe someday we'll see that name on a famous perfume."

Lucinda was trembling inside, and she wondered if Chance could see the pulse pounding at the side of her neck. Did he have any idea of the chaos he made of her senses?

"Then you don't mind about the clothes? Sarah Jane actually thought you'd be pleased because it will save you money."

His expression was suddenly full of amusement. "I'm sure she probably made me out to be a miser."

"No," Lucinda replied, then felt her face growing warmer with each passing second. "She didn't say anything of the sort. She said you'd probably kiss me."

Disbelief widened his eyes. "Kiss you? She said that?"

He sounded incredulous and Lucinda couldn't help but feel a little insulted. Was the idea of kissing her that horrible to him? "Uh—yes, because you'd be so grateful. But then your mother said no, you wouldn't kiss me because of Jolene."

Lucinda bit down on her lip, but it was too late. The words were already out.

His expression remained oddly fixed as he stared at her, then finally his eyelids drooped until he was watching her through two narrow slits. As she waited for him to say something, anything to break the crackling silence, Lucinda's heart began to pound so loud it roared in her ears.

"Well, she was wrong," he suddenly growled.

"Wrong? Who?" she asked breathlessly.

"My mother."

Before she could untangle the meaning of his words, Chance grabbed her shoulders and pulled her to him.

"If she thinks I won't kiss you, then she's going senile."

"Chance—"

His name was all she managed to get out before his head bent down to hers. Knowing he was going to kiss her, Lucinda braced herself for a quick smack on the lips. It didn't happen.

Long seconds began to tick away as his arms moved around her, drew her against him, then locked her there.

While his lips tasted, feasted on the full softness of hers, Lucinda felt herself being tugged to a place she'd never been, a hidden, exciting place where a mystical, intoxicating warmth seeped into her bones.

She clung to his shoulders as though he were the only solid thing in the world and moaned silently with regret when he finally lifted his lips from hers.

Chance had only meant to take one sweet, little taste of her lips. Now as he looked down into her flushed face, he felt dazed, rocked to the very soles of his feet by what had just happened between them.

"Do—uh, you always make a point of proving your mother wrong?"

Her voice was husky and trembling and he realized the sound of it was as alluring to him as the closeness of her just-kissed mouth.

"What do you think?" he murmured, his arms still anchoring the soft warmth of her body against his.

She thought if he really hadn't kissed a woman in years, then his memory of how to do it had certainly come to life a few moments ago.

"I think you're the sort of man who'd take on any challenge."

His brows lifted with wry speculation. "And you think kissing a woman is a challenge for me?"

"Yes. From what your mother said—"

Without warning, he released his grip on her waist and stepped back. "Dee had no business saying anything about Jolene to you!"

"And you think what you did to me a few moments ago *was* your business?" she asked, incredulous that he was displaying such anger over a wife who had obviously been out of his life for a long time.

"I wasn't in that kiss alone and you know it!"

He was right. There was no use denying that she'd been

just as much a part of the kiss as he'd been. But he'd
started it, and she wanted to know why.

"What difference does it make if your mother brought
up Jolene's name? Is it supposed to be a secret that you
two were once married?"

His face was suddenly a stony mask. "No. It isn't a
secret. But all of that was—that's my private life. It's not
something I share with anyone."

He couldn't have said anything that could have hurt
Lucinda more. But then she'd asked for it, she told herself.

Turning slightly away from him, Lucinda stared with
burning eyes at the ornament Chance had made for his
mother so many years ago. She was stupid, she realized,
to think she could ever mean that much to anyone.

"Well, I know what you're trying to say. I don't normally share my mother's death or the fact that I was raised
in an orphanage with anyone, either. I guess I just had a
momentary lapse with you." Stepping around him, she
started out of the room. "If you'll excuse me, I'll get back
to my work."

As Chance watched her limp away, her head up, her
long hair swinging against her back, he hated himself.
He'd never meant to hurt her, damn it! But Jolene was—
dead, he forced himself to finish. When was he ever going
to be able to put her memory to rest?

"Lucinda, wait!"

She didn't stop. Not until his hand came down on her
shoulder. She looked up at him then, her expression as
cool and distant as she could make it.

Chance's features twisted with anguish. "Look, I didn't
mean that the way it sounded."

"Yes. You meant it."

He let out a long breath. "Okay. So maybe I did. But
I was wrong."

Surprised by his admission, she turned around to face him. "No. I was wrong, Chance. I was wrong to think that one little kiss between us gave me any rights to bring up any woman in your past."

One little kiss? Is that how she thought of the embrace they'd shared? It had seemed more like instant combustion to Chance.

"But I expected you to tell me about yourself. And then I—" The frustration of wanting to make her understand made him shake his head. "I'm not used to talking about Jolene with anyone."

She shook her hair back away from her face. Chance watched a strand of it slide against the peak of her breast, then finally settle against her arm.

"Why not?" she asked.

During those moments Lucinda had been in his arms, Chance had forgotten all about Jolene. His mind had emptied of everything except for the taste of Lucinda's lips, the feel of her warm curves pressed against him. And he supposed that was the thing that had really angered him. He'd finally met a woman who could make him forget Jolene and he felt very guilty about that.

Releasing a tired breath, he said, "Because, like you, I don't want to look at painful memories."

She should have never started this conversation, Lucinda realized. Because now she was seeing more than just a cowboy who'd rescued her from a wrecked car. He was a man who'd once loved and lost, a man who wanted to keep his thoughts and his heart to himself. A man she was becoming hopelessly attracted to.

"You must have cared for her deeply," she murmured.

"I did care for her. But that didn't keep her from dying less than a year after we were married."

His words literally stunned the breath from Lucinda.

The last thing she'd expected to hear was that Chance had been widowed. He must have been devastated.

"I'm sorry," she said, her voice barely above a whisper.

Chance was sorry, too, he realized. Sorry that he was afraid to take Lucinda back in his arms and let himself forget the past.

Shrugging, he said, "Yeah. Well, you wanted to know. Now you do."

She didn't know everything. Especially why he'd kissed her so passionately, but Lucinda wasn't going to remind him of that. She was going to put the whole thing down to a sudden whim and do her best to forget that she'd ever spent one moment in Chance Delacroix's arms.

"So now we're even. You've told me all about you and I've told you all about me," she said. Then forcing a smile on her face, she added, "And now I really am going back to my room. I promised your mother and sister some new clothes and I want to make sure they get them before I leave."

Chance watched her limp out of the room and, as he did, it dawned on him that he didn't want her to go. Not because his mother and sister were gone and the house was quiet. He simply wanted to have her in the same room with him. He wanted to be able to look at her, talk to her. *And touch her.*

Damn it, Chance, didn't you learn anything tonight? he asked himself. Kissing Lucinda hadn't turned out to be a simple meeting of their lips. It had been the meeting between a man and a woman, a precious glimpse of what could be.

But Chance knew what love could be. When it filled your heart the whole world was a magical place. Once it was gone, life became a living hell.

Chapter Six

The next morning Lucinda rose long before dawn, took a quick shower, then dressed in a pair of winter white corduroy pants and a cowl-necked, emerald green sweater.

After brushing and tying her towel-dried hair back from her face with a green velvet ribbon, she left the bedroom and headed to the kitchen.

She found it as dark and quiet as the rest of the house. Obviously the Delacroix family didn't rise quite this early in the morning, Lucinda decided as she flipped on a light over the kitchen sink.

Yesterday she'd learned where the coffee makings were so she quickly started a pot dripping, then went to look out the plate glass door leading onto the back porch.

Cupping her hands around her face and eyes, she could see the sky was clear and twinkling with stars. The white snow covering the ground gave off an eerie illumination, allowing her to see as far out as the barns and feedlots.

Sarah Jane had told her that in the spring and summer months, hundreds of acres of grain were grown in the nearby area, turning the fields into a sea of green. Right now it was hard to imagine the sight. Just placing her hands against the glass door told Lucinda the temperature outside was probably in the single digits.

The sound of the coffeepot gurgling its last few drops called her back over to the cabinet area. She filled a mug then poured in a bit of half-and-half cream she'd found in the refrigerator.

Lucinda drank the first few sips standing beside the cabinet before she carried her cup over to the breakfast counter and sank down onto one of the stools.

Even though she'd gone to bed early, she felt tired this morning. But that was hardly surprising when she'd spent the better part of the night flopping from one side of the mattress to the other.

No matter how hard she'd tried, she couldn't quit thinking about Chance, how distant he'd been because she'd mentioned Jolene and the expression on his face when he'd told her that his wife had died.

Lucinda could come to only one conclusion. Chance had never stopped loving the woman. Even though she was dead, she was still living in Chance's heart. It was no wonder he hadn't kissed anyone in years, she thought. He probably saw it as cheating on Jolene's memory.

Well, she wasn't going to be the one to tell him he was living in the past. She had her own problems to think about. She certainly didn't want to compound them by letting Chance get under her skin. It was bad enough to be running from one man, she didn't think she could survive two.

The unwelcome thought of Richard reminded Lucinda that she hadn't yet called Molly. She glanced at her wristwatch, then at the phone sitting on the bar a few feet down from her.

Her friend would be up now, getting her husband off to work and her children ready for school. Lucinda still had the kitchen to herself, so she wouldn't have to be worried about what she could safely say in front of the Delacroix family.

Before she could change her mind, she moved to the end of the bar and punched the operator for a collect call.

A few seconds later, Molly was squealing in her ear. "Lucy! Where in the world are you? I've been worried out of my mind!"

"I'm sorry, Molly. I meant to call you last night, but I—got sidetracked. I thought I'd catch you before you headed out to work this morning."

Molly breathed a long sigh of relief. "It's a good thing you did. I've been trying to decide whether to contact the police—"

"Molly, no! God forbid! You know Richard would be the first one to start looking for me!"

"I know. I know," she quickly assured Lucinda. "That's why I've tried to keep patient. So where are you now?"

"Actually, I'm stranded."

"Stranded! Lucy, come to your senses and catch a plane back to Chicago."

"Never. I'm not about to go back to that life." Especially now that she'd met the Delacroix and glimpsed for herself what living within a family really meant. She had to go on to California and hope that someday she'd have a real Christmas tree with ornaments made by her own children. And under the tree, she'd have gifts wrapped with love.

"Look, I'm fine, Molly. I'm staying with a family southwest of Amarillo. The way things stand right now, my car is wrecked, my ankle is sprained and the highways are covered with ice and snow. It looks like I'll be here for a few days. Possibly until after Christmas.''

Molly groaned loudly. ''You're staying with a family you don't even know? My lord, Lucy, don't they have motels out there?''

Lucinda realized the whole thing probably sounded strange to Molly, who considered a ten-mile trip to her mother's house an adventure. ''The way things happened I couldn't make it to a motel. Besides, the Delacroix are very nice people. Their home is a big ranch called the D Bar D.''

''You're on a ranch with real cows and cowboys?''

Lucinda couldn't help but laugh. Molly made it sound as though being on a ranch was the next thing to visiting Hollywood.

''That's right,'' Lucinda told her, then gave her the ranch's phone number just in case the other woman needed to contact her. ''Now I'd better get off the line. I'm running up your bill.''

''When can I expect to hear from you again?'' Molly wanted to know.

''I'll call when I leave here. And Molly, if Richard happens to come snooping around, don't even hint that you know where I am.''

''You know me better than that,'' Molly assured her. ''I'll act like you haven't even left the city.''

''Thank you, Molly.''

''You can thank me by taking care of yourself,'' the other woman said.

''Don't worry about me. Once I get my car back and head on to California things will all work out.'' Footsteps suddenly sounded behind her. Lucinda looked over her shoulder to see Chance entering the room. ''Uh, I've got to go, Molly. Have a good Christmas.''

Before Molly could make a reply, she quickly slapped down the receiver and turned to Chance. "Good morning," she said. "You're up early."

He glanced pointedly at her, then the telephone. "Obviously not as early as you."

Before Lucinda could stop it, a flush of heat spread over her face. Damn him! He made her feel like a little girl caught with her finger in the sugar bowl.

"I guess I should have asked about using the phone first. But I called collect. So I thought—"

Frowning, he turned toward the coffeepot. "I'm not worried about the cost. I was only wondering who you'd be calling at such an early hour. Since you don't have family—"

"That was—my friend, Molly. Well, actually she's more than a friend. She was my seamstress. I promised to keep in close contact with her until I reached California."

"I see."

No, he couldn't really see, Lucinda thought, as she watched him reach for a mug. He didn't know that Molly was concerned for her safety, any more than he knew what it was like to have someone torture him with threats, to play sick games with his mind until it was impossible for him to eat, sleep or make sense of anything.

Chance poured the mug full of coffee then carried it over to where she sat at the breakfast counter. "Do you usually get up this early?" he asked.

She nodded. "During the workweek."

She didn't add that she'd gotten up this morning because it had been useless to remain in bed when she couldn't sleep. The tired lines on her face had probably already told him she'd spent a restless night.

"What about you? Is this your regular rising time?"

"Yeah. I like to have enough time to feed the horses before breakfast."

Propping her elbows on the breakfast bar, Lucinda leaned forward to put him out of the line of her vision. Yet her attempt to keep her eyes off him didn't work. Before she could stop herself, her head was turning to look at him. And blast it all, he still looked as damnably handsome as he had last night.

He was dressed similarly to yesterday, only this morning his shirt was black denim with pearl snaps. The top two at the throat were undone, giving her a view of his undershirt. Something about the white fabric lying against his darkly tanned throat struck her with the unexplainable urge to lean toward him. More than anything, she wanted to lay her hands upon his chest and slowly open the remaining snaps holding his shirt together. She wanted to push the tough denim aside and feel the soft cotton and warm muscles she knew she'd find beneath it.

"I have twenty head right now," he went on, unaware of the direction Lucinda's thoughts had taken. "All of them what we call 'using' horses. It costs like hell to feed that many, but I couldn't run the ranch without them. The D Bar D covers more than four thousand acres. That equals a lot of ground and cattle to look after. I know many ranchers use four-wheelers now to do some of the things horses do. But I don't cotton to those things."

Clearing her throat, she looked away from him, then pressed her fingers against her eyes. What was the matter with her? She thought she'd learned her lesson last night.

"You, uh, prefer the traditional ways," she said as she did her best to collect her thoughts.

"In the case of horses, I do."

And what about women, and marriage, and babies? she wanted to ask him, then gave herself another mental shake. Chance had already been married once, and from the way he'd acted last night he wasn't about to love, honor and cherish any woman except his dead wife. The idea left a flat feeling inside of her.

"I'd like to see your horses sometime before I leave the ranch. Would you mind showing them to me?"

He looked at her with raised eyebrows. "I'm surprised you asked."

She frowned at him. "Why? Because I'm a girl from the big city and I only know about fashion and fabric and living out of a scrunched-up little apartment on the tough side of town?"

He twisted the bar stool so that he was facing her. As Lucinda took in his closeness, the broad width of his shoulders and the sensual curve to his lips, she felt the room shrink around them.

"No," he said to her question. "I figure most city people, from either side of the tracks, would like horses if they had the opportunity to be around them. I was talking about last night."

Lucinda's heart gave a couple of hard thuds against her breast then seemed to want to stop completely. "What about last night?" she asked, unaware that her voice had dipped to a cautious murmur.

His eyes met hers, lingered there, then dropped to her lips. Lucinda suddenly began to ache with the want to touch him, to have him kiss her again. The same way he'd kissed her last night.

"You were angry with me. I expected you to still be that way this morning."

She was surprised by his notion. Mainly because his thinking was so far from the truth. "I wasn't mad at you. If I recall, it was the other way around."

His expression rueful, he glanced down at his coffee

mug. He didn't think he'd slept more than two hours last night. All he'd been able to think about was Lucinda and the way she'd looked when he'd told her he didn't share his private life with anyone. He'd hurt her. It had been all over her face. And though he'd never intended to do it, he couldn't forget that he'd caused her a moment's pain.

"I was a lot more angry with myself than I was with you. Hell, it's been so long since I've been around a woman for any length of time I—well, I guess I've gotten pretty rough around the edges."

"You live with two women," she pointed out.

He grimaced. "They're kin to me. You're different."

And she was making him different, Chance realized. Two days ago it wouldn't have mattered to him if he'd hurt Lucinda, or anyone who dared to bring up Jolene around him. He'd figured he had the right to lash out and protect his privacy. Losing Jolene and the baby had given him that right. But that was a crazy way of thinking. He could see that now and the revelation staggered him.

"I'm different? How do you mean?"

A wry smile twisted his lips. "I don't go around kissing my mother or sister—the way I kissed you."

Just having him mention the time she'd spent wound tightly in his arms set her heart to thumping. "Forget the kiss," she said huskily. "I already have."

Had she? Chance wondered. Then why didn't she look him in the eye instead of staring at the wall behind his head?

"How's your ankle?"

Relieved that he'd changed the subject, she stuck her foot out and showed him that her ankle had regained some of its former flexibility. "It's feeling better. It only pains a little to walk on it now."

"Then maybe you'll feel like walking through the horse

barn after lunch. If I get things caught up, I'll come fetch you.'' He slid off the bar stool and carried his cup over to the kitchen sink. ''Right now I'd better get to work. See you at breakfast.''

See you at breakfast. The simple little phrase stayed with her as Chance left the room and she walked over to the plate glass door.

Yes, she would see him again at breakfast, she thought as she stared out at the early dawn sky, and she would be waiting for that time to come.

The admission frightened Lucinda. Sooner or later, she would have to head down the highway and get on with her life. She didn't want it to hurt when she left this place. She'd already dealt with enough pain in her life. She didn't think she could survive any more.

Later that morning, after learning the main highway was reasonably clear enough to travel, Dee and Sarah Jane headed to Hereford to do some last-minute Christmas shopping.

Lucinda declined their invitation to join them. Her ankle was better, but she didn't think it was quite up to that much exercise. Instead, she used the time to work on a pantsuit she'd started for Sarah Jane.

A few minutes before noon, the two women returned with a carful of presents. After everything was carried in, Dee began preparing lunch while Lucinda offered to help Sarah Jane wrap the gifts the two women had purchased this morning.

''How do you like these?'' Sarah Jane asked Lucinda as they worked at the breakfast counter.

Lucinda looked at the earrings dangling from Sarah Jane's fingers. They were at least four inches long and made of pink, orange and red plastic beads. Lucinda figured whoever wore them had to be bold or crazy—or both.

"Well, they're—uh, bright," she said, trying her best to be polite and honest at the same time.

Across the room, Dee burst out laughing. "Lucy, you don't have to be so nice. They're the gaudiest things Sarah Jane could find."

"And believe me, I hunted hard," Sarah Jane said with a giggle.

"I'm almost afraid to ask who the earrings are for," Lucinda said, unable to keep from joining in on their laughter.

Sarah Jane carefully arranged the jewelry in a small box and fastened down the lid. "These are for Great-Aunt Bess. She'll love them."

"She's my aunt, on my mother's side," Dee spoke up. "She's a spry eighty-five and she loves dressing up. The wilder looking, the better."

"Sounds like a lady with fashion sense," Lucinda said.

Laughing, Sarah Jane handed the box to Lucinda. "Just wait until Christmas Day. You'll get to meet her then."

One by one the gifts were wrapped in bright foil paper and tagged with a name. A tie for one cousin and a bottle of Scotch for another, a box of candy for the closest neighbors and a furry stuffed kitten for their foster daughter. Each name had a story behind it and Lucinda enjoyed hearing Dee and Sarah Jane describe their friends and relatives. It made her feel a part of the family somehow.

"I wish you could have gone shopping with us this morning," Sarah Jane said as they worked their way through the gifts to be wrapped. "You might have found something you wanted to buy."

"Oh, I doubt it," Lucinda replied. "But I enjoy looking."

"Do you do much Christmas shopping?" Dee asked as she carried a bowl of salad to the table.

The question jerked Lucinda back to reality and the life she'd led back in Chicago. She'd never had the family and friends that the Delacroix had. But at one time she'd had a fairly large circle of friends and acquaintances. Yet Richard had changed that for her. Slowly and methodically, he'd cut her away from anyone close to her until finally her life had centered solely around him.

Now that Lucinda was away from him, it was easy to see that he'd been doing what nearly every abuser tried to do. Isolate the victim. Yet back then she'd been blinded to the fact of what he was doing to her life. She'd so desperately needed, wanted someone to love her that she'd ignored the first warning signals pointing to Richard's possessive behavior.

"I don't have much shopping to do," she answered Dee's question, unaware that Chance had walked into the room. "I gave my friends their gifts before I left Chicago."

"Don't you have distant family living somewhere in the States?"

Lucinda shook her head as she wound a red ribbon around the box in her hands. "No. My mother was killed in an accident when I was small and since I was placed in an orphanage I can only assume that she had no family."

"I told Lucinda she was lucky," Chance said as he walked up behind Lucinda and his sister. "She doesn't have to buy a lot of gifts. Like these."

With a curious smile on his face, he picked up a pair of red long johns and held them out in front of him.

"Those are for Doc," Dee spoke up before he could

ask. "He's always telling me he's cold. I figure those will warm him up."

Laughing, Chance draped the underwear around his sister's neck. "Mother, he wants you to warm him up. Not a pair of long johns."

Dee snorted. "Well, he can stay cold till spring then."

"He wants to marry you, Mother," Sarah Jane pointed out.

"The old man doesn't know what he wants," Dee said with a wave of her hand. "He's got to convince me all that sweet talk of his is for real before he ever gets a yes out of me."

Lucinda glanced up from her task to see Chance grinning at his mother. After a moment, he looked at Lucinda and winked.

Why did he have to do that? she silently groaned as she jerked her eyes back on the ribbon she was tying. It made her feel flustered and even more foolish. Because for some reason, when Chance looked at her and winked, it made Lucinda believe she was special to him. And that kind of thinking was crazy. Lucinda Lambert wasn't special to anybody.

"Well, who's getting this for Christmas?" Chance asked, picking up a coiled lariat rope from the pile of gifts on the counter. "Me?"

"No. That's for Tim," Dee told him. Then to Lucinda, she said, "He's one of Chance's hired hands. Roping calves is his hobby."

In the flash of an eye, Chance built a loop then began twirling it about a foot or two off the floor.

"Chance! Quit!" Dee shouted at him.

Amazed, Lucinda watched as Chance jumped agilely inside the whirling loop, then back out again. She'd seen such a thing done in western movies before, but she'd believed it was probably done with a trick of the camera.

Waving a metal spatula, Dee ran at him. "Damn your hide, Chance, you're going to knock over my poinsettias! Now stop it!"

Laughing at his mother's scolding, he allowed the lariat rope to settle on the floor around his boots. As he coiled the braided nylon back together, he said, "I want Lucinda to know she's in West Texas, where the cowboys are real."

Sarah Jane groaned. "The cowboys are not only real, they love to show off, too."

Lucinda met his eyes and suddenly she was smiling at him. Whether he'd been showing off for her or not hardly mattered. She'd enjoyed seeing his playful antics.

"Can you do anything special with those other gifts?" Lucinda asked him, her smile turning impish.

He glanced at the pile of things the two women hadn't yet wrapped. "No. I'll leave those to you and Sarah Jane. Otherwise, Mother might send me out to the doghouse."

"No. I'm sending everyone to the table," Dee corrected her son. "Come on, girls, we'll finish all that wrapping later. It's time to eat."

After lunch, the three women finished the gift wrapping, then Lucinda went back to working on the designs for Sarah Jane's clothes. Normally she had plenty of time to allow her imagination to dwell upon certain styles and fabrics. But in this case, she only had a few days to complete her work. She was going to have to hurry in order to have everything ready to hand over to a seamstress before she left the ranch. Although Sarah Jane still had a few months before the wedding, Lucinda didn't want to mail anything back and leave a trail for someone to follow.

Even so, when Chance came for her later that afternoon, she didn't hesitate. She grabbed her coat and mittens and followed him outside.

The sun had steadily grown warmer throughout the day, and now melting snow dripped off the roof and left mushy puddles along the track leading down to the barns.

As the two of them stepped off the porch, Chance nodded toward a horse tied at the backyard gate.

"I brought taxi service," he told her.

Lucinda's mouth fell open as she looked at the horse, then her eyes swung back to Chance and she burst out laughing. "You can't expect me to ride a horse!"

"You don't want to strain your ankle by walking all the way down to the horse barn. And even though you don't weigh very much, Traveler can carry you a lot easier than I can."

Lucinda's gaze whipped from him to the sorrel horse standing quietly by the fence. He seemed docile enough. But she'd never been on a horse in her life!

"I know. But Chance, the closest I've ever been to a horse was in the grandstands at Maywood Park!"

Chance chuckled. "Well, Traveler is hardly a racehorse. He won't go anywhere unless I tell him to. And he's got one pace. Slow."

Lucinda wasn't a coward. But she knew if she didn't climb on Chance's horse, he would peg her as one. "Then I guess I'll put myself in your hands. Just remember I'm no Dale Evans."

"What? You mean you can't sing?" Chance joked as the two of them walked toward the horse.

She shot him a dry look. "No. I can't sing. Nor can I ride."

"Sure you can. Just because you've watched some old western movies on late-night TV, you think all horses rear straight up on their hind legs, whinny, then take off in a wild gallop. Believe me, Lucy, if they really did act that way, there wouldn't be any cowboys left. We'd all have broken necks."

"Well, now that I'm finally seeing you in the sunlight, yours does look a little bent," she said while studying him with exaggerated concern.

So Lucy did have a little humor in her, he thought, a smile tilting the corners of his roughly hewn lips. He liked that about her. But then Chance had to admit he was beginning to like quite a few things about her.

After untying Traveler's reins, Chance linked his fingers together and held them, palms up, near the stirrup.

"Give me your foot. The good one," he instructed. "And I'll help you into the saddle."

"If you insist." Taking a deep breath, Lucinda put the toe of her boot into his hands.

"I do insist. Now, when I lift, you grab hold of the horn and slide your leg over the saddle."

"What's the horn?" she asked frantically.

He patted a round thing wrapped with black rubber.

"Here we go," he warned, then gave her a boost upward.

Before Lucinda could figure out how she'd done it, she was sitting astride the big red horse. Chance quickly swung himself up behind her, then reined the horse away from the fence and toward the horse barn.

Lucinda was immediately swamped with sensations. The rhythm of the horse's walk rocked her gently from side to side and the ground looked to be a long way down. But it was Chance's nearness that was affecting her the most. His chest was brushing against her back and his thighs felt molded to the back of hers. If she turned her head slightly to the right, her forehead would bump into his chin. He didn't have to be that close, did he?

"Now what do you think about horseback riding?" he asked, his voice little more than a murmur in her ear. "Not nearly as scary as you thought it would be, is it?"

Lucinda wanted to groan as a shiver ran through her body. How could she think about the horse, or riding it, when he was touching her like this? "Oh, no. I'm not scared."

That much was the truth. She knew Chance could control the animal and he'd never allow her to fall. But riding a horse with a man who turned her senses haywire was not what she'd planned to do when she left Chicago.

"That's good. I like a woman who isn't afraid. I've tried for years to get Mother to ride. But she's terrified of horses. She's lived her life on this ranch for thirty-five years and never has been in the saddle. That's frustratin'. Real frustratin'."

I like a woman who isn't afraid. Well, he certainly wouldn't like her, Lucinda thought dismally. Not if he really knew her. If he knew how many nights she'd spent shaking in the darkness of her bedroom, afraid to close her eyes and sleep, he'd probably label her a helpless coward.

Maybe she was. Leaving Chicago certainly made her look that way. But she'd tried to confront Richard. She'd even tried getting help from the police. She'd personally gone down to the station to file a complaint. They had eyed the whole thing in a different light. To the police, she'd simply been an angry ex-fiancée out for revenge. Richard Winthrop was one of their own, a real asset to the homicide division, he would never stalk a woman!

Lucinda had come away from the whole thing looking

foolish and even more embarrassed. After that, she'd never looked to the law for help. She'd realized it would be as useless as trying to climb a brick wall without any toeholds.

Chance pulled the horse up beside a long barn, slid off Traveler, then reached up to help Lucinda down. Seeing no other way to get to the ground, she placed her hands on his shoulders and allowed him to lift her from the saddle. As he set her to one side of him and the animal, Lucinda's hands slid off his shoulders and lingered on his forearms.

"Thanks," she murmured, her eyes carefully avoiding his.

"You're welcome, Lucy."

His quiet reply had her eyes darting up to his, and for a moment their gazes locked. Even with the coldness of the snowy ground all around them, Lucinda felt heat rise up within her, spread to her limbs and stain her cheeks with color. Something on his face, the strange light in his eyes told her that he hadn't forgotten the kiss they'd shared and he knew she was still thinking about it, too.

With one gloved forefinger, Chance reached out and touched her face. Lucinda trembled as the need to step closer to him argued with the sensible part of her that was screaming for her to move away.

"I don't think I've ever known a woman who blushes like you do."

"It's—my skin. It's very fair and sensitive to the cold," she said, hating the breathy sound of her voice.

Chance's dark eyebrows cocked up in speculation. "And here I was thinking I'd caused all that," he drawled.

Was he flirting with her? After the way he'd reacted to Jolene's name last night, it was hard to imagine Chance Delacroix flirting with any woman, much less Lucinda.

There was nothing special about her. But he had kissed her, she mentally argued with herself. And that kiss had felt like a lot more than flirtation.

The whole, scary idea had her quickly turning away from him and looking at the barn. "Are you ready to show me the horses?"

No, Chance wasn't ready to show her the horses. He was thinking more on the line of taking her into his arms right then and there, just to prove to her that she wasn't as indifferent to him as she was trying to let on.

But that wouldn't be wise, he tried to tell himself. He hadn't brought her here for that reason. He'd invited her to the stables because she'd intimated an interest in the horses and he'd wanted to show off his herd to her. Hell, he'd gone for more than ten years without a woman in his life. Just because Lucinda was giving him certain urges didn't mean it was time to get another wife, or even a lover.

Besides, the argument in his head went on, Lucinda was a woman on the move. She was young and unsettled and she had her own career to think about. She wasn't his type of woman at all.

The reminder had him grabbing her upper arm and guiding her toward the barn. "Yeah, Lucy, I'm as ready as you are," he said.

But as they stepped through the door and Lucy's shoulder brushed against him, Chance wished like hell the hired hands hadn't gone into town for a load of feed. Without them around, he didn't know how he was going to keep his hands off her.

Chapter Seven

The first moment Lucinda stepped inside the huge structure, she noticed the pungent smell of alfalfa hay and the unfamiliar scent of horses. Sunlight slanted through the roof where sheets of corrugated iron had been replaced with a white, lighter weight material to create skylights at regular intervals.

Rows of stalls lined the back wall of the building, while to the front and the right of them was a closed-off room where, Lucinda guessed, feed and tack were stored. To the left of them were more empty stalls.

"The only time I keep all the horses in the barn is when the weather is as bad as it has been the past couple of days," Chance told her as he guided her over to the nearest group of animals.

"Where do they stay in summer?" she asked.

"In warm weather, all the horses are turned out to pastures. Except for the stud. He has to be separated from the rest for his own safety, as well as that of the herd."

She cast him a curious glance. "You raise horses, too?"

He nodded. "I've got about six or seven new foals coming this spring. Not a great amount. What we don't keep to use here on the ranch, I'll take to Clovis and sell."

As she and Chance approached the stall nearest to them, a tall black horse with a blazed face hung his head over the metal gate that served as a door.

Chance gave the animal's jaw an affectionate pat. "This is Big John. He's one of the smartest cow ponies here on the ranch. I wouldn't sell him for any amount of money."

"What is a cow pony? He looks a lot bigger than a pony to me," Lucinda said, carefully standing a good two feet away from Big John's head.

Chance chuckled and Lucinda shot him a defensive look. "Obviously my ignorance about ranch life amuses you."

Frowning, he shook his head. "I don't think you're ignorant about anything. I'd be just as lost if you showed me a dress pattern. As for your question about the cow pony, that's just a term we cowboys use for a horse or mare that can be used on a ranch to head or cut cattle from another herd. Or if need be, we can rope off them."

Lucinda's chin lifted a fraction higher. "Well, something is making you laugh."

Chance grabbed hold of her hand and pulled her toward him and the horse. "I'm laughing because you're standing back there like Big John is going to take a bite out of you."

"How do you know he won't?"

Before Lucinda could protest, Chance took her hand and placed it on the horse's face. "This horse wouldn't bite a fly. Unless that fly was biting him. Go ahead, give him a good pat. He loves it."

Cautiously at first, Lucinda stroked her hand down the horse's nose. Big John didn't bare his teeth at her, so she rubbed his face again. However, the moment she drew her hand away, the horse nudged her shoulder.

"Is he trying to tell me to keep petting him?" Lucinda asked with surprise.

"Sure he is," Chance answered. "Most horses are very affectionate. They'll follow you around like a dog."

"I didn't realize that," Lucinda admitted, moving closer to the horse. "But then I don't know anything about horses. Or dogs, either, for that matter. Except for the strays I encountered on the city streets."

"You never had a pet? Or you just don't like animals?"

With a shake of her head, Lucinda said, "We didn't have pets in the orphanage. I guess there were already too many human mouths to feed. After I was out on my own, I moved to an apartment where pets weren't allowed." She shrugged one slender shoulder. "I always thought it would be cruel, anyway, to house an animal up all day by itself while I was away at work."

"Having four thousand acres, it's hard to imagine not having a yard big enough for a dog to run in."

"I'm sure it is. But to me, having four thousand acres to care for would be mind-boggling."

Chance guided her to the next stall. As they walked, he said, "It's a challenge. But I wouldn't want to do anything else. I guess raising cattle and horses is in my blood. My grandfather first started the D Bar D. Dad took over after he died. Now it's gone to me."

Even through the material of her coat, Chance's arm against the back of her waist felt warm. Lucinda tried to tell herself she didn't like it, that she wished he'd quit touching her altogether. But she knew she'd only be lying to herself. Having him walk beside her like this made her feel secure. Something she hadn't felt in a long, long time.

"You don't ever feel like the ranch is too much for you?"

The two of them paused at the next stall long enough for Lucinda to see a sorrel mare bedded down in the loose wood shavings covering the floor.

"The ranch has never been too much for me," Chance said as he guided her down the alleyway. "But I have to admit that it's sometimes been a little rough trying to take care of Mother and Sarah Jane. Especially after Dad died. They both turned to me and there wasn't any way I could take the place of a husband and father."

"It must have been an awful time for all of you."

He sighed. "It was. Mother was desperately depressed and nothing I did seemed to help bring her out of it. Sarah Jane was just a fourth grader, who thought her big brother could work miracles and bring her father back. I'm sure I let both of them down back then."

Lucinda couldn't imagine a man like Chance thinking he'd let anyone down. He seemed so strong, so sure of himself and his family. "As long as you stayed here on the ranch and tried to help them, then you couldn't have let them down."

Chance didn't agree. He'd always felt as though he'd let everyone down. Especially Jolene and his unborn daughter. She'd loved him, expected and depended on him to take care of her. Instead, he'd let her die giving birth to his child. The wound of that went so deep inside him, he doubted a lifetime would heal it.

His hand slipped away from her shoulder and Lucinda knew he'd set himself apart from her now. He was back in his own private thoughts. A place where she wasn't welcome. And though Lucinda tried to ignore it, a cold, deserted feeling began to seep through her.

Needing to change the subject, he said, "Come on.

There's a little fellow down here that I think you'll like to see.''

The fellow turned out to be a colt. His white coat was splotched with bay red spots and his unruly mane stuck out all directions. The moment he saw Chance and Lucinda he nickered and trotted over to them.

''He was born in May, so he's nearly eight months now. You like him?''

Just when she was telling herself that Chance was a stranger and she wanted him to stay that way, he had to go and smile at her as if she were somebody special to him. Why did he have to torment her like that?

''He's adorable. What's his name?''

''I haven't registered a formal name for him yet. I'm going to let Sarah Jane do that. She doesn't know it, but this little guy is going to be her wedding present from me.''

She turned her head to look at him. ''She can ride?''

Chance chuckled. ''Don't let her know it, but Sarah Jane can outride me any day.''

Lucinda had always believed gray was a cool, somber color. In fact, she rarely used it in her designs. But as she looked into Chance's gray eyes, she realized they were anything but cool. They were warm and inviting and quickly dissolving her last bit of common sense.

''You must love her a lot,'' Lucinda said quietly.

The expression on Lucinda's face was like that of a lost little girl, Chance thought. One that was always peering into the window and wondering what it was like to live like the rest of the world. And suddenly he wanted more than anything to wipe that look away. He wanted to draw her to him. Not just because it would feel good to have her soft body pressed to his. No, he wanted to show her, tell her that she wasn't alone and unloved. Dear God, what was happening to him? he wondered.

"She's my sister. I want her to be happy."

Even though I can't be. Chance hadn't spoken the words, but Lucinda had heard them just the same. She suddenly yearned to ask him about Jolene. Why couldn't he let go of her memory and give himself a chance to find happiness with someone else?

But Lucinda kept the questions to herself. Chance's life, or what he did with it, wasn't her business. She was just a temporary guest and she knew that Chance wouldn't hesitate to remind her of the fact.

In silent agreement, they moved on through the barn, lingering long enough at each stall for Chance to introduce its occupant to Lucinda. Eventually her ankle began to ache and she told Chance she'd better go back to the house.

"There's one more thing I want to show you before we go," he said.

Curious, she followed him through a door and into a dark room. Chance pulled a string hanging from the ceiling and a light bulb glared to life. Blinking from the sudden light, she glanced around her.

Covered barrels lined one wall, while the back end of the room was stacked several feet deep with feed sacks. Saddles, some new looking and some old and worn, hung by their horns from ropes thrown over the rafters. The sweet smell of molasses mixed with the scent of leather and saddle soap filled the room.

Intrigued by the unfamiliar sights and smells, Lucinda stood in the middle of the room and drank it all in. "Is this what you wanted to show me? What do you call this? A feed room? A tack room?"

Chance smiled as he watched her eyes roam over an

intricately carved fender on a saddle. Her curiosity pleased him, because each saddle and horse were like old, familiar friends to him. He wanted her to like them as much as he did.

"Actually, it's a little bit of both. But the room isn't what I wanted to show you. Come here."

She wound her way through the saddles to where he squatted near a pile of empty feed sacks. Behind them, curled up on an old saddle blanket was a brindle-colored mother cat with four kittens.

"Oh, how precious!" Lucinda exclaimed with undisguised pleasure.

Kneeling down beside Chance, she leaned over for a better look. "Will the mother let you touch them?"

"Sure. She's an old hand around here. She knows we won't hurt her babies." To prove it, he reached over and scratched mother cat between the ears, then picked up one of the kittens. It was a yellow-striped tabby with four white feet.

"Here," he said, handing the kitten to Lucinda. "Hold him and see how you like him."

Even though she knew it was probably childish, she couldn't help oohing and aahing over the furry little animal.

"He's beautiful," Lucinda murmured. "I'm sure he'll look very regal when he grows up."

She was cuddling the ball of fur to her cheeks as if he were more precious than a diamond. And the sight touched a place inside Chance that he hadn't even known existed before now.

"I want you to have him," he told her.

Lucinda lifted her eyes to Chance. His face was only inches away, so near she could see the pores in his skin, the faint ragged line of his bottom lip, the warm light in his eyes. And in that moment she felt very close to him, closer than she'd ever felt to anyone in her life.

"You want me to have him?" she asked, unaware that her voice had dropped to an awed whisper.

She made it sound as if he were giving her the world, and for the first time in a long time, Chance felt a sense of pure joy fill his chest and spread a smile across his face.

"Yeah. I want him to be yours. Don't you like him?"

She glanced down at the kitten cradled gently in her palms, then back to Chance. "I love him. But Chance, what would I do with a cat? I'm headed to California."

Suddenly some of the pleasure of his gift faded. "Well, surely cats live in California, too," he reasoned.

"I'm sure they do. But I'll probably be in a city. I might not have a yard, or a place for him to roam."

His eyes studied her face. "That's important to you, isn't it? That living things have enough space to roam free."

Suddenly Lucinda was back in the orphanage in the long drab room she shared with several other girls. After several years passed, it had become a cage to her. "When I lived in the orphanage," she said quietly, "I used to wish I were a bird so I could fly free, go anywhere I wanted. I wouldn't have people telling me when to go to bed, or wake up, when I could or couldn't eat."

A wry slant to his mouth, he said, "Most kids resent being told what to do, no matter where they live."

"You're right. But living by such a strict schedule made me yearn for my independence. When I was finally old enough to get it, I cherished it. Then Richard, my ex-fiancé, he came along and—"

She broke off abruptly, amazed that she'd been about to open up that private part of her life to him.

"And what?" he urged.

With her forefinger, Lucinda stroked the little yellow tom between the ears. "Richard did his best to take away my hard-earned independence. He wanted to control everything I did and said. Right down to who I could have for friends. Even the color of my clothes. I couldn't bear it. No matter where I am, or whomever I'm with, I have to be me. Just me."

Reaching over, Chance gently touched her arm. "I have a feeling this little guy will understand. He'll give you your space and you can give him his."

Lucinda tried to swallow down the lump of emotion filling her throat. "I just don't want his space to be city concrete. It wouldn't be fair."

His eyebrows lifted with speculation. "Maybe it wouldn't have to be. Maybe you could live somewhere else."

Why did she suddenly get the feeling he was talking about more than this little kitten's future home? "I suppose it's possible. I guess it isn't written in stone that I have to live in a city. But where my work is concerned, it would make things easier."

A brief smile touched his face. "Well, whatever you decide about that, I'm sure you'll give this little guy a good home."

"You really do want me to have him, don't you?" she asked again, as though she still couldn't quite believe it.

"I do. He's my Christmas gift to you."

Lucinda knew she'd never received anything that meant more to her. She didn't know why. Pets were given all the time as gifts. And if she'd really wanted a kitten that badly she could have purchased one at a pet store. But this was different. This kitten represented more than a pet.

He was the idea that she really could have a better life. And Chance had given it to her.

Gently she placed the kitten down with the other three, who were wrestling playfully beside their mother. "I'll leave him with his family until I'm ready to go," she told Chance, then smiled. "I think I'll call him Caesar. He has a noble-looking nose."

Chuckling, Chance rose to his feet and pulled Lucinda along with him. "All tomcats have big noses. But you don't have to tell Caesar that."

Before she could stop herself, Lucinda reached up and laid her palm against his cheek. It felt warm and stubby with whiskers, and incredibly precious to her.

"Thank you, Chance. You're a generous man."

No. He wasn't generous, Chance thought. He was selfish. Years ago he'd wanted Jolene, and because he had, she'd died. Now he was wanting Lucinda the same way and he knew that whatever she did or said, he couldn't give in to those wants. Not if he really cared about her. And he did care about her. The realization of it was becoming stronger and stronger, no matter how he tried to deny it.

"You're welcome," he said huskily, then clearing his throat, he pulled her hand down and led her out of the feed room. "We'd better get back to the house. It's cold in here and you've been on your ankle too long."

As they left the horse barn, Lucinda knew the tender moment they'd shared was gone forever. But she would always remember it in her heart and no one could take that away from her.

When Chance reined in Traveler back at the ranch house, Lucinda's car was parked near the fence. Pulled up next to it was a white patrol car with the word *sheriff* written across it.

Fear rushed through Lucinda, turning her blood to ice water. What was the law doing here? she wondered frantically. Had Richard somehow tracked her down through his network of police friends? Dear God, if he had, all the miles she'd fled would be in vain. Her chance for peace and happiness would be gone.

Chance had just helped her down from the horse when a tall, dark-haired man strolled out of the house and on to the back porch. He was wearing a khaki uniform with a pistol belted at his hip. The shiny badge pinned to his shirt pocket signified his authority.

"Well, hello, Chance. Is all this sunshine agreeing with you?"

Lucinda stood immobilized as she stared at the Texas lawman. On the other hand, Chance seemed glad to see him. Taking her by the arm, he led her toward the house and the waiting sheriff.

"I could use several more days like this," Chance told him. "What brings you out here today?"

"Just wanted to say hey to everybody. I ran into Mike down on the highway. He said he'd been instructed to bring this car up here to the ranch." He motioned with his head toward Lucinda's car.

"That's right," Chance told him. "It belongs to Miss Lambert here. She's staying on the ranch with us for a few days."

The sheriff tipped his cream-colored Stetson at her. "Nice to meet you, ma'am."

Lucinda could scarcely breathe. "Are you here to give me a driving ticket?" she asked him.

Chance immediately burst out laughing. As soon as he did, the young sheriff smiled at her. Totally confused by their behavior, Lucinda glanced frantically from one man to the other.

"No, ma'am. I figure your sliding off in the ditch was due to Mother Nature and not your driving. I just like to check in on my cousin every few days and make sure he's not getting into trouble."

Surprised, she looked from one man to the other. "You two are cousins?"

"On my Dad's side," Chance told her. "So there are two Delacroix men in this county."

"Yeah, and Chance is the ugly one."

Lucinda was beginning to see the resemblance between them now. She was also trembling with relief. Apparently Richard hadn't sent him looking for a Lucinda Lambert from Chicago.

"Yeah, but it's obvious that I got the brains," Chance told him.

The sheriff, who looked to be around the same age as Chance, laughed and clapped his cousin on the back.

"Are you going to be here for Christmas, Miss Lambert?"

She nodded at him hesitantly. "I think so."

"Then you're in for a big treat. Aunt Dee's the best cook this side of the Pecos."

"Too bad you'll have to miss it," Chance spoke up.

He shot Chance a mocking glance. "That's what you think. I just gave her a pheasant to bake for Christmas dinner."

"We're having turkey."

"I'm having pheasant, too," he told Chance, then laughing, he climbed into the patrol car. "You two behave. That's an order."

With a good-natured groan, Chance waved him out of the driveway. "That boy is—" Chance's words came to an abrupt halt as he turned around to see Lucinda limping hurriedly toward the house. "Lucinda?"

She didn't answer or acknowledge that she'd heard him. Cursing under his breath, he trotted after her. Just as she was about to step up onto the porch, he caught her by the arm.

"What's the matter? Are you in that big of a hurry to get away from me?"

Lucinda darted a glance at him, then as quickly looked away. "I'm—just cold."

She looked more than cold to Chance. Her face was as white as the snow on the ground and she was trembling so badly her teeth were chattering. "You look like you've seen a ghost! What's frightened you?"

Frustrated with herself and with him, she tried to shake the hold he had on her arm, but her efforts only made him tighten his grip.

"There's nothing wrong with me," she said, trying her best to sound convincing.

"I see. That's why you're quaking like a leaf. That's why you were running to the house. Are you trying to completely ruin your ankle?"

Something about the tone of his voice struck a nerve inside Lucinda, making resentment flare in her eyes as she glared up at him. "If you really must know, your cousin scared me. So there! Can you quit questioning me now? Because I don't like it!"

His brows shot up, then pulled into a disbelieving line above his eyes. How could she be scared of Troy? And why was she suddenly so defensive? This wasn't the woman he was talking to a few minutes ago in the barn.

"Troy scared you? That's crazy!"

Gritting her teeth, she jerked her arm free of his grasp. "Then I guess I'm crazy!"

Not waiting around to be badgered with more questions, she ran into the house. Dee was at the kitchen sink, but Lucinda hurried on past Chance's mother and down the hall to her bedroom.

Once inside with the door shut, she tore off her coat and sank onto the edge of the bed. Her hands were shaking and her cheeks, which had been ice-cold a few moments ago were now flaming with heat.

Pressing her palms to her face, she groaned out loud. What was the matter with her? She'd gotten upset over nothing. Now Chance was going to think she was crazy or worse!

But the fear that Richard might have tracked her down and sent the sheriff after her had been so great she'd been frozen with it. By the time she'd learned differently, aftershock had taken over.

"Lucy!"

Chance's roar was followed by a knock on the bedroom door. Before Lucinda could yell at him to go away, he strode into the room as if he owned it.

Lucinda jumped up from the bed. "What do you want?"

"I wasn't through with you," he said angrily.

The authoritative tone of his words infuriated Lucinda. Richard had treated her as if he owned her. He considered her to be his object to be questioned, insulted or discarded whenever he chose. She'd be damned to hell before she'd allow another man to treat her that way.

"Well, I was certainly through with you," she retorted, then swiping her tousled hair away from her face, she turned and walked over to the armchair where she'd left her sketch pad. "Now I'd like to get back to work. If you don't mind," she added coldly.

Chance didn't understand her anger or where it was

coming from. At least, he thought with some relief, it had brought some color back to her face. A few moments ago, she'd been so pale he'd fully expected her to keel over in a dead faint.

"I do mind," Chance told her. "I'd like to know why Troy set off such a scare in you. He wasn't about to give you a ticket or anything like—"

Whirling back around to him, Lucinda clutched the sketch pad to her breast. "I wasn't worried about a ticket! I just don't like policemen. They—" She glanced away from his searching eyes. "They frighten me," she finished, her voice suddenly quiet and resigned.

"Frighten you?" He echoed her question as though he weren't certain he'd heard her right. "That doesn't make sense. If you can't trust a policeman, you're living in a pretty scary place."

Lucinda *had* been living in a scary place. But Chance would never understand if she tried to explain about Richard. From what he'd just said, it was obvious he was like all the rest, she thought wearily. Richard would never harm her, he was a trusted law official. Was everyone blind, or was it she who wasn't capable of seeing things clearly?

Chance didn't know what to think as he watched an array of emotions race across Lucinda's face. There was sadness and resignation. But more than that, the look on her face said she was hiding something. Something that she didn't want him or anyone to know about.

"Lucy?" he began quietly. "Did you leave Chicago because you were in trouble with the law?"

The fixed stare of her gaze suddenly jerked off the floor and up at him. Outrage widened her eyes and made her bottom lip quiver. "You think—I've broken the law? You think I'm a thief or a murderer, or—"

Stepping forward, Chance grabbed her by the shoulders. "You see a sheriff and you nearly collapse with fright. What am I supposed to think?"

She'd only known this man for little more than two days. It shouldn't matter if he thought she was a fugitive, or worse. But it did. It cut her to the very bone. Less than an hour ago in the barn, she'd thought that he actually cared for her, that he believed in her as a person. God, how wrong could she have been!

Hopeless tears burned her eyes and threatened to spill over onto her cheeks. Desperate to hide them from him, she twisted her head away and squeezed her eyes tightly shut. "I guess you can think whatever you want to think," she said, her voice wobbling around the lump in her throat.

"That's all you have to say?"

"What do you want me to say?" she asked, defeat pouring through her, settling around her heart like a ring of cold rock. "Do you want me to tell you all about myself? What good would that do? You wouldn't believe half of what I told you. And even if you would, I don't want to tell you. Just like you don't want to tell me about Jolene."

Anger swiftly set Chance's jaw like a piece of concrete. "Why do you keep bringing Jolene into things? You think because I've lost my wife that I've lost my manhood, too?"

Lucinda didn't know where his thinking was coming from, but if he wanted to be insulting, she could, too. Raking a glare up and down his tall, muscular body, she said, "It's obvious you lost your heart. As for your manhood, I'm not in any position to say."

The words were hardly past her lips before he yanked her up against him. "I can remedy that for you. Right now!"

Before Lucinda could jerk away, his thumb and forefinger caught her chin and held it fast. She stared defiantly up at him. "You don't want to kiss me, Chance! You think I'm a felon. Or—or something equally bad."

His mouth twisted into a mocking sneer. "Oh, you're bad all right, Lucy. Very bad for me."

"And you're—"

Lucinda didn't go on. She couldn't. Suddenly his mouth was on hers, hard, hot and demanding. She squirmed against him and tried to wedge her hands between her and his broad chest, but he was holding her so tightly she doubted a piece of thread would slide between them.

Seconds later, it didn't matter. The pressure of his lips softened and the tight grip he had on her waist eased. His hands took a slow, spiraling path up her back until his fingers finally reached her hair. Once they did, they threaded themselves into the silky strands, pressed against her scalp and begged her to answer his hungry lips.

Lucinda didn't disappoint him. With a soft groan, her lips parted beneath his and her hands slid across his shoulders, then gripped the back of his neck.

Kissing Chance was like stepping into a warm, mysterious cave. She knew it was dangerous to continue onward, but she wanted to see, to feel what the next step would bring. And when his tongue invaded her mouth, she savored its taste and texture, reveled in the heat that was pooling in the center of her body.

Lucinda wanted to make love to him. It was that simple. She wanted to give her body to a man who doubted her character. A man whose heart was buried with another woman.

That last thought was enough to give Lucinda the strength to tear her lips away from his. "I can't—don't do this to me," she pleaded, twisting her head to one side and gulping in a deep breath.

Chance released his hold on her, then slowly took a step back. He didn't know how things between them had escalated to this point. But one thing was for sure, he didn't want the passion to end. He wanted to lift her off her feet, pitch her backward onto the bed and see her arms reach out to him. He wanted to see a look of love in her eyes and know that it was only for him.

As he studied her bent head, her slumped shoulders, her trembling hands, he wondered if he'd gone crazy. He didn't know this woman! And from what she'd just told him, she didn't want him to know her.

"I wasn't doing anything to you that you didn't want," he said finally, his voice low and rough.

Lucinda's head whipped around to him. "Well, I'll not want it again! I may not have much in this world, Chance Delacroix, but I do have my pride and my independence. I won't let you take those away. Not you or any man!"

Did she honestly think that's what he wanted from her? And why would she? Shaking his head in confusion, Chance stepped toward her. "Lucy, you're crazy if you think—"

"Yes, I'm crazy all right," she furiously interrupted him. "Damn crazy for thinking you might be different!"

"Different from what? Who?"

She looked at him, opened her mouth to answer, then just as quickly closed it. She wasn't going to argue with him. She wasn't going to look at him, and most of all she wasn't going to want him. She was going to put an end to everything here and now. It was the smartest, safest thing she could do.

Her lips compressed in a tight line, she pointed toward the door. "Get out!"

Chance couldn't ever remember a woman shouting at him. Nor could he think of a time he'd ever been more furious.

"Gladly," he yelled back at her, then turned and slammed out of the room.

Chapter Eight

After the windows quit rattling and she was certain he wasn't coming back, Lucinda walked on shaky legs to the closet and quickly pulled out her suitcases. She couldn't stay here now. The mere idea that Chance believed she was a—a what? she asked herself. He hadn't accused her of doing or being one certain thing. But he'd certainly doubted her innocence and that was enough to convince Lucinda it was time to leave. That and her melting all over him as if he were her long-lost lover.

What had she been thinking? Why had she goaded him like that about Jolene? It was clear that he didn't want to share anything personal with her. But that hadn't stopped her from wanting him to. Nor had it stopped her from wanting to kiss him. So she'd taunted him.

Well, she'd had her foolish, reckless moment with him and now it was over. Now it was time to get back to the real world where she belonged. Chance, his mother and his sister were beginning to matter to her, she realized, and that was a mistake. She couldn't let herself get at-

tached to people. Attachments only meant pain further
down the line.

She was tossing undergarments into a suitcase when the
bedroom door suddenly flew open and Dee burst into the
room.

"Lucy! What in the world is going on? I could hear
you and Chance shouting all the way down to the kitchen.
Now he's slammed out of the house in a black temper."

Keeping her head bent, Lucinda wiped frantically at the
tears on her face. She'd never been a crier. She'd learned
long ago it was useless to shed tears. But this time they
continued to pour down her face in spite of her determination to stop them.

"Chance and I—had a disagreement," she said to Dee.
"I'm sorry if I've upset you."

"Upset me?" Dee asked, incredulous that Lucinda was
putting her feelings first. "Don't worry about me. I want
to know what my son has done to you. Why are you
crying? And why are you packing?"

Lucinda swallowed, then said, "I can't stay here any
longer, Dee. It would be too uncomfortable for me and
your son."

Her forehead puckered with concern, Dee studied Lucinda's tear-blotched face. "But why? Did my son make
a pass at you?"

Lucinda groaned miserably. Dear Lord, what would
Dee think if she knew just how far things had gone between her and her son? She would probably think Lucinda
was just a gold digger, roaming across the country in
search of a gullible man. Chance certainly believed she
was a no-good.

Rising up from the suitcase, Lucinda wiped her cheeks
with the backs of her hands. "It's nothing like that—"

"Well, it should've been!" Dee swiftly interrupted.

"My son needs his head turned by a woman. I thought you'd be pretty enough to do it."

Surprised and touched by Dee's words, Lucinda shook her head. "Pretty isn't enough to turn Chance's head. I'm afraid your son is a closed book, Dee. I pity any woman who tries to read him."

Moving closer, Dee placed her hand on Lucinda's shoulder and gave it a reassuring squeeze. "Then what were you two going on about? Surely it wasn't important enough to make you leave."

Drawing in a shaky breath, Lucinda closed her burning eyes. It wasn't right to shut Dee out. The woman had been too kind to her. She deserved some sort of explanation. "Chance believes I left Chicago because—well, because I did something wrong and I'm running from the law."

For a moment there was dead silence. Lucinda opened her eyes just in time to see Dee tilting her head back and roaring with laughter.

"Oh, my!" she said after a moment. "That's a good one. I didn't realize my son had such a wild imagination."

Lucinda looked at her skeptically. "You don't believe him?"

Dee began laughing again. "Of course not! Chance is a good judge of horseflesh, but people?" Shaking her head, she tapped her chest with her forefinger. "I'm the one who knows people. And I knew the moment I looked at you that you were someone I'd be proud to know."

"But Chance—"

Dee interrupted with a wave of her hand. "Chance is—I wouldn't say he's a suspicious person. But he is very cautious. I guess that comes from losing Jolene and—well, it's made him overprotective, I think."

Lucinda was still trying to digest the older woman's

words when Dee reached around her and flipped over the half-packed suitcase.

"You put all those things back where they belong and forget about Chance."

"But he—" Lucinda tried again, only to have Dee quickly intervene with a firm shake of her head.

"If Chance questioned you, Lucy, it's because deep down he wants to know you better. And subtlety never was one of my son's virtues." She patted Lucinda's cheek, then started toward the door. "Now dry those tears," she tossed over her shoulder. "I don't allow crying in the Delacroix house at Christmastime."

Atop a gentle rise, Chance reined Traveler to a stop and slowly scanned the snow-laden plains. He didn't know where the hell that cow was. Back at the feed troughs, he'd counted forty-nine head. Three times. In this particular pasture there were supposed to be fifty head. None of which were due to calve for at least two more months.

Muttering a curse under his breath, he turned the horse back toward the feeding grounds and jammed his gloved hands into the pockets of his coat.

The sun was rapidly falling and the temperature along with it. He'd been riding for at least two hours now and his feet had long ago gone numb from the cold. There was no use in staying out longer, he realized. Soon it would be too dark to see his way home, much less find a downed cow. When he got back to the house, he'd call his neighbor, Jim Freeman. If Chance was lucky, she'd gotten through the fence somehow and had taken up with his holsteins.

It took thirty more minutes for Chance to ride his way back to the feeding grounds. The herd of black Angus was still there, feeding on several round bales of hay that he and Tim had hauled out here earlier in the day.

Should he count again? Maybe she had walked in from the west side of the pasture while he'd been searching the east side. Deciding to give it one last try, Chance reined his mount to a stop several yards away from the milling herd and quickly began to count in twos.

Fifty! He counted again. Then again. All fifty cows were there and from what Chance could see in the falling twilight, they all looked healthy. Had he simply miscounted earlier?

Hell, it wouldn't surprise him if he had, he thought as he nudged Traveler into a fast walk. He hadn't been thinking straight at all since Lucinda had arrived on the ranch. And after this afternoon, he wasn't able to think, period.

That's what a woman did to a man, Chance mused as he miserably ducked his face against the cold north wind. It wasn't enough for a woman to tie a man's body into frustrated knots. No, they had to go for the heart and the mind, too. Right now Chance didn't know which of the three was giving him the most problems. Worse than that, he didn't know how to fix any of them.

"Chance, I was about to get on a horse and come looking for you myself!" Dee scolded him, when more than a half hour later he walked into the kitchen. "It's been dark for ages!"

Leaning down, Chance kissed his mother's cheek, then tiredly pulled off his hat. "If I'd known you were about to get up enough nerve to ride, I'd have stayed out later."

Shaking her head at him, she hurried over to the stove where she was frying pork steak in a huge iron skillet. "Where have you been anyway? The hands have been gone for at least an hour or more."

"A cow was missing over in the east pasture. I was looking for her."

Dee glanced up from the frying meat to see her son swipe a weary hand over his face. "Did you find her?"

He nodded. "Finally. Is supper ready?"

"By the time you wash, it will be," Dee told him.

Down the hallway, in his bedroom, Chance sluiced his face with hot water, cleaned his hands, then changed his muddy denim shirt for a plaid flannel. His jeans were also muddy and splotched with manure, but he didn't have time to change them or his boots. He'd do that later when he got ready for bed. And the way he felt at the moment, that wouldn't be too long from now.

"Tea or coffee, Chance?" Sarah Jane asked as he took a seat at the dining table.

"Coffee. I need something to unthaw me."

She poured him a cup and passed it down to him. Dee joined them at the table with a platter of biscuits.

Chance glanced from his mother and sister, then to Lucinda's empty chair. When he'd passed her bedroom in the hallway, he'd noticed a light coming from under the door, but he'd figured she'd simply left it on.

"Lucinda isn't coming to eat?" Dee asked Sarah Jane.

Sarah Jane shook her head glumly, then slanted an accusing look at her brother.

"No. She said she wasn't hungry."

"The child has to be hungry," Dee reasoned with a frown. "She didn't eat but a few bites at lunch."

"I tried my best," Sarah Jane said. "She doesn't want to join us. She says she wants to finish that pantsuit pattern she's been working on all evening."

Dee held the platter of biscuits out to Chance. He forked three to his plate before passing them on to his sister.

"There isn't any need for her to finish each one of those

designs before she leaves here," Dee told Sarah Jane. "Your wedding isn't until May. She can mail the patterns back to us, if need be."

"I'm going to tell her that," Sarah Jane said with a nod of her head. "And I'll take her a tray of something later. Maybe she'll eat then."

Chance suddenly slammed down his fork. "What the hell are you going to do that for? She doesn't need to be coddled!"

Sarah Jane turned a glare on her brother. "No. She needs to be treated like a human being. Something, it appears, that you've forgotten how to do."

Chance frowned at her. "What's that supposed to mean? It isn't my fault that Lucy doesn't want to come out and face us!"

"And just whose fault is it, Chance? Mother and I weren't the ones who accused her of being a fugitive from the law!"

"She told you that?"

He was close to shouting the question. Dee looked at him calmly. "I had a talk with Lucy, Chance."

"And now I'm supposed to feel guilty because I questioned her about leaving Chicago? That shouldn't have insulted her. Unless she's guilty of something."

Sarah Jane made a snorting noise while Dee said, "Perhaps it was the way you went at it?"

Chance's eyes lifted to the ceiling. "She's supposed to be handled with kid gloves. Is that what you're trying to say?"

"I'm just saying you could be a little more sensitive," Dee suggested.

Frowning, Chance stabbed a biscuit with his fork, then ripped it open. "Why should I be? The woman pumps me for private information."

Sarah Jane groaned. "Chance, it's a good thing you've never been inclined to marry again. The way you are, I doubt you'd have much luck keeping a wife."

A cold, distant look crept slowly over his features. "I doubt I would, either. After all, I didn't with the first one, did I?"

Sarah Jane's expression was suddenly remorseful. "Oh, I—I'm sorry, Chance. I didn't mean it like that. I wasn't talking about Jolene."

Chance was suddenly too weary to eat. Picking up his coffee cup, he rose to his feet. "Forget it, sis."

Tears welled in Sarah Jane's eyes. "I'm sorry, brother," she said quietly.

Stepping around to her chair, Chance bent down and kissed her cheek. "Don't be sorry. Forget it and eat your supper before James throws you over for a woman with some meat on her bones."

At the far end of the house, there was a study that Chance used as an office. He hated paperwork and usually put it off until his desk was running over with statements and receipts. But tonight he was looking for anything to get his mind off Lucinda.

In the small room, he switched on a desk lamp, then turned on the radio. The Amarillo station, which normally played country music, was now into the Christmas season. Brenda Lee was belting out "Jingle Bell Rock."

On the right-hand corner of the desk, feed bills were stacked elbow high. One by one Chance began posting them in the ledger. As he came to the last and latest one, he growled a curse word under his breath.

Horse feed had taken a sharp rise. Twenty cents a sack. With his ink pen, he scratched out a quick tabulation on the margin of the ledger book. At that rate, he'd be paying eighty dollars more a ton. Three hundred and forty dollars more a month.

Tossing the bill to one side, he leaned back in his chair and linked his hands at the back of his neck. The ranch could absorb the extra expense, but he'd definitely rather be spending the money for new fencing.

Chance supposed he could get rid of two, maybe three of the older horses, but in the long run that wouldn't save the ranch all that much money. Besides, he might as well face it, he was attached to all of them, and deciding which two or three to sell, would be like deciding which leg or arm he wanted to give up. That's why he'd been eager to show the horses to Lucinda. They were like his children and he'd wanted her to enjoy them as much as he did.

Lucinda! Why did she keep coming back to his thoughts? Why couldn't he forget about the way he'd kissed her? The way she'd kissed him back!

A knock on the door interrupted his thoughts. Knowing how his mother hated it when a person didn't eat, he expected to see her come waltzing into the room with a loaded tray of food.

Without looking around, he said, "Mother, I'm not starving to death, I'll eat—"

"It's not your mother."

Chance's head whipped around, then his breath drew in sharply as he saw Lucinda standing just inside the door.

"Lucy."

No man had ever said her name that way, with his voice somehow both soft and rough, so full of emotion. The sweetness of the sound lifted her eyes to his face and for long moments she simply looked at him.

"I—don't want to disturb you," she said, then nervously licking her lips, she took one step closer.

She'd already disturbed the hell out of him. And he'd

already decided that she was going to stay in his head whether she was in this room with him, or some other part of the house.

"You're not disturbing me. Come in."

Reaching behind her, she gently pushed the door shut, then clasped her hands in front of her. The room was small and dimly lit. One small lamp burned on the desk. Its light pooled on the pages of the open ledger and reflected up to Chance's face. She could see that his gray eyes were red with fatigue while black whiskers shadowed his chin and jaws and upper lip. She'd thought about him all evening, the things she'd said to him and the way she'd felt in his arms. Now that she was standing here looking at him, all she could think about was going to him and laying her cheek against his.

"Was there something you wanted?" he asked.

Dear God, yes. She wanted him. Couldn't he see it all over her face? Each time she looked at him, even thought of him, a surge of yearning poured through her like kerosene on fire. And she seemed powerless to stop it.

Taking another step closer, she said, "Yes. I—I've been thinking about—" She breathed in deeply and tried again. "The way I behaved this afternoon. I know you didn't understand—"

"I still don't understand," he swiftly cut in.

"I'm not a bad person, Chance."

"I don't think you are," he replied, his eyes quietly studying her troubled face.

Surprise lifted her eyebrows. "But you implied—"

Shaking his head, he said, "Lucy, you looked like the devil himself had taken a seat on your shoulder. What was I supposed to think? I was worried about you."

Worried about her? No. Lucy couldn't imagine Chance Delacroix being concerned about her. She was just a stranger passing through, a momentary disruption in his life. Still, like a child drawn to the magic of Christmas, Chance's words drew Lucinda to him.

"I know I overreacted. But—" Pausing, she spread her hands in a helpless gesture as she tried to assemble the best words to explain herself. "It wasn't Troy, personally, you see. He seemed like a very nice man."

"He is a very nice man. Even if he is my cousin."

She tried to swallow, then brought her hand to her throat when it refused to cooperate. "But all policemen aren't nice guys," she finally managed to say. "I know, because Richard was a policeman."

Rising to his feet, Chance closed the three steps that separated them. "Your ex-fiancé was a policeman?"

Her face solemn, Lucy nodded up at him. Once she'd left Chicago she'd planned to keep all this information to herself. But no matter what consequences came out of this, she couldn't let Chance go on thinking badly of her. She couldn't bear that.

"He was—is a homicide detective on the Chicago police force."

"I see," he said, his expression suddenly thoughtful.

"I doubt it. You're probably thinking that doesn't explain my reaction to Troy. But believe me, Chance, Richard turned out to be—well, he could be very unpleasant at times. He ruined my impression and my trust for the law. I know that doesn't exactly make sense, and the logical part of me knows that all law officials aren't like him, but I still can't seem to make the separation."

"Why didn't you tell me this before?"

Her mouth twisted wryly. "For the same reason you don't want to tell me things. It hurts."

Oh yes, Chance knew how the past, and retelling it,

could hurt. As it had obviously hurt Lucinda, he thought grimly.

He didn't know what had prompted her to come to him and open up like this. But now that she had, Chance felt like a bastard. No, he more than felt like one. He *was* one. From the moment he'd picked Lucinda up from her wrecked car on the highway, he'd questioned her motives, her past, her future. He'd expected her to give out any information he wanted to know while, like a miser clutching his pennies, he'd held the biggest part of himself back from her. But then, he'd been doing that for more than ten years now. And the hell of it was, no one but Lucinda had pointed it out to him. Or maybe they had and she'd been the only one he'd listened to?

"So I guess I'll say good-night. I just wanted you to know how things were with me," Lucinda went on with a shrug of her shoulder. "I didn't want you thinking I had a suitcase full of stolen money stashed away in the car trunk and my being here would implicate you and your family."

Turning, she started toward the door. But before her hand reached the knob, Chance grabbed her shoulders and spun her back to him.

"I didn't really think that, Lucy," he said, his face bent close to hers. "I was just angry at you because you were being so damn closemouthed."

The warm light in his gray eyes made Lucinda believe him. It also made her quiver with longing. "Like you?" she couldn't help asking.

Chance couldn't be angry with her. How could he be, when everything inside of him wanted to pull her into his arms, cherish her warmth and her softness?

"It's been a long time since a woman has made me want to look twice," he admitted in a husky voice. "And now that you've come along, I don't know what to do about it.''

At first Lucinda thought she'd heard him wrong, then when she realized she hadn't, her heart began to pound. "You—shouldn't do anything about it," she breathed.

His hands on her upper arms, he guided her back a step until she was pressed against the closed door. "Why? Because you're still in love with your policeman?"

The mere thought of loving Richard made her shiver with revulsion. "No! I'm not so sure I ever loved the man. At one time, I believed I did. But now I think I only accepted his engagement ring because I wanted security in my life. I've never had that before, you see."

"Maybe you wanted love to go along with that security," he suggested softly.

His hands were burning through her sweater, right down to the tips of her fingers. His lips, just inches away, were hypnotizing her, making it impossible to tear her eyes away from them. "I did want love. I'd wanted it very badly. But I didn't get it."

One hand lifted to touch her cheek, then tunneled into the side of her hair. "I didn't get it, either," he murmured.

His touch stirred Lucinda's senses, but it was his words that tugged at her heart. "But you—didn't you love Jolene? Didn't she love you back?"

All of a sudden, he moved away from her and went to stand by a single window. The drapes were parted, and beyond the glass panes, Christmas lights twinkled on the eave of the porch. Lucinda thought the cheerful decoration was an odd contrast to the twisted look of anguish on Chance's face.

"Oh, we were married," he conceded. "And we were in love, or so we thought. But I was barely twenty at the time and Jolene was nineteen. I think she was more in love with the idea of marriage and babies than she was with me.''

"And you?"

"I wanted her. Physically. And back then I was too young to know physical desire wasn't what love was all about."

Lucinda didn't know what to say. All this time she'd believed he was harboring a great, deep-seated love for his dead wife. If that wasn't the case, why had he avoided women for so long? Why did he look so tormented now?

"Do you know how guilty that makes me feel?" he asked, when she failed to make a reply.

Frowning, Lucinda walked over to where he stood. "Why should you feel guilty? Jolene wanted to marry you, didn't she?"

A wan smile suddenly touched his features. "Oh yes. In fact, we eloped because she was afraid my parents would try to stop it." He looked at Lucinda. "You see, Jolene was from a poor family and she believed all the Delacroix resented her."

Lucinda couldn't imagine Dee being the sort of person to resent another just because they were less fortunate. But where their children were concerned, people often behaved differently. "Did your folks resent her?"

"No. But they didn't approve of us living in Amarillo."

A frown puckered her brow. "You didn't live here on the ranch?"

Chance shook his head. "Jolene didn't want to live around my family. Since she'd never had much of a home, she wanted one of her very own. So I tried my best to give her one. I got a job on a ranch just outside of the city and we rented a little house not far away from it. I worked during the days and went to college at night for a degree in agriculture."

"That must have been difficult," Lucinda said as she tried to picture a very young Chance struggling to become a husband and a man all at once.

He shrugged. "I'm sure you did the same thing. You obviously had to."

"Yes," she agreed. "But I only had the responsibility of taking care of myself."

With a long sigh, he turned his gaze back out toward the dark night. "Well, we made it somehow. Even up until it was time for the baby."

"The baby!" Lucinda gasped.

His face turned back to hers and Lucinda was suddenly haunted by the shadows she saw in his eyes.

"Yes. I figured Mother had already told you. Jolene died trying to have my child."

Stunned, Lucinda slowly shook her head. She'd expected him to say anything but that. "No. I didn't know. I—can't imagine such a thing happening to you."

His face full of bitterness, he said, "Neither could I. But there I was in the hospital waiting room, certain I was giving my wife the best of care, when the doctors came out and told me she was gone and so was the baby. A girl. Perfectly formed, but gone. Like her mother."

Lucinda's heart squeezed with pain for him. In less than two years, he'd lost his wife and child, then his father. How had he endured such pain?

"What happened to her and the baby?" she asked.

One of his shoulders lifted, then fell. "Oh, the doctors gave me all sorts of medical excuses, most of which I couldn't understand. I just knew that something had caused her to hemorrhage so violently they couldn't stop it. At the time, I didn't care to hear their reasons or explanations, anyway. Jolene and the baby were dead. As far as I was concerned I'd killed them."

"Chance!" she gasped. "That's crazy."

"Maybe so. But I'm the one who made Jolene pregnant in the first place."

"And that's supposed to make you a murderer?"

Pinching the bridge of his nose, he sighed, then said, "I've always thought so."

Determined to reach him, Lucinda grabbed both his hands and held them tightly. "Then it's high time you stopped," she told him. "You need to put all of that behind you—leave it in the past where it belongs."

His eyes lifted and locked with hers as slowly his fingers folded around hers and squeezed. "Do you think you're the woman who can make me put it all in the past?"

She wasn't expecting him to ask such a thing. Even so, the moment her heart had heard the question it had known the answer. She wanted to be that woman. His woman. The woman to give him true love and happiness. But that wasn't possible. Not with Richard hanging like a dangerous cloud just behind her shoulder.

"Chance, I'm not—I can't be that sort of woman to you—or any man."

"Why not?"

With an anguished groan, she turned away from him. "Because it isn't possible. Because I can't forget—"

Before she could get it out of her mouth, he snatched her arm and spun her back around to him.

"You just told me I needed to forget the past. Put it behind me. Why can't you? Or is this a case of do as I say, not as I do?"

"This is different," she said, her voice full of torment. "I have reasons to steer clear of a relationship with a man."

His hands came up to gently frame her face. "For years

I've had lots of reasons hanging in front of my eyes. Now you've come along and made them all look not so important anymore.''

Oh, dear God, he shouldn't be saying this to her, she thought. And she shouldn't be wanting to hear it. But her heart reveled in his sweet confession, glowed with a love as warm and bright as the Christmas candle burning on the living room mantel.

"I'm glad, Chance." With one hand she reached up and traced his cheek with the tips of her fingers. "You deserve to be happy. But not with me."

"You might be wrong about that, Lucy," he murmured. "In fact, I'm pretty sure you're wrong."

As if she were under some sort of spell, she stood totally still and watched his face bend to hers. "Chance—"

"Don't talk, Lucy. Just close your eyes and let me kiss you. The way I've wanted to kiss you since the first night I saw you."

The last was said against her lips, and by then Lucinda had already surrendered to him. Like butter sliding down a stack of warm pancakes, she melted against him, opened her mouth to him and welcomed the sweet invasion of his tongue.

The smell of him, the feel of him had already become achingly familiar to her, and knowing these moments would have to last her a lifetime, she held on to him tightly. Urgently.

By the time Chance finally lifted his lips, the room was spinning around Lucinda's head. Her breaths were coming in short pants and her knees were close to buckling beneath her.

"You say you don't want a relationship with me," Chance murmured, his lips pressing tiny kisses down the side of her throat. "But your body is telling me something else."

It was telling Lucinda something, too. She wanted to make love to this man. That was bad enough. But even worse, she realized she not only wanted to give him her body, she wanted to give him her heart. Something she'd vowed to guard with her very life.

"Chance, you don't know—"

Her words were smothered as his mouth found hers once again. At the same time, his hands delved beneath the hem of her sweater, spread upward against her back, then slowly inched forward to her breasts.

Once his fingers closed around their fullness, Lucinda was lost. Arching her hips against his, she urged him to deepen the kiss. Even though his teeth were grazing hers, his tongue was already exploring every intimate curve of her mouth.

Never had anything felt this good, or this right to her. And maybe that was the thing that frightened Lucinda the most. She was rapidly losing herself to Chance. She was letting another man take control of her again and she knew she must never let that happen.

Twisting away and turning her back to him, she gulped in deep, ragged breaths. "I'm not going to let you change my mind," she whispered hoarsely.

Long moments passed without a word from him. Finally, unable to keep her eyes off him, she turned to see him smiling at her. It was a knowing smile, full of pleasure and a dash of smugness.

"I think I already have, Lucy."

Terrified that he might try to prove it, Lucinda stepped around him and rushed out the door. She wasn't going to give him another opportunity to work his charms on her, she vowed as she ran down the hallway to her bedroom. Because next time, she might not be strong enough to resist.

Chapter Nine

The next afternoon Lucinda held a pattern piece up to Sarah Jane and carefully eyed the fit.

"This will drape over to your left shoulder and tie in a knot like this," Lucinda said to Sarah Jane.

"And that will make a collar?" the younger woman asked.

Nodding, Lucinda placed the thin piece of paper on the dining table, picked up another one and fitted it against Sarah Jane's midriff. "The rest of the bodice will fit tightly. I think the whole thing will look young and romantic and flirty. What do you think?"

The younger woman sighed with pleasure. "Oh, Lucy, you're a genius. You seem to have known exactly the sort of clothes I was looking for without me even telling you!"

"That's why she does that for a living, Sarah Jane," Dee spoke up from across the kitchen. "She's good at it."

"So what sort of fabric will this dress be made of?" Sarah Jane asked as Lucinda carefully continued to fit all the pattern pieces against her.

"Something that will give the skirt a pretty flow. Maybe silk georgette. A peach-colored print, I think. A solid color might make it look too severe. Unless you'd like something else?"

"No. Oh, no! Whatever you say, I trust you completely," Sarah Jane assured her.

"Lucy, you've worked all morning and nearly half of the afternoon on those patterns," Dee said. "Put them away and take a break. There's no need for you to get them all done so quickly."

"That's right," Sarah Jane said. "Like we told you, what you don't finish you can mail back to us. Or better yet, you can stay with us longer. Like until my wedding in May."

Lucinda laughed at the younger woman's outrageous suggestion. "As much as I'd love to see your wedding, Sarah Jane, I've got to be heading on. It's about time I found a place of my own and started back to work."

"Well, I don't know why you can't just make your home around here, close to us," Sarah Jane insisted.

"I'd like that, too, Sarah Jane," Dee said as she poured flour into a big mixing bowl. "But how could Lucinda make a living around here?"

Sarah Jane hopped up onto a stool at the breakfast counter. "Easy," she said. "Every few months she could take her things to Dallas. They have those big fashion buying shows over there all the time. And from what I've heard, everyone from department store buyers to small boutiques purchase merchandise at them."

"Hmm. That's not a bad idea," Dee said thoughtfully as she dumped more ingredients into the bowl. "What do you think, Lucy? Think you'd like being a Texan?"

Lucy began gathering her patterns, scissors and silk straight pins and putting them away in her workbasket.

Sarah Jane's idea had caught Lucinda by surprise. Firstly, because it was such a good one, and secondly it was something she wished she could really do. It would be wonderful to live somewhere nearby, to have these two women for friends. She'd never been around anyone she felt more at home with. And she knew she was going to miss them terribly once she left here. But that was the way it had to be.

"I've never really thought about living in Texas," she told Dee. "But I believe I'll do better with my work on the West Coast."

"I wish you didn't feel that way," Sarah Jane said to Lucinda. "I think you'd like it here."

Lucinda *knew* she would like it here. But until she was certain that Richard wouldn't harm her or her friends, she couldn't really begin to make a home for herself. And right now she wasn't sure of anything. He might be on the road looking for her, and if she led him here to this ranch, she would never forgive herself.

A few minutes later, after the women had shared a cup of coffee, they all got busy making Christmas cookies. Lucinda had never had a reason to do any baking for Christmas before and she was surprised at how much enjoyment she was getting from cutting the dough into stars, wreaths, and Christmas trees, then decorating them with sprinkles and frostings.

She was standing at the kitchen counter, flour on her face and in her hair when Chance came in the back door. The weather had turned cold and cloudy again and he'd been working in it for most of the day. Before he'd stepped into the kitchen he'd been wondering if he would ever feel warm again. But now the sight of Lucinda in a pair of tight blue jeans and a pink shirt with the sleeves rolled up to her elbows was quickly filling him with heat.

He hadn't seen her at breakfast. Then right before lunch, he'd gotten a trailer loaded with hay stuck in one of the back pastures. By the time Chance and one of the other hands had pulled it out, he'd skipped eating altogether. He'd also missed seeing Lucinda. And after what had transpired between them last night, that wasn't something Chance had planned to do.

"What's cooking?" he asked to no one in general as he pulled off his hat and wiped his muddy boots on a rug by the door.

"Christmas cookies," Sarah Jane told him.

"Already?" he asked.

Lucinda could feel him coming up behind her, but she kept her attention firmly on what she was doing. She didn't want to send any sort of signal his way. She wanted to give him the impression that last night and the moments they'd shared in each other's arms were something she didn't intend to repeat.

"It's only two more days until Christmas Eve," Dee pointed out to him. "We've got to get on with it, to finish all the baking I plan to do."

Reaching over Lucinda's shoulder, Chance dipped his finger into the stiff cookie dough. Lucinda twisted her head around to see him eating the raw dough from his fingers. It was the first time she'd seen him since last night. Memories of his kisses, the feel of his rough-skinned hands moving so tenderly against her flooded her thoughts and darkened her eyes with unbidden desire.

"Mmm. That's pretty good stuff."

She jerked her gaze back on the work in front of her. "It will be when it's baked," she told him while trying to keep her voice as casual as she could manage.

"And you're not to get into these, or the others," Sarah Jane spoke up as she pulled a tray of freshly baked cookies from the oven. "These are going to the church tonight for refreshments."

Chance frowned at his sister. "Tonight isn't church night."

"Charles Delacroix!" Dee scolded. "Have you forgotten about the Christmas pageant? Sarah Jane and I will be singing a duet. I know I told you this morning."

She probably had, Chance thought wryly. But he'd had other things on his mind. Like what he was going to do about Lucinda and the way he was beginning to feel about her. He wanted her. And she wanted him, or so her kisses had told him. But did that mean he was really ready to put all the past behind him? He'd married one woman and lost her. And since then he'd vowed he would never set himself up for that kind of hellish pain again. But Lucinda was doing something to him. She was blurring his memories, making him believe the future could be different.

"I guess I didn't hear you," he told his mother, then winking at Lucinda, he reached over her shoulder once again and broke the point off a star she was sprinkling with red sugar.

"Chance! You've ruined that one!" she exclaimed.

He popped the point into his mouth and chewed with obvious pleasure. "It isn't ruined," he assured her with a chuckle. "Four-pointed stars taste just as good as five-pointed ones."

Sarah Jane groaned as she arranged some of the already cooled cookies into a round tin. "Keep your paws to yourself, Chance. We don't come down to the barn and interfere with your work."

He crossed the room to the coffee machine and poured a mugful. "I wish somebody had come to help. I was stuck half the morning, then when I finally got the tractor back to the ranch, a water line had frozen beneath the horse barn. We've spent all afternoon digging it up.''

Dee handed him a freshly made ham sandwich. ''Well, I don't know which is worse. Winter, when everything is frozen. Or summer, when everything is dry and roasted.''

Chance swallowed a sip of the hot coffee and found himself wishing his mother and sister were out of the room. More than anything he'd like to go over to Lucinda and kiss the dab of flour from her cheek, nuzzle her neck and draw her back against him until every curve of her body was touching his.

''You are coming to the pageant tonight, aren't you? Your sister and I are counting on you being there.''

Realizing his mother was talking to him, Chance turned his head in her direction. ''Of course, I'll go. I wouldn't miss seeing you and Sarah Jane dressed up as angels.''

Dee smiled happily at him. ''Good. Then you can bring Lucinda with you. Since Sarah Jane and I have to be there very early, there's no need for her to ride with us and have to sit for more than an hour before the program starts.''

Hearing her name mentioned in their plans, Lucinda twisted around to look at the two of them. ''I didn't realize I was going anywhere.''

Chance smiled at her. ''Sure you are. You're coming with me. And make sure you're ready by six.''

He put down the coffee mug and carried the rest of his sandwich out the back door.

Once he was out of sight, Lucinda released a long sigh. How in the world was she going to handle this?

A little after six that evening, Lucinda sat staring out the pickup window, her fingers absently toying with the pearl choker she wore around her neck. It had been a long time since she'd been to church, and she'd missed it greatly. But after Richard had begun threatening her and following her every move, Lucinda had stopped going anywhere that wasn't absolutely necessary.

For the past months, she'd only left her apartment to go to work or the grocery market. And just doing that had made her a nervous wreck. It made her furious to think how her life had gradually been taken away from her, narrowed down to just the basic necessities. She'd nearly forgotten what it was like to dress up and go out to celebrate Christmas or any special occasion.

"If you'd quit frowning, you'd look perfect," Chance told her as he turned the pickup onto the main highway toward Friona.

She glanced over at him and told herself not to be impressed. But she was anyway. He was wearing western-cut khaki trousers, a white shirt, and a brown leather jacket. None of which were special, or dressy. In fact, the jacket looked as if he'd had it for a long time. The leather was scarred and worn in several places. But it matched his old black hat, and with his dark, good looks and lean, rugged body, he made it all look special.

"I'll do my best to look happier," she told him.

"You didn't want to come with me tonight. I can tell."

Lucinda smoothed her hand nervously down the lap of her deep green skirt. "I haven't said anything of the sort."

"No. You haven't said *anything*. That tells me a lot."

Frowning, she turned her gaze back to the windshield in front of her. "It should simply be telling you I'm all talked out."

"It's funny how you should say that. For a long time now I've hated talking. Mother and Sarah were constantly chattering and they always expected me to join in. I would, but it was an effort at times. The ranch hands were always swapping stories and gossip and they would include me in their conversations. I gritted my teeth and said as little as I could get by with. Now you've come along and picked and prodded at me until you've got all sorts of words comin' out of my mouth.''

She looked at him again, this time her lips parted with surprise. "I haven't picked and prodded at you.''

"Then what have you done to me?''

A warm flush seeped into her cheeks. "Nothing. And I don't intend to. I told you that last night.''

Chance's gaze traveled over the beautiful picture she made in her white silk blouse and Christmas green skirt. "If we weren't on our way to church, I'd pull this truck over and prove you wrong.''

Just the mention of being back in his arms shook Lucinda all the way down to her toes. "Well, we are on our way to church," she reminded him primly, then shot him an annoyed glance. "You really want to know what I've done to you?''

"I'm all ears," he said, enjoying this time alone with her.

"I've simply wakened your libido. And now you're beginning to think I'm someone special.''

She sounded weary, even a little cynical. Chance wanted to shake her. "Oh, my libido was always awake. I just never wanted to acknowledge it. Till I found you.''

Lucinda started to point out that he hadn't found her. But she stopped herself. He had found her. Rescued her. And now he thought they were headed toward something more intimate between them. How had this happened? she wondered miserably.

"I've been thinking a lot about last night," he went on, "and some of the things you said to me.''

Her head bent, she fixed her gaze on the toes of her

black dress boots. "I said them because I—meant them." Suddenly she turned on the seat and allowed her eyes to glide over the shadowed angles of his face. It seemed incredible that this man had come to mean so much to her. She'd only known him for a few days. Yet she felt closer to him than she'd ever felt to anyone in her life. "And I do truly hope you can put Jolene and everything that happened back then, behind you. If you do, I know you can be happy again."

Chance *was* becoming happy again and she was the reason. That much he already knew. What he didn't know was how to make Lucinda believe that she could be happy with him.

So far she seemed determined to follow the course she'd mapped out for herself when she'd first left Chicago. But there were still a couple of days left until Christmas, he told himself, and from now until then he planned to use that time to do some mighty big persuading.

The church the Delacroix attended was some eight miles away from the ranch house. By the time Chance and Lucinda arrived, the parking lot around the brown brick building was almost full.

Inside, the wooden pews were quickly filling with people of all ages. The two of them found a seat next to James, Sarah Jane's fiancé. He was a quiet young man with light brown hair and a slender build. Lucinda had never met him before, but from the few minutes of conversation they shared with him before the start of the program, she decided Sarah Jane was going to be in good hands.

The Christmas play turned out to be a much bigger production than Lucinda had imagined it would be. Several times throughout the program, she couldn't help but remark to Chance on the beautiful settings, which had been made to look like the streets and buildings of Old Bethlehem.

Chance enjoyed watching the story of the birth of Christ being acted out in word and song on the small stage. Though he'd seen it many times down through the years, he always looked forward to seeing it again. Yet this time, with Lucinda sitting next to him, her face shining with awe and reverence, it had all taken on a special meaning to him.

When Dee and Sarah Jane stepped onto the stage to sing "Silent Night" Lucinda couldn't stop herself from reaching over and curling her small hand around Chance's.

"You must be so proud of them," she whispered, her eyes suddenly misting over with emotion.

Tightening his fingers around hers, he smiled. "Very proud, Lucy."

He wanted to tell her that he was proud of her, too. Proud that she was sitting here beside him, sharing this special time with him and his family. But the feeling was so new to him, so fresh and tender that he didn't know how to put it into words. Instead, he held on to her hand, while inside him, the last haunting memories of the past faded away.

A few minutes later, the program ended and the socializing began. Chance took Lucinda over to the refreshment table, where they were immediately swamped by his friends and relatives. One being his cousin, Troy.

This time when Lucinda saw him, she knew there was nothing to fear and she smiled warmly as he shook her hand.

"It's nice to see you again, Miss Lambert. Have you tried your car since Mike returned it to you?"

Lucinda glanced at Chance, who seemed to be watching her closely. "No. But Chance did. Other than having a tire blown out, he says it didn't seem to be hurt."

"You're lucky," Troy told her. "That was a nasty ditch you drove into. You and the car could have ended up in a bad way."

"Yes, I was lucky," she agreed. Over the rim of her punch glass, she glanced at Chance. "Especially lucky that Chance rescued me."

Troy gave his cousin a pointed grin. "Looks to me like Chance is the lucky one," he told Lucinda. "The only thing he ever gets to rescue is a sick calf or cow. Beautiful women aren't his forte."

Smiling down at Lucinda, Chance asked, "Did I tell you that besides being the sheriff of Parmer County my cousin is also its biggest flirt?"

Tonight, for the first time in ages, she felt like a woman again. She felt wanted and desired and the nearest thing to happiness that she could imagine. Chance actually seemed proud to bring her into his circle of family and friends and she couldn't help loving him for that.

"No," she answered Chance's question. "I don't believe you told me that about him."

Laughing, Troy slapped Chance on the shoulder. "What did you tell her about me, buddy?"

Chance put his arm around Lucinda's shoulders and edged her away from the young sheriff. "Not anything that would ruin your reputation, cuz."

They moved on through the crowd, where Chance introduced her to several neighbors, an uncle, another cousin and a second cousin. Stories and news were swapped, a table of food eaten, and Merry Christmas wished to everyone before the crowd finally broke up and headed home.

On their way back to the ranch, Lucinda leaned her head against the seat and sighed with contentment.

Chance glanced away from the highway to look at her. "Did you have a good time?"

A wide smile curved her lips. "Oh, yes. The play was so beautiful and your mother and sister's duet was wonderful. And all your friends and relatives were so—"

"Hayseed?" he asked with a chuckle.

She grimaced. "There's nothing wrong with being hayseed or homespun. I liked all of them. They made me feel so welcome and a part of everything."

"I'm glad."

The quietness and the fact that they were alone again began to settle in on Lucinda. Trying her best to ignore it, she looked at him and smiled again. "Thank you for bringing me. I'll never forget this night."

Chance would always remember it, too. He would only have to think of Christmas and Lucinda would be there in his mind. After this week, he doubted he would ever be able to separate the two. And what would it be like without Lucinda this time next year? he wondered. Where would she be? What would she be doing? Spending her Christmas with some other man and his family?

It was a good thing they were already in the driveway at the front of the house; otherwise, Chance would have simply stopped the pickup on the side of the highway.

"Chance, what are you doing?" she gasped as he grabbed both her hands and tugged her toward him.

"Making damn sure you don't forget tonight, or me," he growled softly.

Forget him? How could she, when her heart, every fiber of her being seemed to be beating just for him?

One hand slid into her hair, cupped the back of her head and urged her face up to his. Lucinda couldn't deny him.

A soft sigh parted her lips and caressed his face with a silent invitation.

Groaning, Chance bent his head and closed the small gap between their lips. Lucinda lifted her arms around his neck, smoothed her hands across his back and sank herself into the heat of his kiss.

Chance had never tasted anything as sweet and intoxicating as Lucinda. Each time he touched her, kissed her, it was like a whole new journey for him. She hadn't just awakened his sex drive. No, she'd shaken up everything inside him. And where Chance had only been existing before, now he felt alive and thirsty for all the things he'd been without. The touch and the love of a woman. Hope for tomorrow and the next, and the next.

Breaking the contact between their lips, he gasped, "Oh, Lucy, Lucy! I want to make love to you."

More than anything, Lucinda wanted to simply draw his lips back down on hers, guide his hands to her breasts and let her body show him how much she wanted the same thing. But she couldn't do that. She had a dark, unsettled past. She had to move on from here, make sure it never followed her or spilled over onto Chance or his family.

"Chance, I—don't go around having sex with—"

Suddenly his hands were cupping her cheeks, his gray eyes were delving into hers. "Lucinda, you're not hearing me. I didn't say I wanted to have sex with you. I said I wanted to make love to you."

Was he trying to say that he loved her? Both joy and fear burst inside her, making an anguished groan slip from her throat.

Laying her palms against both sides of his face, she said softly, "I'm not the person you think I am, Chance. You—"

Suddenly his hands were on her shoulders, urging her

down on the pickup seat. "I don't want to hear about your past, Lucy. I want to know if you want to make love to me, too?"

With the heat of his body covering hers, his finger delicately outlining the edge of her lips, she couldn't lie to him. How could she say no, when all she could think about was the fire in her body and the exquisite pleasure of having Chance cool the flames?

"Yes. I do want to make love to you," she whispered truthfully.

A groan, exultant and deep, ripped from his throat and then his mouth was back on hers, tasting, teasing, begging her to show him exactly what she wanted.

She returned his kiss with a fierce passion. At the same time, Chance reached for the buttons on her blouse. Before he could get the last one undone, he lowered his head to the curves mounded above the cups of her lacy bra.

Lucinda gasped as his teeth grazed her soft skin, nipped delicately at her nipples through the thin French lace. Fire was racing along her veins, mounting an attack on her senses and creating an ache inside her such as she'd never known.

"Oh, Lucy. My sweet love," he mouthed against her, his fingers fumbling with the button on her waistband.

Far beyond resisting him now, Lucinda reached to help him. At the same moment, the sweep of headlights flashed the cab of the pickup.

Dazed, they looked at each other as though neither of them were sure of where they were. Finally it was Chance who cursed under his breath.

"It's Mother and Sarah Jane."

Galvanized by his words, Lucinda snatched her blouse together and tumbled out of the pickup. Ignoring the pain in her ankle, she raced into the house and down the hallway to her room long before the other two women parked the car.

Chance, however, remained in the truck. Like a man who'd been running for miles, his forehead dropped against the steering wheel and his lungs sucked in long breaths of cold night air.

By the time he felt collected enough to go in, the lights in the house had long gone out and his hands had grown cold. But there was warmth in his heart. And for a man who'd been close to death for nearly ten years, that was a hell of a feeling.

Chapter Ten

"I am dead on my feet," Sarah Jane groaned.

"I think Dr. Campbell would tell me I've overdone it," Lucinda replied, flopping down onto one end of the couch and flexing her aching ankle.

The two women had spent the entire morning and a big part of the afternoon making a shopping trip to Amarillo and back. They'd purchased several yards of material for Sarah Jane's new clothes and at the last minute, Lucinda had decided to purchase a Christmas gift for Chance.

After what had happened between the two of them last night in the pickup, Lucinda wasn't sure if giving him a gift would be the right thing to do. She didn't want him to get the wrong idea and think he was becoming special to her.

He has become special to you, Lucinda. The inner voice taunted her and dared her to deny it. But Lucinda couldn't argue with the little voice, or herself. Chance had somehow managed to fill her heart. Somewhere between the moment he'd carried her out of her wrecked car and now, she'd fallen in love with him.

She knew it was foolish and crazy and something she could never hope to act upon, but it was there in her heart anyway. As for the gift, she couldn't let Christmas pass without giving him something.

A knock at the front door caught both women's attention.

"I wonder who that could be in the middle of the afternoon?" Sarah Jane mumbled as she pushed herself off the couch and headed to the door.

Seconds later, Sarah Jane turned away from the door with a huge Christmas bouquet and a bubbling smile on her face. "It was the florist truck! Look at this!"

"James really splurged on you," Lucinda exclaimed.

"Sarah Jane, who was at the door?" Dee asked as she stepped into the room. The moment she saw the bouquet, she gasped with surprise. "Wow! Someone felt mighty generous! If James sent you those, Chance is going to kick his butt. You know he thinks you two kids should be saving your money."

Sarah Jane set the arrangement on the coffee table in front of the couch. "Chance is going to keep his feet and his opinions to himself," she said, quickly prowling through the holly and red carnations for a card.

Dee laughed and winked at Lucinda.

"This little white bear is adorable," Lucinda said, touching the button nose of the stuffed animal nestled among the leaves and flowers.

Sarah Jane finally found the card, then immediately gasped with surprise as she read it. "This isn't for me! They're for you, Lucy!"

Stunned, Lucinda's head began to wag back and forth.

"Me? But they can't be. No one around here would send me something like this? No one even knows me!"

Giggling at the mistaken assumption that James had sent them to her, Sarah Jane handed the card to her. "Well, someone did."

"Merry Christmas, Lucinda," she read aloud. "Is that all? Does the envelope have the sender's name on it?"

Sarah Jane shook her head as she flopped the square of white paper over in her hand. "Not a thing."

"Well, perhaps it was Chance," Dee spoke up. "Maybe he wanted to do something nice for Lucy."

"Oh, no! These aren't from Chance," Lucinda quickly countered. "I don't think your son is the bouquet type."

"Lucy's right. I've never known of Chance sending flowers to anyone. Besides you, Mother."

Dee shook her head. "It beats me. Unless the—"

"The flowers are from someone Lucinda met at church last night," Sarah Jane finished her mother's sentence. "Troy probably. He always was a romantic."

Lucinda didn't think Troy was the sender. She'd gotten the impression that the sheriff considered her Chance's property, and she'd said or done nothing to make him think otherwise. No. The flowers were from someone else. And the sick fear in the pit of her stomach told her that someone else was probably Richard.

"Troy or not," Dee said wistfully, "it's a beautiful Christmas gift. Too bad Doc didn't think of sending me one."

"I'll put in a hint for you, Mother. The flowers will go perfectly with that diamond engagement ring he's getting for you."

Dee waved her hand airily. "That old man isn't getting me a ring! I wouldn't take it anyway."

Sarah Jane laughed, but Lucinda didn't. Her mind was

in turmoil as she stared at the flowers and the little white bear.

"Oh, yes, you will, Mother," Sarah Jane went on. "You'd die before you let Doc give that ring to some other woman."

Dee stuck her chin out. "He doesn't want any other woman. He wants me."

Laughing, Sarah Jane gave her mother an affectionate hug. Across from them, Lucinda rose to her feet.

"If you two will excuse me for a while I think I'll go for a walk," she said.

Her expression suddenly serious, Sarah Jane quickly pointed out, "You've been on your ankle too much already, Lucy. Don't you think you need to rest?"

Lucinda couldn't rest. Nor would she be able to, until she was absolutely sure Richard hadn't sent her those flowers.

Pulling on her coat, she said, "I'm fine. I'd just like some fresh air. I think I'll go look in on Caesar and make sure he's doing all right."

Since the weather had turned out to be another cold and cloudy day, there hadn't been much thawing. Snowdrifts were still piled next to most of the buildings and the fence posts.

With her head bent and her arms wrapped around her waist, Lucinda picked her way around the slushy puddles of ice and water. The cold air helped clear the fatigue of driving back from Amarillo, but it did little to push away the nagging fear that Richard had somehow tracked her here to the ranch.

"Have you lost something? Or are you just counting all the piles of cow manure you've stepped in?"

Lucinda looked up to see Chance approaching her on Traveler, the horse she'd ridden with him. Had that been only three days ago? No, surely it had been longer. So much had happened since then. Chance and his family had changed her. Her heart, her wants and dreams were so very different now.

"I'm trying to stay out of the mud holes," she told him.

He reined the horse to a stop and stepped down from the saddle. Lucinda stood to one side of the path and waited until he was standing next to her. Even though her mind carried a constant vision of him, it never compared to the real thing. The shape of his long, muscular legs were evident beneath the blue jeans he'd jammed into the tops of his black cowboy boots. The brown suede sheep-lined coat he was wearing made his broad shoulders appear that much wider. Although he'd been clean shaven for their outing at church last night, he'd obviously neglected the chore today. Black whiskers shadowed his jaws and chin and upper lip, giving him a hell-for-leather look. It suited him. Just as the ruggedness of these great Texas plains suited him, she thought.

"I see you and Sarah Jane made it safely back from Amarillo. Did you have a good time?"

It was such a simple question, but his asking it meant more than she could possibly ever tell him. To think that he wanted her to be happy, that he wanted her day to be a good one, filled her with an undescribable joy.

"Yes, I did. Sarah Jane is such fun to be with. I'm going to miss her terribly once I leave here."

So she was still planning on leaving after Christmas, Chance thought. Why did that surprise him? She'd been saying that very thing all along. Because, damn it, he argued with himself, she'd very nearly made love to him last night. If his mother and sister hadn't shown up when they did, nothing would have stopped them. Just thinking about it now left a ball of heat in the pit of his stomach.

"Are you going somewhere in particular?" he asked.

"I was going to visit Caesar. Where are you going?"

"I was coming to fetch you."

She glanced up at his face, which was partially shadowed by the brim of his hat. Nothing on his features hinted that he was expecting her to mention flowers.

"Me?"

Taking her by the arm, Chance began to walk her toward another barn situated several yards beyond the one that housed the horses.

"Yeah, there's something I want you to see."

Inside the building two other cowboys were spreading alfalfa in a long hay manger. They glanced around as Chance and Lucinda walked nearby.

"We're gonna check on the new additions, guys," Chance told them.

"They're doin' fine, Chance. Already been eatin' like they were starved to death," one of the men called to him.

Chance gave him a thumbs-up signal, then guided Lucinda to a pen toward the back of the building.

At first, all Lucinda could see was a big black cow chewing a mouthful of hay.

"Look behind her on the ground."

Lucinda bent her head in order to see under the cow's feet, then squealed with soft delight as she spotted the two baby calves.

"There's two of them! And they look exactly alike! Isn't it unusual for a cow to have twins?"

Resting his forearms across the top board of the pen, Chance smiled at her excitement over the newborn calves. "It happens about as often as it does to humans."

"Then it's a special event," she said, her eyes still on the matching pair of calves. "When were they born?"

"About forty minutes ago. I've been down here watching her the biggest part of the day. We thought we were going to have to pull the first one, but once she had him, the little heifer wasn't any problem at all."

Lucinda was amazed. Looking up at Chance she asked, "You mean this cow gave birth less than an hour ago and she's already up eating?"

Chance nodded. "If everything goes all right during birth, a cow gets up immediately afterward and begins to clean her baby. Before the calf hardly has time to dry, it will stand and begin to nurse."

Marveling at the whole idea, Lucinda glanced back at the babies. "A few days ago, I didn't know what living on a ranch meant, or what it was like to be around animals." Feeling suddenly foolish, she shook her head, then looked up at Chance. "Of course you know that. I guess what I'm trying to say is thank you for wanting to show it all to me."

Reaching over, Chance slid his hand down her arm, then curled his fingers around hers. "I've never met a woman like you, Lucy. Such simple things please you."

Disturbed by the sudden intimacy of his touch, Lucinda's eyes dropped from his. "That's because I'm a simple person, Chance."

He shook his head. "No. You're not simple at all. You're special."

"I don't want you to think that."

"Why not?"

She didn't answer immediately. Chance tightened his hold on her hand and drew her a step closer to him. "Why not, Lucy?" he repeated.

Lifting her eyes to him, she said, "Because it would be better if you'd just think of me as your friend."

"I do think of you as my friend. My closest friend. And a whole lot more," he murmured.

Lucinda's heart began to thud heavily beneath her breast. "Did you—" She broke off, swallowed, then started again. "Someone sent me flowers. Was it you?"

As soon as the question was out, Lucinda knew there wasn't any need for him to answer. The look of total surprise on his face assured Lucinda that he hadn't been the anonymous sender.

"Someone sent you flowers, but you don't know who?"

Her spirit plummeting to her feet, Lucinda shook her head. "The card wasn't signed."

He grimaced. "Well, it wasn't me," he said, then his eyes gently probed her face. "Do you wish it had been?"

Of course she did! That's what made the whole thing even worse!

"Don't ask me that, Chance," she said with an anguished groan.

The tug of his hands urged her closer, until their bodies touched, their breaths mingled. "For whatever it's worth, Lucy, I wish I had sent you those flowers. But right now a whole garden of them couldn't begin to tell you what you're doing to me."

"Chance, we're ready to go doctor that bull," a cowboy called from the other side of the barn. "You wanta take the Jeep?"

Cursing under his breath, he glanced over Lucinda's shoulder at his hired hand. "Yeah, I'll be there in a minute or two, Tim."

Looking back down at Lucinda, he said, "There's four-thousand acres on this ranch, but for some reason we always seem to have an audience.''

Which was probably for the best, Lucinda thought. Otherwise, she might be tempted to give in to him. "It—doesn't matter. I need to get back to the house and help your mother with supper anyway.''

With a sigh of frustration, Chance caught her hand and began to lead her back outside to where Traveler stood tied at a fence post.

As he loosened the girth on the saddle, Lucinda's hand closed around the gift she'd slipped into her coat pocket before she'd left the house. She had brought it with her, thinking if she ran into him down here at the barn she would give it to him now, instead of waiting until Christmas Day, when the house would be full of family and friends. That day would be her last day here on the D Bar D. She didn't think she would be in a gift-giving mood then.

"Chance?''

Glancing away from the breast harness he was unbuckling, he was stunned to see Lucinda extending a brightly wrapped package toward him. "What's this?''

She placed it in his hands. "My Christmas present to you.''

"I didn't expect one.''

Lucinda hadn't expected a lot of the things she'd gotten from him, either. Maybe when she was far away in California this gift would let him know that she really did care about him, that even though she was gone, he was the most special thing that had ever come into her life.

Smiling gently up at him, she said, "I know you didn't expect it. But I thought you deserved something for rescuing me.''

A grin suddenly spread across his face and he tore into

the paper like a kid who knew he was about to get what he'd always wanted.

"Spurs!" he exclaimed, his voice conveying just how much she'd surprised him.

She took the torn paper and box from him. "I thought all cowboys liked spurs. And the man at the tack store assured me these were a good sturdy pair. I started to get a pair with fancy silver on them, but then I figured you would only put them up and never use them. And I want you to wear these."

He ran his fingers over the basket-weave design on the leather strap, then twirled each of the small brass rowels.

"You do wear spurs, don't you, Chance?" she asked when he failed to say anything.

Laughing, he grabbed her and hugged her to him. "I have about twenty pairs of spurs, Lucy. But not one pair are as special as these!"

A lump suddenly collected in her throat. "You're not just saying that to be nice?"

Laughing again, he set her from him and quickly began to fasten the spurs around his boot heels. "I'm not a particularly nice man, Lucy. I thought you knew that by now."

Moving back a few steps, he grinned and asked, "How do I look?"

He looked incredibly like the man she loved. But she couldn't tell him that. Not now. Not ever. With a sad little ache in her heart, she smiled at him. "You look like a man with a new pair of spurs."

A few yards away from them, the hired hands pulled up in the Jeep. Ignoring their honk, Chance bent his head and kissed her on the cheek. "Thank you, Lucy."

"You're welcome, Chance."

Stepping away from her, he gathered up Traveler's reins

and started toward the barn and the waiting men. Halfway there, he looked over his shoulder and waved to her. "Wait till the guys see these," he shouted to her. "They're gonna be as jealous as hell."

She smiled and waved back at him. Yet the moment she turned and started toward the house, hot tears oozed from her eyes and rolled down her cheeks.

Giving Chance the spurs had been her way of saying goodbye to him. And nothing had ever hurt her so much.

Lucinda was setting the table for supper when the telephone rang. Dee, who was busy at the cookstove, asked Lucinda to answer it.

"If it's for me," she said, "I'll have to call them back. And if they want Sarah Jane, she's gone to see James."

Lucinda hurried over to the ringing phone. "I'll take care of it," she told Dee, then to the receiver she said, "Hello. Delacroix's residence."

"Well, isn't that something. Just out of nowhere I call a ranch in West Texas and I hear your voice. I'd say that had to be pure fate, honey."

Her first instinct was to slam the phone down, but she knew she couldn't. He would only ring the number again. Lucinda gripped the phone as the room began to whirl around her head. These past few days, she'd prayed night and day that she would never hear Richard's voice again. Apparently God hadn't heard her.

"You sent the flowers, didn't you?" she asked in a hoarse whisper.

A malicious laugh came back in her ear. "Why sure I did, baby. You know I couldn't let Christmas go by without giving you something. And I plan to give you more than just flowers. A whole lot more."

Desperately Lucinda darted a glance at Dee and was

thankful to see she was busy digging for something in the refrigerator and wasn't listening.

"How did you find me?" she murmured under her breath.

"It wasn't hard at all, once I put the fear of God into that friend of yours."

"Molly? What did you do to her?" she demanded, uncaring now if Dee heard her or not.

"She's fine," Richard snorted. "But those kids of hers weren't gonna be if she hadn't spilled her guts and told me where you were!"

My God, he'd threatened to harm Molly's children, she thought sickly. The man was totally deranged!

"What do you want, Richard?" she whispered fiercely.

He made a tsking noise. "Lucinda, living among Texans must have warped your mind. You know what I want. You."

Squeezing her eyes shut, she tried to stop the quaking that had started in her knees and had now spread to her hands. "Where are you?"

"Close. Real close, baby."

She breathed in a ragged, shallow breath and turned her back to Dee, who'd returned to the cookstove. "You're not to come near this ranch, Richard! Do you hear me?"

He laughed mockingly. "Or what? You'll sic some rednecked cowboy on me? The one you've been hanging around these past few days?"

Surely he didn't know Chance, she thought wildly. How could he? "No. I'll have you arrested."

His laughter grew harsh. "That's a good one, Lucinda. All I'll have to do is show them my Chicago badge and those hick town lawmen will be falling over their feet to make me feel welcome."

Rage shook her body. "I'm not coming back to you, Richard." She spoke through clenched teeth.

"Then you better warn those cowboy friends of yours to get ready for some fireworks. I've brought Sally with me. She's strapped right to my heart, and you know, Lucinda, I'm not a bit afraid to use her."

Lucinda very well knew that Sally was the name Richard had given his .38 revolver. She also knew that he wouldn't hesitate to kill with it if someone pushed him.

"You're sick!"

"I'm giving you until morning to leave that ranch, Lucinda, and come back to me."

"I'd rather die first!"

"You may just have to," he drawled softly, then clicked the phone dead.

Realizing he'd hung up on her, Lucinda placed the receiver back on its hook and took several deep breaths. It was nothing new for Richard to threaten to kill her, but it was something entirely different to draw Chance and his family into his demonic plans.

"Who was it, Lucy?"

Trying to collect herself as best she could, Lucinda went back to setting the table. Please God, she prayed, let her act normal. She couldn't let Dee suspect that anything was wrong.

"Actually, it was for me. My—friend in Chicago decided to call and wish me a Merry Christmas."

Dee carried a bowl of salad over to the table. "That's nice. But—" She frowned as she looked at Lucy fumbling with the cutlery. "Are you all right, Lucy? Your hands are shaking and you look pale!"

Lucinda forced herself to give Dee a reassuring smile. "Oh, I'm fine. I just heard some disturbing news, that's all. An old friend has been ill. But she's going to get better.''

"That's good," she said patting Lucinda's shoulder. "I don't want you to be worried. Especially here at Christmastime."

Lucinda nodded, then turned away from Dee as a tidal wave of fear roiled through every fiber of her body.

Dear God, Richard had found her! What was she going to do? How was she going to protect Chance and his family now?

Chapter Eleven

Doctoring the bull turned out to be a bigger job than Chance had anticipated. By the time he and the other two hands got back to the ranch, it was well past dark and he was wet, cold and hungry. Most of all, he was eager to see Lucinda.

Chance hardly thought of himself as an authority on women. But he did know a woman's way of thinking was nothing like a man's. They usually acted on their feelings instead of logic. At least that's the way it was with the few women he'd know, including his mother and sister. So he could only believe that Lucinda wasn't any different. He believed her giving him the gift was more than just a Christmas gift. Just like he believed the passionate way she responded to him was more than just sexual. And tonight he intended to find out how she really felt about him.

"Have you and Lucy already eaten?" he asked a few minutes later as his mother placed a plate of warm food in front of him.

Dee took a seat at her son's elbow. "We gave up on you and ate about an hour ago."

He took up his fork and sliced into a cheese enchilada. "We would have been back earlier but that damn bull kicked down a panel and got away."

"I thought he was sick," Dee said.

"He is, but he decided he'd rather be sick than have us jabbing a needle of antibiotic into his neck."

"What did you do?"

A wry twist to his face, he said, "Chased him down with the Jeep."

"Oh? You were going to run him to good health?"

Dee poured him a cup of coffee and slid it over by his plate. Chance took a sip, then chuckled. "No. I got out on the front bumper and roped him. He jerked me off and dragged me for about twenty yards before he finally decided to give in and stop."

"Charles Delacroix! What possessed you to do such an idiotic thing? Why didn't you let go of the rope?"

He shook his head. "We were in the southeast pasture. It's so big that if he'd gotten completely away, we probably wouldn't have found him until the buzzards circled his carcass."

"Well, it's a miracle you weren't hurt," Dee scolded. "I told Lucy something unusual must have happened for you to be out so late in this weather."

He glanced around the quiet room and had to admit he was disappointed because Lucinda wasn't here sharing his supper and the day's happenings with him.

"Where is Lucy?"

"I think she went to her room. She said she was tired." Dee drummed her fingers against the tabletop. "Someone sent her flowers today."

Chance grimaced. "Yeah. She told me."

Dee studied her son's face. "It wasn't you?"

Frowning, he shook his head. "No. Damn it!"

"Well, there's no need for you to get hot about it. I just asked."

"I'm not hot about it," he muttered as he whacked off another bite of enchilada.

"Sarah Jane thinks Troy sent them," Dee went on.

A shaft of jealousy stabbed deep into Chance. "Troy has women falling all over him. He doesn't need to try to charm Lucy, too."

Dee's smile was thoughtful. "Troy will marry someday. But until then I don't think any young, beautiful woman like Lucinda is safe from him."

Like hell, Chance cursed inwardly. He loved his cousin, but he wasn't going to step aside and let him, or any man, have a clear path to Lucinda. She was meant for him. Each time he looked at her, touched her, his heart told him they belonged together. Not just until Christmas. But together for always. Somehow he had to convince her of that.

Two hours later, Lucinda was still shaking. Even though she kept telling herself that once she left in the morning, Chance and his family would be safe, she couldn't put the horror of hearing Richard's voice out of her mind.

Lucinda was thankful she'd worked so hard on the designs she'd made for Dee and Sarah Jane. They were all completed, except for a few details on Dee's dress. If she could ever get her hands to quit trembling, she could finish those tonight. In the morning, she'd be able to hand over the sketches, measurements, pattern pieces and fabric to Sarah Jane and feel confident that a good seamstress could complete the clothing.

She was attempting to mark a piece of pattern spread

out over the bed when a knock sounded on the door. Before she could say to come in, Chance strode into the room.

Stepping away from the bed, Lucinda turned to face him. Immediately her gaze was drawn to the front of his jeans, which were caked with half-dried mud. His boots and the spurs she'd given him weren't in much better shape. But the sight of him was precious to her. So precious that tears stung the back of her eyes.

More than anything she longed to go to him, hold him close to her heart and pour out all her fears. But she couldn't take that risk. There was little doubt in her mind that if she didn't leave the ranch, Richard would carry out his threat. And she loved Chance too much to put his life in jeopardy.

"It looks like you've been in a wreck," she said.

"I was. With a bull."

Taking one step closer, she suddenly noticed a long scratch down the side of his face. "I hope you won."

One corner of his mouth lifted. "I did. This time."

He didn't say more and Lucinda wondered why he'd come to her room like this. To tempt her and make her more crazy than she already was?

"Did you—want to tell me something?"

Only about a thousand things, Chance thought as he closed the few small steps between them.

"I missed you at supper."

His words were like fingers clutching her heart. Glancing away from him, she said, "It was getting late and I had work to do."

She sounded so cool and aloof, nothing like the woman who'd squealed with pleasure at the sight of the newborn twin calves.

Raking his hand through the side of his hair, he said,

"I know we talked today, Lucy. But I didn't get to say any of the things I wanted to say. That's why I'm here."

"Chance, if this is about last night," she said quickly, "I think it would be best if we forgot that completely."

His nostrils flared as he drew in a deep breath. "You mean forget that we nearly made love?"

She nodded, then finding it unbearable to keep looking up at his face, her gaze dropped to the toes of his boots. "We were—behaving recklessly, Chance."

"No. We were behaving naturally."

She looked up at him, her eyes questioning.

A brief smile touched his face. "Don't you think it's natural for a man and woman to be physically attracted to one another?"

"Yes, but—" Unable to explain the turmoil inside her, she turned away from him and went to stand next to the armchair by the window.

Chance stayed where he was and drank in the picture she made dressed in the same leggings and sweater he'd first found her in. But this time he didn't tell his eyes to stop their looking. Instead, he let them linger on her eyes and lips, her throat and breast, then on to the curvy line of her hips and legs. She was the most sensual woman he'd ever known and it turned him inside out just to look at her. But she was also much more. Like him, she was a survivor, a fighter, and he wanted her to be his wife, the mother of his children.

The certainty of his feelings compelled Chance to cross the room and place his hands upon her shoulders.

"You wanted me last night," he whispered. "Just as much as I wanted you."

The touch of his hands, the raw emotion on his face left a yearning so deep within Lucinda she wanted to weep.

"Yes, I did," she said, her voice solemn.

A light glinting in his gray eyes, he slid his hands up her throat, then cupped them both around her chin and jaws. "Then why are you saying we should forget it?"

Her heart banging against her ribs, she whispered, "Because it was just sex."

His face inched down toward hers until the curve of his lips was just a breath away from hers.

"You know that isn't true."

Her knees were beginning to feel like jelly and she wondered how much longer she could resist. If he didn't get out of here soon, she was afraid she was going to fall apart, tell him the truth about Richard's stalking and beg him to love her and keep her safe.

But Lucinda knew that Chance was the sort of man who would never back down from a fight. If she made him aware of Richard's threats, he'd make it a point to confront him. Chance was a strong, physical man, but that would hardly keep him safe from a psycho with a loaded revolver!

"I know that you're trying to seduce me," she murmured.

A grin parted his lips and exposed the edge of his teeth. The sight reminded Lucinda of how it had felt to have them nipping and tugging at her nipples, how it had felt to have a knot of desire burning inside of her.

"I'm trying to do that and a whole lot more," he said.

Drawing on every ounce of self-control she possessed, Lucinda brought her hands up against his chest and pushed him away. "I can't do this, Chance. I told you—"

He grabbed her hand and jerked her back to him. "You've told me a lot of things! None of which are the truth."

As she looked up at his grim face, everything inside
Lucinda froze. "Like what?" she asked.

"Like you saying you didn't want a relationship with
me or any man."

"That wasn't a lie," she shot back. "After what I've
been through—" She stopped, horrified that she'd very
nearly spilled the truth. "I don't want a man telling me
when I can take a step, or eat. Or breathe. Or sleep!"

The vehemence of her words shocked him. "You think
I'd be like that!"

No, she didn't really believe it. Chance would be a kind,
passionate, loving man. She'd come to that realization
some time ago. But it would be simpler to let him go on
thinking otherwise.

"I don't know. I don't know you," she lied, her eyes
carefully avoiding his.

"Then stay here and get to know me!"

Her eyes swung desperately back to his face. "I can't
stay here and have an affair with you. Or whatever it is
you want from me!"

Groaning with frustration, he shook his head. "You
think I want you to have an affair? My God, Lucy, hasn't
anything I've done or said registered with you?"

She swallowed in an attempt to free her throat of the
painful knot choking her breath and stinging her eyes.
"You don't understand, Chance. And I can't begin to explain—"

"No. *You* don't understand." Folding his hands around
hers, he tugged her warm body up against his. "I'm asking
you to marry me, Lucy. I want you to stay here on the
ranch with me. Be my wife and the mother of my children."

She gasped softly as the impact of his words hit her.
"Ma—marry you?"

His hands closed over her shoulders. "Lucy, I know you want to continue on with your career. And I know I'd be asking a lot of you to stay here, but—maybe you could ship your designs to sellers in the cities."

"You want to marry me?" she repeated in an awed whisper.

"Why are you so surprised? I've been trying to tell you—show you how I felt."

Dazed, Lucinda shook her head. "But after everything you told me about Jolene, I thought you never wanted to marry again."

"A week ago I would have cursed a blue streak if someone had told me I'd marry again. But you've changed me, Lucy. You've changed everything."

So had he, Lucinda thought desperately. A week ago, she'd had nothing on her mind but getting away from Richard's threats and starting up her career on the West Coast. She was still plagued with Richard's harassment, but everything else in her life had changed. For a short time, she'd seen what it was like to live within a family. She'd seen what it could be like to have a man really love her. Not possess her. As for her career, compared to her love for Chance, it was inconsequential.

"I—I'm glad that you feel differently now," she said as a lead weight began to fill her heart. "You're a wonderful man. You deserve to be happy."

His eyes delved gently into hers. "If you want me to be happy all you have to do is say yes."

With an anguished groan, she turned her back to him and bit down hard on her lip to keep from crying. "I—can't do that. I can't marry you, Chance."

Chance closed his eyes and told himself to be calm and patient. "Why? You don't want to be my wife? Are you fraid that if you become pregnant with my child, you'll lie like Jolene did?''

Sick that he should think such a thing, Lucinda whirled back around to face him. ''No! I don't think that at all!''

He shrugged. ''I wouldn't blame you if you did. I believed that very thing for years.''

''Well, I don't! Jolene's death was never your fault. I want you always to remember that.''

Groaning, Chance drew her to him, pressed his cheek against hers. For a moment, Lucinda gave in to the pleasure of touching him, of filling her head with the scent of him. Soon the memories of these moments would be all she had. It wasn't fair. But then she'd learned years ago that life rarely was.

''I don't understand then, Lucy. Why can't you marry me?''

Why did he keep questioning her? she wondered miserably. Why was he going to force her to lie to him, to say something that would break her heart into a thousand tiny pieces?

Knowing she had no other choice, she pushed herself away from him and stared with burning eyes out the window. She'd been right when she'd told Chance that Santa never visited her, she thought. And obviously this year wouldn't be any different.

''I can't marry you, Chance, because I—I don't love you.''

Chance felt as if someone had whacked him in the heart with an ax. He'd come to Lucy tonight eager to tell her how he felt about her and sharing the rest of his life with her. But now he was sick and angry for ever believing the two of them could have a future together as man and wife.

''Well, I—'' A self-mocking laugh took over his words. ''I didn't lie when I said I wasn't used to being around a woman. I guess I let my imagination run away with me. I thought last night was—it wasn't an act.''

"It wasn't an act!" she whispered fiercely as pain began to seep through every inch of her body.

"I thought your gift today meant more than just a thank-you," he went on, his voice angry and accusing.

"It did mean more!" Dear God, he would never know how much more, she thought sickly. He would never know how much she wanted to fling herself in his arms, cry out how much she really adored him and how much she wanted to give him children, to love him for the rest of her life.

"If that's true, then no amount of time would be enough to figure you out. I sure as hell don't understand you, Lucy!"

Clenching her hands together to keep them from shaking out of control, she looked over her shoulder at him. "A woman can feel close to a man without loving him."

A cold, stoic look hardened his features. "Well, you've certainly proved that to me, Lucy. Besides showing me what an ignorant fool I am!"

"Chance—"

Before she could say more, he turned and strode angrily toward the door. Lucinda hurried after him and managed to grab his arm before he turned the knob to open it.

"Chance, you're not a fool!"

His head turned back to her and Lucinda suddenly realized she'd never really known what it was like to love someone until now. The pain she saw in his eyes was tearing into her, wounding her so deeply that she knew she would never heal.

"Then what am I, Lucy? What am I to you?"

She couldn't stop the rain of tears that began to pour

down her face. "A wonderful man," she whispered
hoarsely. "Always remember that."

With a muffled oath, he jerked her to him and kissed
her with desperate, furious passion. Then suddenly he was
out the door and slamming it behind him.

Lucinda fell against it, sobbing and shaking and wondering how she would ever survive to see tomorrow.

The next morning after breakfast, Lucinda went down
to the horse stables to fetch Caesar. No matter what
Chance thought of her now, she still wanted the kitten
he'd given her.

Once she'd settled the animal into a cardboard box that
he could travel comfortably in, she loaded it onto the front
seat of her car, then went back into the house for her
suitcases.

Her movements were stiff and automatic, her eyes dry
and achy as Dee and Sarah Jane followed her outside to
the waiting car.

"Lucy, this is crazy!" Dee exclaimed as Lucinda
pushed the cases into the small back seat. "You'd already
planned to stay for Christmas."

Lucinda slammed the door shut, then turned to face her
friends. "I thought about that, Dee, and I've decided that
it will be better if I leave now. Christmas is a time for
family and I don't want to intrude on yours."

Looking around, Dee was relieved to see Chance approaching the three of them. "Thank God, you've shown
up! Tell her not to leave, Chance. Tell Lucy that she *is* a
part of this family."

He glanced at Lucinda and the look in his eyes dared
her to admit to his mother why she was really leaving. If
the whole thing hadn't been so horrendous, Lucinda could
have laughed. Neither Chance nor Dee, would ever know

the real reason she was leaving. They would never know how much she loved them all, how much she was willing to sacrifice, everything she'd ever wanted or dreamed of having in life, just so they would remain safe. And it was the right thing to do. That was the only thing holding Lucinda together now.

"Lucy knows what's best for her, Mother. And we have to respect that."

Dee stared incredulously at her son while Sarah Jane went to Lucinda and put her arms around her. "Lucy, we all love you and want you to be with us to celebrate. And to help us cook," she added jokingly.

"That's right," Dee spoke up. "Turkey and dressing. Pheasant and pumpkin pies. Lord, we'll never get it all done if you don't stay and help."

A quivering smile touched Lucinda's lips. "I'm betting you will. And I'll think about you. All of you," she added, her eyes going to Chance, "on Christmas Day."

His expression remained as stiff as it had been when she'd first looked at him this morning over the breakfast table. Unable to bear it any longer, Lucinda turned and climbed into the car.

"Goodbye now. And thank you for everything."

"Write to us," Dee called as the car engine sprang to life. "We'll send you pictures of the wedding."

Lucinda nodded and waved, then pressed down hard on the accelerator. She couldn't let them see that she was breaking apart.

It's all for the best, Lucy, she fiercely told herself as she guided the car away from the D Bar D. Once she left Texas behind, Chance and his family would be safe. And maybe, if she was lucky, she could dodge Richard long enough to make it across New Mexico. She'd take it one state at a time until she made it to California.

Once she got there, Lucinda was going to carefully change her looks and try to lose herself in the masses of San Diego. But then what? What was she going to do? How was she ever going to forget Chance and the love he'd offered her?

By the time she reached the end of the lane, Lucinda's eyes were so blurred with tears she was forced to pull to the side of the road and stop. With her forehead resting against the steering wheel, she sobbed so violently that her shoulders shook, tears drenched her face and soaked into the neck of her sweater.

She was so lost in her misery that she didn't hear another car pull up beside her, or the click of the driver's door as it swung open.

"Lucinda, this is all wrong. You sitting here crying, wasn't what I had planned, at all."

Icy fear shot through Lucinda as her head whipped around and she looked straight into the face of her darkest nightmares.

"Richard!"

A snarl on his face, he grabbed her arm and began jerking her out of the car. "It's high time you learned where you belong, little woman."

Chance had hoped that once Lucinda drove out of sight he could put her from his mind. But it wasn't working that way. He'd never felt so empty and lost in his life and the sad looks on the faces of his mother and sister weren't helping at all.

"I can't understand it," Dee said as she piled dirty dishes into the sink. "I was sure Lucy was enjoying herself here on the ranch. Then suddenly this morning she up and says she has to go."

Chance took a bite of a blueberry muffin, but it lodged

in his throat like a wad of cotton. Cursing, he threw the rest of it into the trash and went to pour himself a cup of coffee. The hired hands were waiting on him down at the barn. They were going to have to doctor that damn bull again today, but at the moment Chance couldn't bring himself to go back outside and behave as though nothing were wrong.

Lucinda's leaving was all wrong. And he'd never be normal again.

"I feel like I've lost my sister," Sarah Jane said glumly as she plopped down at the breakfast counter. "Do you think she'll write to us?"

"I think so," Dee answered. "She'll surely want to know how the clothes for your honeymoon turned out. By the way," she added, "Lucy left the fabric and everything in a box in your room."

"I'll take it to Margie after Christmas," she told her mother, then with a thoughtful frown, she asked, "I wonder if Lucy remembered to take her flowers with her?"

Dee began to scrub the dirty breakfast plates. "I don't know. But her getting those flowers out of the blue like that still seems a bit odd to me."

There were a lot of things that seemed odd to Chance, he thought, as he carried his coffee over to the plate glass door and stared absently down at the barns.

Lucinda had said she didn't love him, but the look on her face and the tears in her eyes had spoken just the opposite. She'd said she hadn't been acting that night they'd come close to making love. She'd admitted the spurs were more than just a thank-you. What had she really been trying to say to him? That she loved him but was just afraid to admit it? But why? he wondered as frustration clawed at his insides. Why should she be afraid to love him? She'd said he was a wonderful man. To always remember that.

Suddenly, like the flashing frames of a movie, Chance's mind was filled with scenes of Lucinda. Her first night here and how frantic and desperate she'd been to get back on the road, the terror on her face when she'd first seen Troy and his patrol car. She was afraid of policemen, she'd told him. Because Richard had been a policeman. When Chance broke all that down, he realized she'd simply been saying she was afraid of her ex-fiancé.

"Damn!"

Dee turned around to see Chance slamming his coffee cup down on the dining table. "Where are you going?" she asked as he started out of the kitchen.

Ignoring his mother's question, Chance hurried to Lucinda's bedroom. He found it neat and everything in its place. She hadn't left a thing behind that might give him a hint as to where she was headed. Even the Christmas bouquet he'd seen last night on her dresser was gone now. Or was it?

Jerking up the small wastebasket beside the bed, he found the red flowers shredded to tiny bits. Even the little stuffed bear had been torn into several pieces and tossed in with the rest as though it were all nasty garbage.

This wasn't like Lucinda at all. She was a woman who loved beauty in any sort of form. She wouldn't deliberately destroy a gift. No, this was an act of helpless desperation.

"Mother! Mother!"

Hearing the urgency in her son's voice, Dee raced down the hallway and met her son coming out of Lucinda's bedroom. "What is it? What's wrong?"

"Did anything strange or different happen to Lucinda yesterday? Or last night?"

Not sure how her son's mind was working, Dee looked at him blankly. "Something strange? What do you mean? Why?"

He let out an impatient breath and took his mother gently by the shoulders. "Did she get a letter, or a phone call? Anything?"

"She got flowers. But you knew that," she said, then her brows puckered together as something else registered. "Now that you mention it, she did get a phone call right before supper. She said it was a friend from Chicago."

"Did she say anything else? Please, Mother, think! It's important!"

"Well, all that I remember is that she was pretty shaken after she'd hung up the phone. She said something about it being bad news but that everything was going to be all right."

"That's it!"

Spinning away from his mother, Chance jogged toward the front door. "Call Troy and tell him to head toward the ranch. If he sees Lucy along the way, stop her!"

Stunned, Dee stared at him. "Stop her? But Chance—"

"Just do it! I'll explain later," he shouted, already halfway down the steps.

Right now he had to find Lucinda, he thought desperately, as he raced toward his truck. He had to find her before she drove into danger. Before Chance lost her forever!

Chapter Twelve

The moment Richard attempted to shove Lucinda into his car, she went at him kicking and clawing for all she was worth. Cursing a stream of threats at her, he wrenched her arm behind her back and bent her head towards the open door.

Knowing she'd never escape if he got her inside the vehicle, Lucinda called on every bit of strength she had in her and slammed her knee into his groin.

The unexpected pain caused his grip to loosen just enough for Lucinda to wrench herself away from him. Her breaths coming fast and labored, she raced down the muddy graveled road in the direction of the ranch.

Before she had traveled twenty yards, Richard caught up to her and tripped her from behind. She fell face forward, her hands and belly grinding into the rocks and mud and gravel.

When Chance drove up on the scene, Richard was jerking her up by the arm and a handful of hair at the back of her head.

Wild with fear, he stomped on the brakes, sending the pickup into a sideways skid. It had barely come to a stop in the middle of the road before he jumped out and ran toward Lucinda and her attacker.

"Let go of her, you bastard!"

With a death grip on Lucinda's arm, the crazed man reached into his coat and drew out a revolver.

Lucinda screamed as he pointed the .38 at Chance.

"No! Get back, Chance! He's crazy, he'll kill you!"

"You better listen to her, cowboy. I'd sooner shoot you than her. But if I have to, I'll kill you both."

"You're not going to shoot anybody," Chance growled. His face dark with rage, he continued walking toward Lucinda and her captor. "You're going to let Lucy go and then you're going to throw down that gun."

Richard cocked the pistol and began to laugh. "Like hell!"

Sobbing now, Lucinda looked frantically around her, searching for anything to divert Richard's attention. Like a miracle from heaven, she saw a sheriff's patrol car pulling off the highway and heading toward them.

"Here comes Troy!" she shouted.

Richard twisted his head to look at the approaching car. The moment he did, Chance pounced. Grabbing the arm holding the gun, he whammed it across his raised knee.

The blow knocked the gun loose from Richard's hand. Without the weapon, he was no match for Chance's physical strength. With a right fist in his eye, Richard staggered backward and released his grip on Lucinda. Another blow from Chance's left fist and Richard toppled into the ditch.

As he lay there groaning and helpless, Chance turned to Lucinda. Sobbing, she fell into his arms. He gathered her tightly against him, buried his face in the side of her neck and stroked his hand down the back of her hair.

"It's all right, Lucy. Don't cry, darling. Everything is going to be all right now."

"But Richard will get away! He'll come back and—"

"No! He'll never come back here, Lucy. He'll never hurt you again. I promise you that."

Troy pulled Richard from the ditch and handcuffed him. As the young sheriff prodded his prisoner back to the patrol car, Chance found the .38 where it had fallen and gave it to his cousin. Dazed and shivering, Lucinda clung to Chance's arm as the four of them headed to the patrol car.

"He was threatening to kill us," Chance told Troy.

"I know. I saw the three of you when I drove up. Who is he anyway? Do you two know him?"

Lucinda nodded and spoke as best she could through chattering teeth. "He's Richard Winthrop from Chicago. And he's been stalking me for the past several months."

"You don't have anything on me," Richard snarled. "I never stalked this woman! She's lying!"

"Sure, buddy," Troy said, "that's why you were trying to kill her."

"I'm warning you, I'm a homicide detective on the Chicago police force," he threatened the sheriff. "I'll have your head for this!"

Troy shoved him into the patrol car. "Well, Mr. Homicide Detective, you did the wrong thing when you came to Parmer County. I can assure you of that. I'm gonna see that you're put away for a long time."

He slammed the door shut, then turned back to Chance and Lucinda. "Are you two going to be okay?"

Chance nodded soberly as his arm came around Lucinda's shoulders. "We are now. Do we need to come in and give statements?"

"You can do that later," Troy said, seeing the way

Lucinda was still shaking and clinging to his cousin. "When Lucy feels up to it will be soon enough."

As Troy drove away, Chance gently led Lucinda back to his pickup. Once they were inside on the bench seat, he didn't say anything, he simply wrapped his jacket around her and held her tightly to him.

Finally, after several minutes had passed and the quaking of her body began to subside, she said, "I'm so sorry, Chance. So very sorry."

Pressing his cheek against the top of her head, he asked, "What is there for you to be sorry about?"

She brought her head up to look at him, her eyes begging him for forgiveness. "I nearly got you killed! Last night Richard called and—he threatened to kill you and your family if I didn't leave! I should have never stayed at your ranch. I led him here and he almost—"

"Shh! Don't do this, Lucy. Don't blame yourself for anything. The man is obviously deranged."

Shaking her head, she cupped her hands around the sides of his face. "You know why I had to leave you now, don't you? You know why I couldn't accept your proposal?"

He shook his head with regret. "I know you were afraid. What I don't understand is why you didn't confide in me. I love you, Lucy. Don't you know I'd fight any demon for you?"

Tears began to roll down her face. After the heartache of leaving Chance this morning and then experiencing the wild fear that he was going to be killed in front of her very eyes, she couldn't believe that he was really holding her, telling her that he loved her.

"That's what I was afraid of. I knew if I told you about Richard, you'd go after him. And I knew he carried a gun and I didn't want you to put yourself in that kind of danger. I'd rather he killed me first than for you to be hurt.''

Lucinda shuddered as she relived the fear that had paralyzed her when she'd looked up to see Richard standing outside her car door. ''I've been afraid for a long time now, Chance. For months and months I've lived in fear. I tried getting protection from the police, but that turned out to be a joke. Richard *was* the police. I couldn't get any help there, and since I had no family, my last hope was to leave Chicago and find a new place to make my home.''

''You found it, Lucy. With me. Are you still going to say that you don't love me?''

She wiped at the tears that continued to streak down her face. ''Forgive me for lying to you, Chance. But I did it because I do love you. More than my life.''

He lifted her palm to his lips, then grimaced as his lips tasted the salty blood of her scraped and cut skin. He knew it would be a long, long time before he'd be able to forget the image of Lucinda being manhandled by that maniac, the sight of her helpless and weeping and begging Chance to save himself rather than try to help her.

''You just proved that to me, Lucy. Now if you'll say you're going to marry me, I'll forgive you anything.''

He smiled at her, and the warm, loving light in his eyes made all the terror of the past few minutes fade away like a bad dream.

''Then forgive me,'' she whispered. ''Because I am going to marry you. I'm going to give you children. And I'm going to love you with all my heart for the rest of our lives.''

His sigh was full of elation and contentment as he leaned his head toward hers and gently kissed her lips.

"Then living on a ranch with a cowboy isn't going to be a problem for you? I know your career is—"

With a shake of her head, she quickly pressed her lips back to his and kissed him with all the fervor of her love. "My career will be just fine," she murmured against his cheek. "I'll find some way to get my designs on the market. In fact, your sister had a great idea about that. But you and our children will always come first in my life. Just remember that."

"Well, one thing is for sure, Lucy," he said, rubbing his nose against hers. "You'll never have to be afraid of anything or anyone again. I'll always be around to rescue you if you need it."

At this moment he couldn't have said anything that would have made her feel more safe and secure and loved. Her heart was fairly bursting with it as she smiled and sighed with utter contentment.

"If you'll go get Caesar, I'll be ready to go home," she told him, then in afterthought, she asked, "What about my car?"

"I'll send a couple of the hands for it," Chance assured her.

He went after the kitten, who was still safely ensconced in his box on the front seat of Lucinda's car.

Once Chance was back at the pickup and had settled the animal in the crook of Lucinda's arm, he started the engine, then winked at her and grinned. "You know what tonight is. It's Christmas Eve. And on Christmas Eve, Santa always comes to the Delacroix's house."

"Does he really?" Lucinda asked as she did her best to look skeptical.

"I promise."

Her expression suddenly turned very provocative. "I believe you."

"You do?" he asked, his brows lifted with surprise.

Her face wreathed with joy, she laughed. "Well, he is going to give me a cowboy for Christmas, isn't he?"

Chance's eyes were bright, shining with the love he promised to give her tonight and always.

"He is," he said with certainty. Then leaning over, he murmured against her lips, "Merry Christmas, darling."

A month later, Lucinda was in the kitchen trying her hand at making piecrust when her husband came in carrying the mail.

Stomping the snow off his boots, he tossed a stack of letters onto the breakfast counter, then carried a single envelope over to Lucinda. "You know," he said, glancing around the kitchen. "It's still hard to believe we have the house to ourselves. With Mother and Doc leaving for their honeymoon yesterday and Sarah Jane gone on a skiing trip with her friends, we won't know what to do with ourselves."

Lucinda slanted her husband a provocative look. "Oh, I'm sure you'll think of something."

Chuckling softly, he grinned sexily at her. "I'll try my best. But I'll let you read your letter first."

Before Lucinda took the envelope from him, she kissed him, then handed him a cup of hot coffee.

"Oh, it's from Molly," Lucinda said as she glanced at the return address.

"Open it and see what she has to say," Chance urged.

Lucinda ripped open the envelope. Inside it there was a short note with a newspaper clipping attached to it.

Dear Lucy, I was so happy to hear about your marriage and the happy life you've found out there in Texas.

I found this clipping in the newspaper yesterday and thought you might like to read it. Take care and I promise to write more next time.

Love, your friend, Molly

Smiling, Lucinda turned her attention to the scrap of newspaper. It was small, but as far as Lucinda was concerned, the significance of what it said couldn't be measured.

"What is it, honey?" Chance asked as he watched a myriad of emotions cross his wife's face.

Smiling as though a thousand angels had suddenly descended on the kitchen, she handed the piece of paper to Chance.

"It's about Richard. Molly found it in a Chicago newspaper. I'm glad that his friends and fellow policemen up there finally know that he's serving time in a Texas jail and is undergoing psychiatric therapy. And not only that, after some internal investigations back in Chicago, the state has found Richard guilty of taking bribes from criminals. So after his jail time is up here in Texas, he'll be locked up in Illinois for a long time to come."

Chance shook his head with disbelief. "Too bad it couldn't have happened sooner. When you needed their help, they all believed Richard and pegged you for a scorned woman out for revenge because of your broken engagement. I can't begin to imagine the terror you must have lived through back then."

Yes, her life had once been one long nightmare. But now, surrounded by Chance's love, she was putting it all behind her. "It was like being condemned to hell with no way out. But thank God, that's all in the past now and Richard has been put away where he can't harm anyone else. And he'll be there for many long years."

"The man got exactly what he deserved," Chance said with conviction.

Lucinda tossed the clipping into a nearby trash basket, then curling her arms around her husband's neck, she whispered, "And we got just what we deserved, too, my darling. We got each other."

* * * * *

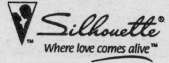

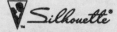

If you enjoyed what you just read,
then we've got an offer you can't resist!

Take 2
bestselling novels FREE!
Plus get a FREE surprise gift!

Clip this page and mail it to The Best of the Best™

IN U.S.A.
3010 Walden Ave.
P.O. Box 1867
Buffalo, N.Y. 14240-1867

IN CANADA
P.O. Box 609
Fort Erie, Ontario
L2A 5X3

YES! Please send me 2 free Best of the Best™ novels and my free surprise gift. After receiving them, if I don't wish to receive anymore, I can return the shipping statement marked cancel. If I don't cancel, I will receive 4 brand-new novels every month, before they're available in stores! In the U.S.A., bill me at the bargain price of $4.74 plus 25¢ shipping and handling per book and applicable sales tax, if any*. In Canada, bill me at the bargain price of $5.24 plus 25¢ shipping and handling per book and applicable taxes**. That's the complete price and a savings of over 20% off the cover prices—what a great deal! I understand that accepting the 2 free books and gift places me under no obligation ever to buy any books. I can always return a shipment and cancel at any time. Even if I never buy another The Best of the Best™ book, the 2 free books and gift are mine to keep forever.

185 MDN DNWF
385 MDN DNWG

Name	(PLEASE PRINT)	
Address	Apt.#	
City	State/Prov.	Zip/Postal Code

* Terms and prices subject to change without notice. Sales tax applicable in N.Y.
** Canadian residents will be charged applicable provincial taxes and GST.
   All orders subject to approval. Offer limited to one per household and not valid to
   current The Best of the Best™ subscribers.
® are registered trademarks of Harlequin Enterprises Limited.

BOB02-R   ©1998 Harlequin Enterprises Limited